NOVELS BY VINCE FLYNN

AND BY KYLE MILLS

AND BY DON BENTLEY

VINCE FLYNN

DENIED ACCESS

A MITCH RAPP NOVEL
BY DON BENTLEY

SIMON &
SCHUSTER

London · New York · Amsterdam/Antwerp · Sydney/Melbourne · Toronto · New Delhi

First published in the United States by Emily Bestler Books / Atria Books,
an imprint of Simon & Schuster, LLC, 2025

First published in Great Britain by Simon & Schuster UK Ltd, 2025

1 3 5 7 9 10 8 6 4 2

Simon & Schuster UK Ltd, 1st Floor
222 Gray's Inn Road, London WC1X 8HB

Simon & Schuster Australia, Sydney
Simon & Schuster India, New Delhi

www.simonandschuster.co.uk
www.simonandschuster.com.au
www.simonandschuster.co.in

The authorised representative in the EEA is Simon & Schuster Netherlands BV,
Herculesplein 96, 3584 AA Utrecht, Netherlands. info@simonandschuster.nl

Simon & Schuster strongly believes in freedom of expression and stands against
censorship in all its forms. For more information, visit BooksBelong.com

A CIP catalogue record for this book is available from the British Library

Hardback ISBN: 978-1-3985-3303-5
Trade Paperback ISBN: 978-1-3985-3304-2
eBook ISBN: 978-1-3985-3305-9
Audio ISBN: 978-1-3985-3312-7

Printed and Bound in the UK using 100% Renewable Electricity
at CPI Group (UK) Ltd

MIX
Paper | Supporting
responsible forestry
FSC® C013604

To Kyle Mills—thank you for your friendship, support, and incredible storytelling. Because of you, **MITCH RAPP LIVES!**

AUTHOR'S NOTE

FELLOW Mitch Rapp fans—like you, I've always wondered how Vince intended to complete the trilogy he began with *American Assassin*. While none of us knows exactly what Vince had in mind, I hope you find *Denied Access* to be a fitting conclusion to our favorite assassin's origin story. As always, happy reading!

DENIED
ACCESS

PROLOGUE

MAY 1945
ORANIENBURG, GERMANY
SUBURB OF BERLIN
SOVIET UNION SECTOR

THOMAS Stansfield was sick of war.

Sick of the killing, sick of the destruction, sick to death of watching friends, comrades in arms, and civilians alike rendered corpses by the giant meat grinder that was war. Though he was barely in his mid-twenties, Stansfield knew that something inside him had prematurely aged. Perhaps terminally so. Thomas might be sick to death of war, but now, only days after the Allies had finally captured Berlin, he was terrified that he might just be the catalyst for a new one.

"Is that the convoy?"

Though he was almost certain of his answer, Stansfield still pressed the Zeiss binoculars to his eyes before replying. The trio of nondescript vehicles could have been among any of the hundreds currently poking through the smoking remains of the Third Reich's capital like jackals swarming the still-cooling corpse of a wildebeest on some African plain.

They were not.

Though the day's last light was draining away from a crimson sky, enough illumination remained for the binoculars. BA-64 armored scout cars guarded the front and rear of the three-vehicle column, but it was the center vehicle that garnered Stansfield's attention. The Soviet ZIS-5 cargo truck lumbering along in a cloud of exhaust featured a single vertical scratch on the metal toolbox mounted just about the right rear wheel housing. The scratch was jagged enough to suggest that its origin was accidental.

It was not.

A fourteen-year-old member of the Resistance had etched the mark two evenings prior at considerable risk to her life. When he'd been fourteen, Stansfield had been focused on perfecting his curveball in the hopes of making the high school baseball team. The notion that he and his fellow spies used children to do the work of men had appalled him at first.

No longer.

Innocence was one of the first casualties of war.

But not the last.

"*Ja*," Stansfield said, lowering his binoculars. "Give the ready signal."

Stansfield's answer, as was the original question, had been spoken in German. He had been horrified by the vicious attack against Pearl Harbor by the Imperial Japanese. Like many of his friends, he had set off for the Army recruiting station that very day, determined to enlist and do his part to avenge his countrymen. But unlike so many others, Thomas's enlistment had been circumvented. He had filled out the required paperwork and waited for the official notification that would provide the time and date of his physical exam.

It never came.

Instead, one of Thomas's professors had requested that he come to his office to sort out an administrative detail. Stansfield had dutifully complied, but the person waiting in his professor's office had not been his professor. In fact, the trim, bespectacled man wasn't a member of the faculty at all. He'd explained in a precise Ivy league diction that Stansfield had come to the notice of a select group of people. A group who'd been tasked to aid America's war effort in an unconventional manner. Rather than enlist, Thomas was encouraged to complete his degree while incorporating two additional fields of study into his course load—French and German.

Thomas did as he was asked. A year later he graduated with honors and walked into the waiting arms of the organization that would later be known as the Office of Strategic Services, or OSS. Other men his age served as soldiers, sailors, or Marines, but Thomas became something else.

A spy.

"Moment of truth."

Andre's whispered comment thundered in Stansfield's ears.

His work with the OSS had taken him the length and breadth of Europe. From gathering information on the state of German munitions factories, to coordinating airdrops for the French Resistance, to scouting possible landing zones for D-Day paratroopers, Stansfield had interfaced with countless Allied counterparts. As with anything else in life, the quality of agents and assets could be graded on a bell curve. Some he would have trusted with his life, while others he'd been convinced would get him killed through pure stupidity.

And then there was Andre.

Stansfield had first made the boy's acquaintance in Paris, where Andre had worked as a runner—someone charged with conveying messages to Resistance cells scattered throughout the city. Though fanatical about hunting down spies and traitors, the Germans tended to ignore preadolescent boys. Especially boys whose asthma made it difficult for them to walk any significant distance without wheezing.

This was a mistake.

Though he looked no older than twelve, Andre was actually sixteen. In a sane world, this distinction might not mean much, but as Thomas knew firsthand, sanity had departed the European continent long ago. The German forces responsible for Berlin's final defense had consisted in large part of old men and young boys. If he had been fighting for the Nazis, the French boy might very well be a squad leader by now.

Andre wasn't fighting for the Nazis any more than he was plagued by debilitating asthma. Though French by birth, he had grown up in an eastern border town and could speak German like a native. A gifted polyglot, Andre was also fluent in Spanish, Italian, and English. Lately he'd been honing his skills with a language that might prove even more relevant to future conflicts.

Russian.

"Come on," Stansfield whispered. "Come on!"

He was perched atop a rocky outcropping that overlooked a small village to the east. A north–south flowing river wound past the settlement's western edge, separating him from the village. The river's placid surface concealed a surprisingly deep body of water.

The village itself was unremarkable. A collection of houses, a bakery, butcher shop, and the prerequisite pub. There wasn't much of Germany that hadn't been ravaged by war and this went doubly so for Berlin's suburbs. Case in point, several of the village's dwellings sported gaping holes hastily covered by tarps and the like. A smoking crater denoted where another building had once stood, and the furrows torn into the fields by the metal tracks of countless armored vehicles were visible even without the aid of Stansfield's binoculars.

Nothing that should be of interest to a Russian column.

Nothing except for the one hundred tons of uranium oxide housed in a metal barn.

This was the moment of truth in more ways than one.

The convoy had been approaching the village from the west, but the road they'd been following emptied into a north–south farm trail that paralleled the river.

The column slowed as it approached the intersection. To the left lay a packed dirt trail that meandered north for one hundred yards past a barren field before arriving at a bridge. The wooden span had been reinforced with metal girding, but the bridge still looked a bit rickety to Stansfield's eye. To reach surer footing, the convoy would need to turn right and proceed south for another two miles to where a bridge constructed of much sturdier river stone spanned the river.

Sturdiness aside, Stansfield had wagered that the shortcut would prove too tempting for the road-weary Russians. The convoy was in a race with a collection of American and British scientists and soldiers who were also intent on claiming the German uranium oxide. Time was of the essence.

"What are they doing?" Andre punctuated his question by reaching for the binoculars.

Stansfield intercepted the teen's questing fingers and pushed them away. Though it was often easy to forget, Andre was still a boy, and boys liked to see. "No binos," Stansfield said. "Can't risk a glint from the glass."

As if hearing Stansfield's thoughts, the lead scout car's passenger door opened and a Russian soldier exited. A soldier with his own set of binoculars. Though he couldn't be sure without using his binos to check the shoulder boards on the soldier's uniform, Stansfield was willing to bet that the man was a member of the Russian military intelligence organization known as the GRU.

Stansfield sensed motion to his left and instinctively grabbed Andre's shoulder. "Be still. We're well hidden. At these distances motion is easier to detect than a human form."

Andre's muscles stopped twitching beneath Stansfield's grasp. "What are they doing?"

This time the question carried more frustration than curiosity. Stansfield sighed. The boy's body might no longer be in motion, but his mind was never idle. "Trying to decide which bridge to take. Safety to the right or speed to the left."

"Will they choose left?"

"The Russians know they're on borrowed time. Multiple countries are looking for that uranium just like multiple countries are trying to capture Nazi nuclear scientists. If it were me, I'd turn left."

Unfortunately, it was not up to Stansfield, and while his reasoning was tactically sound, if the intelligence was correct, the Soviet convoy was not composed of just tactical men. Though he understood very little of the underlying science, Stansfield knew that the world's top physicists were feverishly working to be the first to develop a weapon that unleashed unfathomable destructive power by splitting the atom.

Rare uranium oxide was critical to this endeavor.

Differentiating between uranium oxide and other remnants of the German nuclear weapon's program was not a task for common soldiers. This column was rumored to contain two Russian physicists who had been rushed to the front lines for just this purpose. Scientists by their nature were slow, methodical creatures taught to plod through experiments with an eye toward reproducibility and bulletproof data.

Spies were a different breed.

Men and women whose livelihood depended on short, and often frantic, bursts of communication. An existence lived both figuratively and literally under the gun in which speed was its own variation of safety. Russian physicists might be the ones charged with validating that the strange material wrapped in tarps in an otherwise unassuming barn was the uranium the Soviet nuclear weapons program so desperately needed, but it was the GRU minders who were responsible for ensuring that they obtained the prize before the Americans or British did. Intelligence officers would choose speed over safety any day of the week.

At least that's what Stansfield hoped.

As with everything the Resistance had used to wage their covert war against the Axis, German-manufactured RDX plastic explosives were in short supply. With only enough material to rig one of the two bridges, Stansfield had put all his chips on the closer one.

Now his wager was about to be put to the test.

For an impossibly long moment, the convoy remained stationary.

Not for the first time, Stansfield considered revising his plan and ambushing the vehicles outright. While traditional military doctrine stated that an attacking force must outnumber defenders by three to one, the Resistance had grown adept at adapting tactics to suit its perpetually numerically inferior members. The men and women who staffed its ranks had become experts in the art of sabotage and were quite proficient at engaging Germans with hit-and-run attacks. Skirmishes in which the goal was to inflict maximum casualties in the minimum amount of time.

The military maxim of gaining and holding terrain was just that—a maxim for conventional forces. Stansfield thought his band of ruffians stood an excellent chance of disabling the convoy and killing most of its members, but most wasn't good enough.

There could be no one left alive to report what had transpired here.

The Soviets were still the notional allies of the Americans and British. Stansfield didn't think this détente would survive the year, but for the time being, West and East were working together. It wouldn't do for the Russians to discover that their convoy had been ambushed by American-aligned Resistance fighters. For this to work, the scientists and their minders had to die in a manner attributable to one of the few remaining pockets of German resistance.

A bridge destroyed by German explosives fit the bill.

Just as the tension gripping Stansfield's stomach began to seep into his chest, the armored car at the front of the convoy lurched forward. Stansfield's heart stopped as the hood swung to the right. Then his breath came back in a shuddered gasp when the car nosed back left.

"Pothole," Andre said. "The driver must have been steering around it."

Stansfield nodded in reply, not trusting his voice just yet.

While there was widespread division throughout the ranks of the OSS with regard to the Soviets, he was firmly in the camp that it was better to act now than to wait for the cancer growing in Eastern Europe to fully metastasize. He'd weathered several lifetimes' worth of trauma over the last couple of years. The naïve college graduate was long gone, replaced by a hardened killer. A person who'd seen the depravities of men in unfiltered detail. He'd scouted the Buchenwald concentration camp shortly after its liberation. He understood evil at a visceral level.

Others might pretend otherwise, but the truth was that Stalin and Hitler were two sides of the same coin. The Soviets could not be allowed to develop an atomic bomb. The OSS chain of command was uncharacteristically indecisive when it came to whether they should prevent the Russians from obtaining Germany's uranium oxide.

Stansfield was not.

"They're on the bridge."

Stansfield refrained from pointing out that he could see that convoy just as well as Andre. In some ways he found the boy's observations refreshing. Stansfield had at least enjoyed a normal childhood before being thrust into war. War was all the French boy had ever known. Perhaps if someone as jaded as Andre could still feel excitement, there was still hope for the world.

Perhaps.

"Ready the signal," Stansfield said.

He and Andre were not located with the demolition team. The charges emplaced on the bridge had to be denotated on command via an electronic switch. The only spot close enough for the demolition team to accomplish this while still remaining hidden did not offer an adequate view of the road leading to the structure. Accordingly, Stansfield had split the attacking force into observation and demolition elements. Leon, the demolition team leader, was experienced, but too headstrong for Stansfield's liking. This operation required finesse, which usually meant his would be the hand holding the firing mechanism. Since that wasn't possible, he'd drilled a set of simple instructions into Leon's head—the explosives were not to be detonated until he gave the word. In this case, the word would come in the form of the electric flashlight Andre was holding.

The bridge shuddered under the convoy's weight and for a moment Stansfield was worried the structure would give way prematurely. That would be almost as bad as if the bridge failed to collapse at all. The center of the river had both a treacherous current and the needed depth, but the first several feet featured a gently sloping riverbed that gave way to a precipitous drop-off. To obtain the desired result, the convoy had to be over the deepest part of the river when the bridge fell.

The aged timbers stopped swaying, and the convoy continued at a stately, if slow, pace. Stansfield sighed, but his relief was short-lived. Rather than follow the first two vehicles onto the bridge, the second armored scout car remained on the riverbank. Perhaps the driver was waiting for the first vehicle to make it to the far side before adding his vehicle's weight to the rickety-looking span. Stansfield's heart rate quickened at the implication.

He needed all three vehicles in the river.

By the same token, he couldn't allow the lead scout car to reach the far side. His sources inside the village claimed that the uranium cache was unguarded by Nazi soldiers, but if he had assets among the townspeople, logic dictated that the Soviets probably did too. If the second scout car didn't join the rest of the convoy, he would have to drop the bridge, ambush the remaining vehicle, and then push it into the river.

This would stretch his little band of partisans to the limit, but the mission was a no-fail operation. He would trade all of their lives if it meant keeping the uranium out of Russian hands. Stansfield was in the process of planning the ambush when the trail scout car rolled onto the bridge in a cloud of smoke.

"The driver must have stalled it," Andre said. "Good thing you knew to wait."

Stansfield considered coming clean with the boy, but didn't. Casualties were all too common in this line of work and treachery and double-dealing were the norms. Life as a Resistance fighter was usually both bleak and short. Partisan fighters needed to believe that they would defy the odds, and if following a commander with a fox's cunning helped them sleep better at night, so be it.

The lead scout car was now two-thirds of the way across the bridge. Stansfield was running out of time. The trail vehicle hadn't yet reached the drop-off, but with a little luck, its forward momentum would carry it into the river's depths.

"Send the signal," Stansfield whispered.

Andre slid the flashlight's power switch forward.

Nothing.

Cursing, Andre toggled the switch on and off.

Still nothing.

The French boy flipped the flashlight on end and was reaching for the battery cap when Stansfield snatched the torch from him. The scout car had less than ten yards to travel. No time to mess with the batteries. Stansfield struck the metal cylinder against the ground and felt the jolt travel the length of his arm. Then he aimed the flashlight and slid the power switch to the on position. The bulb glowed a warm crimson through the filter he'd fitted over the lens. Like a madman, Stansfield waved the torch in a circle, praying that his demolition team got the message.

His prayers were answered.

A series of flashes flared across the bottom of the bridge as the charges detonated. A low rumbling followed, but by then the bridge was already collapsing. With a groan, wood splintered and pylons bent. The scout cars and truck followed the debris into the swirling river. The turbulent water swallowed the convoy and its occupants, leaving no trace of the Russians.

They'd done it.

"Look," Andre said.

Stansfield followed the boy's pointing finger and swore.

A single head bobbed in the water. Then the man began to stroke toward shore. The survivor was too far away for Stansfield to determine whether he was a soldier or scientist, but the distinction didn't matter. Snatching the German Karabiner 98k sniper rifle from where it was lying beside him, Stansfield sighted on the swimmer and pulled the trigger.

The shot missed, raising a geyser of water to the swimmer's right.

Taking a steadying breath, Stansfield adjusted his aimpoint left, exhaled, and fired again. The swimmer jerked and then sank beneath the surface. Stansfield swept the river with his rifle's ZF-41 optic, checking the turbulent water for additional survivors.

There were none.

After waiting another minute, Stansfield slowly lowered the rifle. "Let's go."

The boy nodded. "Do you think we just prevented war or fired the first shots in a new one?"

"Prevented one," Stansfield said before tousling Andre's hair. "Most certainly."

His battle-weary heart hoped that was true.

His cynical intellect feared otherwise.

CHAPTER 1

M ITCH Rapp could feel the surveillance team.

Like an itch that he couldn't quite reach or the buzzing of an unseen mosquito, he could sense their presence. If asked, he could point toward their watching eyes in the same manner in which a compass needle unerringly swung toward magnetic north. For most people, the notion that a person could intuitively detect an unseen observer was ridiculous.

He was not most people.

Over the course of the last hour, the team had grown bolder. As Rapp had followed his companion's lead through the winding warren of Barcelona's streets, the sensation had progressed from a buzzing at the edge of his consciousness to shapeless forms just outside his field of view. More than once he'd felt the compulsion to quickly turn his head in an effort to catch a glimpse of the unseen watchers.

Rapp had ignored that urge.

If the surveillance team realized that they'd been made, the members would have to make a decision—withdraw or escalate. Rapp knew the team represented a tactical problem that he would have to solve, but he intended to do so on his terms, not theirs. In addition to the standard mental checklist he addressed before choosing a time and place for possible kinetic action, this afternoon he had another factor to consider.

The blonde seated across the table from him.

"Something the matter, darling?"

Though she knew English, the woman asked the question in French in keeping with their agreement. Rapp spoke the language like a native, and the passport resting in his back pocket proclaimed him a resident of *la République française*.

This was a lie.

One of many.

"Everything's fine," Rapp said, studying his girlfriend.

Greta Ohlmeyer possessed the sort of magnetism that caused would-be suitors to make fools of themselves. The Nordic beauty was a statuesque five feet eight with bright blue eyes, high cheekbones, and a strong jaw that tapered to a little apple chin. The Swiss woman's hair was almost always pulled back into a high ponytail, and though they'd been dating for a little over a year, Mitch was often at a loss for words in her presence. He'd lost count of the number of suitors who had gone to ridiculous lengths in the hopes of garnering a smile from her. Collisions between members of the male species and inanimate objects were almost a daily occurrence around Greta.

"You're not behaving as if everything's fine."

"I need to use *les toilettes*," Rapp said. "Could you please order me another glass of sangria?"

"Of course."

The brief change in her countenance suggested that Greta was not buying what he was selling. A slight narrowing of her eyes, a pursed lower lip, and a single worry line that marred her otherwise smooth forehead. Someone who had not spent hours memorizing her every feature might not have noticed the minuscule differences in her expression.

Rapp noticed.

Reaching across the table, he squeezed Greta's hand. Her soft fingers sent a jolt of electricity crackling up his arm. She smiled. It was tentative, but a smile nonetheless.

She knew the effect she had on him.

She also knew what he did for a living.

Rapp slid his gaze across his surroundings as he stood.

He and Greta were seated among a cluster of tables that served as the outdoor eating area for a café located on the southwestern corner of the Plaça dels Àngels. The open-air plaza was anchored to the northwest by the Barcelona Museum of Contemporary Art and a municipal building to the southeast. To Rapp's eye, the museum's edgy lines and endless panes of glass seemed at odds with the municipal building's stodgy faded stone façade, but the throngs of pedestrians who transited the plaza didn't seem to mind. Mothers pushing baby strollers jostled with young professionals on their way to or from lunch, while tourists clustered in twos and threes armed with cameras and maps.

The shops and restaurants lining the courtyard made Plaça dels Àngels a natural gathering point for Catalans and tourists alike, but another, more distinct clique also made use of the slate walking area. A coterie of skateboarders incorporated the museum steps and tiered concrete entrance into their aerial performance. While predominately male, a handful of women also numbered among the dozen or so skaters.

A redhead wearing a tank top and loose cargo pants broke from the pack, riding her board straight at the concrete ledge adjacent to Rapp's table. The velocity she generated in the run-up to the trick was impressive. Her twin braids streamed behind her, reminding him of a crimson battle ensign snapping in the wind. He guessed her to be about his age, but with her face scrunched up in concentration, she looked much younger. The ledge was only a few board lengths away, but the woman was determined to go faster still. Risking her balance, she shifted her trail leg off the board for a final, monstrous push. Then she stomped the tail of her board and went airborne.

The ollie was expertly done.

The redhead's board cleared the ledge with room to spare. The same could not be said of her rear foot. The edge of her toe clipped the concrete lip, sending skateboard in one direction and woman another.

Over the course of the four years he'd spent on the Syracuse University lacrosse field, Rapp had developed the ability to mentally slow down a developing play and determine its probable outcome in real time. Imagining the skateboarder as an attacker hurtling down the field with the ball in her crosse's pocket and a clear shot at goal made the rest easy. In the blink of an eye, Rapp analyzed the woman's flight path and computed a likely point of interception. Sliding left, he interposed himself between the redhead and the unforgiving pedestrian walkway. A millisecond later, she slammed into his chest. Rather than attempting to arrest her momentum, Rapp went with the flow, cradling her unhelmeted head as they both tumbled to the ground.

The jarring collision between the unforgiving stone and his arms and shoulders foreshadowed bruises to come, but he was able to take the majority of the impact across his thick back muscles. Maybe not as clean as the countless falls he'd practiced in the jiujitsu dojo, but it got the job done. For a moment he was flat on his back and nose to nose with the startled woman.

He wondered what she saw in his coal-black eyes.

A startled tourist?

A Good Samaritan?

Or maybe something else.

Rapp unlocked his arms, and the skateboarder shot to her feet. He couldn't understand the torrent of Spanish pouring from her lips, but judging by her embarrassed smile and flushed features, he could guess.

"*C'est bon,*" Rapp said. "*C'est bon.*"

The woman loosed a final bit of Spanish before grabbing him in a surprisingly strong hug. Then she picked up her board and headed back to the circle of skaters. Rapp watched her go before turning to Greta.

He smiled.

She did not.

Chuckling, Rapp summited the steps and entered the museum.

CHAPTER 2

THE Barcelona Museum of Contemporary Art had a rather uninspiring lobby.

Rapp already knew this because he'd spent an agonizing four hours traipsing through the museum the day before as Greta regaled him with details about each exhibit. This was not to imply that he was uncultured. In addition to English and French, Rapp spoke Arabic and Italian fluently and could get by in Persian. He'd forgotten more about the inner workings of the Fertile Crescent than most academics knew, and he'd graduated from Syracuse with a degree in international business and a minor in French. He did not think much of modern art, but he was smart enough not to voice this opinion to his girlfriend.

In a nod to its contemporary sensibilities, the museum eschewed the traditional soft lines, vaulted ceilings, or murals that made Barcelona a destination for architecture aficionados. Instead the lobby consisted of sharp edges, boxy walls, and uninspiring displays. Rapp would not have termed anything that graced the ample wall space *art*. Indeed, the most inspiring vista did not come from within the museum's Soviet-style decorum at all. That honor belonged to the floor-to-ceiling

tinted windows that offered an unobstructed view of the skateboarders'
courtyard antics.

Rapp approached the ticket counter and tried to catch the eye of
the disinterested twentysomething manning the register. He did not
succeed. When it became apparent that the young man was content to
indefinitely ignore Rapp in favor of his paperback novel, he spoke.

"One ticket, please," Rapp said in French-accented English.

With a long-suffering sigh, the man slapped the book onto the
counter and looked up at Rapp. "*No hablo inglés.*"

This was an interesting, not to mention unforeseen, development,
since the same young man had been only too happy to speak English
with Greta at great length just yesterday morning. Normally, Rapp
reserved his ire for actual problems rather than just inconveniences.

Normally.

But the thought of a surveillance team lurking just out of sight had
him in no mood to deal with the man's bullshit. "Listen to me, you arro-
gant fuckstick. I know you speak English. Now sell me a ticket before I
lose my patience."

The twentysomething swallowed and his eyes traveled over Rapp's
face as if seeing him for the first time. He reached for the ticket dis-
penser and ripped one off from the roll. His paperback was apparently
forgotten, and this was a shame. *The Cardinal of the Kremlin* was a fantastic read.

The man handed the ticket across the counter with shaking hands.

Rapp was accustomed to this reaction. In sticking with his legend
as a French tourist on holiday, he was dressed in European casual. A
button-down shirt, slacks, and Italian loafers. On the surface, he looked
about as dangerous as a pastry chef.

On the surface.

A closer inspection revealed an olive complexion, thick black hair,
and muscular build, but it was his eyes that really told the story. Rapp's
eyes were so dark as to be black, and when he was angry, they communicated an unnerving intensity. The museum worker might not have

been able to explain his reaction, but he would have no trouble naming the emotion gripping his heart.

Terror.

"Enjoy the museum, monsieur."

"*Gracias*," Rapp said with a smile as he dropped a handful of pesetas on the counter. "Keep the change."

Rapp took the ticket and made his way toward a spiral staircase, ascending the stairs with quick, even strides. Contrary to what he'd told Greta, his hurry had nothing to do with the toilets located on the second floor. Neither was his urgency driven by a desire to experience for a second time the avant-garde exhibit consisting solely of discarded paper napkins. Instead Rapp was anxious to make use of the added height offered by the second floor's towering windows.

After confirming that the corridor's handful of patrons was more interested in the exhibits than him, Rapp stepped to the tinted glass. Though he'd already examined the windows while outside and determined that their reflective surface didn't offer a view into the museum, Rapp still positioned his torso behind the thick concrete wall. As his mentor and onetime instructor Stan Hurley had beaten into his head, safe was better than dead.

Stan would know.

Though he was more accustomed to the role of hunter than prey, the events from ten days ago had driven home the precarious nature of Rapp's current profession in rather unambiguous terms. Betrayed by his own countrymen, ambushed in the middle of a job, and subsequently hunted across France by several intelligence services and a national police force, Rapp knew that his honeymoon period with the Central Intelligence Agency was officially over. As the dull ache in his shoulder and puckered flesh from a still-healing gunshot wound could attest, he was not invulnerable.

To make matters worse, the surveillance team Rapp had been sensing all morning had found him despite his intentions to disappear. This was troubling. Prior to the almost life-ending events in a French hotel room, Rapp had plied his trade with relative impunity. While not every assassination had gone exactly as planned, Rapp had no reason to believe that his cover had been compromised. He'd been living his Paris-based software-salesman legend while hunting his nation's enemies on their own turf for over a year. Now, in less than two weeks, he'd been burned twice. Rapp accepted that Murphy's Law was real.

Sometimes shit happened.

Sometimes.

But a formerly airtight cover repeatedly breached over the course of a relatively short period of time suggested that pure dumb luck was not to blame. He could think of only one explanation for the surveillance team's presence.

They'd had help.

Now that he was no longer pretending to be just another diner, Rapp surveyed the courtyard in a methodical manner more akin to the way in which a countersniper hunted an enemy shooter. A good surveillance team was maddeningly hard to detect if its members were disciplined enough to resist the urge to crash the subject, and equipped with a big enough bench to frequently rotate the member charged with close surveillance.

Put another way, the technique used to determine whether or not you were under observation hadn't really changed in the thousands of years the art of espionage had been practiced. Seeing an identical face across multiple locations and times meant that you were being followed. To avoid detection, a surveillance team needed to ensure that its target never glimpsed the same person twice.

Though he'd yet to see a familiar face staring back at him from a shop window's reflection, Rapp had identified other tells. A male coffee drinker who'd ignored Greta when the Swiss beauty had passed by his table. A flurry of motion that had exploded from an adjacent park bench when he and Greta exited a store, and a scooter engine roaring to life the moment they'd turned a corner. These tells all had viable explanations, but Rapp was not interested in the evidentiary standard practiced by courts of law. He knew what his instincts were telling him. Rapp no longer entertained the question of whether or not he was being followed. Instead, his thoughts were focused on a different dilemma—how to deal with the surveillance team.

One story below and fifty feet in front of him, Greta checked her watch.

Over the last several weeks, she'd had an up close and personal view of his life. The kind of up close view that resulted in his dried blood beneath her fingernails after she'd bandage his gunshot wound. Rapp was still trying to navigate a world in which his professional life had so thoroughly intruded into his personal. This quasi vacation had been suggested by Hurley as a way to allow the events in Paris to blow over.

Rapp had also thought it would be an excellent opportunity to sort through his relationship with Greta. While an assassin paired with a beautiful woman might be a spy-movie staple, it didn't work quite so well in real life. Besides trying to decide how much to tell her about his work for the CIA, Rapp also needed to balance the danger this information might pose to Greta.

Danger like the sort represented by the man rapidly approaching Greta's table.

CHAPTER 3

J OE Gaunt took a mammoth swallow of his Valmiermuiža beer. The amber lager glided across his tongue before disappearing down his throat in a pleasant rush. Many, many times he'd questioned his life choices, usually when he was bent over double with a hundred-pound rucksack on his back and boot-deep in mud or snow, with moisture dripping from the brim of his boonie hat. Those were the days when he wondered why he'd ever thought it a good idea to drop out of law school in favor of earning the coveted Green Beret.

And then there were days like today.

"This ain't a bad gig."

Joe nodded and wiped the beer remnants from his lips with the back of his hand. "Almost makes the last twelve months worth it, right?"

His companion, a tall, slender man with a mop of brown hair, paused before answering. "Jury's still out on that one."

Joe nodded again and took another swig of beer to hide his smile. His grin was partly because he was pleased that the young recruit had answered correctly, but also due to the man's thick Bronx accent. His companion could have played an extra in *Goodfellas*.

At just twenty-one, David McCloskey was barely old enough to drink beer in his native New York. Had he chosen a normal vocation such as plumbing, David would now be in the third year of his apprenticeship program and still functioning under a master plumber's watchful eye. If he'd stayed in college, where he'd been majoring in theater, David might be auditioning for a coveted role on Broadway.

David had chosen differently.

Instead he'd decided to serve his country first in the Navy as a cryptologic technician and then by volunteering for one of the most demanding and least-known units within Joint Special Operations Command, or JSOC. The organization went by several names, each meant to be more confusing than the last, but among its initiates it was simply called the Unit. The selection process boasted an attrition rate of around 75 percent, while the operator training course, or OTC, that followed graduated less than half the recruits who began.

As Joe had remarked more than once, the training was supposed to be hard because the Unit's unique mission was equally challenging—something David had learned firsthand over the last ten days. As Joe's first team sergeant had told him when he'd first reported to Tenth Special Forces Group as a newbie Green Beret, the more you sweat in training, the less you bleed in combat.

But he didn't say that to David.

This was partly because he was trying to avoid the label of crotchety old team sergeant. But only partly. The real reason was that at that moment he was more interested in something else.

The disagreement brewing in the far corner of the bar.

"What are they saying?" Joe said, nodding toward the group.

The pub in which the pair were seated could most charitably be described as *intimate*. A pair of large picture windows at the front of the room helped to disabuse the stereotype of a dimly lit bar, but the rest of the establishment's features were more traditional. A freestanding structure of brown, scarred wood served as the room's centerpiece. Two busy bartenders dispensed alcohol from behind the island of oak, and serving glasses hung upside down from racks above their heads.

Patrons gathered in twos and threes around circular tables of the sort that would have looked more at home in a drawing room than the neighborhood bar. Illumination came courtesy of a trio of glittering chandeliers, and music was delivered by a retro turnstile upon which was propped an album cover displaying Bob Marley's smiling face. On a good night, the space probably held thirty customers.

Tonight, Joe counted half that.

Most of the customers were quietly talking over glasses of frothy beer. Most, but not all. In the opposite corner of the bar, four seated men were vigorously arguing with two newcomers standing over them. Though he couldn't put his finger on why, Joe had a feeling what they were discussing might be important. To his credit, David didn't turn in his chair toward the loud voices. Instead he set his beer on the table and slouched as if he hadn't a care in the world.

It was an act.

David might have demonstrated the physical and mental fortitude required to join the ranks of a Tier One unit, but beneath his bushy beard and shaggy hair, he was still a twenty-one-year-old kid. When he was really concentrating, the former thespian scrunched up his nose. At the moment, he looked like he'd just bitten into a grapefruit.

"Everyone's speaking Russian, but I hear two distinct dialects."

Joe knew they were speaking Russian.

Army Special Forces commandos were unique among the greater special operations community in that every Green Beret attended language school as part of their postselection training known as the Q Course. Tenth Special Forces Group's area of responsibility included both Europe and the Soviet Union. As such, Joe had spent several months studying Russian after completing the Q Course. He worked hard to maintain conversational proficiency, but he was by no means fluent.

David was in another league altogether.

As the son of a Polish father who'd traded in his ethnic name for one he considered more American and a Russian mother, David had grown up in a home in which multiple languages were spoken. His family had immigrated to the United States when he was in elementary school, and he'd added English to his repertoire within months of landing in New York City. As was often the case with first-generation immigrants, David fiercely loved his adopted homeland. When the money he'd saved for college had dried up, it had been an easy decision to express this love through national service.

He'd disclosed his polyglot abilities to a Navy recruiter, who in turn had pitched him on the job of cryptologic technician interpretive— a billet tasked with collecting and translating foreign communications. David's sterling work had brought him to the attention of yet another recruiter. This one from the Unit. The secretive organization was built around pairing special operators like Joe with linguists who had signal-intercept experience like David.

In a mission that was a Unit staple, the two men had spent the last week emplacing clandestine devices around the periphery of the former Soviet air force base located in the Latvian city of Lociki, about nine miles to the northeast of Daugavpils proper. The low-profile receivers were designed to intercept radio communications and telemetry transmitted by the Russian fighter-bomber squadron that called the airstrip home. The MiGs were capable of carrying nuclear weapons and the American intelligence agencies that provided the Unit's operational taskings wanted to keep tabs on the aircraft in an effort to decipher Moscow's thinking.

Like many Baltic states, Latvia was still on unsteady ground with its former parent nation. Tensions had erupted a little over a year prior when Soviet paramilitary forces had attempted to brutally suppress a series of dissident protests that had engulfed the Latvian city of Riga. After the Soviet Union's dissolution, Russian paramilitary units continued to attack Latvian border stations, killing several Latvians in the process.

While emplacing the clandestine receivers was his primary mission, Joe's overall tasking was to develop intelligence. Many in the West feared that Latvia was on the brink of an armed conflict with its Russian agitators. As such, Joe's secondary objective was to gather on-the-ground insight into how the ethnic Russian people who called eastern Latvia home might respond to an armed Russian incursion. At the moment, his operational sixth sense was telling him that the conversation across the room might be useful in that regard.

Which was where David came in.

"Why don't you take a leak and see what you can hear?"

The red door leading to the facility's restrooms was conveniently located near the quarreling group. David nodded before downing half his pint in a single swallow. "What?" he said in response to Joe's raised eyebrow. "I'm a Method actor."

True to form, David got to his feet and started toward the bathrooms. His gait was a bit unsteady, and he flashed the bartender a disarming smile as he passed. Joe had been skeptical about the former thespian at first. The Unit normally had a hard-and-fast rule that no one with less than five years' military experience could attend selection, but the kid was proving to be a natural.

Maybe JSOC should be recruiting more theater majors.

Joe gave his partner a couple of seconds' head start, then downed his own beer. He wasn't usually one for amber brews, but this one had sucked him in. He only wished he'd paid a bit more attention to the alcohol content before ordering. Grabbing his mug, he headed toward the bar for a refill, conveniently arriving at the same moment David drew even with the quarrelsome men.

Joe set his mug carefully on the polished wood and angled his body so he could see as well as hear the action. David did his part to linger as long as possible as he approached the bathroom door, but he didn't try to feign a reason to stay. That was the right play, as things at the table had just escalated. One of the newcomers shouted a couple of choice epithets that Joe recognized from the crash course his partner had provided on Russian curse words.

The seated man closest to the offender seemed remarkably calm considering what the agitator had just said about his mother. Without even acknowledging the other man, the seated patron grabbed his beer mug and lifted the glass to his lips. Joe had heard the phrase *patience of Job* before, but this was the first time he'd seen it embodied. Maybe patience was just in the Latvian blood.

A millimeter before the beer's foamy head touched the seated man's lips, he had a change of heart. A considerable one. With an expertly executed flick of his wrist, he rocketed the contents of his mug at the offender. The standing man pawed at his face, no doubt to clear the burning alcohol from his eyes.

He didn't quite make it.

The moment his midsection was unprotected, the seated man fired a right hook into his opponent's liver. Joe cringed in sympathy. The punch's recipient never stood a chance. One moment he was digging the heels of his hands into his eyes. The next he was on the ground in the fetal position.

As if on cue, the table's occupants swarmed to their feet. No weapons had been drawn, but Joe still would have thought twice about mixing it up with the men had he been the offending party. The four had the heavy shoulders and meaty hands of laborers, and their expressions didn't speak so much to anger as quiet resignation. They were not barfight novices.

The remaining aggressor seemed to share Joe's assessment.

With hands raised in the universal symbol of surrender, he crouched over his fallen comrade and hooked his hands beneath the unconscious man's armpits. Then he dragged his companion out the door and into the night.

While Joe was fine with the notion that all's well that ends well, he was still suspicious. Very rarely did a drunk retreat from the field of battle with his tail tucked between his legs. More often than not, the night air revitalized his fighting spirit. Were he a betting man, Joe would lay odds that the agitators would return with friends or lurk outside in ambush.

Or both.

With this in mind, he reached into his pocket for his stash of currency, dropped a few lats on the bar, pointed to his empty mug, and held up two fingers.

"*Nyet,*" the bartender said. "*Za schyot zavedeniya.*"

Joe was a little iffy on the literal translation of the second half of what the bartender said, but he thought it equated to something along the lines of *it's on the house.* The bartender seemed to confirm Joe's hunch by pushing the bills back across the polished wood before filling two glasses with Valmiermuiža. After setting the steins in front of Joe the big man said, "*Zah zdah-rohv-yuh.*"

"*Zah zdah-rohv-yuh,*" Joe echoed back.

Life was good.

He had a beer in his hand, a completed mission under his belt, and a teammate who was well on his way to earning a permanent spot in the Unit. Latvia might not be Club Med, but Joe had certainly been on assignments that were worse. Much, much worse.

Life was good.

"We've got a problem."

Joe turned to find David at his elbow. For a former theater kid, David was pretty good at moving silently. "Maybe, maybe not. Drink your beer. If those two knuckleheads don't come back with reinforcements by the time we finish, I think we're in the clear."

Joe had intended his words to be reassuring. David didn't seem to be taking them that way. Rather than grabbing the mug, he gripped Joe's shoulder and leaned closer. "I'm not talking about the fight. I'm talking about what I found in the bathroom."

Joe should have known this was too easy.

Latvia was no longer part of the Iron Curtain, but its proximity to Poland and thereby Western Europe made the nation a convenient transit point for black-market goods destined for Russia. From hash-ish to heavy weapons, there was literally no telling what David had discovered stashed in the shitter.

Bracing himself for bad news, Joe asked the inevitable question.

"What'd ya find?"

"A bomb."

CHAPTER 4

FOR a long moment, Rapp tracked the man's progress in silence, attempting to reconcile what he saw with what he'd expected to see. Though she'd become an initiate into the world of shadows, Greta's pathway to that community ran through him. Yes, her grandfather had done some clandestine money-laundering on Hurley's behalf back when the banker had lived in East Germany, but Carl Ohlmeyer was not a spy.

Neither was Greta.

Rapp had therefore assumed that the surveillance team was targeting him.

Erroneously assumed.

The man confidently striding across the courtyard was locked on to Greta's table. He threaded through the gaggle of skateboarders without missing a step, moving unerringly toward the Swiss beauty like an arrow fired from a hunter's bow. With calm, deliberate motions that belied his thundering heart, Rapp withdrew a flip phone from his pocket and thumbed the speed dial.

A two-tone beep indicated the call had gone through.

Greta reached for her purse.

"Allo?"

"Inside the museum. Now."

Greta might not have been trained as a clandestine operative, but she'd begun to behave like one. Grabbing her purse, the Swiss beauty pocketed the phone, tossed a handful of pesetas onto the table, and made for the museum's beckoning door.

Rapp lived in a world bound by distances and angles.

An existence in which the difference between a successful hit and one in which his body acquired another bit of puckered flesh came down to inches and degrees. Though the cold metal of his Beretta's frame still pressed comfortingly against the small of his back, Rapp knew the pistol was not the solution to this problem.

Not yet, anyway.

Greta moved toward the museum's door with quick, distance-eating strides, but her pursuer was also determined.

It was going to be close.

Then it wasn't.

One moment Greta was just feet from the door. The next, the red-headed skateboarder tried another ollie. What was meant to be a hop onto the smooth wall that fenced the museum's entrance off from the courtyard became a pile of tangled limbs and curses. Once again, the skateboard shot from beneath the woman's feet like a wheeled missile. Rather than following the board's trajectory, the woman tumbled to the cobble-stones directly in Greta's path.

The Swiss beauty stopped.

Her pursuer did not.

Rapp felt more than saw the equations governing angles and dis-tance change. Greta was not going to make it. Time for plan B. Turning from the window to the wall, Rapp saw salvation in the form of a red metal square with the word FUEGO stenciled in white block letters across the top.

Rapp smashed his elbow into the safety glass.

Then he pulled the fire alarm with his knuckle.

An electronic Klaxon sounded accompanied by flashing strobes. The handful of art aficionados sharing the second floor with him froze as if unable to reconcile the blaring alarm with the tranquil environment they'd been enjoying just moments before.

Not Rapp.

He was already in motion.

Rapp bounded down the staircase, taking two steps at a time. Sprinting past the welcome desk and the much more animated employee, Rapp shot from the front doors like a pinball launched by a spring. The fire alarm's Klaxon echoed across the courtyard, and the skaters had largely paused their antics and were gesturing at the lights flashing from the building's exterior.

The crowd of diners and streams of meandering pedestrians were similarly frozen. Several café patrons had gotten to their feet but remained tethered to their tables as if unsure whether to stay or go. The man hunting Greta did not suffer from the same indecisiveness. As everyone else remained poised on the brink of motion, he closed the remaining distance to the Swiss beauty and snared her elbow.

Greta was no wilting flower.

Wrenching her shoulder, she tried to rip her arm away from the man's grasp. Against a slighter opponent, the maneuver might have worked. The man gripping her elbow was not slight. Heavy shoulders bunched beneath his dress shirt, and though the man was shorter than the statuesque Swiss woman, he more than made up for his lack of height with muscle. Slipping forward with an agility that seemed out of place for his thick, blocky build, the man kept hold of Greta as she stumbled backward.

No matter.

Greta did not have to escape. She just needed to buy time for Rapp to flip the equation governed by angles and inches to his favor. With a burst of speed, Rapp flowed down the museum's steps while formulating the manner in which he would deal with the threat. His concealed Beretta was the most obvious answer, but Rapp was loath to employ the pistol in broad daylight, especially since the stubby suppressor was not screwed onto the pistol's muzzle. The knife hidden in his belt buckle was another option, but that weapon required time to retrieve.

Time that Rapp did not have.

Instead, he would have to rely on two things he possessed in abundance—speed and violence of action. Rapp tightened the knuckles of his dominant hand into a fist and selected his target. Haymakers to the jaw made for great TV, but these sorts of strikes often did as much damage to the attacker as the recipient.

During an early sparring session in the Lake Anna, Virginia, training center he ran for potential Orion Team members, Stan Hurley had boiled the art of hand-to-hand contact down to a simple parable—use hard things on soft targets and soft things on hard targets. Case in point, Rapp intended to embed his hard, bony knuckles into the soft flesh lining the man's muscular neck. If he hit the vagus nerve, so much the better, but the strike didn't require that level of precision. The punch only needed to stun the man and thereby open a pathway for a follow-on blow from Rapp's pointy right elbow.

Rapp surged across the courtyard. The Swiss girl was still struggling, but her assailant was undeterred. Lifting Greta from her feet, the fire hydrant of a man shouldered his way past the tables and advanced toward the confluence of streets to the west.

A Good Samaritan moved to intervene.

The newcomer was rail-thin with narrow shoulders and shaking hands. He seemed to have as much expertise with unarmed combat as Rapp did with quantum mechanics. Still, what the man lacked in martial skills he made up for with courage. While his fellow diners seemed content to watch a man kidnap a resisting woman, he acted. The Good Samaritan reached for Greta with a pianist's delicate fingers.

The kidnapper was unimpressed.

With the same disregard he might show a puppy attacking his trousers' hem, the kidnapper cuffed the man with an open-handed slap to the head. The heavy *thunk* generated by the flesh-on-flesh collision echoed across the courtyard. The Good Samaritan spun in a half circle and crumpled. He tried to arrest his fall with a limp hand, but succeeded only in overturning a chair.

A chair that tumbled directly in Rapp's path.

The stricken man struggled to his feet on unsteady legs. That his efforts thus far were proving to be unsuccessful didn't seem to register. Or perhaps his addled brain was still trying to reboot after bouncing off the inside of his skull. Either way, Rapp figured he stood a better-than-even chance of joining the man on the cobblestones if he tried to leap over the prone figure.

Instead, he deviated to the right.

The distance and angles changed again.

The kidnapper gained a step.

Greta's wide eyes found Rapp's. The fear radiating from their depths became something else.

Resolve.

Greta tucked her knees against her chest like she was about to cannonball into a swimming pool, held the position for an instant, and then rocketed both legs toward the ground. The abrupt change in her center of gravity caused her assailant to stumble. Like a yo-yo winding back up its string, Greta used the man's motion to her advantage by arcing her head toward his face. She missed his nose but connected solidly with his chin.

Her abductor stumbled a second time.

Rapp did not.

Sprinting past the still-addled Good Samaritan, he closed the remaining distance to Greta and reached for her wrist.

Missed.

Reached again.

Brushed her fingertips.

Greta elbowed her abductor in the torso twice, turning her shoulders into each blow. The kidnapper grunted and faltered, trying to restrain his captive.

A step later, Rapp was on him.

Or at least he would have been were it not for the Citroën that barreled into the courtyard from a narrow side street. Rapp heard the redlining engine and instinctively leapt skyward. The car's bumper missed his leg but caught the bottom of his foot, spinning him in midair. Rapp crashed into the sedan's hood, tumbled off the metal, and fell. His head bounced against the hard stone and his vision swam. For a long moment the world seemed far away as he drifted on the euphoria of semiconsciousness.

Then a shrieking engine birthed a single thought.

Greta.

Rapp groaned and pushed himself to his feet just in time to see the kidnapper bundle a flailing Greta into the rear seat before climbing in after her. The passenger door slammed shut and the car's engine revved. The driver made eye contact with him through the windshield. Rapp tried to get clear of the car's bumper, but his sluggish legs weren't responding.

The driver popped the clutch, and the Citroën lunged.

Backward.

With equal parts bewilderment and disbelief, Rapp tracked the car as it reversed out of the courtyard, executed a precise J-turn, and sped away in a cloud of exhaust.

Rapp shook his head, trying to clear the cobwebs.

The driver's actions made no sense. The man had had him dead to rights. Maybe he hadn't wanted to cause a scene by running over a pedestrian in broad daylight, but Rapp had been at this game long enough to know that displaying mercy on the battlefield was a recipe for disaster. An enemy permitted to live today too often translated in an enemy that would have to be faced tomorrow, often on less favorable terms.

Thoughts about the Citroën's driver brought with them something else: a revelation fluttering at the edge of his consciousness. The man's startled expression was important somehow. Rapp thought he could decipher the expression's significance if he just pushed a bit harder, but another matter demanded his attention.

A motor scooter.

CHAPTER 5

S AY that again," Joe said.

"A bomb. There's a freaking bomb in the stall of the men's bathroom."

Joe stopped himself from asking the obvious question—*Are you sure?* Before coming to the Unit, David had been part of a team that manned listening stations designed to scoop up RF energy transmitted by foreign adversaries. These stations were often situated on remote hillsides and mountaintops, meaning the men and women who lived there had to be able to repair the sensitive radio equipment if it malfunctioned.

David knew the difference between a bomb and a bundle of wires.

"Could you tell what kind?"

David shook his head. "I don't know shit about bombs, but it looked straight out of central casting. A bunch of nails wrapped around a couple of sticks of dynamite and a glass bottle full of liquid. Maybe gasoline."

Perfect.

Just perfect.

The prudent course of action would be to get the hell out of Dodge, but even if they could convince the patrons to leave with them, there would be questions after the device exploded. Questions asked by trained professionals, who were suspicious by nature. He and David were traveling as tourists on Canadian passports. Joe was confident that their legend would stand up to the coming scrutiny, but he was less sure about their ability to withstand sustained questioning by Latvian or Soviet counterintelligence officers. Members of the Unit often traveled surreptitiously, but they were not CIA officers trained for deep-cover operations.

Joe needed to resolve this situation in a way that didn't lead to an interaction with the police, but neither could he walk out of the bar and hope for the best. Latvia wasn't an ally at the moment, but neither were the Latvian people enemies. Joe didn't pretend to be a geopolitical analyst, but it didn't take a genius to see that the tiny country's populace yearned to be free of Russian oppression. Joe couldn't stand by and allow innocent people to perish in the name of operational security.

Which left just one option.

"Let's take a look," Joe said.

"Thought you'd never ask," David muttered, but the thespian headed for the bathroom all the same.

The bartender fired a burst of Russian at Joe as he followed David's lead. The man's accent was too thick and his diction too quick for him to understand what he'd said, but based on the laughter that echoed from the other patrons, Joe could make a guess.

Nothing like being the butt of a joke from the very people you were trying to save.

Joe quickened his stride and entered the bathroom on David's heels. Closing the door behind him, he threw the bolt home on the simple latch screwed into the wood and then turned to see what awaited. David had already opened the cabinet above the toilet. "I was looking for toilet paper and found this."

This was a package of wires and dynamite about the size of a child's lunch box.

Joe leaned closer, careful to keep his hands at his sides. Only now did the enormity of the situation fully register. He knew as much about bombs as he did calculus, which was to say not a whole hell of a lot. He supposed he'd been hoping to see something that looked familiar from the movies. Perhaps a bright red LED with numbers steadily counting downward or maybe even an old-school alarm clock connected to a pair of red and black wires. Instead Joe was confronted with five sticks of dynamite, a bundle of wicked-looking roofer's nails, and a brown glass bottle filled with an ominous liquid.

Not great.

"Now what?" David said.

"I'm thinking," Joe said.

"Love that for you. Maybe think faster?"

"I don't know how to disarm a bomb. Do you?"

"Of course not, but I'm not the one who said we should take a look. Remember?"

Joe did remember and that decision was beginning to feel dumber by the second. He had to imagine that whoever had planted the device had done so with the intention of detonating it. He had assumed that the trigger would be linked to a timer of some sort, but he didn't see anything that looked like a clock. Nor did the bomb appear to have buttons or dials that would enable someone to set a countdown timer.

Maybe he was approaching the problem the wrong way.

"You're a radio guy, right?" Joe said.

"And a theater major. I also have a decent singing voice, but I'm not sure any of that's gonna be super beneficial at the moment."

"Stay with me, jackwagon. Could this thing be designed to be detonated remotely? Like with a radio?"

David shrugged. "Possibly. Lemme take a look."

That David hadn't dismissed his hypothesis outright seemed like a good sign. Or maybe the new operator was just happy to have something to think about besides what it would feel like to be disemboweled by a piece of ten-gauge galvanized steel. And if the nails or concussive shock wave didn't kill him outright, he could always look forward to being burned alive courtesy of whatever accelerant was probably sloshing around in the glass bottle.

Maybe David wasn't the only one who needed something to focus on.

"I don't see any antennas, so it's probably not radio-operated. I've heard of bombs that were configured to use pagers or cell phones as receivers, but I don't see those either. Maybe there's something at the back of the bomb. Should I take a peek?"

In for a penny, in for a pound. "Yeah, but try not to jostle it too much. Sometimes they have anti-tamper devices."

"Care to specify what constitutes *too much*? Never mind, it's probably better if I don't know." David balled his hands into fists and then shook them out. "Here goes nothing." The thespian cleared his throat. "*We few, we happy few, we band of brothers.*"

"What are you doing?" Joe said.

"I quote from *Henry V* when I'm nervous. Want me to pick a different stanza?"

"Maybe just concentrate on the bomb?"

"If you'd like to switch places, say the word."

Joe bit back his reply and tried to remember that David was a newbie operator on his shakedown trip. Aside from the snide comments and weird theatrical tics, he wasn't doing half bad.

"Gonna take that as a no," David said. "All right, I'm leaning into the cubby to see if I can see the backside of the device. Here we go—"

A *boom* shook the room.

Fortunately, it was the boom of the bathroom door slamming against its frame as someone tried to gain entry. Unfortunately, that distinction seemed lost on David. A second boom followed closely on the heels of the first. A boom caused by the newbie operator's skull smashing against the wooden enclosure.

"Mother of God," David said. "I—"

Joe shouted in Russian, hoping to drown out his partner's English.

"Why did you say that?" David hissed.

"I told whoever's pounding on the door that the bathroom's occupied," Joe whispered back.

"No, you did not."

The thunderous laughter from the far side of the door seemed to confirm David's statement. No matter. The bar's patrons had just witnessed two men head into a single bathroom together. Whatever faux pas Joe had committed would only serve to help their cover.

Probably.

"Nothing on the back side either," David said. "I stand by my earlier statement that I don't know shit about bombs, but I don't see anything that looks like a receiver or timer. Maybe you're right about the detonator being rigged to some kind of anti-tamper device. Didn't the Russians do that in Afghanistan?"

"Yeah," Joe said, standing to one side so David could climb down from his perch on the toilet. "They put bombs in toy trucks, dolls, teddy bears, you name it. Thousands of Afghan kids were maimed or killed."

"Animals," David said, reaching to brush a stray hair from his face.

Joe grabbed his partner's wrist. "Don't fucking move."

"What?"

Rather than answer, Joe snared the thin filament draped across David's forehead between his thumb and forefinger. Lifting the wire from his face, Joe gently followed it back to the cubby. The filament was attached to the bomb.

"Think I found the trigger," Joe said.

Like watching a match flare to life, Joe could tell the exact moment his companion made the connection. The thespian's emotions flitted across his face, changing from irritation to confusion to the final stop—terror. David's mouth opened, and his eyes widened. For a blissful moment the operator was silent.

Then he began to speak.

"If we are mark'd to die, we are to do our country loss—"

"Cut that out," Joe said as he gently settled the filament back into the cubby.

"You kidding me? I almost got a face full of roofing nails. I think I'm entitled to a little Shakespeare therapy. *This story shall the good man teach his son—*"

"If you don't stop, I'm going to rip out your tongue."

"Okay, okay. I'll use my inside voice. Is that a trip wire?"

Joe wondered the same thing. Hopping up on the toilet, he examined the cubby's interior, looking for the tamper mechanism. Obviously, the bomb wasn't rigged to blow if the wire went limp or else David would now be reciting his favorite play face-to-face with its author. His gaze tracked to the cupboard door. Then he understood. "Here," Joe said, pointing at a divot in the wood. "This is where the filament was attached."

His partner clambered onto the toilet next to him. "How do you know?"

"How many times have you seen a nail or tack embedded on the inside of a cupboard door? Whoever set the bomb must have secured the wire to something they pinned to the wood. Did you open the door fast or slow?"

"Slow."

"Why?"

David shrugged. "I was afraid the hinges would squeak, and I didn't want everyone in the bar to know I was looking for toilet paper."

Joe began to chuckle.

"What?" David said.

"Sorry," Joe said, his chuckle progressing to a full-fledged laugh. "Just trying to wrap my head around the idea that your prudishness is the only reason I'm not a human pincushion."

David pointed to the toilet paper holder. "It was empty."

"Because whoever planted the bomb wanted the next person in here to yank open the cupboard door," Joe said. That sobering thought put a damper on his humor. "They didn't have a specific target. Anyone who used the toilet would have been fair game."

"Like the Russians in Afghanistan."

"Yeah," Joe said, his mind replaying the earlier argument between the two groups of men. "Were you able to understand what they were yelling about?"

"A bit. The folks seated at the table were ethnic Russian Latvians like most of the people who live in Daugavpils. The pair who got their asses beat were probably members of a Latvian nationalist militia. Some offshoot of the Popular Front of Latvia I'd guess."

"The what?"

David rolled his eyes. "Did you read *any* part of the briefing book?"

"I just saved your life. Maybe dispense with the smart-ass comments."

David glanced at the cubby and swallowed. "Yeah, okay. Tensions have been high between the Latvian citizens of Russian descent, who reside primarily in the eastern section of the country, and Latvian nationalists like the Popular Front, ever since the Soviet Union tried to institute a coup in Riga a year or so back. Six Latvians were killed and a bunch more were wounded in the fighting."

Joe digested this in silence. There was something about the argument that was nibbling at the edge of his subconscious, but he couldn't work out its significance. Maybe because the five sticks of dynamite were still demanding his attention. "We can't leave this here," Joe said, pointing at the cubby. "It might still explode."

"So we'll what—walk out of here with it under one arm like it's a loaf of bread?"

Joe wanted to tell David to can it, but he didn't. For one, his partner's objection was a solid one, but perhaps more importantly, the kid hadn't raised the most obvious objection—the bomb could detonate if they moved it. David might be a bit too sarcastic for his taste, but the newbie operator possessed another trait that was much harder to find—courage.

"Exactly," Joe said. "But first I need you to earn your language pay."

"The extra one hundred dollars per month? Can't wait to hear what I have to do for that fortune."

"Go back to the bar and tell them I had an accident in here."

Watching David's cocky smile wilt was almost worth standing eyeball-to-eyeball with a stack of dynamite.

Almost.

"What kind of accident?"

"The kind that requires cleanup. Ask them for a towel or something. Maybe a couple of towels. I'll throw one of them over the bomb and then we'll walk out of here like it's a loaf of bread. How's that grab you?"

Judging by his expression, Joe's plan didn't grab his partner well at all. David opened his mouth, but his reply was drowned out by something equally unpleasant.

An explosion.

CHAPTER 6

T HE motor scooter careened around the blind corner doing almost forty.

For a second time, Rapp thought he was about to become a victim of vehicular homicide. Fortunately, the rider handled his scooter with a deftness that, while not excusing his excessive speed, helped atone for it. Downshifting, the man braked while simultaneously piloting the scooter to the left, passing within inches of Rapp's torso. The scooter fishtailed as the rider stopped, nearly tipping over. Turning, the rider flipped up his helmet's shaded visor to reveal an irate visage.

His flashing brown eyes centered on Rapp.

"Eres estúpido?"

Even for a non-Spanish speaker, the meaning wasn't hard to intuit.

Are you an idiot?

"Lo siento," Rapp said.

The man could be forgiven for assuming Rapp was apologizing for standing in the middle of the road.

He was not.

Snapping his arm in a tight circle, Rapp buried his elbow into the side of the rider's helmet. The man's head drooped, and he slid from the motor scooter. Rapp caught him beneath the armpits and eased him to the ground. Other than showing the bad sense to drive too fast on Barcelona's notoriously crowded narrow streets, the rider hadn't done anything wrong. Hopefully his motorcycle helmet meant the man would wake with nothing more than a bad headache.

A bad headache and one less motor scooter.

Climbing aboard the scooter, Rapp gunned the throttle and tore off down the street.

The winding passage, while large enough to fit a car, definitely favored the smaller scooters and motorcycles that were ubiquitous on Barcelona's streets. Unfortunately, Rapp's scooter was not what anyone would call a sport bike. The 50cc engine was designed for fuel economy rather than raw acceleration. Snarls from the Citroën's racing motor still reverberated from the side streets' narrow confines, but the sound was already growing fainter.

If Rapp didn't do something to change the equation, he would lose Greta.

Rounding a corner, Rapp caught a flash of the sedan's taillights as it slowed for an intersection. Then the car nosed into an adjacent street heading west. Braking, Rapp put his left foot onto the ground, added throttle, and spun the scooter in a tight left turn before rocketing down an alley that paralleled the sedan's route. The alley east-west-running side streets emptied into the larger north–south Ronda de Sant Antoni, but all paths were not created equal. Most of the side streets doglegged through additional intersections, while one or two flowed straight west. Rapp believed the alley he was following fell into the latter category, but he wasn't certain.

Only one way to find out.

The pedestrian traffic during this time of the day was thick, but most people stuck to the meager sidewalks. Most. A few braved the motorists by brazenly walking down the center of the street. Thankfully these daredevils were the exception. Between Rapp's liberal use of the motor scooter's anemic horn and his unwillingness to yield ground, the majority of the Spaniards he encountered gave way.

After nearly clipping a man who'd clearly paired his afternoon vermouth with breakfast, Rapp felt the bike sliding from beneath him. With a display of agility worthy of a former collegiate lacrosse player, he steered into the wobble, touched the ground with his right foot, redlined the engine, and shot back down the alley.

A string of angry Spanish phrases chased him, but Rapp was already focused on what lay ahead—a pair of plastic garbage bins marking the junction with the busier Ronda de Sant Antoni thoroughfare. While he didn't pretend to understand the intricacies of Spanish vehicular courtesies, he had learned something of Barcelona's rules of the road during his forays with Greta. Driving through some of the narrower alleys was frowned upon, and to discourage collisions between man and machine, refuse containers were strategically placed to block the entrance and exits to the tighter side streets.

Side streets like the one Rapp was currently hurtling down.

Gritting his teeth, Rapp edged the motor scooter onto the curb and drew both feet as close to the center of the scooter as possible. To dissuade motorists of the two-wheel variety, the city planners had lined the sidewalks with anti-traffic barriers resembling slender fire hydrants. Rapp estimated six inches of clearance between the concrete barriers and his scooter. Forcing himself to ignore the bone-crunching cement, he concentrated on the narrow, pedestrian-sized gap between the refuse bins.

With a final burst of speed, Rapp bounced from the sidewalk back to the street. He cannonballed between the bins and arrived on the far side mostly intact. A wrenching of the scooter's steering mechanism accompanied by a shriek of rending metal suggested that the bike that shot from the bins was not an exact replica of the one that had entered. A quick glance away from the road confirmed his thesis. His left mirror was gone and the right hung by a collection of wires. Still, he'd made it.

That was the good news.

The great news was that the Citroën's red two-toned bumper poked from a second side street to Rapp's right. The sedan was waiting at a traffic light.

A traffic light that had just turned green.

CHAPTER 7

R APP did not stop to think.

Instead, he revved the throttle with his right hand and reached for the small of his back with his left. Being left-handed was often an inconvenience.

Not today.

Steering and managing the throttle with his right freed Rapp's dominant hand to do what it did best: shoot. Though he would have loved to have fitted the suppressor to the Beretta's muzzle, there wasn't time. If Greta's abductor made it to Ronda de Sant Antoni, they were as good as gone. A constant stream of motorists flowed toward Plaça Universitat to the north and the busy Mercat de Sant Antoni to the south. Once the Citroën joined the vehicular artery, Rapp's opportunity to interdict the kidnappers would vanish.

Now or never.

He gunned the motor scooter and its underpowered engine responded with a whine that was more bark than bite. A horn sounded to his right as Rapp narrowly missed colliding with a delivery van, but the risk had proven worth the reward. He was moving, while the Citroën was still stationary. The sedan's driver was already nominally within pistol range, but Rapp didn't fire. Instead he held the Beretta alongside his leg, muzzle angled downward, as his scooter closed the distance to the car.

Surprise was his only advantage.

Each shot had to count.

Rapp numbered the men in the snatch team to be at least three. A driver and passenger in the front seat with the remaining team member in the rear with Greta. Precision shooting from a moving platform through a vehicle's safety glass was difficult, but the angles and distances favored him. He was approaching perpendicular to a stationary vehicle. If he shot through the driver's window, his bullets would only impact the car's front two occupants. Killing the driver would render the vehicle inoperable, which meant that Rapp would have time to reposition in order to deal with the situation in the rear seats—whatever that might be. Had it been up to him, Rapp would have delayed engaging the driver until his front tire was kissing the Citroën's door frame.

It was not up to him.

The traffic light finished cycling as Rapp closed to within ten feet.

The sedan edged forward.

Bringing the pistol up in a singular, smooth motion, Rapp aligned the front sight post on the driver's head and eased the slack from the trigger. The driver turned toward Rapp and his blue eyes widened.

He was too late.

Rapp had fired thousands of rounds through his Beretta. The pistol might as well have been an extension of his arm. The first shot would break in the next millisecond. Like an unwary skier caught in an avalanche's path, nothing could save the driver now.

Nothing but a blond ponytail.

Cursing, Rapp jerked the pistol off-target, sending his first shot into the Citroën's engine block instead of the driver's skull. Why Greta had chosen that moment to wrestle with the driver was baffling, but unimportant. His target line was now obscured.

Time for plan B.

Braking, Rapp slowed the motor scooter until he could jump clear. The bike slammed into the sedan's front bumper before crashing to the ground, but Rapp was no longer aboard. Once again, he stood atop the Citroën's hood. This time he had a pistol in his hands. Rapp indexed the Beretta's stubby front sight post on a dark-haired man in the passenger seat. A man who was frantically trying to draw a pistol from his waistband.

He wasn't going to make it.

Rapp was applying smooth pressure to the trigger when his shot was interrupted.

Again.

This time by a scream.

"Don't shoot!" Greta said. "Mitch, don't shoot!"

Rapp looked over the pistol's sights to see Greta stretched the length of the front windshield. "They are bodyguards! My grandfather's bodyguards!"

Once Rapp decided to kill someone, very few people could change his mind.

Greta was an exception.

So was her grandfather.

CHAPTER 8

A N invisible fist smashed into Joe's back and hurled him against the wall.

Through more luck than skill, he interposed his forearm between his skull and the exposed brick, but the collision still left him seeing stars. Joe groaned and tried to make sense of what had happened. His ears rang and his eyes burned from the sudden grit in the air. For a long moment he couldn't seem to breathe.

Then his quivering lungs began to function.

He inhaled, drawing much-needed oxygen into his chest, and then promptly coughed it back out. The air tasted of soot and smoke.

"David?" Joe croaked.

His partner lay on the dirty floor in a crumpled heap, blood trickling from the back of his head. Joe knelt by the newbie operator's side, reaching for his neck to check for a pulse. The moment his fingers brushed David's skin, his teammate reacted.

"*Blyat*," David growled as he came awake swinging.

"Easy, tough guy," Joe said, parrying the strike. "It's just me."

David hadn't been able to put much force behind the blow, but Joe clamped his teammate's arms to his sides anyway. The punch stung, but he didn't mind. The guy had just been knocked unconscious and he came to cursing in Russian and throwing a right hook.

He definitely had a future in the Unit.

"What happened?" David said. His words were slurred and his voice raspy, but his eyes were focused.

Progress.

"Great question," Joe said. "Can you stand?"

David closed his eyes and gritted his teeth. "Think so. Why aren't we dead?"

Another great question.

"Our bomb didn't explode," Joe said, helping his teammate to his feet, "so I'm guessing the bomber was an overachiever. Something detonated in the other room. The brick wall and thick wooden door must have attenuated the blast's shock wave and prevented the box of fun in the cupboard from sympathetically detonating."

"My head doesn't feel like anything got attenuated," David said.

"The door blew open and brained you," Joe said. "You're bleeding, but the cut looks superficial. Come on, we gotta get moving."

As if to emphasize Joe's statement, a resounding *snap* echoed from beyond the door followed by an equally ominous *thunk* as something heavy and once solid collapsed. The pub occupied the basement floor of a multistory building. There was bound to be structural damage after a blast of that magnitude.

"What about that?" David said, gesturing toward the cupboard.

"Leave it," Joe said. "No chance we're sneaking out of here now. Besides, the heat and secondary explosions might cause it to explode. Let's go."

The thespian frowned but didn't argue.

Joe understood.

Leaving the bomb felt wrong, but there was nothing he could do. He had come to terms with the idea that his chosen vocation was never going to be without risk, but Joe drew the line at outright suicide. Looping his teammate's arm over his shoulders, Joe staggered toward the door. The maneuver took a bit more out of him than he'd anticipated.

The world wasn't spinning, but it had developed a strange tilt.

"Wait," David said, gesturing at the door as they cleared the bathroom's threshold.

"Right," Joe said.

Propping his teammate against the wall, Joe limped back into the bathroom and pulled the door closed. The hardwood frame sported a series of new divots, but the length of oak still swung on its hinges. The shock wave had destroyed the latching mechanism, so it didn't shut completely, but most of the way closed was better than open. Hopefully the barrier would keep the fire's heat from the bomb for a bit longer.

David pushed himself from the wall and managed a step before he began to sway. Joe caught his teammate just as he started to crumple. "Easy there, tough guy. No sense bouncing your noggin off the floor. I'm gonna need you awake enough to throw some Russian around once we get outside."

David grunted something unintelligible, but he quit struggling.

Joe threaded David's arm over his shoulders a second time and then staggered into the bar proper. A blast of heat greeted him followed by a cloud of choking smoke. The room looked as if it had been hit by a tornado. The island of oak was somewhat recognizable, but what had once been the centerpiece of the establishment now more resembled a pile of scrap lumber. The base was intact, but everything higher than about four feet had been reduced to jagged splinters. A pair of legs lay on the floor like parts from a discarded mannequin, but only bits of gore remained of the bartender's torso and face.

"Oh, God," David said.

"Breathe through your mouth and keep moving," Joe said. "Nothing we can do."

Tongues of fire were already licking up the wall while separate flaming tentacles stretched for the floorboards. Only a matter of time before the bomb in the cupboard kicked off. Joe was grateful for the good fortune that had allowed him to survive the first detonation, but anyone who'd done this job more than a day knew that luck was a fickle mistress.

"What about them?"

Joe followed his teammate's pointing finger and sighed. He'd been focused on the bar's exit to the exclusion of the rest of the room. He wanted to believe that this was because he was concentrating on navigating the smoke-filled interior as quickly as possible, but this was only partly true. The less noble portion of the explanation was that he couldn't hold himself responsible for what he didn't see. Now, thanks to David, he knew about the bodies strewn across the opposite side of the bar. One of which was still twitching. Of all the news guys in the Unit, he was partnered with Jiminy Cricket.

"Lemme get you out. Then I'll come back for them."

"Why?"

"Someone needs to tell any Good Samaritans or first responders to stay the hell out of the building because of the second bomb. Any other helpful questions?"

David remained silent. Joe didn't know if that was because he really didn't have any more questions or because he was smart enough not to answer.

He'd take the win.

"Check on them now," David said as he pulled his arm away. "I can make it to the door."

Joe thought about reminding his teammate that he was in fact the team leader, but he didn't think it would have done any good. Besides, David was right. The fire would probably prevent him from reentering the bar once he helped David outside. If he intended to assist the other survivors, he had to do so now.

Joe paused to make sure David was capable of getting to the door. His teammate's steps were unsteady, but he was heading in the right direction, and the door leading outside was already open. Unit operations were often accomplished by two- or three-man teams, and working under these conditions was only possible if each team member trusted the other to do their job. David knew his assignment was to get clear of the building and warn first responders about the second bomb.

That was enough for Joe.

A *crack* split the air as another ceiling timber tumbled to the floor. Flames danced along the wood, searching for something else to consume. Between the waiting bomb and the roaring fire, the bar didn't have long.

Neither did Joe.

Putting a hand to his face, Joe tried to shelter his eyes and mouth as he stumbled toward the prone men. The heat had been present before, but it felt different now. More oppressive. As if he were standing naked beneath the desert sun. Wisps of smoke rose from his sleeves and the hem of his pants. A flaming piece of wood landed on his shirt. Joe beat at the fabric, extinguishing the ember.

He needed to get out of here.

The smoke was thicker closer to the wall and Joe crouched, searching for cleaner air. He didn't find much of that, but his proximity to the ground did make it easier to see the huddle of bodies. The unnaturally positioned head of the first casualty told him all he needed to know, as did the length of metal protruding from the chest of the second.

The third man, the one closest to the wall, showed promise.

Like his friends, the man's extremities were riddled with shrapnel and his leg was twisted at an obscene angle, but the fingers of his right hand were reaching toward the exposed skin around his neck. Moving closer, Joe saw smoke drifting from the man's shirt collar. He was alive and could feel pain.

Joe couldn't let him burn to death.

Hooking his hands beneath the man's armpits, Joe yanked the casualty clear of his companions. The man screamed as his broken leg flopped across the bodies, but Joe kept pulling as he backed toward the door. Either the explosion had rung his bell harder than he thought, or the man was bulkier than he'd expected, or both. Joe's legs quivered and his back muscles screamed, but he kept putting one foot in front of the other.

He took a giant breath and instantly folded double as a coughing fit racked his chest. He didn't dare drop the wounded man to wipe his mouth, for fear he would never be able to lift him again. Instead, Joe ignored the acid burning up his throat, the mucus streaming down his nose, and the vise squeezing his lungs. His vision tunneled, but he kept pulling, each step taking him closer to the beckoning door. The entrance was behind him, but Joe imagined the cool, fresh air just feet away as he tried to ignore the significance of his narrowing field of view.

Just a couple steps more.

Joe stumbled as the man's weight seemed to double. Peering down the length of the casualty's body, Joe saw that the patron's pant leg was caught on a bit of debris. The logical solution would be to set the man on the floor and try to work the fabric free, but if he did this Joe was afraid he'd never summon the strength to lift him again.

While in Ranger School, an instructor had told Joe that Rangers came in two types—strong or smart. Joe had always believed it was better to be part of the second category, but today he was praying to be counted among the first. Bending his knees, Joe lowered his center of gravity while worming his arms deep beneath the man's armpits. Then he clasped his hands in the Gable grip he'd first learned as a high school wrestler. The modified bear hug better distributed the bulk of the man's weight and Joe extended his legs, trying to pull the man free.

On the fourth step, Joe heard the gonging in his ears that announced his oxygen-starved brain was about to call it quits. He had no doubt that if his eyes were open, his vision would be wavery with the bright starburst that signaled a pending loss of consciousness. His eyes were not open because he didn't need to see.

He just needed to keep moving.

His legs wobbled and he sank to his knees, still holding the wounded man to his chest. The air was no longer just warm. Heat radiated across his skin, bringing to mind the time he'd almost stumbled into his grandfather's woodburning stove. The old man's gnarled hand had been surprisingly strong that day, grabbing him by the shirt collar before Joe's face had pushed through the open grate into the waiting flames.

There was no one to save him now.

"*Razreshite.*"

The Russian phrase seemed to drift at the edge of Joe's consciousness as he struggled to render the word into English. Something about getting moving maybe? He tried to formulate a response, but the required rejoinder flitted about like dandelion fuzz, just out of reach.

"*Razreshite.*"

This time the word came with more force. Force and action. Rough hands grabbed the man he was dragging and struggled to tear him from Joe's grasp. For a confused instant, Joe fought the attacker. Then he understood. Relinquishing his grip, Joe allowed the newcomer to bear the dead weight. Without the burden of the injured man, he was able to find his feet and continue moving. The first step almost brought him to his knees, but by the second, his muscles were able to compensate. Joe sucked in a breath, coughed, and opened his eyes. His savior was a man dressed in business casual with a pair of readers perched on the end of his nose.

Fantastic.

Joe, a former Ranger and Green Beret, had just been rescued by an accountant. In that moment he was both pissed that David had left him to be burned alive and grateful that the newbie operator hadn't been there to witness his shame. The Unit was primarily staffed with Army veterans, but a few Navy SEALs had also joined the ranks. When it came to his frogmen rivals, Joe would rather be dead than embarrassed.

A ball of fire erupted from behind the bar, peppering Joe's face with something sharp. The shrapnel missed his eyes, but judging by the sudden stickiness dripping down his forehead, not by much.

The accountant hadn't been so lucky.

The man screamed and began clawing at the jagged chunk of glass sprouting from his right eye socket. Reaching deep inside, Joe summoned his final reserves of strength. He looped his arms beneath the bar patron's armpits and began dragging him toward the door as he called to the accountant. He thought he was telling the man to follow his voice, but his raw throat made the words largely unintelligible.

Two agonizing steps later, he was out the door and into the refreshingly crisp air. Joe resisted the urge to drop the man on the street, choosing instead to drag him to the far curb. The sound of sirens cut through the air and he didn't want the wounded man to be accidentally run over by responding emergency vehicles. As if summoned by his thoughts, headlights played over him accompanied by the roar of an approaching engine. Setting the bar patron on the ground, Joe was turning toward the vehicle when his world went white.

He woke up facedown on the street to someone whispering into his ear.

In English.

"Get up, Joe. Get up, we've got to move."

Joe wasn't so sure about that. The pavement felt delightfully cool against his cheek, and while the cobblestones weren't exactly soft, he'd slept on worse. Unfortunately, whoever was whispering in his ear was pretty damn insistent.

"Get your ass moving."

Joe jerked, wondering for a moment if his grandfather was somehow speaking to him from beyond the grave. Then he realized the truth—Ulysses Dieck would have never stooped to using profanity.

Especially profanity spoken with a Bronx accent.

"Where . . . were . . . you?" Joe said, huffing between each word.

"Getting the car. Get up and get in. Now."

Joe turned to see the open door to their rented Lada sedan beckoning. His pounding head and rolling stomach suggested he'd been concussed, but his foggy thoughts struggled to make sense of what was happening. Something about leaving didn't feel right.

"What—" Joe said.

Or at least he tried to.

The contents of his stomach came rushing up right about the time he was searching for the next word. Turning his head, he vomited.

Definitely a concussion.

"I thought you Army guys could hold your liquor. Up you go."

Once again, strong hands grabbed Joe beneath the armpits, but this time they propelled him into the car. None too gently. Joe kept his pulsing head from crashing into the door, but his face bounced off the dashboard.

"What the—"

A slamming door drowned out his question. Then David was in the driver's seat next to him. A moment later, the Lada's little engine revved and Joe smashed into the upholstery as the car accelerated forward. He couldn't say whether it was a surge of adrenaline or just good old-fashioned anger that cleared the cobwebs, but the result was the same. He found his way through the mental fog.

"What the hell are you doing?" Joe said.

That he'd finally completed the sentence he'd tried three times to voice seemed like a major victory. So did the fact that his shaking hands managed to find and buckle the seat belt.

Progress.

"Chasing Russians," David said.

"What Russians?"

"The ones who planted the bomb."

CHAPTER 9

ONCE again, the words Joe was hearing seemed to be coming from far off. This time, it wasn't translating them from Russian that was giving him problems. It was the meaning of the words themselves.

"Russians planted a bomb?"

David slalomed to the left in order to make way for a police car hurtling in the other direction. The strobing emergency lights felt like ice picks stabbing into Joe's eye sockets. He closed his eyes, but the damage was done. Cranking down the passenger window, he stuck his head into the cool air and emptied his heaving stomach a second time. Thankfully, there wasn't much left to vomit, but the bile still burned his throat and left an acidic taste in his mouth.

"You okay?" David said.

"Peachy," Joe said, wiping his mouth with the back of his hand. "I somehow bounced my head off the cobblestones."

"Not somehow. I was coming around the corner when it happened. The second bomb must have detonated. The shock wave tossed you to the ground like a rag doll. A tongue of fire shot out of the door just above your head. You got lucky."

Joe did not feel lucky, but compared to the bar's other patrons, he'd won the lottery. Closing his eyes, he began to massage his temples, but the lack of visual references made his nausea worse. David was still driving like a bat out of hell and the way he was jerking the steering wheel made the little Lada bounce around like a rowboat in a typhoon. He opened his eyes just in time to see a motorcycle flash by.

A pair of red brake lights glowed in the distance.

"The bomb," Joe said. "Tell me about the bomb."

"Our friends from the bar were waiting outside in an RAF minivan across the street. I thought they were going to help at first, but they didn't. Instead, one of them flashed me the bird while the others laughed. That seemed strange, but I was having trouble thinking clearly. I knew I had to get the car, but I couldn't remember where we parked it."

"Guess I'm not the only one with a concussion."

David shrugged. "I haven't puked yet, so I think I'm okay. Besides, I only got blown up once."

As medical diagnoses went, this one wasn't exactly ironclad. Still, Joe wasn't in a position to argue. The throbbing in his head had begun to recede, but he sure as hell didn't feel up to weaving between traffic at 130 kilometers per hour on A13, a sleepy two-lane road probably rated for less than half that pace. Excessive speed aside, his teammate wasn't doing a half-bad job driving.

If only Joe knew what they were chasing.

David redlined the engine, and a boxy silhouette resolved into a knockoff Volkswagen minivan.

"Got you!" David said.

"Back off the gas," Joe said. "If you get too close, the driver will be able to see us in his rearview mirror."

David dutifully reduced his speed, and the minivan pulled ahead.

"There," Joe said once the minivan was about fifty yards in front of them. "That's the perfect distance. Now, walk me through how a drunk flashing you the middle finger makes him and his crew Russian operatives."

"Right," David said, nodding. "So when I came around the corner to get you, the agitators from the bar were standing by the van, but they weren't just watching. I had the windows down so I could hear them."

"Hear them?"

"Yeah. They were catcalling. Mocking the survivors and yelling insults. It was as if they wanted to be noticed."

Joe frowned.

While the men's behavior was callous, trying to read the purpose behind a belligerent drunk's actions was a fool's errand. Small slights often led to exaggerated outcomes when mixed with alcohol. There was a reason rowdy bars employed bouncers. "I'm still not following."

"The men wanted to be heard and seen," David said, enunciating the words as if he were speaking to a child. "They could have gotten away before anyone saw them, but didn't. The agitators wanted to be remembered."

"That makes no sense."

"It makes no sense if the men were what they seemed to be—Latvian nationalists picking a fight with their ethnic Russian countrymen. I've got a hunch they're something else. That second explosion was a doozy. It seemed to surprise the agitators as much as it did you. The shock wave knocked one of them into the van, and he let loose a string of curses."

Joe thought he was beginning to see. "In a different language?"

David shook his head. "Same language. Different accent."

"Russian?"

"Exactly."

Joe massaged his temples. It was thin, but he could see where David was heading with his theory. "You think the bombing was a false-flag operation?"

The minivan picked up speed as it exited Daugavpils proper for the more sparsely populated outskirts.

David kept pace.

"Daugavpils is unique among Latvian cities in that there are more ethnic Russians here than Latvians, right?" David said.

"Yep."

"And the ethnic Russians and Latvians don't always get along, right? Especially after the coup in Riga a couple of years back?"

"Yeah," Joe said. "Mostly low-level stuff, but there's definitely been an uptick in race-related crimes in Daugavpils. Latvian nationalists are naturally suspicious of their fellow citizens. Especially since some provinces openly supported the Soviet-instigated coup."

"Exactly," David said. "The coup failed for a number of reasons, not the least of them being world opinion. Images of unarmed Latvian citizens gunned down by Soviet paramilitary forces didn't play well on the nightly news. I'm not saying this is the only reason the Soviets backed down, but the narrative that innocents were being killed was a powerful one."

"Powerful enough for the Russians to give it a try?"

David nodded. "Think about it—Latvians of Russian descent get blown up by their own countrymen. If the Latvian government can't protect its citizens who are of Russian descent—"

"Then the Russian government might just have to do it for them," Joe said, waving away the argument. "I get the theory, and I agree that what you've laid out is certainly possible. What I don't understand is why we're chasing a van full of potential Russian operatives."

"Ah, sorry," David said. "I left out part of the story. The man that was smashed against the van was hemorrhaging pretty heavily. I think he got hit by a piece of shrapnel. Something big. I'm betting that he'll need a trauma center."

Joe was preparing to ask what that had to do with anything when he saw a road sign and put two and two together. A road sign for the Soviet air force base that was now a Russian facility. "You want to see where they take him for help?"

"Exactly," David said, flashing him a smile. "Now that we're out of Daugavpils, the nearest civilian hospital is in Preili, which is another twenty-five miles to the north. But if you're a Russian operative—"

"You'll want to use the level-one trauma center at the former Soviet air base in Lociki. That's pretty good thinking for a theater major."

"Like I said, I only got blown up once. Okay, here we go—moment of truth."

The minivan zoomed up to the turnoff for the air base. Continuing straight on A13 meant the Preili hospital and back to square one. Right meant the air base and a potential validation of David's theory. For a long moment, the Volkswagen's silhouette hung motionless.

Then the minivan's turn signal activated.

The right-turn signal.

CHAPTER 10

THE Hotel Casa Fuster was one of Barcelona's most luxurious accommodations. Tucked away just off the iconic Passeig de Gràcia, the hotel was a study in stunning architecture, fantastic dining, and a service staff that embodied old-world sensibilities. The hotel was not anywhere near Rapp's price range, which was why he'd never entertained the idea of staying there let alone renting the grand suite in which he currently found himself.

Then again, money didn't really factor into the decision-making criteria of the man seated across the coffee table from Rapp. Though he'd been born and raised in East Germany, Herr Carl Ohlmeyer had escaped to West Berlin shortly after receiving his degree in economics from the prestigious Humboldt University. He excelled in the field of finance and found work in one of West Germany's most important banks, where he eventually made the acquaintance of a brash young American intelligence officer by the name of Stanley Albertus Hurley. Together the two men wreaked financial havoc on the East German banking system and the Soviet patronage that kept the corrupt system afloat.

Now that the Cold War was over, Ohlmeyer ran his own family bank with the help of two of his sons and his favorite granddaughter. Officially, he was out of the intelligence business. Unofficially, he still helped his lifelong friend Stan Hurley obtain the occasional off-the-books passport or financing for operations too sensitive to be traced back to the CIA's collection of shell companies.

Ohlmeyer was a serious man who'd spent the entirety of his adult life engaged in the serious business of fighting on behalf of freedom-loving people against the ravages of fascism and communism.

He also happened to be Greta's grandfather.

"What are your intentions toward my granddaughter?"

Rapp resisted the urge to take a swallow from the cup of coffee he held in his left hand. Herr Ohlmeyer was a savvy businessman and had deep connections into the world of espionage. In addition to the support he provided to Hurley's official capacities, Ohlmeyer ran a retirement service for Stan and several other Orion operatives in the form of numbered Swiss bank accounts and safe-deposit boxes containing cash, passports, and the other assorted credit cards and licenses needed to establish a new identity.

Ohlmeyer was quite literally Hurley's get-out-of-jail-free card, and he provided these same services to Rapp. In turn, Rapp had repaid the banker's kindness by fomenting a clandestine romantic relationship with his granddaughter. A relationship that had exposed Greta to the dangers of the covert world he inhabited. Rapp had been dreading this conversation, but it was time to face the music. Squaring his shoulders, he did something extremely difficult for a spy.

He told the truth.

"I love her."

The words rolled off Rapp's tongue a little easier than expected, partly because he'd been practicing them on Greta, but also because he really did love Ohlmeyer's granddaughter.

This had not always been true.

In the beginning, their relationship had mostly been built on lust.

He and Greta were young, attractive, and available. Rapp had been taken with Greta's fierceness as much as her physical beauty. Though he couldn't read her mind, he believed that part of her initial attraction to him centered on his vocation.

She was bedding an assassin. A wolf among sheep. A member of a select cadre to whom her grandfather afforded a special kind of respect, while making it abundantly clear to her that such men were not appropriate targets for his beloved granddaughter's affection. Had it not been for Paris, the torrid sex would probably have fizzled out, and Greta would have gone the way of the women who'd preceded her.

But Paris had happened.

Finding himself with a gunshot wound to the shoulder, betrayed by his country, and the target of an international manhunt, Rapp had reluctantly brought Greta into the clandestine side of his existence. He'd fully expected her to bolt after experiencing the bloody reality of an assassin's life in all its gory detail.

She hadn't.

Instead, Greta had risen to the occasion and Rapp found himself responding to her sacrificial love in a way he hadn't since . . . since his college girlfriend had perished in the wreckage of Pan Am Flight 103 in Lockerbie, Scotland, in 1988. It had taken Rapp longer to echo Greta's proclamation of love, but once he'd spoken the words he did so with the single-minded intensity that he applied to all aspects of his life.

Rapp did love Greta.

Whether that love would survive her grandfather's scrutiny remained to be seen.

Herr Ohlmeyer stared back at Rapp for a long moment, his flinty blue eyes giving away little. This was the face of a man who'd helped Hurley run operations against the Stasi, the nickname for East Germany's secret police. The face of the man who had the ability to keep Rapp looking over his shoulder for the rest of his life with just a few well-placed phone calls.

After an eternity, the patriarch slowly nodded.

"I believe you. More importantly, I believe she loves you, but she doesn't understand you or your world. Not the way I do."

"I think she understands more than you think," Rapp said. "It was never my intention to put her in danger, but—"

"Danger still found her," Ohlmeyer said, waving away Rapp's argument with slender fingers. "This is precisely my point. You of all people should understand that she will never be safe so long as she is with you. My friend Stan Hurley says that you're good, Mr. Rapp. Perhaps one of the best he's ever trained. But being good wasn't enough to keep you from getting shot, was it?"

Despite his best efforts to remain cordial, Rapp felt his blood pressure beginning to rise. "That's a bit hypocritical, don't you think? When most everyone else in West Germany was content to ignore the menace of communism, you used your position in one of your nation's most important banks to facilitate clandestine operations against East Germany. Are you telling me that your actions didn't put your family and loved ones at risk?"

"They absolutely did!" Ohlmeyer slammed his fist against the coffee table as his German accent grew more pronounced. "My work came at a price. A horrible price. One I would spare my granddaughter."

A flush crept across the old man's cheeks and his chest heaved as he fought to catch his breath. His physical reaction, more than the substance of Ohlmeyer's argument, persuaded Rapp to hold his tongue. Rapp did not run agents like a traditional CIA case officer, but he didn't need to be a master spy to realize that he'd struck a nerve. One of Ohlmeyer's bodyguards vacated his position by the door in response to the old man's outburst, but this seemed to only further anger the banker.

"I'm all right, damn you."

Greta's grandfather did not appear to be all right. Though Ohlmeyer had always looked every bit of his sixty-odd years, the former spy didn't seem to be himself. His face was puffy and his eyes bloodshot from lack of sleep, too much alcohol, or perhaps both. Rapp had originally chalked Ohlmeyer's appearance up to worry about his granddaughter, but now realized that the banker's concern was a symptom, not the problem. Something had caused him to fly to Barcelona and dispatch members of his security detail to round up his granddaughter. Judging by the man's genuine surprise at finding Greta sequestered with Rapp, their relationship wasn't the catalyst for Ohlmeyer's behavior.

The old man was spooked.

After several deep breaths, Ohlmeyer's breathing returned to normal, and his expression turned from irritation to a look Rapp couldn't quite read. The banker rubbed his chin and his gaze traveled across Rapp as if seeing him for the first time. "You truly love my granddaughter?"

Rapp nodded. "I do."

"Then let's see if your words have conviction. She needs help."

Rapp again felt his temper stir. He was not accustomed to having his veracity challenged and Ohlmeyer had done so twice in a single setting.

"Help with what?"

"Someone who wants to kill her."

CHAPTER 11

RAPP stared at Ohlmeyer, waiting for the old man to elaborate.

When he didn't, Rapp sighed and bit the bullet. "Who?"

The banker slowly nodded. "That is a reasonable question. The question of an assassin preparing to service his next target, but in this case, it's the wrong question. It is the *why* rather than the *who* that must inform our response to this threat."

Again, the banker paused and again Rapp refused to immediately take the bait. Instead, he took a swallow of coffee and engaged his most fearsome weapon.

His mind.

In keeping with European traditions, the coffee was a latte, since it was now late afternoon. The brew was both strong and flavorful, but Rapp unexpectedly had a craving for good old-fashioned American drip java. He'd been living his legend as a Paris-based traveling computer salesman for almost two years. While the idea of calling one of Europe's most desirable cities home had seemed great on paper, the reality was different. He missed America and all her eccentricities. He'd become somewhat of a soccer fan in order to fit in with the locals, but nothing beat *Monday Night Football*. In fact, had it not been for his relationship with Greta, Rapp thought he might have already requested a move back stateside.

Greta.

Ignoring Ohlmeyer's exasperated expression, Rapp surveyed the room.

The hotel had a distinctively European feeling without the postmodern vibe that seemed to be all the rage. Rather than monochromatic decorations, hard edges, and uncomfortable furniture, the décor was warm and the plush leather chair could have been fitted for his backside. A carafe of freshly squeezed orange juice stood glistening next to a bowl of mixed fruit and a plate of meats and cheeses on the low table that separated him from the German banker. Cut-glass tumblers filled with mineral water completed the entourage. One of Ohlmeyer's men hovered in the background, but the remainder of the banker's security detail was absent.

As was Greta.

After arriving at the hotel under the care of the agitated, but otherwise no worse for wear, security detail, Greta had been warmly embraced by her grandfather and then told in no uncertain terms to wait in an adjoining suite while the family's patriarch had a private conversation with Mr. Rapp. Since he had more than a passing familiarity with Greta's stubborn streak, Rapp had expected fireworks. Instead the woman he loved had brushed his cheek with a kiss and then done her grandfather's bidding. It wasn't lost on Rapp that the sign of physical affection had been its own form of rebellion, but he was also a little shocked to see his headstrong spitfire behave like a church mouse.

He hadn't understood then.

He did now.

Greta was not as ignorant of her grandfather's past as the banker believed. Or at the very least, she realized that the man who'd secreted her pieces of chocolate as a child was more than just a financial tycoon. Greta understood Ohlmeyer, which went a long way toward explaining why she understood Rapp.

But perhaps the kiss had a deeper meaning.

Beyond just demonstrating her affection for Rapp, Greta had also communicated the opposite with equal clarity. She loved Ohlmeyer with the entirety of her heart, which meant that if Rapp truly cared for her, he needed to see the old man in the same light. Like it or not, the banker's problem had just become his. After a final swallow of coffee, Rapp set the ceramic mug neatly on its coaster. Then he turned his attention back to the man seated across from him.

"How about we dispense with the cloak-and-dagger nonsense?"

"Easier said than done, my young friend. Cloak-and-dagger nonsense is the exact reason why I sent a detail of the best Swiss security specialists money could buy to augment my own personal protection team when they recovered my granddaughter."

Rapp refrained from pointing out that if these men were the best money could buy, Ohlmeyer might want to ask for a refund.

Or at least a discount.

As security details went, the men had performed adequately, but against an operative of Rapp's caliber, adequate wasn't enough. And while Rapp was good, perhaps very good, he was not an invincible killing machine. If he had been able to get to Greta, the real person or persons who'd prompted such a response from Ohlmeyer would be able to do the same.

Like it or not, Rapp was in this now.

Biting back another irritation-laced response, Rapp tried a different track. One that he didn't often employ.

Humility.

"How can I help?"

Ohlmeyer sighed and settled deeper into his seat. "I am not trying to be obtuse, it's just that a problem that has been thirty years in the making is not so easily put into words. To reciprocate the simplicity of your question with an equally simple answer—I need you to visit someone and ask him a series of questions."

"You're a man of considerable resources, Herr Ohlmeyer," Rapp said. "Why would you need my help to ask someone questions?"

"The person in question is beyond my reach."

Rapp studied the banker, waiting for the other shoe to drop.

On the far side of the room, the valet fussed with a stainless-steel monstrosity affixed to the far wall. Steam hissed, milk frothed, and espresso gurgled. Two additional mugs sat within easy reach.

Herr Ohlmeyer was expecting company.

"I wasn't aware that any place on earth was beyond your reach."

"The man in question resides in Russia. Moscow to be exact."

Touché.

While Moscow wasn't the Arctic Circle, it would definitely qualify as out of reach for a man who'd once gone head-to-head with the KGB during the height of the Cold War.

"Let's say for argument's sake that I was able to have a conversation with this man. What would you have me do with him once our question-and-answer session was over?"

"Kill him."

Though he'd half expected that answer, Rapp was still a little unnerved at Ohlmeyer's sudden frankness. Moments ago, the conversation had been all subterfuge and innuendo. Now the man he'd known only as a friend of Stan's and an enabler of clandestine operations was asking him to interrogate and kill someone.

On the other side of the room, the valet was topping off mugs with frothed milk and arranging them on a platter. While he was far from an expert on banking, Rapp understood that the management and movement of large amounts of money did not happen in a vacuum. If something or someone had prompted the Swiss banker to take such extraordinary measures to protect his granddaughter, chances were that the threat did not end at his doorstep. Ohlmeyer was a banker, which meant that he had customers.

Customers who would need to be reassured that their investments were still safe.

"I am not a killer for hire," Rapp said.

"That's good because I don't intend to pay you. Think of this as a target of opportunity. A chance to right one of the greatest wrongs ever leveraged against your nation."

In spite of himself, Rapp was intrigued.

Whatever Ohlmeyer might be behind the façade of gentleman financier, he was not a blowhard. Stan Hurley did not trust his life to unserious men. That said, what Ohlmeyer was asking of Rapp was not insignificant. The Iron Curtain might have fallen, but the former Soviet Socialist Republics were not exactly bastions of freedom and democracy.

Until now, Rapp's talents had been directed toward targets more suitable for his appearance and aptitude for Arabic, but that didn't mean he was ignorant of the seismic shifts upending governments and alliances all across the European continent. While many of the Western-based foreign policy intelligentsia were dancing in the streets and proclaiming the end of history, Rapp viewed the Soviet Union's demise with a more skeptical eye.

Yes, the collapse of communism was undoubtedly a good thing, but he wasn't convinced that rainbows and unicorns were about to spring from the ash heap. Based on his own study of history, Rapp didn't believe in a bias toward good or morality. The United States was an exceptional nation precisely because the values and ideals on which it had been founded were the global exception rather than the norm. More often than not, the collapse of an empire birthed chaos, and the forces that filled the ensuing void were not benevolent. Swirling undercurrents of greed and corruption were already choking Russia's fledgling attempt at democracy.

"Who are we talking about?" Rapp said.

"Alexander Hughes."

Despite the fact that he was employed by the agency, Rapp had deliberately limited his exposure to the organization. He was a member of the Orion team. A black program with a singular goal—the elimination of his nation's enemies.

Rapp was not an intelligence officer.

He was an assassin.

He did not concern himself with agency politics, bureaucracy, or lore. He had no ambition to one day rule an empire from Langley's seventh floor or serve as a chief of station for one of the CIA's coveted overseas postings. Rapp neither knew nor cared how the CIA ran its clandestine service because as far as he was concerned, he was not part of the agency. His handler was Irene Kennedy, and his mentor, Stan Hurley, was the senior member of Orion and a fellow contractor.

That said, even Rapp knew the name Ohlmeyer had just rhetorically tossed onto the table. The damage done by Alexander Hughes rivaled the havoc wrought by Julius and Ethel Rosenberg, the American husband-and-wife spy team who provided the Soviet Union with the means to construct their first atomic bomb. While Hughes hadn't upended the world's nuclear strategic balance, his espionage had hamstrung British and American intelligence efforts for a generation.

Hughes had been a CIA officer assigned to the Berlin Operations Base, the most important intelligence posting during the Cold War. Hughes had used his access to funnel sensitive information to the Stasi and the KGB. Information responsible for decimating American and British espionage efforts in East Germany and the Soviet Union. The total butcher's bill was difficult to calculate, but even conservative estimates put the number of executed Russian CIA agents at close to a dozen.

To make matters worse, Hughes was able to escape to East Germany before his espionage was discovered. He accepted a job with the Stasi, then thwarted justice a second time by fleeing to Moscow after the Berlin Wall fell. Once in Moscow, he resumed his espionage activities against the United States, this time in the KGB's employ.

Alexander Hughes was definitely a man who needed killing.

But was Rapp the person to pull the trigger?

"My taskings come from my handler," Rapp said, "not you or anyone else. Unless you'd care to explain exactly what this has to do with Greta, I'm leaving."

Rapp got to his feet.

The lone bodyguard moved closer.

Rapp locked gazes with him and the man stutter-stepped. It was apparently not lost on the guard that the same Beretta that had been pointing at him through his sedan's windshield was still holstered at the small of Rapp's back. Rapp felt a bit of sympathy for his fellow shooter, but only a bit. To paraphrase another Hurleyism, people who played stupid games won stupid prizes.

"Two days ago, a message arrived at the doorstep of my house in Zurich. An unmistakable message."

Rapp remained standing, but he changed his focus from the bodyguard to Ohlmeyer. "I'm listening."

"An intricately wrapped gift box like the sort you might receive from a designer store. My wife, Elsa, is fond of such stores and I am well acquainted with their appearance."

"Did Elsa open the box?"

Ohlmeyer shook his head. "Thankfully not. I saw it first and something made me pull on the scarlet ribbon tied in a bow across the top. Maybe it was curiosity or the compelling nature of a length of satin just waiting for a tug. Or perhaps it was the dregs of the intuition that kept me alive during my early days in East Germany. You're too new to know this just yet, but once that instinct has been awakened it never fully goes to sleep."

Rapp was indeed relatively new at this game, but he was not new to killing. Stan and Irene had kept him busy. Very busy. And while Rapp wasn't the type to keep notches on his Beretta's pistol grip, Hurley had once let slip that Rapp was the most successful graduate of the Orion program to date.

Men in Stan's line of work only measured success one way.

"The box," Rapp said, not bothering to hide his exasperation. "What was in it?"

Ohlmeyer held eye contact with Rapp for a beat before looking at a point somewhere over his shoulder. The banker's facial muscles contracted, pulling his still-handsome features into a mask of rage. "Two things. An old friend's head and a piece of stationery."

"What was on the paper?"

"A handwritten message and a series of numbers. The message said that the next box I received would hold the head of someone who was even dearer to me."

"Greta," Rapp said.

Ohlmeyer nodded.

Rapp processed that scene in his mind's eye.

Hollywood had done its part to desensitize the average moviegoer to violence, but there was something horribly effective about presenting an adversary with a companion's head. Perhaps that was because, setting the visceral nature of the act aside, it was the ultimate degradation of a person. A separation of their most recognizable feature—their head—from the body that had kept them alive. It forced a victim's friends and family to associate a final image with pieces of a whole rather than the personage.

"Who was the victim?" Rapp said.

"Someone who began as an adversary before becoming a compatriot, and finally, a friend. The head in the box belonged to Felix Bauer. We first met on the Cold War's battlefield."

"He was Stasi?"

Ohlmeyer nodded, a slow, ponderous movement as if the weight of his head had suddenly grown too heavy for his neck to bear. "After a fashion. It's more accurate to say that he was my counterpart for the Stasi. An East German banker who facilitated the East German intelligence service's operations against the West. Over time, he became disenchanted with the communists and their Soviet puppet masters."

"So he defected?"

Another nod. "He escaped to West Berlin and brought with him a treasure trove of information in the form of financial documents and other insights into how the Stasi and KGB were operating."

"And you think Alexander Hughes had him killed? Why?"

Ohlmeyer shrugged. "As to your first question, most certainly. The series of numbers annotated to the stationery corresponded to an off-shore bank account. Or to be more accurate, a former offshore bank account. The account that held the not-inconsiderable funds the Stasi and KGB had jointly deposited in exchange for the classified information Hughes passed to them."

Rapp was beginning to understand where this was headed. "I take it Mr. Hughes was never able to access these funds?"

"Correct. Felix Bauer brought the account information with him when he defected, and I used it to drain his funds. To put it mildly, Hughes was not happy."

A hiss originating from across the room became a gurgle as the steward added a final mug of steaming brew to the trio resting on the gilded, silver tray. Apparently, Ohlmeyer was expecting a quartet of visitors.

"How much did Hughes lose?" Rapp said.

"The current value of that account would be somewhere in the neighborhood of five million US dollars. Hughes was a shrewd investor."

Rapp sucked in a breath. Five million dollars was certainly reason enough to carry a grudge, but something else about this entire affair didn't make sense. "But that was what, ten years ago? Why would Hughes suddenly start settling old scores now?"

"I do not know. I was rather hoping you would put that question to him."

"What about Greta?" Rapp said. "How does she play into this?"

Ohlmeyer shrugged. "I haven't the slightest idea. She's important to me; maybe that is reason enough for Hughes to target her. Either way, a

credible threat has been made against her life, so I've taken steps to protect her. She's being moved into hiding as we speak."

Rapp didn't respond, but judging by Ohlmeyer's reaction, the set of
his jaw still said plenty.

"Let me explain," Ohlmeyer said, holding up a liver-spotted hand.
"I did this not as leverage against you but as protection from you."

Rapp leaned toward the banker. "If you think I'd ever—"

"I don't. At least not intentionally. But you have been in this business long enough to know that the notion that someone can hold out
indefinitely against torture is rubbish. Make no mistake, the task I've
laid at your feet is not insignificant. The odds of you making it into
Moscow, interrogating and killing Hughes, and then escaping unde-
tected are not great. I'm asking you to do this because I believe the risks
are worth the reward, but I didn't live to old age by placing my fate in the
hands of chance. I'm prepared to weather the storm if you're captured and
must give up what you know about me. My granddaughter is not."

Rapp slowly leaned back in his chair. While he still thought what
Ohlmeyer had done was underhanded, he understood the banker's
reasoning. He might have suggested something similar to insulate
Greta had Ohlmeyer bothered to consult him. Then again, he hadn't
exactly consulted Ohlmeyer before he'd begun to date his granddaughter.

"You understand," Ohlmeyer said.

The banker's words were phrased as a statement rather than question. Rapp's role as a clandestine operative necessitated subterfuge and
he normally prided himself on his ability to mask his emotions.

Normally.

When the subject matter was Greta Ohlmeyer, the word *normal* no
longer applied.

"Who else are you asking for help?" Rapp said, gesturing toward the
silver tray laden with coffee cups. Ohlmeyer smiled.

"I'm glad thoughts of my granddaughter haven't completely blunted
your instincts. I don't believe in playing fair. You are my best option to

unravel this plot, but I would not trust Greta's life to a single man. And before you ask, no, I will not tell you anything about the people I'm about to meet any more than I will discuss you with them. Now, I'm afraid the time for choosing is upon you, Mr. Rapp. Will you help my granddaughter?"

In the year or so since Rapp had graduated from Hurley's version of the Farm and begun to work operationally, he'd learned a great deal about himself and his enemies. He'd also discovered quite a few things about his supposed allies. He trusted Irene Kennedy, and Stan Hurley had begun to grow on him, but the job gone wrong in Paris had only reinforced something he'd instinctively known from the beginning of his clandestine career—there was just one person on whom he could completely rely.

Himself.

Technically, Rapp shouldn't be agreeing to undertake an operation without permission from Kennedy or Hurley.

Technically.

His final set of instructions from Hurley came to mind. At the time he'd issued them, Hurley had been driving Rapp away from a Paris hotel in which Rapp had just killed four men, one of whom happened to be a French intelligence officer and another the presumptive director of the CIA. That the American, Paul Cooke, was a traitor and had been plotting with the others to kill Rapp made the choice to engage in the unsanctioned assassinations a no-brainer, but Hurley had known that the deaths would hit the international press with the subtlety of a nuclear blast.

Accordingly, Stan's final instructions had been both simple and unambiguous.

Lie low for a while.

To Rapp's way of thinking, this meant that he was off the government clock until such time as Hurley, or more likely Kennedy, rescinded those instructions. While Stan had been direct from the standpoint that he expected Rapp to remain off the grid, he hadn't specified what Mitch should do during his vacation.

Or what he *shouldn't* do.

With this in mind, if he decided to take a sightseeing trip to Moscow and drop in on Alexander Hughes, Rapp couldn't imagine that Hurley would object.

Actually, he could very much imagine Stan objecting.

Loudly.

But what Hurley, Kennedy, or even Thomas Stansfield would think of his choices didn't much matter to Rapp. This wasn't about spies, national secrets, or old grudges. Greta had been there for him when he was at his most vulnerable. If someone was foolish enough to threaten the woman he loved, he intended to help them see the error of their ways.

Permanently.

Rapp turned from the tray of coffee mugs to Ohlmeyer's expectant blue eyes. "I'm in."

"Excellent. First-class tickets on Emirates airline to Moscow are waiting for you at the airport. I took the liberty of purchasing them under your French legend. I'm certain you and Mr. Hughes will have a productive conversation and that you'll be reunited with my granddaughter in no time."

Rapp wasn't so sure.

CHAPTER 12

IRENE Kennedy walked through the hallway at a pace that was just short of a run. Her haste was partially due to the fact that she was late for a meeting with the acting director of the Central Intelligence Agency.

But only partially.

While she'd become more accustomed to the ebb and flow of the headquarters building, Irene was still a field officer at heart. She purposely avoided the bureaucrats who landed a coveted spot in Virginia with the intention of never venturing back to the real world. Though she wanted to believe that such people made up a far smaller percentage of employees in the nation's premier intelligence organization as compared with the other sprawling governmental agencies that called the greater Washington, DC, area home, recent events were putting this thesis to the test. The man many had figured as the odds-on favorite to become the next CIA director, Deputy Director Paul Cooke, had been found dead in a hotel room having been in the process of passing classified information to a couple of other equally dead bad guys.

And Rapp had been the one who'd killed him.

Irene wasn't normally one for office intrigue. Yes, she was a legacy employee who counted the legendary Stan Hurley as a sort of uncle and Thomas Stansfield, deputy director of operations and current acting director, as a surrogate father, but she had zero interest in the political jockeying that went along with moving up the ranks at the agency. Instead, she'd approached her mandatory headquarters rotation with the attitude that she would keep her head down, work hard, and get back to an overseas posting as quickly as possible. Her failure to return to the field in a more timely manner had more to do with Stansfield's gravitational pull than her hard work, but even after several years, Irene still refused to consider Langley home. But home or not, Irene was a spy and keenly attuned to things normal people didn't notice. Things like the sense of morale a place projected. And Langley's current morale could be summed up in one word.

Bad.

"He's expecting you."

Irene smiled her thanks at Meg, Stansfield's assistant, pretending not to notice the implied rebuke. With a force of will cultivated through countless hours of training at the CIA's school for fledgling spies known as the Farm, Irene kept her expression placid until she was behind the woman. Only then did she stop to nervously tuck her shoulder-length auburn hair behind her ears.

Though she'd yet to celebrate her thirtieth birthday, Irene was already reporting directly to the man who would probably occupy the seventh floor's corner office. She knew that Stansfield would have never promoted her so quickly had her work as a case officer not justified her rapid accession, but the same couldn't be said for her coworkers. A CIA case officer's promotion was tied to successful asset recruitments. Irene agreed with the philosophy of basing promotions on merit rather than time in service, but when peers succeeded at different rates, jealousy was a natural by-product. Irene had to be better than anyone else because Thomas Stansfield had been her surrogate father after her own was killed when a Hezbollah terrorist detonated an explosive-laden van in front of the US embassy in Beirut, Lebanon.

But that wasn't the only reason.

Surrogate daughter or not, Thomas Stansfield treated all his employees the same. If you produced, he rewarded you. If you didn't, you were out. His management style was as simple as it was effective. So far, Irene had more than earned her mentor's respect.

So far.

"Irene—nice of you to join us."

Stansfield's comment was delivered with a smile, but the implied warmth didn't quite reach the discerning eyes behind his black glasses. The last several weeks had been trying for multiple reasons. Rapp's sanctioned assassination of a former Libyan intelligence officer in Paris had been a setup. An ambush designed to kill the American assassin facilitated by information leaked by the treacherous CIA officer, Paul Cooke. Though wounded, Rapp had escaped the killing zone with his life. The same could not be said of the several innocent Parisian bystanders who had been murdered by the terrorists gunning for Rapp.

But that wasn't even the worst of the news.

The fallout from the compromised operation had brought to the surface tensions that had long been simmering between Rapp and Hurley, while at the same time compelling Stansfield to acknowledge the shit show that had developed under his watch.

Irene suspected it was Stansfield's forced realization of his blind spot toward Stan Hurley and the toxic environment this forbearance had created that really had her boss on edge. In the space of a week, years of work had nearly been undone. Though Rapp had managed to plug the leak before Cooke's damaging information had left the hotel room, France was a mess, the Orion program was being rethought, and Stansfield was reexamining his thirty-year history with Hurley in a new, much more critical light. Morale might be bad for the rank-and-file agency employees who had learned that one of their own had been murdered in France, but for the handful who were truly in the know, Irene would use a different descriptor for their collective state of mind.

Abysmal.

"Sorry, sir," Irene said. "A cable came in downstairs that I thought might be pertinent to this discussion. I wanted to get a final update."

Though Irene's actual role was to run the Orion program, that project was so black as to be nonexistent, so she needed a "cover" job. Accordingly, the agency's org chart listed Irene as loosely attached to the Counterterrorism Center, located in the basement of the Old Headquarters Building. Normally this meant that the information she was privy to had a nexus to Islamic terrorism.

Normally.

But since Rapp's handiwork in the French hotels had been labeled as terrorism, Irene had started perusing classified cables from CIA stations and bases across the continent to determine the fallout from the deaths. In doing so, she'd stumbled across something interesting concerning a potential terrorist attack in the former Latvian Soviet Socialist Republic.

Stansfield eyed her over the top of his reading glasses before waving her to a seat at his conference table. He didn't arch his right eyebrow, which she took as a good sign, but Irene knew she was on borrowed time. While Stansfield had been staring down enemies for most of his life, this morning he had an appointment with a group of interrogators that caused even someone with his impressive résumé trepidation.

The United States Senate Select Committee on Intelligence.

Paul Cooke's death had been sensational and his employment with the CIA well-known. The details were simply too juicy to pass up and the series of front-page stories that had run in the *Washington Post* and *New York Times* were starting to mirror the writing style of the *National Enquirer*. The cold, hard facts were that politicians made their living by attracting voters and donors, and that was easier to do when elected officials were in the news. In a rare show of bipartisanship, ranking members from both parties on the Senate committee had declared their intention to hold public hearings into Cooke's murder.

Stansfield had considered appealing to the coterie of legislators known to be friendly to the CIA to cancel the hearings altogether, or at a minimum close them to the press and uncleared visitors, but Irene had argued against the idea. More than just the CIA's reputation was at stake.

Cooke's murder had the potential to expose the Orion program, not to mention the fallout that would occur if it became known that an off-the-books CIA assassin had killed an agency executive. To Irene's way of thinking, Stansfield's best option was to come before the committee, handle the questions, and let the opportunists score their political points.

The French government had a vested interest in keeping the true nature of their DGSE operative's role from coming to light and was doing what they could to characterize the gathering as an asset meeting gone bad. Stansfield's voluntary testimony would take the air out of many of the conspiracy theories currently circulating among the Beltway elite, while also engendering some goodwill from the very senators who would be voting on his eventual confirmation as head of the CIA. It was the logical course of action and Stansfield had eventually agreed with Irene's reasoning.

But agreeing to testify and testifying were two very different things.

"Another development in the investigation?" Stansfield asked.

Irene shook her head. "No, but perhaps something that will take their minds off Cooke."

"Please tell me that Mr. Rapp hasn't upstaged himself by killing the potential director of yet another intelligence service?"

Stansfield delivered the question with a ghost of a smile, but Irene knew the question was only half in jest. The people murdered in that Paris hotel room had not been on the Orion kill list and their deaths had not been sanctioned by Irene or Stansfield. Hurley had claimed that he'd given Rapp the go-ahead before the assassin had done his work, but

Irene had her suspicions. So did Dr. Tom Lewis, the agency shrink in charge of vetting members of the Orion team.

Like Stansfield, Hurley was off his game because his judgment had been inadequate. Stan's number two man in the Orion program, Victor, had proven to be a traitorous murderer who had passed the program's classified kill list to Cooke, who in turn was preparing to sell it along with information on program operatives to a pair of terrorists when Rapp intervened. If it also came to light that Rapp had decided to assassinate four people without Stan's go-ahead, Hurley's future with the agency might just be over. This contingency would have beggared belief only days ago, but Irene was willing to bet that Stansfield was now considering this exact course of action.

"No, sir," Irene said. "As per his last directive from Stan, Mitch has stayed off the radar. He calls the message service every twenty-four hours to check for instructions, but otherwise he's a ghost."

"A ghost with Greta?"

Irene shifted in her seat.

This topic was a source of friction. While he was certainly no stranger to the stress that came with living a clandestine existence and the torrid romances that often resulted from this lifestyle, Stansfield viewed Greta differently. The Swiss girl's grandfather was one of his oldest friends and a comrade in arms. After learning about the relationship from Hurley, Stansfield had provided more than one thinly veiled hint that perhaps Irene should issue an ultimatum to her assassin to end the dalliance. These suggestions had not taken the form of orders yet, which gave her a bit of latitude, but Irene recognized the thunderclouds gathering on the horizon all the same.

"I think that's a safe assumption," Irene said.

"You didn't ask?"

"No. Orion program members are trained to operate without supervision. Rapp is no exception."

Irene wanted to respond with something much more pointed. That Rapp was an exception in every sense of the word certainly wasn't lost on Stansfield. Neither was the notion that he was treading on the toes of one of his most capable and trusted case officers. Irene wasn't conflict-averse, but she was judicious about where and when she picked a fight. With her boss just minutes from leaving for a meeting with a bunch of salivating jackals and a roomful of cameras, now was not the time to address Stansfield's double standards toward Rapp.

But that fight was coming.

"Sorry," Stansfield said with a sigh. "I know I'm taking my frustrations out on the messenger, but this thing with Cooke has me worried. If the truth of what he was doing in that hotel room becomes more widely known, the congressional outrage will make the Church Committee look like a PTA meeting. But that's a problem for later. I believe you were going to bring me up to speed on something in Eastern Europe?"

Irene stared at Stansfield.

Her mentor smiled back. "Yes," he said, "I do still have a mole or two down in the Counterterrorism Center. Unfortunately, the quality of their reporting isn't what it used to be. I knew you were headed this way with information about Europe, but not the specifics. Now, out with it."

Irene filed Stansfield's revelation away for future consideration, determined to figure out who in her basement office was the informant. And just that quickly she realized she'd been played. The cover sheet on the folder in her right hand bore the alphanumeric designator indicating the reporting inside concerned the Near East Division, which included both Europe and Russia. Maybe the old spymaster still had a source or two in the basement, or maybe he was just trying to keep her on her toes. Either way, Thomas Stansfield was still a formidable opponent.

She hoped the waiting senators would soon learn this lesson first-hand.

"This reporting comes from an American clandestine special operations team on an intelligence-gathering mission in Latvia," Irene said.

"They witnessed a bombing at a popular bar in downtown Daugavpils. Latvian media is calling the incident probable domestic terrorism perpetrated by members of a nationalist militia who intended to target Daugavpils's ethnic Russian population. This is a plausible explanation, since tensions between ethnic Russians and Latvian nationalists remain high. The bloody crackdown against protesters in the Latvian city of Riga and the ensuing skirmishes between Soviet or Russian paramilitary forces and Latvian border guards are both still fresh in the minds of the general populace."

"Plausible but incorrect?"

Irene nodded. "Our special operations team saw the altercation between the alleged Latvian nationalists and the bar's patrons prior to the bombing. One of the nationalists was critically injured after the explosion. Rather than take him to a civilian hospital, his comrades evacuated him to the Russian air base at Lociki."

"That is an interesting development," Stansfield said.

"It gets better. As per their standard task organization, one of the special operators is a linguist. He heard the nationalists speaking with Russian accents as they rendered first aid to their injured comrade."

"Hmm. So you think this is a false-flag operation?"

"I think we should find out. The runway at the Russian air base is twenty-five hundred meters long. That length will permit Russian Il-76 military transport aircraft to land fully laden."

"Meaning that if the Russians intended to use the Latvian government's apparent inability to protect their ethnic Russian citizens from domestic terrorism as an excuse to launch a 'peacekeeping' operation into Latvia, the Lociki air base would make an excellent spot to establish a beachhead."

"Exactly."

Stansfield removed his glasses and twirled them in his right hand. "How do you propose we handle this development?"

Irene was a bit taken aback by the question, but she didn't let her surprise keep her from answering. "The special operators have done great work, but this has now evolved beyond the capacity of a two-man clan-destine team. I think the CIA should be running point on this. We can take over the spec ops tasking from JSOC and then decide what other assets need to be brought to bear. We need to understand what the Rus-sians are doing in Latvia and whether they are planning to use this bombing as a pretext to invade a sovereign nation."

"Let me get this straight," Stansfield said with a frown. "You want to undertake a high-risk collection operation against the Russian Federa-tion on another nation's soil at the exact moment our agency is squarely in Congress's crosshairs? Maybe we should stay out of the limelight and let a different agency take lead. Perhaps DIA?"

Were it not for the serious expression on his face, Irene would have assumed that Stansfield was joking. Had someone else relayed this con-versation, she would have instantly discounted them. Thomas Stans-field did not subscribe to Hurley's view of operations, which was often heavy on execution and light on planning, but neither was he risk-averse.

Or at least he hadn't been.

Maybe the Cooke affair had affected him more than she'd under-stood, or maybe his mind was on his looming testimony. Either way, Irene knew that her course was clear.

Like her mentor, she did not back down from a fight.

"We are the Central Intelligence Agency," Irene said. "Our mission is to collect and analyze foreign intelligence so that our political leaders can make informed decisions. The situation in Latvia is rapidly evolving and may turn into a shooting war. The president will need answers, and there's no time to fight a turf battle with a dozen members of the intelli-gence community. Max Powers should be helming this. He's the Near East Division chief and both Latvia and Russia fall within his area of re-sponsibility."

Her last sentence seemed to hang in the air and Irene half wished she could take the words back. Who was she to be lecturing Thomas Stansfield on the importance of proactive intelligence operations?

Legendary was too generic a term to describe her boss. Some of the operations he'd undertaken during World War II were still classified at the code-word level. If he was expressing caution, there had to be a good reason. Something she hadn't seen or an angle she didn't understand. Irene mentally girded herself for the dressing-down she was certain was coming.

"Well said." Stansfield gave an approving nod. "For the most part. There's one aspect of your assessment with which I disagree—Max cannot be the one to run this. Moscow Station has something major in the works, and I need him solely focused on that operation for the next forty-eight hours."

"Okay," Irene said, sorting through the implications of Stansfield's instructions. "Do you have someone else in mind?"

"Of course," Stansfield said with a smile. "You."

CHAPTER 13

KRIS Henrik pulled her shawl tighter as she fought off a shiver.

A gust of wind howled down Klimentovskiy Pereulok sending bits of trash tumbling across the narrow pedestrian walkway. The morning had seemed mild enough when she'd dressed for the outing, but the weather, as with everything else in Moscow, could not be trusted. Where before the sun had streamed down from a perfectly blue sky, clouds the color of the gray stone walkway now gathered overhead. Temps had dropped noticeably in the last thirty minutes and the breeze that ruffled her skirt and gripped her bare skin with icy fingers came more frequently. The slate sky suggested that rain was imminent, or perhaps even sleet.

In Moscow, one never really knew.

Kris suppressed another shiver and recrossed her long legs. The plunging mercury or the foreboding wind could have been the cause of her discomfort, but they were not. Kris had to suppress the urge to shiver for another reason altogether.

She was terrified.

"Would you like my coat?"

"No, thank you."

Kris tempered her response with a warm smile at odds with her thundering heart. At five foot ten with shoulder-length auburn hair, green eyes, and a collegiate athlete's physique, Kris was accustomed to standing out in a crowd. Though it had been ten years since she'd served her last point for the Ohio State University volleyball team, she still exercised daily. Physical activity had long been her method of dealing with stress—something that wasn't exactly in short supply in Moscow.

Kris had hit her growth spurt in high school and had for a time slouched and stooped so that she wouldn't tower over her friends or even potential boyfriends. She'd detested the way both her flame-colored hair and stature made her stick out in a crowd, but a full ride to a Division 1 college helped change her perspective. Meeting Barry her freshman year solidified that change. Her football-playing boyfriend's broad shoulders towered above her and she loved living life at his side. Kris still wasn't the life of the party, but neither was she a wallflower. Marrying Barry had brought her a wonderful sense of balance.

Until Moscow.

"Please, take it. A beautiful girl like you should not be shivering on a cold bench."

In a nod to the burgeoning influx of Western tourists, the bench in question sat adjacent to a two-story building that doubled as a fast-food eatery and gift shop. The north side of the east-west-running Klimentovskiy Pereulok was resplendent with such establishments along with an assortment of cafés, gift shops, and the like. All of these commercial entities lived in service to the main attraction, which sat on the southern side of the pedestrian walkway just across from Kris's bench—an iconic red and white building topped with five unmistakable domes.

Kris smiled again, looking past the man standing over her to the doorway of the church behind him.

The doorway through which she was expecting Barry to appear.

"Quite beautiful, isn't it?" the man said, shrugging out of his coat.

"St. Clement's Church is one of the wonders of our city." Settling onto the bench next to her, he draped his jacket across her bare legs. "There—that's better now, isn't it?"

Though the heavy coat did feel nice, things were not better.

Not by a long shot.

The man's appearance alone should not have elicited feelings of uneasiness. He was dressed in a suit of impeccable tailoring and his black shoes shone with polish. Though he appeared to be in his seventies, he was still trim, with an erect bearing and confident movements. His full head of gray hair seemed at odds with his black bushy eyebrows, but his lined face spoke of wisdom rather than age. His eyes sparkled and his smile was kind.

He could have been someone's favorite grandfather.

Could have been.

But for all his outward signs of normalcy, something about the man's presence had Kris on edge. For one, he'd switched to English even though she knew her Russian was perfectly understandable. And while the man's attention wasn't desirable per se, it did serve a purpose. Or rather it confirmed Kris was serving her purpose. She was seated on the bench wearing a skirt several inches short of her knee in questionable weather for a reason.

Kris was the distraction.

Unfortunately, the person for whom she was serving as a distraction was late.

And spies were never late.

"Thank you," Kris said, resisting the urge to glance at her watch, "but I need to be going."

"So soon? But the church is right here, and you haven't even been inside."

The statement was delivered with an odd certainty.

Kris had done a two-year stint as a missionary in Siberia after college. She and Barry had thought they would spend the rest of their lives sharing the Gospel with the Russian people. She knew a thing or two about fending off advances from Russian men, but this gentleman took things to a new level. It was almost as if he'd been watching her since she'd taken a seat on the bench in the then-warm sunshine thirty minutes ago.

Maybe he had.

"My husband is the architecture buff," Kris said, getting to her feet. "Now if you'll excuse me—"

"You're being modest. Barry Henrik wrote his dissertation on the architectural styles of Byzantine and Gothic churches. Your husband is one of the world's foremost experts on the topic. Among other things."

The man's familiarity with Barry should have unsettled Kris even more, but it didn't. Perhaps because her fight-or-flight response was focused on something else—the cold fingers wrapped around her biceps like bands of steel.

"Let go of me," Kris said, attempting to pull away.

"I think not."

The man wrenched her biceps downward. Burning needles exploded the length of her arm and into her shoulder. She gasped as the man transferred his grip to her collarbone and she involuntarily plopped back onto the bench to stop the pain.

"That's better. Can't have you running off, now can I? Especially since we've just met."

"My . . . husband . . . is . . . coming." Kris grunted each word between clenched teeth. Though she was less than half his age, Kris couldn't move. The joint lock forced her to bend double in order to ease stress on her shoulder. "Help me. Please!"

Kris had the presence of mind to make the plea in Russian, but her quick thinking didn't yield the results she'd imagined. Rather than the sound of footfalls announcing the approach of a Good Samaritan, she heard something else.

Laughter.

"You still have some things to learn about my country, my dear.

Things not covered in textbooks or language classes. The Russian people are proud, but practical. A proud man might come to the aid of a beautiful woman screaming for help. A practical one knows better. Especially when the person causing that woman to scream is a lieutenant general in the Federal Counterintelligence Service."

His words almost made her forget the tongues of fire burning up her arm. She had guessed that he might be Russian intelligence, but supposing something to be true and knowing it were two different things. "What do you want?" Kris said, hating the way her voice quavered.

"Exactly what you're giving me. I apologize for the unpleasantness. It shouldn't be long now. Ah, yes. Here we are."

Kris couldn't make sense of the Russian's words.

Then again, it was hard to concentrate on anything beyond the agony enveloping her arm and shoulder. Unlike Barry, her collegiate area of study had been more sensible—sports medicine. Her plans to become a physical therapist hadn't materialized, but she'd done enough practicums to recognize what was happening to her shoulder. If the man didn't ease the pressure he was exerting on the joint, her rotator cuff might tear. As if hearing her thoughts, the pressure on her shoulder vanished.

Kris nearly sobbed with relief.

Nearly.

Until the agony that had enveloped her shoulder reappeared elsewhere.

As if he were scruffing a feral cat, the Russian grabbed her by the hair and yanked her head backward. Kris gasped and reached for the intelligence officer's hand only to have her wrist snared in another joint lock.

"Just a moment or two more, my dear. A little to the left, please."

The hand holding her hair jerked to the right, which turned her face left, bringing a familiar person into view. Someone stood in the center of the pedestrian walkway, flanked by a pair of Russians.

Barry.

The look of horror on her husband's face quickly transformed into rage. She tried to call out to him, but the Russian chose that moment to viciously yank her hair.

Her words came out a sob.

Something pricked her neck.

She felt a rush of cold.

Then, nothing.

CHAPTER 14

"HALLO?"

"Greta, it's me."

"Mitch!"

The instantaneous change in Greta's tone made Rapp smile. This was no mean feat, since he was currently standing in one of his least favorite places.

An airport.

"You okay?"

"Yes, I'm—"

"Don't tell me," Rapp said, turning his back to the pedestrians strolling through the international terminal. As airports went, Barcelona–El Prat wasn't bad, at least from Rapp's perspective. Then again, his evaluation criteria were a bit different than the average air traveler's. Case in point, the custodians who serviced the terminal's floor-to-ceiling windows did an excellent job of keeping the glass free of smudges. Presumably, most people took advantage of their hard work by taking in the view of the beautiful Spanish coastline.

Not Rapp.

He was busy studying the reflections of his fellow travelers.

"Why?" Greta said.

"Your grandfather thought it was better if I didn't know. For now."

"What does that mean?"

Rapp sighed. "It's complicated."

"I think that means you're about to do something dangerous for my grandfather. I think you don't want to know where I am because you don't want to have to worry about saying something to the wrong person if that thing you're about to do goes wrong."

Greta was not a covert operative, but she was smart and had a knack for putting two and two together and arriving at five. Greta acquitted herself well during the chaotic days after the Paris hit went south, but her stubborn streak had also reared its head a time or two. Stubbornness could look a lot like tenacity under the right circumstances.

Maybe he should start thinking of Greta as tenacious rather than mule-headed.

"What did your grandfather tell you?" Rapp said.

"You first."

Definitely mule-headed.

"The CliffsNotes version is that you're in danger—"

"And you're going to fix things."

The irritation coming through the phone was unmistakable and Rapp felt his own blood pressure rising in response. "Yes, I'm going to fix things. Why does that make you angry?"

"Because you and my grandfather came up with this plan without even once stopping to consider me."

"You?"

"Yes, me, you idiot. I understand why he still treats me like a six-year-old with pink ribbons in her hair. I understand, but I don't like it. But you? You should know better."

So that's what this was about.

Rapp shifted slightly so that he had a better view of the terminal's reflection.

He was standing in a blind spot created by a T-intersection. The concourse to his right formed the T's horizonal axis, while the terminal to his left was the vertical leg. His positioning allowed him to surreptitiously observe passengers as they entered the terminal. In yet another plus for the airport, his terminal had just four gates. The even numbers, gates 6 and 8, were on his side of the terminal, while the odds, 5 and 7, were on the far side. Only gates 7 and 8 featured flights that were scheduled to depart in the next ninety minutes. This meant that no one had any business entering his section of the terminal unless they were waiting for a departing flight.

Or tailing someone.

A young woman with a travel bag slung over her shoulder hurried by. Rapp caught a quick glimpse of squinting blue eyes and features scrunched in concentration before she passed his observation post. After reaching the terminal's end, she checked flight information displayed on the TV screen adjacent to gate 7 and sighed.

Loudly.

With a muttered curse, she retraced her steps to the concourse without so much as a glance in his direction. As performances went, it didn't get more convincing. He wanted to believe that she was just another frazzled traveler who'd accidentally selected the wrong terminal, but couldn't.

This was the second time he'd seen her.

"Sorry," Rapp said, not so much because he felt the emotion as he was convinced it was the correct thing to say. "I should have consulted you instead of just riding to your rescue. In the meantime, hopefully no one chops off your head, stuffs it in a box, and mails it to your grandfather. My apologies."

Compassion wasn't really one of his strong suits.

"What? What did you say?"

"Do I have your attention now? Good. Your grandfather has made an enemy or two over the course of his career. Someone did what I just described to one of his oldest friends. Oh, and they also enclosed a note saying your head would be next."

"O mein Gott."

Rapp paused to allow Greta to fully process the barbarity of what he'd relayed. As he'd suspected, Ohlmeyer had not told his granddaughter about the box. He'd deliberately remedied that oversight because he wanted the Swiss beauty to understand the stakes, not so that she couldn't sleep at night, but because he thought a shock of this magnitude might be the only thing capable of overcoming her stubborn streak. Greta had to do her part if this was to work, and in this case, her part was to willingly remain in the company of the men Ohlmeyer had handpicked to protect her.

"Listen," Rapp said as he surveyed the crowd, searching for a second familiar face, "the people who are going after your grandfather are good, but they've already made one mistake. They neglected to factor in something that is going to completely change the tactical equation."

"What?"

"Me. The enemies he's facing have done their homework on him, no doubt. They know how to strike at his weaknesses. The things he values the most—his friends and you—but they don't know about me. I'm going to pay someone a visit, ask him a few questions, and take care of this issue. As soon as I do, my first call will be to you. Until then, I need you to stay with your grandfather's men. Okay?"

"Why can't I be with you? You can protect me."

Rapp sighed. "No, I can't. I won't be able to do what I need to do if you're with me."

This time the silence that followed his answer had a different feel. Contemplative. This was a double-edged sword. Shock and horror meant that Greta would reflexively do what he'd asked, but only so long as it took for those feelings to subside. Contemplative meant that she'd choose what to do based on her own decision-making criteria, but there was a fifty-fifty chance Greta's conclusion would not align with his. Headstrong or tenacious were both too charitable a description.

She was stubborn.

"You're going to kill someone."

Greta's response was more statement than question and a healthy dose of resignation flavored her tone. Had the words sounded like an accusation they might have provoked a different response, but she might as well have been remarking on the fact that it was raining outside. The circumstances weren't what she wanted, but life often reflected circumstances that weren't what a person wanted. She was by no means the perfect woman, but she might just be the perfect fit for his jagged pieces.

"I'll do what needs to be done. You know me. I'm not a nutjob who gets off on violence, but I am a realist. Either I take care of this, or it takes care of you. That's about as clear-cut as my world gets."

Left unsaid was that had Rapp not involved Greta in Paris, she would not truly know him or the hard-edged world he inhabited. But as quickly as the thought came, it vanished. She might not be of his world, but it had found her anyway through her grandfather. Her survival might be far less certain without him in her corner. Perhaps the phone call he'd placed to her after he'd been shot in Paris had saved more than just his life.

"Okay, darling," Greta said. "I don't like it, but I get it. I'll stay with my grandfather's men like a good girl."

"I love you, darling."

"And I you. Mitch—please be careful."

"Of course."

Rapp disconnected the call before Greta could respond. This was partly because he didn't want the Swiss girl to exact promises he didn't intend to keep.

But only partly.

The woman with the shoulder bag was back.

CHAPTER 15

SHE'D done a good job altering her appearance.

A very good job.

Her jeans and blouse were gone, replaced by a long but formfitting dress that hugged her hips and flattered her breasts. The front wasn't overly revealing, but it scooped low enough to catch the eye.

The male eye anyway.

The woman's previous outfit had been chosen for anonymity. A wardrobe meant to render her just another face in the crowd. Her new dress served the opposite purpose. Her hair was now shoulder-length and chestnut brown instead of collar-length and dirty blond. Her features were masked behind stylish glasses with oversize black frames and her shoulder bag was gone, replaced by a large purse.

She even moved differently.

Where before the woman had displayed the hurried stride of a frazzled traveler, this time she swayed with each step. The movement was understated, but the motion still caused the dress's fabric to hug her hips with every stride and accentuate her curves. The transformation was so strikingly complete, Rapp wasn't sure that he would have made her if not for a single oversight.

Her shoes.

Her flowing dress almost obscured the same pair of flats she'd worn with her previous outfit. Almost. Like most people, the woman's stride wasn't perfectly symmetrical, and a brown scuffed toe peeked from beneath her dress's hem each time she led with her right leg. The scuff and hint of brown shoe was barely noticeable, but the profession of espionage often turned on barely noticeable details.

Had she been facing him, the woman probably would have favored Rapp with a smile. Since he was watching her reflection, she continued by without so much as a glance. Her performance was magnificent.

Captivating even.

Which meant that the woman was not where he should be looking.

Turning away from the window and stepping out from the alcove, Rapp began a systematic survey of his surroundings. In the concourse to his left, a deli sold sandwiches, croissants, fresh-squeezed orange juice, and an abundance of the *jamón ibérico* for which Barcelona was famous. Three of the six tables were empty. One held haggard-looking parents who were seemingly at their wits' end with a screaming baby. A man sipping from a ceramic espresso cup as he paged through the newspaper sat at the other. The man's sport coat, slacks, and dress shirt suggested he was a business traveler waiting for his connection.

He was not.

Aside from the broad back and heavy shoulders that were somewhat at odds with his businessman persona, it was the man's choice of tables that confirmed Rapp's suspicions. No member of the male species would voluntarily sit in such proximity to a fussy child. The half dozen vacant chairs scattered throughout the deli suggested there was a reason the pseudo-businessman had chosen that particular table. Rapp was betting it had something to do with the sight line from the table to the mirror that hung behind the deli's counter.

A mirror that offered an unobstructed view of Rapp's terminal.

With a sigh, Rapp completed his scan. While he hadn't been as vigilant as he could have been during his phone call with Greta, he knew the table next to the still-howling infant had been empty the last time he'd conducted a visual sweep. The man's presence coincided with the woman's reappearance. Turning, Rapp saw that the woman was now seated by gate 7 on the opposite side of the terminal. This would allow her to surveil the entire zone, thereby negating the need for a second member of the surveillance team to penetrate the confined area.

Unless what he was seeing wasn't a surveillance team.

Rapp resumed his visual sweep, this time focusing on the terminal's exterior. The gates with scheduled departures, 7 and 8, located at the far end of the terminal, featured the activity he expected to see on the tarmac—baggage carts driving to and fro, men and women in brightly colored vests directing vehicular traffic, and the occasional worker squatting in the shade. Of the two remaining gates, 6 was on his side of the pedestrian area, while 5 was directly across from him. Six sported an unusual concentration of carts and condiment trucks parked circularly in front of the airbridge. Baggage handlers and ground crew members sprawled across the vehicles or squatted in the building's shade.

Gate 5 was also empty.

But it wouldn't be for long.

In the window adjacent to the gate, Rapp could just make out the sleek form of a taxiing business jet.

CHAPTER 16

T HE twin-engine Cessna Citation was painted an off-white with a multicolored racing stripe that ran down the fuselage just below the passenger windows. Other than the required tail number, the aircraft bore no markings. No logos suggesting it belonged to an airline or charter jet company and no seal or flag that pointed toward a national entity.

Rapp was not fooled.

The Citation might be one of the most common business jets in use, but private planes did not just taxi up to open gates at a commercial terminal. Rock stars, A-list actors, CEOs, and foreign dignitaries all followed the same protocol when flying private. They boarded and disembarked at the general aviation fixed-base operator, a separate building kept far from the busy traffic and confined space that had to accommodate wide-body passenger jets. Obtaining the necessary permission to occupy the passenger terminal's prime real estate with a business jet would require an act of God.

Or a shit ton of cash.

Either way, determining who greased the administrative skids in preparation for the jet's arrival would have to wait for later. The plane was here, and Rapp could think of only one reason for its presence.

Him.

As if it could hear his thoughts, the Citation turned to the left and pointed its cigar-shaped nose at gate 5.

He had a handful of minutes.

Maybe less.

When he'd first decided to call Greta from the airport, the idea had seemed genius. While the safety measures were certainly not impenetrable, the assortment of metal detectors, roving policemen, and other security features made those with less-than-honorable intentions think twice about bringing a weapon into the terminal. By the same token, the airport's restrictive airspace and multiple ground checkpoints discouraged aerial or vehicular surveillance, and the plethora of electromagnetic energy emitted by radios, navigational aids, and the like also had the potential to interfere with electronic snooping. Travel by commercial air allowed Rapp to mix with the general populace, while putting him out of reach of hired muscle.

But if he was facing sophisticated adversaries, the airport rendered Rapp weaponless and isolated like a cornered rat. Whether his decision stemmed from overconfidence or was just an honest mistake, the results were the same. Rapp had severely misjudged his adversaries. Anyone thinking of conducting a rendition in a place crowded with witnesses was clearly off their rocker.

Or they had permission.

Turning from the window, Rapp peered past the deli in both directions. Not good. Clusters of uniformed Spanish National Police were positioned in pairs on either side of the T-intersection formed by the concourse and his terminal. The police officers didn't appear to be on edge, but they were openly scanning the faces of travelers exiting the terminal for the concourse and airport proper.

Rapp slid back into his blind spot.

On the far side of the terminal, the Citation was almost to the gate.

Within a minute or two, the aircraft would dock and whatever was waiting inside its sleek cabin would come boiling through the airbridge. To his right, the woman in the formfitting dress was getting to her feet. To his left, the faux businessman seated at the deli no longer seemed interested in his paper. As if feeling Rapp's gaze, the heavy-shouldered man locked eyes with him. The decision was simple: Either wait for the rendition team or fight.

He wasn't much for waiting.

He left his alcove and tracked right, away from the concourse and toward gate 6, located on his side of the terminal. He kept his pace even and unrushed while still trying to cover as much distance as possible with each stride. He checked his reflection in the window to his right.

The pretend businessman was standing.

The man had undoubtedly expected Rapp to make a break for the concourse and airport proper, but since Rapp was headed toward a dead end, he probably wasn't worried. On the opposite side of the terminal, the Citation had finished taxiing and the airbridge was stretching toward the aircraft's fuselage.

It was happening.

The woman in the hip-hugging dress moved to intercept him. She maintained the eye-catching sway even as her pace increased to match his. With a smoothness that only came with practice, she planted herself in Rapp's path.

"Excuse me," the woman said, "I was wondering if—"

Her English was excellent, her smile engaging, and her magnetism palpable.

Rapp didn't pay attention to any of those things. Nor was he focused on the slender fingers reaching for his chest or the hint of cleavage revealed by the scoop-neck dress.

He was watching her other hand.

The one hidden by her purse.

Her fingers brushed his shirt, and Rapp felt a surge of warmth.

There was something about being touched by a beautiful woman, even if the contact was fleeting.

She wasn't just smooth.

Her tradecraft was exceptional.

The purse dropped away the moment the palm of her right hand pressed flat against his pectoral muscles. The Taser hidden beneath her handbag hissed as electricity arced between its two contacts.

The hungry, artificial lighting reached for his torso.

Stepping into the woman, Rapp seized her left wrist with both hands while bending his right arm and smashing his elbow into her chest. The pointy bone struck the woman's solar plexus and the breath surged from her lungs in something that sounded midway between gasp and cough.

She doubled over.

Rapp stripped the device from her and shoved the still-arcing probes into her side. The woman went rigid and then collapsed. He considered snapping her wrist as he lowered her to the ground, but Hurley's voice echoed in his head.

We don't kill women or children.

Someday, he might have to break the first part of the rule.

Not today.

Releasing the woman, Rapp scooped up her purse. Then he sprinted to gate 6, smashed the crash bar attached to the emergency exit, and burst onto the steps leading to the tarmac.

CHAPTER 17

R APP'S linguistic acumen did not extend to Spanish, but he'd learned the utility of mastering a few simple phrases in each country he visited. *Hello*, *excuse me*, and *goodbye* were always part of his repertoire along with a few more that were relevant to his unique profession. He employed one such word as he bounded down the stairs leading to the tarmac.

"*Fuego!*" Rapp screamed, pointing back at the terminal. "*Ayúdame, ayúdame. Fuego!*"

The screeching alarm along with his impeccable acting seemed to do the trick.

Or at least part of the trick.

Of the five workers who were lounging across tractors and baggage carts, four abandoned their makeshift break area for the stairs leading to the terminal.

The fifth was a problem.

Whether the man wasn't buying what Rapp was selling, couldn't hear Rapp's scream through the blue earmuffs he was wearing, or perhaps just wasn't all that interested in charging headfirst into a raging inferno, the results were the same. While his compatriots made for the staircase, he remained sprawled across his baggage tractor's broken seat cushion.

Bad choice.

Still shouting about the nonexistent fire, Rapp careened toward the man like a runaway freight train. With a sigh, the worker got to his feet and stretched out his hand in the universal sign for stop. "*Tranquilo.*"

Rapp rewarded the man's cool head by shoving the Taser into his midsection and triggering the device. The worker collapsed like a pile of dirty laundry. Rapp lowered the man to the concrete and climbed into the seat he'd vacated. The tractor's controls seemed easy enough to master, but something made Rapp hesitate before starting the engine.

The shiny silver key dangling from the ignition.

Pocketing the key, Rapp jumped to the next tractor and swiped that key as well. Then he was in the driver's seat of the third and final tractor. The engine started with a single turn of the ignition. Setting the woman's purse in his lap, he popped the transmission into reverse and backed away from the circle of vehicles. He was preparing to shift into drive when the scrum of bodies roiling down the staircase changed his mind.

So maybe his Method acting wasn't on par with Daniel Day-Lewis just yet.

Leaving the transmission in reverse, Rapp hammered the accelerator. For a vehicle designed for high torque at low speed, the tractor had surprisingly good acceleration. Rapp's chest slammed into the steering wheel as the tractor rocketed backward. Ignoring the shouts and curses trailing him, Rapp looked over his shoulder as he threaded between an adjacent gates' airbridge and one of the fire-engine-red double-decker buses that served as passenger movers.

The bus with its precious cargo of human beings must normally enjoy the right-of-way, because the diesel monstrosity kept coming. For a terrifying moment, Rapp was convinced this game of chicken was going to end with him plastered to the bus's bug-infested grille. Then the bus skidded to a halt amid squealing brakes and a blaring horn. Rapp raised a hand in thanks and then spun the wheel to the right, bringing the tractor's nose around before popping the gearshift into drive.

Decision time.

The airfield was canted to mirror the 060 heading of its largest runway. Rapp was in the northwest corner, which meant that the shortest distance to freedom lay with the fence guarding the airport's western boundary to the right. Unfortunately, this direction also led to a convergence of highways, parking lots, and maintenance buildings.

While Rapp had the element of surprise, this advantage was fading with the passing of every second. The baggage tractor probably didn't top out at much more than twenty miles per hour, which meant that he would be easy prey for the airport police in their sedans. Even if he somehow made it to the fence unmolested, Rapp wouldn't be able to evade his pursuers for very long.

Left meant heading east, which would take Rapp past the remaining terminals along miles of open tarmac. The airfield's eastern boundary was mostly farmers' fields. The rural terrain that would offer him a better chance of escape, but there was zero chance he would get to the perimeter fence unmolested. This left the final direction—straight and south. There was just one problem—south meant crossing all three runways.

All three very active runways.

"*Parar! Parar!*"

Rapp looked over his shoulder. The airport police had joined the chase. They were still on foot for the moment, but that wouldn't last.

South it was.

Rapp gunned the engine, and the tractor surged forward. A siren pierced the air, the wailing audible even over the screaming of jet engines. Rapp glanced left and swore. A blue and white liveried patrol car was racing to intercept him. No matter how he weaved and dodged, the little tractor wasn't going to win that race. He was toast.

Unless.

Unless he was willing to go where the patrol car wouldn't.

Runway 060 Left, the first of three actives, loomed just a quarter of a mile to the south. Rapp had originally intended to detour west to skirt the commercial traffic arriving and departing on the almost two-mile stretch of concrete.

Not anymore.

Rapp adjusted course so that he was hurtling toward the runway even though a wide-body jet was flaring in anticipation of landing. Plowing through the grass, Rapp edged the steering wheel slightly to the right to ensure he passed behind the aircraft. He had no intention of saving his own skin at the expense of the hundreds of innocent passengers.

But his pursuers couldn't know that.

Smoke puffed from the plane's landing gear as rubber met concrete at 170 miles per hour. The aircraft thundered past in a blur and then Rapp rocketed across the runway driving behind and perpendicular to the jet. He gritted his teeth against the jet blast as the wake turbulence created by the several-hundred-ton lifting body tried to tear him from the tractor. Gripping the steering wheel with white knuckles, he turned into the wind as the vortices rocked the tractor against its struts. For an instant the man-made tornado had the upper hand. Then the tractor's front tires found purchase on the grass on the runway's far side.

Cranking the wheel farther right, Rapp sought the protection of the more crowded secondary terminal. Steering like a madman, he roared under one stationary jet, in front of another taxiing aircraft, and then weaved between several parked planes like he was slaloming down his favorite ski run. The persistent warbling from the pursuing sedan's siren faded. Risking a look over his shoulder, Rapp saw the patrol car still on the northern side of the active runway, apparently loath to cross the sacred ground.

Good.

Zooming past Terminal 1, he skirted the approach edge of the diagonally running Runway 020, and then shot across Runway 060

Right, moments before a blue and white liveried Boeing with the Star of David featured prominently on the plane's tail took the active. Rapp thought about waving to the El Al crew but decided that might make matters worse. The Israelis had enough problems back home without thinking that a madman on a baggage tractor had tried to ram one of their passenger planes.

Rapp bottomed out the accelerator as the vehicle's wheels traded concrete for the sandy soil on the far side of Runway 060 Right. The little tractor certainly wasn't designed with off-roading in mind, but he kept the pedal to the metal and hung on for dear life. The uneven terrain and the baggage cart's lack of shocks conspired to nearly toss him from his seat, but after thirty seconds of hard riding, he arrived at the perimeter fence. Bringing the vehicle to a halt with the tractor's blunt nose touching the fence's metal chain links, Rapp grabbed the purse and then scrambled up and over the barrier. He landed in the soft dirt on the far side and bolted for the cover of the surrounding trees.

The smell of salt water saturated the air, and the ocean breeze tickled his face. The ground was sandy and crisscrossed with canals brimming with brackish water. He seemed to be in some sort of estuary, and he paused for a moment to take his bearings. A narrow road provided vehicular access to the marsh, but that wouldn't do. Sure, the pavement would allow him to move faster, but the road probably tracked along the airfield's perimeter with very few secondary branches.

If Rapp risked the road, he would be easy pickings for his pursuers.

Like a mosquito's irritating buzzing, the warbling siren was back. Rapp darted into the estuary, trying to disguise his footprints by keeping to solid ground. He might be able to hide for a time among the scrub brush and stunted trees, but with a canal to his west and a large industrial area to his east, Rapp was effectively boxed in. Any competent team would erect roadblocks, construct a search grid, and eventually find him. It might take the searchers longer if they didn't have access to canines, but either way, hiding in the marsh was a nonstarter.

Which left south.

The shouts echoing from behind him spurred Rapp to action.

He headed south in a distance-eating lope, his pace a product of countless training runs. Trail running wasn't really his forte, but he only had half a mile or so of truly rough terrain to cover. The gritty soil was challenging, but Rapp kept to the rows of oak and catalpa trees. Their root structure helped to hold the earth in place, defeating the wind and water, which eroded the lower-lying stretches of land. The wood line at the estuary's edge paralleled his intended direction of travel and for several hundred yards, Rapp just ran. Then the trees intersected a narrow west-east-running road. At barely two lanes, it was just wide enough to permit cars to travel in opposite directions, but the surface was largely gravel and littered with potholes.

Exactly the type of road one would expect to follow for beach access.

Rapp considered using it, but didn't. While the road boasted plenty of parked cars and beachgoers walked along it in twos and threes, Rapp felt too exposed. The earlier trees and scrub brush that had provided at least a modicum of cover were gone. The south side of the road boasted the occasional hedge or palm tree, but the open expanse was mostly grass. He would be easy to spot on the long stretch of road, especially since he wasn't dressed like the other beachgoers.

Rapp crouched beside a bush as he surveyed the open no-man's-land separating him from the beckoning ocean. His clothes were a liability. The linen slacks, button-down shirt, and loafers weren't beach attire.

He needed to improvise.

For the first time, Rapp opened the woman's handbag. As he'd expected, the purse was configured with surveillance in mind. The interior was surprisingly roomy and featured a plastic liner that could be cinched closed to ward off moisture—a necessity when running surveillance in the rain. Several cleverly placed zippers permitted the purse's size and shape to be reconfigured on the fly, another surveillance must.

A quick inventory of the contents turned up several interesting items—a spare cell phone, a wallet complete with a picture ID, and a couple of benign things like a key chain, makeup compact, and lipstick and the like. Some of the innocent items probably concealed something more sinister that he might be able to suss out with more time.

Unfortunately, time was not something he had in abundance.

Though he hadn't heard or seen his pursuers, Rapp knew they were out there. One did not careen across an airfield in a stolen baggage tractor and expect to waltz away scot-free. If nothing else, sheer embarrassment would motivate the national police and airport security officers to continue to look for him. Rapp needed to disappear, and while he had the beginnings of a plan, something had to be done about his appearance. It would do him no good to elude his pursuers just to have a helpful bystander explain to the police exactly where he'd gone. The ocean was the solution to his problems, but unless he came up with a way to escape into its welcoming embrace, the waves might as well have been four hundred miles distant rather than four hundred feet.

Rapp was considering threading the needle by attempting to follow the road east while remaining concealed in the spotty hedges when salvation arrived in the form of a man.

A very old, very naked man.

Surprise and revulsion blinded Rapp to the possibilities at first. The image of sagging, wrinkled things was now forever seared into his mind. For a long moment, Rapp couldn't fathom why an eighty-year-old man would be strutting down to the ocean in just his birthday suit.

Then he got it.

A nudist beach. After monitoring the old man's progress all the way to the water to ensure that he didn't elicit any outraged reactions from fellow sunbathers, Rapp got busy. Shucking his shoes, clothes, and underwear, he bundled everything together, placed it in the watertight container, and cinched the bag shut. Then he looped the carrying strap over his shoulder and started across the street.

Rapp was not particularly prudish, but neither was he an exhibitionist. Figuring that blushing cheeks would be a dead giveaway, Rapp kept his eyes on the surf crashing against the beach and pointedly ignored a trio of rather attractive young ladies sunbathing to his left. As he drew even with them, one of the women lowered her sunglasses and let loose a burst of Spanish. The words might have been indecipherable, but the woman's tone left no doubt as to her intentions.

Rapp flashed her a smile and then jogged the remaining distance to the water. Without breaking stride, he dove into the breaking waves, doing his best to ignore the chill. While the swim trunks he normally used weren't insulated, the water still felt bracingly cold to his unprotected nether regions. He tempered his strokes in acknowledgment of the still-healing gunshot wound in his shoulder, but before long he'd swum beyond the surf break and into open ocean. After tightening the bag's strap across his shoulder and back, Rapp turned right and settled into an easy rhythm.

Ninety minutes later, Rapp walked from the surf.

His chest heaved as salt water ran down his skin in rivulets. Between his still-sore shoulder and the drag induced by the handbag, the swim had been more strenuous than he'd anticipated.

A lot more strenuous.

Rapp had originally considered swimming east, against the current, in favor exiting the water in one of the less populated coastal areas, but he'd rejected the idea. He would attract much less attention coming ashore in front of one of the many resort hotels than if a random person saw him emerge from the water on one of the secluded sections of sand that bordered the industrial area around the port. Besides, if he swam too far east, he might accidentally wander into the commercial shipping lanes.

After spending the better part of an hour floundering in the surf, Rapp was forced to come to terms with a simple fact he'd been trying to ignore—while his shoulder was feeling much better, he was nowhere near one hundred percent. He had tried to settle into a relaxed swimming cadence, but the pain and tightness had forced him to abandon his more powerful freestyle stroke in favor of flipping onto his back and allowing the current to do most of the work.

Not ideal.

The outcome might not have been anywhere near as rosy if he'd attempted to fight the current by swimming east. The tides probably would have turned him around and sent him west. Probably. But if he'd floundered into a riptide, the results could have been much more dire. Yes, he felt good most of the time, but his body was not done healing and he could not expect to operate at one hundred percent.

He needed to remember this lesson.

This time Rapp received no catcalls from sunbathing beauties. Instead, the stretch of nude beach consisted of mostly elderly men and women basting their sagging bodies under the cloudless sky. The median age had to be about seventy-five. Maybe there was a retirement community nearby. He smiled at the thought of a bunch of old people trekking from afternoon bingo to the beach and back wearing nothing but sandals.

His humor was short-lived.

Besides working on his tan, Rapp had had precious little to do while drifting down the coast besides think.

Think and remember.

Though he no longer had to contend with a fresh bullet wound, the persistent ache in his shoulder coupled with the feeling of floating weightless in the water's embrace was familiar.

Too familiar.

Not that long ago, he'd been submerged in the Seine's filthy water with a fresh bullet wound, floating through Paris as he tried to work out who had attempted to kill him. Today the climate was more agreeable and his body in better shape, but the circumstances were too similar for Rapp's liking. Dangerous people were again hunting him, and he had no idea who they were or how he'd been found.

Entering the beach's public bathroom, Rapp selected an empty stall.

After closing and locking the door behind him, he unzipped the woman's waterlogged bag and uncinched the plastic liner. As he'd hoped, his clothes were dry. Using handfuls of toilet paper, Rapp blotted the worst of the ocean water from his body before flushing the soggy mess.

Then he dressed and considered what to do next.

During his thoughtful float, Rapp had arrived at several unsettling conclusions. While Ohlmeyer's dispute might be with a Cold War adversary, this no longer felt like a grudge match between two onetime combatants. The surveillance and rendition team who had attempted to interdict him at the airport was not just hired help.

He knew a bit about the lucrative world of executive protection. During his time with the Orion program, Rapp had crossed swords with numerous bodyguards ranging from hired goons to former military. High-end mercenaries could match, or in some cases exceed, the competency of their government-employed counterparts, but it wasn't so much the skill of the airport team as the impunity with which they'd operated. Even the wealthiest Saudi prince had limits on what his funds could accomplish. Money could buy perks, but cash alone was not enough to entice the cooperation of a national police service or allow a private plane to use a berth normally reserved for wide-body jets. This was to say nothing of the kind of coercion required to convince the Spanish government to permit a surveillance-and-interdiction team to conduct a rendition in the crowded terminal of one of their busiest international airports.

That sort of pressure came from just one source.

A nation-state.

This realization required a reframing of his task. It was one thing to fly to another country, interdict a private citizen, interrogate him, and end his life. Absent the interrogation portion of the equation, Rapp had been following this exact formula for almost two years.

Going to war with a nation-state was something else.

But this was just one of his concerns, and not even the most pressing. The more pertinent question had to do with location. More specifically, his location. How had the rendition team known Rapp was going to the airport when he himself had only found out during his meeting with Ohlmeyer?

The answer was equal parts simple and devastating.

The team had known because Ohlmeyer had known. Either the banker's inner circle and his extensive security protocols had been breached, or . . .

Or.

Or Ohlmeyer had set Rapp up.

Rapp stared at the final two items in the waterproof bag as he considered that possibility. He didn't know the German man well, but Ohlmeyer had been comrades in arms with two generations of American clandestine warriors—Stansfield and Hurley. Neither CIA officer allowed people into his confidence easily, yet Ohlmeyer was a friend to both. Still, even the hardest of men showed cracks in their iron façade when it came to their families. If the person responsible for lopping off the head of one of Ohlmeyer's oldest friends threatened to do the same to Greta unless the banker gave up Rapp, would he do it?

Rapp didn't know.

If he were in Ohlmeyer's place, it would be a tempting trade to make. He didn't believe Greta's grandfather harbored any ill will toward him, but the German banker had come of age during the Second World War. That conflict had since been relegated to fuzzy black-and-white pictures and dusty history books, but it had been hell on earth. Children had been used as couriers by the Resistance, while teenagers fought in partisan squads charged with sabotaging railroads or ambushing German supply lines. If his formative years had been forged in this crucible, would Ohlmeyer balk at sacrificing an American assassin he barely knew in exchange for the life of his treasured granddaughter?

Probably not.

The pair of phones at the bottom of the bag might as well have been coiled vipers. One of the cells belonged to him, while the other had come with the bag. Rapp had removed the batteries from each, so the electronic devices were harmless at the moment, but as soon as he reconnected their power sources the handsets held the power to kill.

Or save.

Slowly, a plan began to shape. As always, it started with big pieces that rushed together as the concept of the operation crystallized. Was what he was considering risky?

Absolutely.

The best plans always were.

With quick, efficient motions, Rapp cinched the watertight lining closed and slipped the handbag over his shoulder. From the time he'd first detected the surveillance team this morning until he'd dragged his naked body from the surf, Rapp had been reacting to his unseen enemy.

That was about to change.

CHAPTER 18

S HE heard words, but they seemed to be coming from far away. As if the voice were echoing down a long drainage pipe. Kris groaned and tried to rub the grit from her eyes.

She couldn't.

A tightness in her wrist brought her arm up short.

A metallic tightness.

Groaning again, Kris Henrik forced open her eyes.

"There you are! Would you like a glass of water? You must be terribly thirsty."

Blinking away the blurriness, Kris tried to make sense of her surroundings. The single light bulb dangling from the ceiling didn't do much to beat back the shadows. She could see bare concrete walls shrouded in darkness and a face sitting across the table from her.

A familiar face.

"Where—" Kris coughed. "Where am I?"

The man standing over her still resembled a grandfather, but his cold smile and hard eyes suggested otherwise.

The Russian reached for Kris, and she jerked away.

Or at least she tried to.

It was then that her woozy brain made sense of the tightness binding her wrist. She was manacled to the table.

"Please don't struggle," the Russian said. "You'll only hurt yourself. The table is bolted to the floor, as is your chair. Believe me when I say there is absolutely nowhere you can go."

"Why—"

Again, the hoarseness in her voice betrayed her. Kris tried to swallow, but her mouth was bone-dry and her throat felt like sandpaper.

"Here," the man said, pushing a glass of water to within reach. "Take a drink. The drug we used to sedate you is wonderfully fast-acting, but I'm afraid that it isn't without side effects. Waking up after suffering its effects has been termed the world's worst hangover. The water will help. I promise."

As if his words made her aware of the rest of her body, Kris realized her head was pounding in time with her heartbeat. A wave of nausea roiled her stomach and bile raced up her throat.

"Drink. Please."

Kris couldn't see what was in the glass, but decided she didn't care. She'd been at their mercy while unconscious, and she was still just as helpless. If the Russian intelligence officer harbored malicious intentions, they certainly weren't dependent on her ingesting whatever was in the cup. Bringing the glass to her lips, she took a sip.

Water.

Choking back the urge to sob, she finished the glass in two long swallows. Perhaps it was just her imagination, but the headache seemed to ease. Even better, her mouth and throat no longer felt like she'd been gargling with gravel. Setting the glass back on the table with shaking fingers, Kris cleared her throat and tried again.

"Where am I?"

"Exactly where you'd expect to be, I'd expect. Lubyanka Square."

"What? Why?"

"Because that's the location of my intelligence service's headquarters. Conveniently, it is also where we interrogate traitors and spies."

For a long moment, the Russian's words seemed to be lost in the fog enveloping Kris's thoughts. She didn't understand what the man was getting at.

Then she got it.

Like a fuzzy scene suddenly snapping into focus, she saw her accommodations for what they were—a prison cell.

"Spy?" Kris said. "I'm not a spy."

"Of course you are, and a very good one too, but I'm getting ahead of myself. My name is Lieutenant General Grigoriy Petrov. I've served my nation for over fifty years, first in the NKVD, then the KGB, and now in our counterintelligence service. Your name is Kris Henrik, and you are a CIA officer."

"What?" Kris said. "I—"

"Using your husband as a distraction was brilliant by the way. Absolutely brilliant. We know all about the American initiative in which green CIA officers are sent to Moscow posing as low-level diplomats. Since this is their first overseas tour, we don't focus on them, especially since their embassy cover jobs aren't ones typically utilized by case officers. But you've taken things to an entirely new level. Bravo!"

Kris bit her lip, trying to understand what had transpired.

Petrov was speaking to the exact reason she and Barry were in Moscow. Contrary to his State Department cover, Barry was a CIA officer. A CIA officer on his first operational tour. Moscow was a hard nut to crack, and Russian counterintelligence officers were famous for their rough-and-tumble method of operating against foreign intelligence services. Someone had coined the term *Moscow Rules* to describe the intense, often physical interactions the men and women of the CIA's Moscow Station negotiated on a daily basis.

With alarming frequency, the KGB seemed to know which CIA officer was replacing whom before the person even arrived in-country.

Good spies had a penchant for remembering faces, and the proliferation of computers allowed for the much more rapid dissemination of photographs taken of suspected American CIA officers. Russian counterintelligence officers could now identify agency case officers the moment they stepped off the plane at Sheremetyevo International Airport by referencing a database of pictures. The solution to this problem was as elegant as it was simple—send unknown case officers to Moscow.

This is what the CIA officer who had put Kris through her paces had explained during the classroom portion of her training. Along with a handful of other wives, and a female case officer's less-than-enthused husband, the spouses of the Moscow-bound junior officers had been subjected to a week of specialized training geared at preparing them for the rigors of their pending Russia posting.

The exercise had culminated with a mock arrest and interrogation that had felt very real. Apparently, Kris hadn't been alone in this assessment, as the red eyes of several of her fellow spouses could attest. At the conclusion of the training, the same plainspoken CIA instructor had assured his audience that the Russians, while hard, still adhered to the unwritten rules that had governed interactions between adversarial intelligence services for decades. Moscow Rules might be the order of the day for their CIA officer husbands or wives, but a Russian counterintelligence officer would never lay a hand on an American spouse.

"You are mistaken," Kris said, this time putting a bit of steel into her voice. "I'm a housewife. Nothing more."

Her indignation didn't come so much from a newfound sense of courage as much as that what she said was true. While the spouses had been provided with a bit of rudimentary training, they were not employees of the Central Intelligence Agency and were not expected to conduct themselves as such. Sure, Kris had known that Barry was going to unload a dead drop in a location near St. Clement's Church, but she had nothing to do with that. Her role had been to sit on the bench outside and look pretty.

Literally.

Russian men loved Western women. Barry's boss, the chief of Moscow Station, believed that an almost six-foot-tall former collegiate athlete with shoulder-length, flame-colored hair wearing an above-the-knee dress would make an excellent decoy.

"Stop, please," Petrov said. "Your denials are pointless. I have a job to do, just as you do. Admitting your intention to commit espionage against my nation is just a formality at this point, but it's still an important part of the repatriation process."

"I told you," Kris said, "I am not a spy. My husband works for the State Department. This is our first overseas posting and—"

"I'm not interested in Barry. I want to know about you."

The man's grandfatherly affect had melted away, and Kris didn't care for what remained. Petrov no longer resembled a favorite great-uncle or a demanding but fair professor emeritus. Instead he looked devoid of human emotion. Someone confronted with an unpleasant task he was nonetheless duty bound to complete.

Kris shivered. "There's not much to say about me. I lived in Russia before and I wanted to spend our posting exploring Moscow and working on an idea I had for a novel. I—"

"Enough!" Petrov leaned forward to shout into her face. "I was hoping it wouldn't come to this, but you've forced my hand." Turning, he faced the mirror to Kris's right. "Bring it in!"

She'd seen enough cop shows to have suspected that the glass was two-way, but the validation was still alarming. This was actually happening. She was being interrogated by a Russian counterintelligence officer. The door swung inward, and two men entered pushing a cart between them. Kris gulped, convinced that the anemic light would flicker off gleaming implements of torture, but to her relief, this wasn't the case. Rather than blades, pliers, mallets, or rusty jumper cables clipped to a car battery, the cart carried something unexpected—a traditional Russian wooden matryoshka doll and a small plastic bag.

"Look familiar?" Petrov said.

"Not in the slightest," Kris said.

Petrov frowned. Now he resembled a headmaster confronting a particularly troublesome student. "You're determined to play this farce to its conclusion, I see?"

Kris shook her head. "I have no idea what you're talking about."

Rather than answer, Petrov snapped his fingers. The bulkier of the two men emptied that Ziploc bag and a circular, metallic object about the size of a dime fell onto the cart.

"Microfilm," Petrov said. "A dated but still highly effective way to commit espionage. Using a matryoshka doll as a dead drop was a brilliant piece of fieldwork, by the way. They can be found in any of the multiple souvenir shops adjacent to the church. Of course, most of those dolls lack this one's hidden compartment."

"I'm sorry," Kris said, her head spinning. "I—"

"You might have succeeded if not for your Russian agent's poor tradecraft. The traitorous scientist has passed his final bit of technical information to you, I'm afraid. He's in an adjacent interrogation room, so I apologize if you hear the occasional scream. We've done our best to soundproof these walls, but sometimes my men get overzealous."

The words, delivered in such a matter-of-fact manner, hit Kris like hammer blows. A man was being tortured in the next room, and she was sitting across the table from the person who'd ordered it. A flood of emotions washed over her. The fear and bewilderment she expected, but there was one in the torrent that caught her by surprise.

Anger.

"I'm done with this," Kris said, leaning across the table as far as her restraints would permit. "I have no idea what game you're playing, but I am done with it. I am the wife of an American diplomat. I demand to see my ambassador."

Her voice's tenor surprised Kris. Gone was the mouse who had cowered in fear of the strange men who had snatched her from the street. This was the voice of the team captain who had led her teammates to the state championship in her senior year of college. Kris still didn't know what Petrov was playing at, but he'd chosen the wrong person for his scheme.

The Russian looked back at her for a long moment.

Then he slapped her.

Kris never saw the blow coming. One second, she was staring into Petrov's cold eyes. The next, pinpoints of light danced across her vision as the length of her left cheek caught fire. She'd never been hit in the face before and was surprised by how much it hurt. Her jaw ached and it was all she could do to contain the moan that wanted to break free. Probing her teeth with her tongue, Kris confirmed that there were no new gaps, but she did taste the iron tang of blood.

He'd split her lip.

Her storm of indignation dissipated as quickly as it had formed. As a collegiate athlete, Kris was no stranger to physical discomfort. She'd weathered her share of strained muscles, jammed fingers, and even a broken bone. Her sophomore year, a spike she'd misread had given her a concussion and prematurely ended her season. She knew about pain, but the violence that had just been so casually visited upon her was something else. She still didn't know what was going on, but she was certain about one thing—she couldn't take another blow like that.

"I tried to be civil," Petrov said. "To grant you the respect due another professional, but I can see now that you mistook my kindness for weakness. Hopefully, you won't make that mistake again."

Petrov raised his hand, and Kris flinched. She tried not to cower. She really did. But rather than fading, the pain from the blow was increasing. The numb tingling across her cheek had progressed to a dull ache and her jaw moved strangely when she tried to swallow. She didn't think the bone was broken, but the joint might be dislocated.

"Good," Petrov said, nodding in approval. "I think we've reached an understanding, so let's bring this engagement to its conclusion."

Kris took a minute to make sense of what Petrov was saying. She understood after a third man entered the room. A man with a handheld video camera. The gesture she'd mistaken for another slap was actually meant to beckon the newcomer. Tendrils of dread gripped her stomach as he casually extended the tripod's legs and then attached the camera. She didn't know what Petrov intended to tape, but she didn't think she would enjoy it.

The newcomer said something to Petrov. His accent suggested he was from southern Russia, perhaps Rostov, and his words were difficult to decipher. Kris thought he might be indicating that he was ready, but she wasn't sure.

"Excellent," Petrov said before turning his hard eyes back to her. "About a decade ago, our scientists developed a novel method to help us stem the flow of secrets to the West. I believe you call it spy dust. Sound familiar?"

Kris had no idea what the man was talking about, but she also had no intention of weathering another slap. Torn between antagonizing the man with a denial or admitting to something that would further incriminate her, she tried to split the baby. Gritting her teeth, she refused to answer.

Petrov sighed. "Believe me when I say that silence will not serve you any better than your earlier outburst, but for the sake of time, I will overlook your insolence."

Reaching into his jacket pocket, Petrov withdrew a flashlight with some sort of filter attached to the end. After thumbing on the power switch, the Russian pointed the flashlight at the matryoshka doll.

Kris gasped.

The wooden toy's surface shone with bits of brilliance like someone had spilled a container of glitter onto the wood.

"Impressive, yes?" Petrov said. "Spy dust. The powder is invisible, but it fluoresces upon exposure to a specific band of the electromagnetic spectrum. It's impossible to detect by touch or smell and it adheres to everything. Coating sensitive files or items with spy dust allows us to determine who has been touching things they shouldn't. Let's look at the bag we found inside the doll, shall we?"

The Russian angled the flashlight so that its weak-seeming beam focused on the Ziploc bag. Glitter sparkled from everywhere.

"And now for the finale," Petrov said.

Maybe it was her aching jaw, or the effects of the tranquilizer, or perhaps just that she was still coming to terms with her imprisonment. Whatever the cause, the result was the same. Though Kris should have anticipated what was coming, she did not. With a flourish worthy of a stage magician, the Russian snapped the power off, pointed the flashlight at her manacled hand, and thumbed the switch back on.

Kris's fingers shone.

"Did you get that?" Petrov said.

The camera operator answered with a guttural but decipherable "*Da*."

"Excellent," Petrov said. Then he turned back to her. "Now, please say your name for the camera."

She considered refusing, but didn't want her silence to be taken as evidence of guilt.

She wasn't a spy, and she wouldn't behave like one.

Staring into the lens, Kris wet her lips and began to speak.

CHAPTER 19

R APP pressed his hands against the scarred wooden railing as he breathed in a lungful of sea air. Barcelona really was a remarkable city, and the sight line from Castell de Montjuïc was especially stunning. The tourist attraction sat atop Montjuïc Mountain and offered a 360-degree view of Barcelona's port. The scrub brush on the far side of the railing concealed a steep drop-off, and though the cliff's edge had too much litter for Rapp's taste, the vista it revealed was still breathtaking.

Five hundred feet below, the Port of Barcelona glittered in the evening sun. A glance to the right revealed acres of metal cargo containers waiting for transport on one of the several ships docked at the multiple peers. The gritty, industrial feel of this section of the port was starkly at odds with the view to Rapp's left. Dominated by a large traffic circle built around the Plaça de les Drassanes, this was the port's pedestrian area where visiting cruise ships disgorged their passengers. Shops, eateries, and hotels made this stretch of pier a perfect place for a stroll.

Rapp was not here to stroll.

His vantage point at the eastern corner of the sprawling acreage upon which the more than three-hundred-year-old military fortress sat put him about halfway between the industrial and tourist sections of the port. The cafés, bars, and pedestrian areas were about a half-mile straight-line distance to his left, while the container yard and the rows of waiting cargo ships were located about the same distance to his right. He did his best work up close and personal with his silenced Beretta, but he was no slouch with a rifle. Still, a high-angle shot at a target more than a half mile distant was well beyond his abilities.

Fortunately, Rapp wasn't here to shoot either.

"Beautiful, isn't it?"

The question came from the blond woman to his left.

She'd appeared at the railing a minute or two before, and while Rapp had marked her approach, she hadn't triggered his radar. The observation area was strategically positioned to catch visitors exiting the castle, and more than a few lingered by the railing to take in the awe-inspiring seascape. The woman had asked the question in American-accented English, and judging by her stylish designer jeans, tank top, and white leather K-Swiss shoes, she was probably a tourist and thereby harmless.

Probably.

"*Je ne parle pas anglais,*" Rapp said with haughty Parisian indifference.

He'd been proficient in French by the end of college, but living in Paris over the last year or so had done wonders for his accent, and he could now pass as native of the City of Light. The blonde's short *o*'s and flat *a*'s marked her as from the upper Midwest. Northern Minnesota if he had to guess. Hopefully his rudeness would grate on her Midwestern sensibilities, and she'd take the hint and leave him alone.

He'd baited his trap almost an hour ago.

If his hunch was correct, his quarry should be arriving soon.

"*Très bien,*" the woman said, switching to French. "I never get to practice with a native speaker."

Rapp sighed.

As Hurley was fond of saying, stereotypes existed for a reason, and the blonde was Exhibit A.

There was no getting around Minnesota nice.

"Your French is very good," Rapp said, turning toward the woman, "but—"

He intended to say *but I'm not much for small talk*, but the words died in his throat once he faced Minnesota Nice. It wasn't just that she was stunning. Her shoulder-length blond hair, athletic build, and Nordic features could have been a twin for Greta's.

No, that wasn't quite right.

Her laugh lines were a bit deeper, and the first hint of a wrinkle had begun to form on her otherwise smooth forehead. She was Greta ten years from now.

"You were saying?" Minnesota Nice said with a smile.

"*Désolé*," Rapp said. "You remind me of someone."

"I'm sure I do," she said, laughing. "You Frenchmen are all the same. And before you ask, yes, I'm married. My husband is just down there."

Rapp looked to where the woman was pointing and saw a tall, brown-haired man poking about by one of the fortress's World War I–era cannons. "He likes guns?"

The woman shrugged. "He's a writer. Always doing research. I should probably join him. It's been nice speaking with you, monsieur . . ."

"Gervais," Rapp said. "Simon Gervais."

"Great to meet you, Simon. I'm Lysa. *Au revoir.*"

After gracing him with a parting smile, Lysa followed the path toward her writer husband. Rapp watched her for a minute, wondering if he and Greta would someday traipse through the ruins of ancient castles together.

He hoped so.

Putting Lysa out of his mind, Rapp lifted the pair of tourist binoculars hanging from a leather strap around his neck to his eyes. Panning across the promenade below and to his left, he focused on an ordinary-looking bench a little over a half mile distant.

His earlier hunch had been correct.

Someone was nibbling at his bait.

CHAPTER 20

"W HY does your organization still exist?"

Thomas Stansfield gazed up at the speaker, wrestling with a question of his own.

Why did the nation I love entrust its leadership to such idiots?

He resisted the urge to give voice to his inner monologue. As his first-grade teacher had drilled into his head in the single-room schoolhouse of his youth, one did not show disrespect to those in authority no matter how much they might deserve it. The man who'd just spoken might be an imbecile, but he was also a member of the greatest deliberative body in the world.

The room in which they were meeting reflected this stature.

As was the case with anyone who testified before the Senate Select Committee on Intelligence, Stansfield was seated at a small, unadorned table facing the elevated row of seats reserved for his questioners. The room's royal-blue carpeting seemed at odds with the rich nutmeg paneling framing the dais, as did the white, marbled wall that served as the chamber's backdrop. Stansfield took comfort in the sparse and perhaps unconventional furnishings. This was a solemn place populated by serious men and women who discussed weighty topics.

Or at least it was supposed to be.

"I'm not sure what you mean," Stansfield said.

"Maybe some context will help—the Soviet Union crumbled almost two years ago. The Cold War is over. We won. They lost. So why does this Congress still need to spend almost ten percent of the national budget on an intelligence entity dedicated to stealing the secrets of a nation that has already been relegated to the ash heap of history?"

The question was delivered in a thunderous oration that suggested rehearsal. Extensive rehearsal. The image of the ranking member of the opposition party practicing his questions in front of his bathroom mirror almost brought a smile to Stansfield's face.

Almost.

Fifty years ago, Stansfield had been barely into adulthood and surrounded by partisans who were even younger. In the early days of the OSS, no one questioned the need for an intelligence organization dedicated to stealing the secrets of America's enemies. At least no one on the front lines of the fight. Had such an organization been in existence in the 1930s, perhaps a second world war might not have enveloped the globe in death and destruction.

Or perhaps not.

Senator Jefferson Rutledge was not an anomaly. Self-serving blowhards had sought political power since antiquity. Stupidity was hardly a problem unique to the twentieth century, but the fact that this particular useful idiot had amassed so much power might be. The television camera mounted along the far wall telescoped, no doubt zooming in on Stansfield's face. Whether Senator Rutledge really believed what he was spouting, or if this was all fodder for a future reelection commercial, Stansfield couldn't say. He did know that his answer would likely lead the evening news programs, since many of the television anchors shared Rutledge's sentiment.

Stupidity was contagious.

"I appreciate you getting to the heart of the matter so quickly, Senator," Stansfield began. "Your question has been asked with increasing regularity, and I welcome the opportunity to address it in these hearings. As you've elected to make my testimony open to the public, I will have to refrain from providing specifics in order to protect sources and methods."

Rutledge's mic picked up a sudden indrawn breath, and Stansfield paused in expectation of another fiery diatribe.

It did not come.

Instead, the senator reclined in his leather chair and folded his arms across his chest. Like far too many contemporary politicians, Rutledge had a TV-ready look. His black hair was stylishly cut and free of any pesky hints of gray despite his sixty-plus decades of life. His blue suit was perfectly tailored to accentuate his still-trim frame, but it was his expressive face that cameras loved. Had he not pursued politics, the senator might have enjoyed a successful career onstage.

At the moment, his malleable features wore the famous look of exasperation that had graced countless newspapers and television screens. Stansfield was a firm believer in both the rule of law and the importance the United States Constitution placed on the three branches of government, but he detested the theatrics that too often accompanied open hearings.

As per the usual setup, Stansfield sat alone at the witness table. Though executive branch cabinet members or department secretaries called to testify often traveled with a phalanx of aides along with the occasional lawyer, Thomas attended hearings by himself. He needed no administrative bodyguards, and his memory had been honed by decades of practicing espionage. More importantly, Stansfield came to these meetings alone because he did not intend to expose anyone else in the agency's leadership to hostile fire. Though he'd been the acting director since the Cooke debacle, he placed his odds at confirmation at no better than a coin toss. If someone needed to go down with the ship so that his beloved agency survived, it would be him.

Alone.

"My apologies," Stansfield said, sliding into the building silence. "I thought Senator Rutledge was about to comment. As I was saying, the Central Intelligence Agency's mission is not, nor has it ever been, solely focused on defeating the Soviet Union. The men and women I have the pleasure of leading gather and analyze intelligence in order to protect our nation from threats, plural. The Soviet Union was perhaps the largest threat to confront our nation since World War Two, but it was far from the only one. Nature abhors a vacuum. Like all of you, I cheered when the Berlin Wall crumbled just as I cheered when we defeated Nazi Germany and accepted Japan's surrender. But to rejoice in the defeat of one enemy while refusing to acknowledge that this defeat will make room for the emergence of another is the height of naïveté."

"I'm naïve?" Rutledge said. "Is that your testimony?"

Stansfield shook his head. "Senator, I'm simply making the point that this agency has been defending our nation against foreign threats for almost fifty years. Sometimes those threats were easily recognizable. Oftentimes they were not. But rest assured, despotic dictators and rogue actors the world over see America's very existence as a danger to their continued rule. As long as the United States represents a shining city upon a hill, there will be no shortage of barbarians who wish to extinguish that light. My job is to provide intelligence that enables our leaders to make informed decisions that will protect America and its citizens from those who mean us harm."

"Very poetic," Rutledge said, "but also a little self-serving. You're here today for more than just baseball and apple pie. You are testifying so that we can decide whether to advance your nomination for director of the Central Intelligence Agency to the full Senate for a vote. Before we do that, I'd like your response to my suggestion that we cut the CIA's budget by half. Setting aside that the military has already been downsized by ten percent with no appreciable degradation to our national security—"

"Yet," Stansfield said.

Rutledge's face flushed, but he plowed over the interruption without stopping. "As I said, the military's budget has been appreciably decreased, and we are just as safe. More safe I would argue, since we are now able to reinvest this peace dividend into the types of domestic programs that directly benefit the American people. But that's a topic for another day. I'd like to circle back to what you said earlier. About the CIA's purpose. You said that your job was to protect our nation, correct?"

"No," Stansfield said. "I said that my job was to provide the intelligence that—"

"Yes, yes, we've got it," Rutledge said. "My intent isn't to trip you up with legalese. My question is much more basic—is your agency causing more harm than good?"

Stansfield let the question hang in the air as he considered where the senator might be trying to lead him. Rutledge might be a self-important bureaucrat who fancied himself the next JFK, but underestimating him would be a mistake. The senator had the intellectual chops of a Chihuahua, but his bellicose style and good looks made him a perfect spokesman for the anti-CIA sentiment that was becoming ever more prominent. More than once, he'd ambushed Stansfield with an argument or set of facts that suggested that he might be getting help from agency insiders.

"I'm afraid you'll have to be more specific," Stansfield said.

The statement was a gamble, but not a large one. While the killings in Paris had certainly made news, the president had made it clear to his fellow pols that any discussions about the murders had to be done in a sensitive compartmented information facility, or SCIF.

A few well-placed warnings from the executive branch typically did the trick. Congressmen and senators might make a lot of noise, but they were loath to put their security clearances at risk by discussing sensitive matters in open forums. Every member of the legislative branch holding a security clearance had signed the required NDAs that specified the draconian penalties for disclosing classified information. Whatever dirt Rutledge might have on the operation, he certainly wouldn't divulge it during an open hearing and thereby risk a lucrative post-political career spent sitting on the boards of defense contractors, or worse, occasion a visit from federal law enforcement.

"Happy to," Rutledge said, drawing a piece of paper from the stack in front of him. "CNN broke this story moments before this hearing began. The Russian ambassador claims that their counterintelligence service arrested an American spy earlier today. Would you care to comment?"

"Absolutely not," Stansfield said, his anger getting the better of him. "We are in an open hearing."

"Indeed we are," Rutledge said, nodding gravely, "but these are extraordinary circumstances. The alleged spy is an American diplomat's wife. The Russians are threatening to expel our entire US mission from Moscow and try the wife in criminal court. This would be a horrible development. Have you nothing to say on the matter?"

Stansfield had plenty to say, but since the hearing was being broadcast live on C-SPAN, he kept his thoughts to himself. Instead he swept away his anger and forced his features into an impassive expression. "Senator, as is standard practice, I will neither confirm nor deny the specifics of an intelligence operation. This entire line of questioning is inappropriate."

"As I suspected," Rutledge said with a mournful look. "The cowboys running your organization have once again made our nation, and by extension the entirety of Europe, less safe. I agree that continuing this hearing is pointless, but if you won't speak to these charges, we'll let CNN have the last word."

On cue, the twin television screens flanking the dais changed from displaying an image of the seal of the Senate to a picture of a woman seated behind a desk. Her lip was split and blood dribbled down her chin, but it was the woman's manacled hands that demanded Stansfield's attention.

They were covered in sparkling spy dust.

CHAPTER 21

THE surveillance team was smooth.

Smooth enough that their presence only registered with Rapp's subconscious.

A kind of metaphysical itch he couldn't scratch.

At first, he'd wondered if he was jumping at shadows. His nerves had been on edge since the incident at the art museum and the line between operational instincts and paranoia was much finer than most clandestine operatives cared to admit. Maybe he was seeing something out of the ordinary because his adrenaline-saturated brain was chasing ghosts.

Then a plastic bag brought the situation into focus.

To set his trap, Rapp had constructed two rudimentary dead drops. Despite the beauty of their city, Catalonians weren't much for ensuring their litter made it all the way into the trash receptacle. The greenery around public trash cans was covered with plastic bags, soda cans, beer bottles, and other refuse. It had been a simple matter to repurpose a discarded piece of cardboard and a soiled sandwich wrapper into improvised containers for his bait.

A pair of cell phones.

The first phone was his. He'd wrapped the cell in the greasy sandwich bag before wedging it beneath a bench in the port's tourist area. The second he'd found in the handbag he'd taken from the woman at the airport. This mobile went into a cardboard box that he'd placed adjacent to an underused trash can guarding the entrance to the shipping container yard. After activating both phones and emplacing the makeshift dead drops, he'd taken a cab to Castell de Montjuïc and begun his vigil of the two geographically disparate dead drops from the castle's observation area. He was hoping the cells might help with two burning questions—how was he being tracked, and who was doing the tracking?

Someone had discarded a neon-green plastic bag in the vicinity of the dead drop containing his phone. A trio of musicians had taken over the bench beneath which the dead drop was wedged. Two were lustily strumming their guitars, while a third appeared to be singing while keeping time with a handheld shaker.

The green bag swirled at their feet before tumbling across the ground.

Rapp's eyes were drawn to the motion. He panned away from the bench, tracking the cartwheeling plastic with his binoculars until its flight was arrested by the spindly legs of the Torre de Jaume I. The rickety-looking steel tower stood almost four hundred feet high and anchored the southeastern corner of the promenade between the one-way sister streets of Moll 18 C Barcelona and Moll 18 A Barcelona. In addition to serving as the backdrop for countless pictures, the tourist attraction also featured an observation deck that provided an excellent view of the entire pier.

Rapp panned up to the metal structure to the deck.

Empty.

With a frustrated sigh, he was in the process of lowering his binos when another image swam into view. Twin glass and steel structures flanked the tower. The buildings had an art deco vibe presumably designed to match the tower's scaffolding-like construction. The lower levels housed restaurants, bars, and shops, while the upper deck provided an outdoor seating area.

A covered, outdoor seating area.

The seating area of the building to the tower's south was empty, but a scan of the northern one revealed several patrons. Most were eating inside, but one man had selected a table along the balcony, perhaps to soak in the evening's soft light. Conveniently, the table also offered an unobstructed sight line to the promenade and the bench with the musicians. Rapp focused the binos on the watcher's face. His visage wasn't familiar, but his fair features didn't match the olive skin or dark complexion of a native Catalan.

He could be a tourist.

Or something else.

As Rapp watched, the man lifted a cell to his ear and appeared to speak.

Rapp swept the binos across the promenade. The pedestrian area to the tower's west was still clear, as was the area around the bench.

What was he missing?

That question led to another.

Where would he position the rest of the surveillance team?

With the man at the table observing the pier's southeastern corner, Rapp would have put someone in place to monitor the comings and goings from the northwest entrance. Sweeping the binos to the right, Rapp centered on a building situated on the corner of Moll 18 A Barcelona and Ronda Litoral. The two-story structure had a striking reddish-brown exterior that resembled cedar paneling and seemed to be some sort of terminal. The flat roof was empty, and the slit-like windows positioned at irregular intervals across the façade sported reflective glass that made guessing what was inside impossible, but the southern exit, which faced the tower, sported an overhang and several benches.

One of the benches held a pretty woman with a cell phone.

Rapp focused on the woman's face. Talking on a cell wasn't proof that she was part of a surveillance team, but her choice of seating was unusual. Mere feet away, a pedestrian area offered palm tree–shaded benches and a cool ocean breeze.

Instead, the woman had chosen a congested terminal's dingy corner.

Still, dingy or not, the corner provided unobstructed sight lines to the pedestrian promenade as well as the adjacent bus station. The vehicular traffic flowing west and east along Ronda Litoral was also clearly visible. Her position was perfect to lock down the northeastern corner of the pier, but if he were running the operation, he'd employ a surveillance element with more than just two operatives. Shifting from the woman, Rapp checked the choke points along the eastern side of the pedestrian area.

A Mediterranean restaurant located on the northeastern corner offered plenty of outdoor seating and an assortment of benches. Rapp panned across the half-full dining area and marked a couple of possibles. Transitioning from the restaurant to the surrounding benches, he found several occupied. Most of the benches faced east, toward the bus stop and away from the dead drop.

Most but not all.

Two were oriented west toward the ocean and the promenade.

One of the two was occupied.

Judging by the shoulder-length brown hair, clothing, and small frame, Rapp guessed that the seated person was female, but he couldn't determine much else. He was about to shift focus back to the dead drop and the trio of musicians when the woman played with something in her lap. He tried to angle the binos for a better look but couldn't get line of sight past her shoulder.

Then she lifted a cell phone to her ear.

He swept the binos to dead drop 2, next to the container yard's trash can.

No activity.

He shifted back to dead drop 1.

Several bystanders had crowded around the musicians, clapping along with the music and tossing change into the open guitar case lying on the ground in front of their bench. Rapp panned to the woman positioned at the terminal in the northwest corner just in time to catch a trio of sedans entering the traffic circle at the western edge of the pier. The first two took the second right out of the traffic circle and headed southeast down Moll 18 C Barcelona. Other than their slightly elevated speed, there wasn't anything unusual about the vehicles.

The third car was a different matter.

It took the first right out of the traffic circle and proceeded southeast toward the dead drop by driving the wrong way on a one-way street.

The rendition team had just arrived.

CHAPTER 22

THE lead vehicle in the pair of cars heading the correct way down Moll 18 C Barcelona accelerated. Drawing abeam the cluster of musicians, the sedan turned left, blocking both lanes of traffic. The trail vehicle did the same, effectively creating a cordon around the startled group of onlookers. The third sedan swerved right, driving over the concrete curve and onto the stone pedestrian area. Though its speed was now slower, the car continued across the pavement until it reached the musicians, closing the vehicular box.

The doors on each car swung open.

The vehicles' eight occupants converged on the trio of musicians like an avalanche enveloping unsuspecting skiers. One moment the two guitarists and shaker player were happily making music. The next they were surrounded by broad-shouldered men.

Angry broad-shouldered men.

The lead operative, a man whose buzz cut, wide back, and narrow waist all but screamed military, said something to the man with the shaker and gestured toward his car. The musician shook his head. In a blur of motion, Buzzcut snared the musician's shoulder, arm-barred him, and face-planted him onto the ground.

One of the guitarists tried to intervene.

It did not go well.

The operative nearest the guitarist, a blond man whose rippling forearms belied his trim build, fired an open-handed strike into the musician's throat using the webbing between his thumb and index finger.

Clutching his neck, the guitarist fell to his knees.

The second guitarist, a man with shoulder-length dreadlocks, appeared to ascribe to the philosophy of making love, not war. In what looked like a practiced gesture, he lifted his hands above his head, allowing the guitar's sling to catch the instrument. Buzzcut and Blond searched the musicians with quick, efficient motions as the bystanders scattered. While an amusing assortment of drug paraphernalia—several Ziploc bags filled with suspicious green leaves and a single knit hacky sack—were emptied onto the pavement, the items did not appear to be what the men were looking for.

After patting down each man twice, Buzzcut looked over his shoulder at the sedan parked on the pedestrian area and barked out something. Rapp was too far away to hear the words, but he could guess their meaning.

We didn't find anything. What now?

The sedan's rear passenger door swung open, revealing a pair of legs. A pair of very shapely, very long legs. The woman who exited the car looked nothing like the brutes who had accosted the musicians. Rapp's first thought was of a kennel master and her hounds, but that didn't quite capture the relationship either. A queen surrounded by her royal guard might be a more apt description. The woman's auburn hair was cut short, not quite a bob but shorter than collar-length, and the style emphasized her hard, angular features.

A crown of fire.

Her gaze flitted from musician to musician and the men wilted beneath her glare. Buzzcut gestured toward the pile of paraphernalia and then at the hapless trio. The Queen crouched so that she was eye level with the man with dreadlocks. Her lips moved and the man responded by shaking his head in a *no* motion that began slowly and increased with vigor the longer the Queen spoke.

Standing, the Queen turned back to Buzzcut. She gestured at the captives while delivering what appeared to be a reprimand. Buzzcut shook his head and withdrew something from his pocket. His meaty fingers obscured most of the device, despite Rapp's best efforts. After fiddling with the object, he again shook his head.

The Queen held her hand out, palm up, fingers extended.

Buzzcut handed over the mystery device and Rapp saw that it was about the size of a pager. A frown creased the woman's porcelain features as she thumbed something on the front of the device. Then she stepped toward the captives. After waving the device around the men as if she were blessing them with incense, the Queen consulted the object. Moving past the musicians, she approached the bench, crouched, and withdrew the greasy sandwich wrapper. Wrinkling her nose, she unfolded the paper and found Rapp's cell.

Dropping the wrapper, the Queen tossed the phone to Buzzcut.

The mobile hit him in the chest and almost tumbled to the pavement before he caught it. The Queen was no longer paying attention. Instead, she turned away from the bench and looked southwest.

Southwest toward Rapp.

He focused the binoculars on her face, committing the Queen's expression to memory. As if sensing his gaze, the woman gave three exaggerated claps. At first Rapp didn't understand.

Then, he did.

She was applauding.

Turning, the Queen strode back to her sedan, settled into the rear seat, and closed the door. The vehicle pulled a U-turn and departed the same way it had arrived. As the car drove away, Rapp noticed a detail he'd overlooked earlier.

The sedan had diplomatic license plates.

Russian diplomatic license plates.

CHAPTER 23

NINETY minutes later, Rapp was descending into the bowels of the Metro de Barcelona. The subway system was easy to use, reliable, and convenient, but this was not why he was following the stairs into the Paral-lel Metro station. Moving to his right to allow room for the riders in a hurry to flow past him, he followed the winding staircase onto the subway platform. But instead of trailing the crowd to the left and the waiting car, Rapp turned right.

Right toward the bank of public phones.

Selecting a handset equidistant from both the foot traffic and the crowd milling around the boards displaying maps of the Metro and the train schedule, Rapp used his knuckle to punch a set of digits on the phone's keypad.

After three rings, a voice echoed across the line.

An annoyed voice.

"I thought I told you to take a vacation?"

"Had to cut it short," Rapp said. "A new work project landed on my plate."

Rapp heard only silence for a beat. Presumably this was because the person on the other end of the line required a moment to work through the deeper meaning hidden in his deliberately vague answer.

At least he hoped that was the source of the pause.

"Okay. What do you need?"

An excellent question.

After watching the Russian diplomatic convoy depart the pier, Rapp had kept his vigil at the railing long enough to verify that they weren't heading toward the second dead drop at the cargo yard's entrance. Fifteen more minutes of watching nothing happen to the cell phone tucked away in a cardboard box next to the garbage can had been enough to convince him that his phone was the only one that had been compromised. This realization, combined with his experience with the airport, could only mean one thing—the Russians had thoroughly penetrated his legend. He didn't know how or why, but he couldn't ignore the fact that he'd already been lucky twice.

There was no reason to believe his luck would hold a third time.

His next decision had been easy.

He'd hiked down from Montjuïc Mountain, located a phone booth, and dialed a number that had connected him to one of the answering services reserved for the Orion team. He'd left what sounded like a generic voice message but in reality had been a set of very specific instructions detailing whom he wanted to speak with and when. He'd then ended the connection, killed time by playing tourist, and at the appropriate hour descended into the subway for his second call.

The one he was on right now.

"I'm in a bit of a bind," Rapp said. "My flight home was canceled and someone stole my wallet. I need help rebooking my travel."

"Got it. Give me thirty minutes and then ring admin. They'll have your new itinerary. Anything else?"

Rapp hesitated. This was the part of the conversation that would really hurt. "My new project is a doozy. I could use another pair of hands."

"Whose?"

Rapp sighed. "Yours."

Another beat of silence.

"You want help from me?"

"Yes."

"Well, I'll be damned."

"Is that a *yes*?" Rapp said.

"Shit. I'd love to help, kid, but I'm really swamped right now."

Rapp ground his teeth. Why had he ever imagined the old codger would ever have a change of heart? "Fine, I'll—"

"Just busting your balls. Of course I'm in. See you soon."

The humor in Stan Hurley's gravelly voice was almost too much to bear. Rapp wished he could hang up. He couldn't.

Not yet.

"Thank you," Rapp said. "I mean it."

Hurley had already ended the connection.

Rapp swore as he placed the handset back onto its cradle.

He should have felt relieved.

He didn't.

CHAPTER 24

Have you ever provided classified information to a foreign government?"

Zeke Williams had been expecting this question, but hearing it voiced so casually still gave him pause. All polygraphers were not created equal. Some wanted to delve into your personal life for the enjoyment of hearing you confess to cheating on your eighth-grade science test. Still others were all about the steamy details of forbidden office romances or a fling with a friend's spouse. The very best examiners resisted the urge to become a voyeur in a stranger's life in favor of getting to what really mattered—was the person on the other end of the polygraph machine a foreign asset?

The unassuming man with thinning blond hair, oversize black spectacles, and a small paunch seemed to fit that category. He'd begun the interview with a few perfunctory statements about the nature of a polygraph examination, what he intended to cover, and what he did not. This speech was not new to Zeke. As someone who'd held clearances at the secret level and above for almost two decades, he was well acquainted with what would follow. Still, the polygrapher's approach had thrown him off-balance. Usually an examiner started with a few inane questions meant to relax the subject.

Not today.

"Never," Zeke said.

"'Yes' or 'no' answers only, please. Have you ever provided classified information to a foreign government?"

"No."

The faint sound of a keyboard clacking drifted from where the examiner was seated behind and to his left, but Zeke tried not to dwell on the ambient noise. The examiner might be flagging the answer for follow-up, fine-tuning the polygraph, or simply fiddling with the machine to keep Zeke off balance. There was no way to know what the examiner was seeing, so Zeke didn't try to speculate. Instead he kept his attention on the centimeter-sized paint chip that marred the far wall's otherwise flawless beige color scheme.

Like most interrogation rooms, the décor emphasized function over form. The bare walls were devoid of decoration, the carpeting an anemic shade of gray, and the chairs were constructed of a sturdy, but not particularly comfortable, form of composite wood. Something not quite plastic, but still a far cry from anything that had ever taken nourishment from soil or sunlight.

Unlike many government offices that owed their blandness to regulations stating that any decorations purchased with taxpayer dollars must be sourced from companies that checked the two boxes most important to any government contractor—technically feasible and the lowest price—the polygrapher's room was designed to look sterile. In the ever-evolving science of detecting lies, current orthodoxy dictated that while the interviewee shouldn't be made physically uncomfortable, there was nothing wrong with inducing a little mental stress.

In the same way in which the average person filled uncomfortably long silences with idle chatter, a polygrapher wanted his subject to feel as though they had nowhere to hide from his questions. This was why no pictures of windswept beachscapes graced the walls. Instead of artwork or soothing music, the subject experienced only the examiner's voice and the *tap, tap, tap* of his fingers against a hidden keyboard. But this room offered a haven from the sterility in the form of a minuscule blemish on the wall's otherwise uniform surface. Zeke almost smiled at the image of a fellow interviewee scratching the mark into the paint with his fingernail during one of the examiner's numerous exits from the room.

He sighed instead.

No one smiled during a polygraph examination.

No one.

"Please try to keep your breathing regular. Uneven respiration makes my job harder and might require us to revisit earlier questions. I don't want to be here any longer than necessary."

Zeke doubted this very much.

Polygrapher slots were much sought after. Likening the examiners to the inquisitors of old wasn't a fair comparison, but it was one that was often made by those required to endure periodic five-year examinations, or worse yet, an unannounced session with an interrogator.

Zeke hated polys.

As did everyone.

"Sorry," Zeke said.

He was not sorry.

As with anyone who occupied the pressed-wood chair, he had secrets.

Ones he did not intend to reveal.

Whether those secrets remained intact depended in large part on the skill of the examiner and how deeply he intended to probe. *You might beat me, but you'll never beat the machine* was a common refrain voiced by polygraphers. Zeke subscribed to that sentiment after a fashion, but with a very large asterisk. He didn't believe he could beat man or machine, nor did he want to. Instead he was focused on fencing off their conversation to topics he was willing to divulge, while countering the examiner's attempts to shine a spotlight into the dark corners of his mind.

This mental chess match was not unique.

Men and women had been shrouding portions of their lives from questioners for as long as security interviews had been in existence. Everyone had secrets. Zeke hitched a breath as he concentrated on the paint chip. The change in respiration wasn't great enough to garner a reprimand from the examiner, but it would register to the multiple sensors attached to his head, torso, and feet. A deviation in a subject's breathing pattern could signify many things, but in the scope of this conversation, he was hoping the examiner would attribute the blip to contrition.

Zeke was not contrite.

Not in the least.

"Have you ever met with an agent of a foreign government?"

"Yes."

Contact with agents of foreign governments were part and parcel of Zeke's job.

Though this reinvestigation pertained to the security clearance he held as a staffer for the National Security Council, or NSC, this was not Zeke's primary role. He actually worked for Bob Hillman, a former congressman and one-term senator who hailed from a flyover state. Like many of DC's professional class, Bob had come to the nation's capital as a wide-eyed idealist of modest means but had quickly realized that there was money to be made in the District of Columbia. After losing his senatorial reelection bid, Bob had chosen to monetize the relationships he'd developed while serving in the legislature rather than return to Kansas.

Zeke had interned for Bob during the congressman's initial campaign and had been promoted to chief of staff by the end of Senator Hillman's political career. Accordingly, he'd followed his boss to lucrative stints as a K Street lobbyist and campaign advisor. Several years ago, Bob had founded a think tank focused on increasing international trade. He'd been instrumental in helping the current president win the Oval Office and had been awarded a seat on the NSC as thanks. At nearly seventy years of age, Bob wasn't much on attending meetings, so Zeke nearly always represented his principal at NSC gatherings.

But this was just a side hustle.

Zeke's primary responsibility was to meet with foreign entities who wished to invest in or acquire American companies. Many of these meetings included representatives from foreign governments.

"Other than the instances that you previously disclosed in your preinterview questionnaire, have you ever met with an agent of a foreign government?"

"No."

Zeke responded with the rapidity that the examiner expected even as he focused the whole of his being on the paint chip. He made no effort to alter his already steady respiration, but he ran through a mental exercise to slow his pulse.

More faint clicking from the keyboard.

More silence.

Then, "Other than the instances that you previously disclosed in your preinterview questionnaire, have you every mishandled classified material?"

"No."

As if he were opening a boiler's safety valve, Zeke allowed his anxiety to bleed through. The definition applied to the charge of mishandling classified material was so broad as to be almost all-encompassing. From failing to engage your computer's screensaver when stepping away from your desk, to accidentally attaching the wrong cover sheet to a restricted document, almost any common mistake could fall under the category of mishandling classified material.

Prior to the examination, Zeke had already admitted to his most egregious examples in response to the preinterview questionnaire. Times when he'd momentarily exited a SCIF with a classified document in hand, or the instance when he'd forgotten to put his cell phone in one of the lockboxes affixed to the wall outside the facility. Both of these sins had been quickly forgiven after he'd confessed them, but where there was one mistake, others were sure to lurk. Others that reared their heads only after the subject was attached to a polygraph machine and under the duress prompted by an examiner's questions.

This was intentional.

Contrary to what he told participants, part of the examiner's job was to ask questions designed to make his subjects feel uncomfortable. Despite vehement claims to the contrary, analyzing the results of a polygraph was still more art than science. British intelligence refused to use the devices at all, and even in America, the results from a polygraph were inadmissible in court. This was because every individual's baseline was different and therefore subject to interpretation. There was no such thing as a perfect result to a polygraph. In the same way in which human appearances came in all shapes and sizes, a person's mind was as unique as their fingerprints.

At the end of the day, determining whether a subject passed or failed their exam was largely subjective. Any prosecutor worth their salt understood that a competent defense attorney would make hay out of this ambiguity. Failing a polygraph couldn't lead to criminal charges, but for someone who made their living in the national security sector, a failure could result in something almost as dire.

Loss of a subject's security clearance.

So while the polygrapher liked to pretend that this exam was nothing more than a routine question-and-answer session, Zeke understood it to be much, much more.

No one enjoyed polygraphs.

No one.

"Are you an agent of a foreign government?"

"No."

A pause, perhaps longer this time. More clacking on the computer. Then, "Have you ever provided classified information to a foreign government?"

"No."

Zeke tried not to read into the examiner's tone, count the number of times he'd been asked the same question, or estimate the interval between the man's questions.

This was an impossible task.

"Your answer to the last question is giving the machine some trouble. Is there anything we need to discuss?"

Zeke was still facing the wall, which was a good thing. Only the cracked paint chip witnessed the beginnings of a smile that he quickly extinguished. Subjects were not supposed to think that any portion of an exam was amusing, especially if the examiner was expressing concern about an answer, but he was relieved nonetheless. Like a familiar argument between long-married spouses, Zeke was back on firm ground. At some point in every examination, the polygrapher expressed concern about an answer. Sometimes this was because the examiner believed the subject was engaging in deception.

Sometimes.

Other times, this was just an interrogation tactic, a last-ditch effort to exact a confession from a subject who was otherwise passing the exam with flying colors. Though he couldn't see the squiggly lines on the examiner's monitor, and wouldn't have been able to interpret the voodoo even if he could, Zeke was nearly one hundred percent certain this was the case. As with any examination, there were aspects of the questions that gave him trouble. Phrasings or word groupings that brought to mind things he would rather forget.

Not with this question.

He had never, under any circumstances, passed classified information to a foreign government.

"Don't know what to tell you," Zeke said, not bothering to hide his annoyance. "I answered truthfully."

"You have nothing to add?"

"Nope."

"Okay. Just a minute."

An electronic device hummed to life. Zeke turned to see the examiner grab a sheet of paper from the portable inkjet printer. The man lifted his glasses onto his forehead as he read through the results again, as if somehow the analog version of the test might prove different than what was displayed on his screen. With an oversize frown the examiner looked from the flimsy paper to Zeke. "I'm going to need to step out for a second."

"Sure."

Zeke didn't ask the examiner how long he'd be gone.

This was part of the game.

Was there an anomaly on the paper the examiner was clutching? Perhaps, but that was not important. The polygrapher hurrying from the room with the test results was pure theater. This same routine had occurred in every single polygraph Zeke had ever taken.

Even so, he refused to embrace the sense of relief, choosing instead to channel the nervousness he'd felt at one of the earlier questions. Like a politician who accidentally says the quiet part out loud when he doesn't realize that his mic is still live, Zeke was still connected to the machine, which meant that the whirring hard drive was still gathering information. A normal person would still be experiencing unease if not dread at the test's sudden interruption. This was the most important lie he needed to sell.

That he was a normal person.

"Okay, looks like we're all good here."

The examiner's voice startled him. Zeke had been so absorbed in his thoughts he hadn't realized the man had returned. Or perhaps the door's hinges were regularly oiled for just that reason. For the first time, he allowed a smile to break through as he imagined the examiner spraying down the hinges with WD-40 on an hourly basis.

"Something funny?"

"You know what they say," Zeke said. "If you can't laugh, you'd cry."

An hour later, Zeke nosed his BMW 5 Series into his favorite pub's cramped parking lot. While he'd more than earned an afternoon cocktail, this was not why he'd chosen this particular watering hole on this particular day. Turning off the car's engine, he glanced at the freshly painted row house across the street. Technically, an examiner was not allowed to tell the subject whether they'd passed or failed, as the results would have to be verified, but this rule was often stretched. A simple wink or even a warm handshake was enough to communicate the unspoken sentiment.

Nothing to worry about—you passed.

The bespectacled man had not winked, nodded, or even offered a particularly warm handshake. Instead their final conversation centered on the perfunctory admonishment that Zeke was not to talk about the exam or discuss the questions he'd been asked. This was not a cause for concern in itself. The examiner struck him as a bit of a stick-in-the-mud. His deviation from the unofficial practice was probably the sign of a fanatical adherence to policy, nothing more. After all, the role of polygraph examiner attracted a certain type of candidate.

As did Zeke's job.

His other job.

The newly painted row house was one of the many that had been refurnished as part of the gentrification craze sweeping the District. Its exterior was a sparkling shade of white that contrasted nicely with the black door frames and shutters.

Zeke's gaze drifted up to the pair of second-floor windows.

Unlike its companion, the blinds on the right window were drawn.

Zeke looked at the window for a moment longer just to be sure. Then he withdrew a cell phone from his jacket pocket and began to dial.

CHAPTER 25

I T was not an exaggeration to say that Irene Kennedy had known her
boss her entire life. Long before she'd understood the true nature of her
father's employment or the significance of his tragic death, she'd viewed
Thomas Stansfield as a surrogate father. When her mother had gone to
pieces and her family seemed to be self-destructing, Stansfield had been
her rock. During her reflective years in college, it had been Stansfield
who had shepherded her through the turbulent waters of self-doubt
and fear.

Stansfield had been the one who'd broken with agency policy to explain to her the family business, and Stansfield, with Hurley, had been
in the audience at the Farm for the secretive graduation ceremony held
after she'd successfully completed the CIA's clandestine training course.
After he became her boss, the nature of her relationship with Stansfield
had changed. She was a good case officer, but she wasn't perfect. As
with any good supervisor, there had been a time or two when Stansfield
had expressed his disappointment in her performance. In all this time,
Irene had never seen her mentor truly lose his cool.

Until now.

"I think the idiots might actually do it, Irene. The blown CIA operation in Moscow and this nonsense with our case officer's wife couldn't have come at a worse time. Rutledge might finally be able to muster enough votes to bring a motion to defund the agency to the floor for a vote."

Irene let her boss's words wash over her, uncertain how to respond.

It was a testament to Stansfield's state of mind that the conversation was being held over the phone rather than in his office. Though she was on an agency Gulfstream jet speeding east and speaking on a secure line, she still hesitated. Rather than an outlier, the Moscow debacle was a culmination of a string of arrested Russian CIA assets and aborted operations. While the principle espoused by Occam's razor pointed toward a human penetration of agency secrets as the source of these failures, Irene wasn't willing to place all her chips on that bet.

The CIA had conducted numerous successful technical operations against the Soviets and now Russians. From tapping undersea communications cables to attaching listening devices to secure telephone lines, the agency's Directorate of Science and Technology had proven to be quite adept at compromising what had previously been considered impenetrable communication methods. Only a fool would assume that the Russians weren't capable of doing the same.

Irene wasn't a fool.

"Do you think the resolution will pass?" Irene said.

The answering sigh was both long and pronounced. "I normally have a feel for the difference between partisan outbursts and statements that reflect an elected official's true feelings."

"Not this time?"

Another sigh. "Something's happening, Irene. Something beyond the normal idiocy. I think this madness began in the usual way with the usual suspects spouting off for the cameras, but this nonsense with the Russians, along with the continued fallout over the Cooke France affair, has taken the rhetoric to the next level. It's as if a drunk blowhard has suddenly had his bluff called. The situation in Moscow is only adding fuel to the fire. Our agency is leading the news cycle, and the public outcry might just compel Congress to act."

Irene digested this in silence.

Her nation was historically unique because it had been founded on an idea: the notion that certain truths were self-evident and that humanity had been bestowed by its Creator with certain inalienable rights. These precious ideals had birthed a constitutional republic in which the voice of every citizen carried the same weight, and in which disagreements were settled with ballots rather than bullets.

But this form of government was not perfect.

In an age in which TV coverage had become a campaign's oxygen, career politicians had begun to devolve into the type of outlandish behavior that generated headlines and invitations to appear on the Sunday morning talk shows. A government of the people, by the people, and for the people was only possible if the leaders those people elected to the nation's highest offices exhibited the sobriety needed to make the tough decisions that national service required. Unfortunately, sober-minded statesmen who embodied these traits seemed to be dwindling, replaced by Senator Rutledge and his ilk.

"Do you want me to return to DC?" Irene said.

Her question was an honest one and not driven by any inflated sense of her own importance. Stansfield had been in the CIA since the organization's inception. He was well-respected among the rank-and-file officers and had spent the majority of his time as an agent runner in the field. He knew where the bodies were buried both figuratively and literally, but to paraphrase the old Chinese proverb, they were living in interesting times. The CIA was beset with scandals both abroad and at home, and Stansfield was only the acting director.

In times of crisis, this distinction mattered.

Stansfield's *acting* title gave him less weight when testifying before an adversarial Congress and a diminished standing within the organization he was charged with leading. A director's word was law on Langley's seventh floor, but an acting director was more curiosity than dictator. The career executive bureaucrats who led the CIA were not immune to the political contagion infecting Congress, as Paul Cooke had so aptly demonstrated. Until Stansfield was properly coronated as DCI vis-à-vis a formal Senate confirmation, he was at best an interloper and at worst a rival to others seeking the agency's top job.

If leadership was a lonely enterprise, helming the nation's premier intelligence organization was doubly so. Irene's charter now focused almost exclusively on the Orion project, but more and more, her additional duties consisted of acting as an aide-de-camp and confidante to Stansfield. Hurley certainly had a longer history with Stansfield, but he had proven unsuited to office politics so Stansfield had removed Stan from the agency's active rolls in favor of transforming the contrarian operative into a contractor. While this was undoubtedly good for both the CIA and Hurley, it limited his ability to play the role of organizational insider. In a moment when Stansfield was under attack on all sides, it made sense that he would want the confidants he could trust implicitly close by. As far as Irene could tell, that category currently held a singular person.

Her.

"I appreciate the offer, but no. I need you in Russia, now more than ever. The situation in Latvia is getting worse. The ethnic Russians in Daugavpils are demonstrating in the streets against the Latvian government and the Russian president is making noise about sending in peacekeepers. We need to get to the bottom of this and my confidence in Moscow Station is at an all-time low. Max Powers has been an adequate Near East Division chief, but the chief of station in Moscow is his Farm classmate. They're old friends."

"You think Max has a blind spot to Moscow Station's failings?"

"I'm not sure. What I do know is that a potential conflict is brewing between Latvia and Russia. A conflict that could easily spill over to the other former Soviet republics and potentially NATO. It doesn't strike me as a coincidence that the agency station most suited to provide insight into what the Russians are actually thinking has been completely side-lined."

Irene turned Stansfield's words over in her mind. "The false-flag operation in Latvia and the burned operation in Moscow are related?"

"The Russians play the intelligence game better than anyone else, Irene. At the moment, I'm flying blind. I need you to be my eyes."

"I'm on it, sir," Irene said.

"I know you are. My intuition says that we are perilously close to an armed conflict in Europe. We just won a cold war. I'd rather not start a hot one. Good luck."

Stansfield ended the connection.

Irene considered her mentor's words as she placed the red secure phone back into its bulky cradle. She was not a military historian, but she did know one thing about her nation's martial history: When it came to wars, the United States did not often get to choose when to fight them.

CHAPTER 26

RAPP had never been so happy to see Stan Hurley's craggy mug. Okay, that wasn't exactly true. While it was good to see Hurley standing on the pier's edge with his hands on his hips like Patton surveying the battlefield, it was the sight of dry land rather than his mentor that flooded Rapp with a sense of relief. If Rapp never boarded a boat for the rest of his life it would be too soon.

"Hey, kid," Hurley said. "You don't look so good."

"Rough crossing." Rapp leaped from the fishing trawler's deck to the pier before the boat had finished docking. His stunt elicited chuckles from the crew, but he didn't care. Had he thought it would have gotten him to dry land faster, he would have swum ashore.

"I always thought the turning-green thing was a figure of speech, but damned if you don't look like a celery stick."

To Rapp's dismay, putting his feet on the pier's weathered wood planking had not done much to steady the swaying. Though he knew the island wasn't experiencing an earthquake, his inner ear wasn't so sure. Perhaps that had something to do with the twelve hours he'd spent transiting the Iberian Sea as the remnants of a rare Mediterranean hurricane, or *medicane*, battered the fishing trawler. The fishermen crewing the vessel hadn't seemed overly bothered by the rough seas, but Rapp had spent a good part of the trip retching over the side rails and questioning his life choices.

"I need something to settle my stomach," Rapp said.

"I know just the thing. Follow me."

"Beer? Really?" Rapp didn't bother to hide his skepticism as he eyed the refreshments the dirndl-clad waitress had just deposited on their table. The sizzling links of white sausage, Brotchen rolls, eggs, and cheese all looked reasonable enough, but the stein seemed a bit out of place.

"I made my bones running agents in Germany and Austria," Hurley said. "The Bavarians have a thing called *Brotzeit*, which is kind of like a second breakfast. You can't have *Brotzeit* without a *hefeweizen*. It's the law. Now drink up."

Rapp was willing to concede that he was no old German hand. Even so, he remained suspicious. With an eye toward his still-rumbling gut, he took a cautious sip. And then another. Whether the wheat beer was some sort of magical stomach elixir, or the anxiety of the last twenty-four hours was finally beginning to fade, he didn't care. Almost as soon as the alcohol swirled down his throat, the world stopped listing, and his appetite returned.

With a vengeance.

"See?" Hurley said with a smile. "Sometimes we old spies actually know a thing or two. Now, fill me in."

Rapp tore open one of the crusty rolls and loaded it with sliced meat and cheese as he thought. Stranger even than the idea of pairing eggs with beer was the notion that he and Hurley were sitting in a German-themed cantina overlooking the Playa de Palma discussing espionage. Judging by the plethora of *Bundesflagge* draped across buildings and flying from flagpoles, this section of the Spanish island catered to German tourists and Hurley looked to be in his element. It didn't take much for Rapp to imagine his mentor skulking from shadow to shadow, one step ahead of the Stasi as he emptied a dead drop or completed a brush pass with a jumpy East German asset. He and Hurley were seated on an otherwise empty patio situated on a small rise with a breathtaking view of the crashing surf. The beach and a floating dock were just steps away, and the morning sun shone from a cloudless blue sky. But despite the day's warmth, Rapp could still feel the Cold War's chill overshadowing their conversation.

"It started when I made a surveillance team in Barcelona," Rapp said.

In between bites of breakfast and hearty swallows of the frothy beer, Rapp relayed all that had happened from the moment he'd left Greta sitting at the table outside the Barcelona museum to his boarding of the fishing trawler bound for Mallorca per Stan's instructions. In a strange way, it felt good to get everything off his chest. As if the flimsy table and the abandoned patio were some sort of open-air confessional and Hurley his priest.

Hurley fished a package of cigarettes from his pocket as Rapp's story wound down. "Want one?"

"No."

Rapp half expected another lecture on German culinary etiquette, this one emphasizing the importance of the post-breakfast smoke. It didn't come. Instead Hurley shook loose a cigarette, lit it with a wooden match he struck on the table, and then inhaled deeply. Rapp had never been particularly susceptible to peer pressure, but if Hurley had asked again in that moment, he might have obliged. There was something iconic about watching Hurley exhale smoke through his nostrils with his gaze fixed far beyond the watery horizon.

The espionage equivalent of the Marlboro Man.

"I've been expecting this," Hurley said.

"What? The move against Ohlmeyer?"

"No," Hurley said, shaking his head. "That's just a distraction. A skirmish. I'm talking about the real war."

Rapp resisted the urge to point out that to Ohlmeyer and Greta, it was much more than a distraction. He had a feeling whoever's head had ended up in the hatbox probably felt much that same way. Instead, he let Hurley's words tug him in the right direction.

In between bouts of seasickness, Rapp had had plenty of time alone with his thoughts. Ohlmeyer had led him to believe that the killings were the remnants of an old vendetta. Some skeleton in the banker's closet born of his clandestine past. Though he'd only been part of the cloak-and-dagger world for a handful of years, Rapp had already made enemies. It stood to reason that someone who had been in the game in one fashion or another for more than three decades certainly had his share of adversaries looking to even the score.

But this was more than that.

A rendition team had targeted him twice in Barcelona. A well-financed, well-trained rendition team. With the dissolution of the Soviet Union still fresh and the fledgling Russian experiment in democracy already corrupted by oligarchs and the like, there was no shortage of hard men and women willing to sell their skills to the highest bidder. Except that mercenaries typically didn't ride around in vehicles sporting diplomatic license plates. What happened in Spain felt very much like a war's opening salvo, but Rapp was still unsure of his enemy's identity, never mind his aims.

"War between Russia and the United States?" Rapp said.

"Not yet, but I think that's where this thing's going unless we head it off at the pass. You tracking what happened in Moscow?"

Rapp shook his head.

After watching the Russian team zero in on his cell phone lure, he'd deliberately stayed clear of any potential electronic collars. The Spanish fishermen had mostly kept to themselves, and the trawler's single radio was tuned to music rather than news. A meteor could have struck Washington, DC, and he wouldn't have known about it.

"Thought not. The short version is this—Russian counterintelligence officers detained a CIA officer's wife. She's still in custody."

"The FSK arrested a spouse?"

Hurley nodded. "Judging by the photographs, the interrogators weren't too gentle with her either."

"I thought family was off-limits."

"They are—unless they're part of the team. The Russian news agency TASS did a formal press release with still shots. The wife's hands were covered in spy dust, the dead drop she supposedly unloaded was sitting on the table next to her, and the FSK rolled up one of our most productive assets—a scientist who works for a Russian defense conglomerate. Our ambassador is raising holy hell, but it doesn't look good. The situation's pretty hot, and the CIA's Moscow chief of station has already been declared persona non grata along with his deputy."

"That the end of it?"

Hurley shook his head. "Normally, but in this case, I'm afraid the Russkies are just getting started. They still haven't allowed the wife, Kris Henrik, to see anyone from the State Department. The Russian ambassador to DC is making noise about holding a criminal trial."

"Because she's an illegal?"

"Exactly." Hurley used the ember of his already-smoked cigarette to light a fresh one. "The normal rules dictate that they kick out one or two of ours and we return the favor. Then everyone takes a breath and things go back to the status quo. But instead of angling for a concession and jonesing for us to release one of their spies, the Russians seem hell-bent on escalating."

"Is that the war you're talking about?" Rapp said, scratching the stubble on his chin. "A squabble between intelligence services?"

"When I said *war*, I meant it. I think the Russians are planning to invade Latvia."

Rapp felt a tingle go down his spine. "What are you talking about?"

"Irene thinks they're conducting a false-flag operation to make it look like the Latvian government can't protect their ethnic Russian citizens from Latvian nationalist domestic terrorists."

"Leaving Moscow no choice but to intervene for humanitarian reasons."

"Bingo."

"That sounds bad," Rapp said, "but I'm not following what it has to do with me."

"Maybe everything." Hurley stubbed out his cigarette and turned to Rapp. A familiar hardness lurked behind his eyes. "Ohlmeyer is a smart guy, but he's still human. His weakness is his granddaughter. The one you're not supposed to be dating." Hurley paused. When Rapp didn't take the bait, he continued. "The thought of opening a box with her head inside is keeping him from thinking clearly. Otherwise, he'd have never sent you off half-cocked to take care of that traitorous prick Alexander Hughes."

"Why not?"

Hurley reached for his cigarettes again, but rather than shake out another, he scooped up the pack and tucked it into his pocket. "Because Hughes is bait."

"Bait for what?"

"Us. He wants the CIA focused on Hughes instead of the big picture."

"Who?"

"The Russian intelligence officer who ran Hughes. His name is Grigoriy Petrov. He was KGB and now he's FSK. My gut says he's the puppet master pulling everyone's strings."

Rapp laughed. "Sounds like some *Tinker Tailor Soldier Spy* bullshit."

"It's not bullshit," Hurley said.

"How do you know?"

"Because Petrov has been a thorn in my side for two decades."

CHAPTER 27

RAPP stared back at Hurley waiting for an explanation.

An explanation that the old operative didn't appear in any hurry to give.

The silence stretched until the pretty waitress returned and asked whether they wanted their beers refilled. Hurley answered negatively for them both.

She nodded and left. Only once the sliding glass door leading to the outdoor patio slammed shut did Hurley turn toward Rapp. "You heard of the year of the spy?"

Rapp frowned. "Not much into movies."

"It's not a movie, you dipshit. It's CIA slang for the tragedy of 1985. I get that you were still in diapers then, but I thought you'd know at least a little agency history."

Rapp had not in fact been in diapers in 1985, but that was beside the point. He was willing to afford to the codger some latitude, but Hurley's grumpy-old-man routine was getting old. "News flash—I don't know much agency history because the guy in charge of my training didn't think it was an important subject to cover. Also, in case you forgot, you are that guy."

"Yeah, yeah," Hurley said, "don't get your panties in a bunch. I'm just busting your balls. Nineteen eighty-five was the year we figured out that the entire US intelligence community was leaking like a sieve. Hughes had already defected by then, but he was just the tip of the iceberg. Our counterintelligence agents arrested fourteen American traitors, many of whom were spying for the Soviets. Those shitbags helped to explain how we'd lost some of our Russian assets."

"Only some?"

Hurley nodded. "CIA counterintelligence worked the problem for a while, even going so far as to launch an official mole hunt, but nothing came of their efforts. Eventually we stopped losing assets, so the head shed decided to move on."

"Seriously?"

Hurley sighed. "Your experience with our beloved agency is a bit one-sided. You're strictly a field operative, which means you see the CIA at its very best—an organization staffed with cowboys and meat eaters. The place Wild Bill Donovan imagined. But there's another side. One manned by risk-averse bureaucrats more concerned with their pensions and lucrative post-government jobs than stealing our enemies' secrets. Imagine what would happen to those pensions and cushy post-government opportunities if it turned out that our burned Russian assets were actually the result of a concerted intelligence operation that had been successfully run beneath their collective noses."

"That's your theory?"

"Not theory. Fact."

"How do you know?"

"Because I ran a little intelligence operation of my own. Wanna hear a story, kid?"

"Do I have a choice?"

"Shut up and listen."

CHAPTER 28

S TAN Hurley watched the woman exit the apartment building.
Fashionable Western clothes were hard to find, but the fräulein could have made a paper bag look chic. Her hair fell to her shoulders in a midnight wave and her skin was so white as to be porcelain. Blue eyes sparkled behind long, thick lashes, and her sweater and pants flattered her curvy figure. The woman's shy smile made the most self-assured of men stutter, and she exuded a sense of innocent wonder that often manifested in a bubbly laugh. She was somewhere in her twenties, glowing with youth, but delightfully absent the cynicism of her peers.

She was, in a word, lovely.

She was also something else.

A gust of wind tousled the woman's hair. She pushed the black strands from her face as she looked up and down the street. Stan turned his back to the girl, cupping his hands as he lit a Karo *Lungentorpedo* cigarette. He inhaled and the nicotine hit his nervous system like a freight train. There was a reason the Germans nicknamed the brand *lung torpedoes*. The first time he'd smoked one, Hurley had been convinced someone had exchanged the tobacco for cocaine. He was standing in front of a department store, and the large display window allowed him to see the woman purse her lips as she searched for a taxi. In most of East Germany, this would have been a losing proposition.

Not here.

This was Strausberger Platz, home to high-level bureaucrats, ranking members of the Communist Party, and other important officials. Officials like the one whose apartment the woman had just left. A Volga sputtered to life up the street. Its anemic four-cylinder engine powered the taxi to where the woman waited. She took one last look at her surroundings while climbing into the back seat. He felt the weight of her gaze on his back as she marked his presence, but Stan wasn't worried.

East Germany was the definition of a police state.

Here, someone was always watching.

The taxi rumbled away in a cloud of choking exhaust. Stan finished smoking his cigarette in case the woman had the Volga double back. At least that's what he wanted to believe. In actuality, he was steeling himself for what was coming next. In the last twenty-four hours, he'd killed two KGB thugs before they could kill him and left their bodies floating in the Spree. Less than twelve hours ago, he'd paid the man who dispatched the murderers, Mikhail Ivanov, a visit in his East Berlin office. In what passed for restraint in the rough-and-tumble world of espionage, Hurley had put a gun to the KGB officer's head and explained what would happen if any more Soviet wet-work teams plied their trade against American CIA officers.

Then he'd blindfolded Ivanov, tied him up, and pilfered his files.

Taking the files had been an afterthought. A way to further humiliate the KGB officer and keep him off balance, but after skimming through their contents, Hurley realized he'd struck gold. He'd handed the majority of the stash to a courier for transport back to West Berlin.

One page he'd kept for himself.

Tossing the cigarette to the ground, Stan made for the apartment building's door. Unlike much of the new construction in East Berlin, this structure did not appear as if it were one stiff breeze from tipping over. The fourteen-story building looked out on a greenspace replete with fountains. The pedestrian area was free of trash and the entrance featured an arc of worked stone that protected residents from the elements. As with most places behind the Iron Curtain, it paid to be one of the party elite.

Without breaking stride, Hurley pulled open the glass door and stepped into the lobby. A doorman who'd been slouching behind a desk adjacent to the entrance shot to his feet.

"Kann ich Ihnen helfen?"

"Nein," Hurley answered. "I'm here for Herr Volkov."

The doorman's eyes widened.

KGB officers on rotation to East Berlin preferred to keep their living arrangements shrouded. Hurley's Berlin-accented German was perfect, but the fact that he knew the intelligence officer residing on the seventh floor by his true name rather than an alias further burnished his credentials. Only another intelligence officer would have access to that information. In the doorman's mind, this meant the Hurley was Stasi and best left alone.

Or at least that's what he hoped.

"If you'll wait just a moment, I'll ring Herr Volkov to let him know you've arrived."

"You'll do no such thing. Not that it is any of your business, but Herr Volkov left strict instructions for me to come to his apartment unannounced. I will knock on his door. If he is still indisposed, he will not answer, and I will return in one hour's time. His instructions were abundantly clear in this regard. I'm assuming you find them equally as clear."

The doorman swallowed. "Yes, but our procedure—"

"Perhaps I haven't made myself plain," Hurley said, stepping closer. "I am going to enter that elevator, take it to the seventh floor, walk down the hall to Herr Volkov's apartment, and knock on his door precisely three times in accordance with his wishes. If you choose to deviate from those wishes, the repercussions will fall squarely on your shoulders. Understood?"

The doorman swallowed again.

Stan shifted, allowed his suit jacket to drift open. The Walther PPK holstered under his left armpit already had a suppressor screwed onto its modified barrel. The additional length would slow his draw, but in this case, quiet was more important than fast. Herr Volkov was definitely not expecting him, and Stan intended to keep it that way.

"I understand. Please give Herr Volkov my best."

Hurley nodded, pressed the call button for the elevator, and stepped inside. The trip up to the seventh floor seemed to take an eternity. Each second was another opportunity for the doorman to hedge his bets and ring the KGB officer.

If that happened, Hurley was done.

The elevator shuddered to a halt and the doors slid open.

The landing was empty.

With a thundering heart, Hurley strode down the hallway as quickly as he could move without giving the appearance of running. Last night, when he'd still been high on bloodlust and the adrenaline spike that came with getting the drop on Ivanov, this had seemed like a great idea. Now, in the ominous silence, he had a different take.

This was stupid.

Incredibly stupid.

Hurley clenched and unclenched his shooting hand to get the blood flowing as he checked the numbers stenciled on the apartment doors.

711.

712.

713.

This was it.

Easing the pistol from his holster, Hurley held the weapon with the muzzle pointing downward. Then he took a step backward, and before the rational portion of his mind could regain control, he kicked the door just below the handle.

It swung open.

Hurley allowed his momentum to carry him across the threshold. The PPK was already at eye level, and the extra length added by the cigar-shaped suppressor made the weapon feel even more stable. With ease he tracked the tip to the forehead of the man seated on the couch in the apartment's small living area.

"Don't move," Hurley said. "I'm here to save your life."

Dmitri Volkov did not look particularly physically imposing. Though he was of an age with Stan, the Russian already had the beginnings of a beer belly. His eyes were bloodshot and his face veined, probably from too much vodka. He looked like a man who had just finished a night of debauchery with a winsome German girl young enough to be his daughter.

He did not move like one.

In a blur that Stan would not have believed had he not witnessed it, the KGB officer reached behind the couch's cushion.

Volkov was incredibly fast.

Hurley was faster.

The PPK spat a single round, and a tuft of fabric jumped an inch from the Russian's outstretched fingers.

"The next one's in your forehead," Hurley said. "I just want to talk. Give me five minutes. Then I'm gone."

For a long moment, Hurley wasn't sure which way this was going to go. Then Volkov slowly moved his hand back into his lap. "I often have people who wish to speak with me. They usually make an appointment with my secretary. She's quite good."

"Do you know who I am?" Hurley said as he eased the apartment door closed with one hand while keeping the pistol trained on the Russian with the other.

"Of course."

"Then you know why I couldn't call your office."

Volkov shrugged. "There are ways in which these things are done. Kicking down a man's door and sticking a pistol in his face is not one of them."

"I don't have time for formalities. Neither do you. Unless corrective actions are taken, I expect you'll receive an unscheduled recall to Moscow by the end of the day. By this time tomorrow, you'll be a guest of Lubyanka prison. You know what happens next."

For the first time, Hurley saw a fissure form in the Russian's otherwise calm and collected demeanor. The slight frown vanished almost as quickly as it had appeared, but Hurley knew what the look signified. Dmitri Volkov might be a rising star in the KGB, but he would not be the first hotshot officer to have his flame extinguished in one of Lubyanka's dank basement cells. Lavrentiy Beria might be long dead, but his famous sentiment of *show me the man and I'll show you the crime* was still very much alive. "Why should I—"

The phone on the end table next to the Russian rang to life.

Volkov glanced at the handset and then back at Stan.

"Go ahead," Hurley said. "Answer it."

While he hoped the KGB officer took his instructions as a sign of confidence, they were actually an act of desperation. Stan was betting that the caller was the doorman. By now the shock-and-awe campaign Hurley had waged in the lobby had probably worn off. Or maybe the man was just hedging his bets and figured that he had more to lose by not calling the Russian than by angering Stan. Either way, if it was the doorman and Volkov didn't pick up, Hurley knew who the dutiful German would call next.

The Stasi.

With exaggerated motions, Volkov lifted the trilling handset and held it to his ear. "*Ja?*" The Russian listened in silence for several seconds, then thanked the caller and hung up. "That was my doorman. A message just arrived via a courier from the office. They'd like me to come in on my day off."

Hurley nodded like that was exactly the news he'd expected, while hoping against hope that his thundering heart wasn't as loud as it seemed. "Then I guess you have places to be. I'll show myself out."

Stan reached behind him. His fingers were closing on the doorknob when the Russian spoke.

"How did you know?"

Stan sighed.

"The woman you're seeing—Stefanie—she's Stasi. A swallow."

Technically, *swallow* was a Russian term of art. Stan wasn't sure what the Stasi called officers who had been trained to use sex to ensnare potential agents, but he figured the distinction wouldn't matter to Volkov. Judging by the look of rage on the Russian's face, he'd been correct.

"Get out," Volkov said. "Now."

"It's true, and you don't have to take my word for it." Reaching into his coat pocket, Stan withdrew a single piece of paper. "I paid your boss a visit after he sent two men to kill me. We had a constructive discussion about what the rules of engagement between our intelligence services should be going forward. I also helped myself to some of his files. I thought you might be interested in this nugget."

With the pistol still pointed at the Russian's chest, Hurley handed over the single page like he was offering a strip of raw meat to a tiger. It wasn't that Volkov had become more formidable in the last thirty seconds. Quite the opposite. The Russian sagged like a deflated balloon, but he was angry and desperate.

Angry and desperate men did stupid things.

Volkov snatched the paper and began to read. Stan could tell when he got to the damning paragraph. The jerky typewriter-like motion of his eyes stopped. For a long moment, the Russian just stared at the paper.

Then he slowly placed it on the end table.

"Why did you bring me this?"

"Your boss tried to kill me, and according to that, he plans to use the excuse that you fell into a honeytrap to kill you. That means you and I have something in common."

Volkov smiled a tired smile. "Would you care for a drink?"

"Next time. I've been here long enough. Do you want me to take care of the girl?"

The smile died. "I believe a man should clean up his own mess."

"So do I," Stan said. "You're in a tough spot, Dmitri, but I make a better friend than enemy."

"You and I are now friends?"

Stan holstered his pistol. "You know how this works. Your boss wants to kill you. I've risked my life to save you. Doesn't seem like a hard choice to me. I'll be in touch."

Hurley opened the door, ghosted into the hallway, and closed it behind him. As recruitments went, the pitch he'd just delivered to Volkov wasn't exactly textbook.

Then again, neither was he.

CHAPTER 29

RAPP stared at Hurley.

He'd known his mentor was a crazy son of a bitch, but the story he'd just relayed took things to a whole other level. "You recruited a KGB officer at gunpoint?"

"Yep. Ran him personally too. Together we formed an espionage cell I called the Boys from Berlin. You already know some of the founding members."

"Ohlmeyer?"

"Exactly. The man in the hatbox, Felix Bauer, was another. I know from Volkov's reporting that Petrov used Hughes to create his own spy ring. I think some of those bastards are still active."

Rapp considered that proposition as the ocean breeze ruffled his hair.

Counterintelligence was not his area of expertise, but he knew a thing or two about complacency and arrogance. If Hurley had penetrated the KGB and Stasi through a combination of audacity and good fieldcraft, it was the epitome of arrogance not to think that his hard-charging Soviet counterpart couldn't have accomplished the same thing.

But even if this were true, there was still an underlying issue Hurley hadn't addressed.

"Why is Petrov is using Hughes to go after the Boys from Berlin now?" Rapp said.

"That's the million-dollar question, kid. Petrov's around the same age as Stansfield. He began his career during World War Two and has served his nation for the last forty years. Now that nation no longer exists. Watching the Soviet Union dissolve must have been like watching the foundation on which he'd built his life suddenly give way. Maybe now is as good a time as any to balance the checkbook, but this feels bigger than that. It's no accident that the world's best chess players are Russian. They play the game of espionage better than any other intelligence service. Does killing one of the Boys from Berlin and threatening another make Petrov feel good? Sure. But would he give Hughes the green light in an operational vacuum? Not a chance. There's more here. Something we're not seeing."

The rumbling of a turboprop engine grabbed Rapp's attention. He looked up to see a high-wing floatplane pass overhead. After turning into the wind, the plane touched down in a spray of seawater and then taxied up to the floating dock at the edge of the beach.

"Then we pay a visit to Hughes like Ohlmeyer wanted?"

Hurley shook his head. "Not yet. Working in Russia is hard. Working in Moscow is damn near impossible. We'll get exactly one shot at Hughes. We need to interrogate him, not just ask a couple of scripted questions. Before either of us sit across the table from Hughes, we have to understand what Petrov's thinking."

"How?"

"By talking to Petrov's former deputy."

"Dmitri Volkov?"

Hurley smiled. "Now you're getting it."

"Is he stateside?"

"Nope. Like me, Volkov was convinced the CIA's mole problems went beyond just Hughes. After he defected, he refused to be repatriated to America for fear that the KGB would find him."

"Was he right?"

Hurley shrugged. "He's still alive. Either way, I want you to bring him in from the cold."

"Alone?"

"Yep. I've got something else to run to ground. I'm going north and you're heading—"

"East? To Greece?"

Hurley gave him a strange look. "Why Greece?"

"If I were Volkov, I'd want to hole up somewhere my CIA pension would go a long way, but not a country that's overtly Western. Somewhere that has enough tourists that a person with a strange accent wouldn't stand out, but far enough off the beaten path that my former KGB colleagues wouldn't come snooping. Greece seemed to fit the bill."

"Great logic. Wrong country. You're heading southeast, not east. Tunisia."

Rapp's stomach sank. "Another boat ride?"

Hurley smiled. "As much as it would bring me great joy to picture you puking your guts off the side of another trawler, we don't have that kind of time. You're traveling by air."

"Thank God."

"You may want to hold off on the rejoicing. After that bullshit in Barcelona, you're burned. The airport in Mallorca is tiny, and I can't risk the Spanish National Police IDing you. You're not flying commercial."

As if privy to their conversation, the floatplane's cabin door swung open. A man wearing a Hawaiian shirt and board shorts stepped onto the float and then hopped to the pier.

After seeing Stan, the pilot gave a friendly wave.

"You've got to be kidding," Rapp said.

"Cheer up, kid. Beats swimming."

CHAPTER 30

THERE really was no accounting for taste.

As a world traveler, Ilya Lebedev understood the draw of tourist attractions. While it was chic to play down the appeal of Egypt's Pyramids, China's Great Wall, or Spain's Basílica de la Sagrada Família, the truth was that seeing these things in person was often a rewarding if not moving experience. That said, Ilya never imagined he'd be passing a blustery English afternoon sitting next to the Thames while waiting for an Elvis Presley–themed river cruise to disembark.

But there was no accounting for taste.

Especially the tastes of terrorists.

As if hearing his thoughts, the first fat raindrop fell from the leaden sky turning the grime coating the Queen's Walk into full-fledged mud. Ilya sighed and turned up the collar of his Burberry coat. Cold rain, while an inconvenience, was not anything he hadn't endured before. As a boy raised in the Russian steppes, he'd thought he'd understood winter.

He hadn't.

Not until Ilya had spent a month living rough in the Hindu Kush mountains so that he and his Spetsnaz team could use the snowfall as cover to hunt down a particularly wily mujahideen had he truly come to terms with what it meant to be cold. Over the course of those bleak days and frigid nights, every member of his commando team had suffered at least one cold-weather injury. Ilya had lost one-third of a toe to frostbite, but at the end of the hunt the Afghan resistance had one less commander. At the time he'd thought that an even trade.

Eight years later, he was no longer sure.

"Excuse me, sir, where do I buy the tickets for the riverboat cruise?"

The question, posed by an Asian child of about twelve, was asked in English. Accented English. English was one of several languages that Ilya spoke fluently. Actually, more than fluently. After his time in Afghanistan, Ilya had embarked on a career change, leaving the army in search of greener pastures.

He hadn't wandered far.

As with the American military, there was something of a revolving door between Soviet special operations and the nation's intelligence organizations. Between his exemplary military record, his service in Afghanistan, and his deployments to several other less publicized combat zones, Ilya had quickly found employment with the KGB's Directorate V, or Vympel, unit. He'd always had an affinity for languages and already spoke a little English, but by the time he'd left charm school, Ilya could converse like a native and do so with an American accent.

This was important for his current tasking.

"Right over there," Ilya said, pointing to a glassed-in building on the far side of the walkway. Though the child was just feet away, Ilya spoke loud enough for his voice to carry to her waiting parents. The pair might not speak the language, they were not the only people enjoying what passed for fair weather in the UK. Ilya rolled through the foreign consonants and vowels as if he were responding to a question from his notoriously difficult language instructor. The woman from Ohio. American regional-dialect accents were challenging to master, which was why the preponderance of the charm school's faculty hailed from the Midwest.

"Thank you."

The girl flashed a hesitant smile before scampering back to her parents. Ilya didn't return the gesture. This was not because he had anything against Asian people in general or little girls in particular. Like his Midwestern accent, Ilya had an appearance to maintain. A carefully curated appearance in which smiling at a child might seem out of character. Besides, a double-decker tourist boat was nudging up to the dock.

The show was about to begin.

CHAPTER 31

THERE was nothing out of the ordinary about this particular boat. As with the majority of tourist vessels, the craft featured an open-air top with plenty of seating and a glassed-in cabin area where passengers could eat a three-course meal, drink overpriced cocktails, and presumably enjoy the King of Rock and Roll's greatest hits. The boat's blue and white livery made it easy to track against the Thames's muddy-brown water, and judging by the laughter echoing from its deck, the concertgoers seemed to have had a great time.

Ilya did not care about the boat, its amenities, or even Elvis.

He was here for another reason.

His vantage point was a bench on the pedestrian walkway on the south side of the same glass building to which he'd directed the Asian girl. The bench faced west and offered a lovely view of the Thames, Big Ben, and the Palace of Westminster's unmistakable silhouette. A queue of people waiting to buy tickets or board the next cruise snaked across the walkway to his north, while a bored-looking bobby held down the street corner to his east. Though Ilya appreciated the sight line to the Thames, he'd chosen to linger on this bench for a different reason.

The bench was just a few yards from the boat's disembarking passengers.

Getting to his feet, the former Spetsnaz operative conducted a quick but thorough assessment of his surroundings. To his left, the Thames flowed placidly by as other tourist boats competed for space with more mundane nautical traffic. To his right, the multistory County Hall building funneled foot traffic from the south toward the glass building. On the north side of the building, the pedestrian area broadened into the entrance to Jubilee Gardens—a park that encompassed three acres of valuable riverfront real estate.

The bobby noted his movement with a quick glance, but the police officer didn't seem inclined to leave his post. Ilya had already walked the park and surveyed the surrounding shops, side streets, and alleys while assessing the area's police presence. The beat cops seemed to be focused on deterring criminals through a show of force rather than patrolling the milling crowds.

That was just fine with Ilya.

This was his first time in London, but it was not his first time doing a job such as this one. Though if he were being honest, the detailed instructions that had accompanied this operation had been a bit disconcerting. That was saying something considering that his previous assignment had required him to saw off a man's head and mail it in a hatbox.

Though he wasn't thrilled with his current tasking, Ilya didn't question his orders. If he'd ever harbored the naïve notion that men limited the depths of their depravity based on some internalized moral code, Afghanistan had cured him of that. He'd initially recoiled at the idea of seeding the countryside with children's dolls containing explosive devices. That disgust had vanished the first time he and his team of commandos had been beaten to a downed Soviet aviator by the mujahideen. What the Afghans had done to the poor pilot was almost indescribable.

Almost.

Ilya still saw the man's flayed body when he closed his eyes.

Afghanistan had taught him many things, but there was one lesson he'd internalized above all others: Victory goes to those with the fortitude to do what is required to win. The moral high ground is nice in theory, but in the real world, weakness equals defeat.

Someday he would have to atone for his many sins, but that was fine. To atone, one had to be alive.

Ilya's gaze settled on the Asian girl.

This was going to be messy.

CHAPTER 32

THE boat's doors opened, and passengers began to disembark.

The first two were a man and a woman. Americans. The rotund woman had attempted to adopt European fashion, but the stylish clothes didn't sit well on her heavy frame. Her husband hadn't even bothered to try. In defiance of everything that passed for fashionable attire on this side of the Atlantic, he wore high-waisted jeans paired with a button-down dress shirt and sneakers. As if to add insult to injury, a baseball cap sat at a jaunty angle on his shaved head.

Americans.

The couple breezed down the ramp connecting the boat to the dock and then onto the pedestrian walkway. The woman was chattering, and the man was nodding dutifully as he followed his wife. Ilya thought that ridding the world of these two might actually begin his atonement process, but he let the pair go. He was not a fan of Americans, but they were not his target.

A heartbeat later, a pair of men exited the boat together.

Both were dark-complected and about the same height, but their similarities ended there. The first man's broad chest and powerful shoulders strained the fabric of his suit. His head swiveled on a thick neck, scanning his surroundings as he placed his bulk between the second man and any perceived threats.

His charge was rail-thin with expensive taste and hungry eyes. His suit was expertly tailored and his leather shoes were expensive. Like his comrade, the thin man's gaze swept the crowd, but rather than suspicious people or likely ambush sites, his attention lingered on something else.

Women.

Girls, actually.

According to his dossier, Youssef bin Muhammad had a penchant for prepubescent girls. At one point in his life Ilya would have found this practice abhorrent, but fires stoked by moral outrage no longer burned in his belly. The Afghan mujahideen had a penchant for children too, but their tastes ran more to boys. Boys kept chained like animals. Ilya's feelings toward the thin man were more resignation than acceptance. If experience had taught him anything, it was that the world beyond the walls imposed by civilization was a dark place inhabited by dark men engaged in dark deeds. Youssef might be dressed like a cultured businessman, but he was still a barbarian.

After confirming the Syrian's identity, Ilya turned away from the men and lit a cigarette. As he shook out the match, the Vympel operative marked the duo's progress using storefront windows on the far side of the street. The bodyguard looked his way, and Ilya engaged in a fit of fake coughing, bowing his head under the stress of his spasming lungs.

A quick peek in the window confirmed that his subterfuge had been successful.

The bodyguard had continued his scan, perhaps searching for healthier threats.

Still tracking the pair via their reflection, Ilya deposited the lighter and cigarettes deep into his overcoat pocket with his left hand. His right hand was fingering something else. With a final glance at the window,

Ilya took a steadying breath, turned, and drew the pistol from his right pocket in one smooth motion.

The Beretta handgun was chambered in 9mm. The rounds were subsonic, the action well oiled, and the stubby suppressor screwed onto the muzzle was custom-made. While not Ilya's weapon of choice, he understood why another assassin felt differently.

Something triggered the bodyguard's attention.

Whether it was the flurry of motion as Ilya drew the handgun or maybe just honed instincts, the result was the same. The bodyguard turned and his coal-black eyes found Ilya's. Ilya thought that they widened for an instant. Perhaps the instinctual recognition felt by one predator for another.

He would never know.

Just as the bodyguard's massive muscles began to twitch, a 115-grain projectile entered his skull at four hundred yards per minute. The hollow-point slug mushroomed as it tore through the cranial bone. Like a snowplow pushing aside half-melted sludge, the bullet carved an everwidening path through the bodyguard's cerebral cortex before exiting his head in a spray of bone and brain matter.

He was dead before he hit the ground.

The thin man turned as his bodyguard crumpled.

Ilya expected him to run. He didn't. Instead the terrorist snarled as he lunged toward his assailant. Ilya nodded. Though either action would have been futile, the thin man had chosen fight over flight. Ilya hoped that when his time came, he would also choose to go out swinging.

Ilya squeezed the pistol's trigger a second time, and the thin man's head snapped backward, as if he'd been hit by a devastating uppercut. Then he collapsed in a puddle of flesh. Ilya took careful aim at the top of the man's head and fired a third time.

Three shots, two dead men, two seconds.

Not bad.

The beginnings of a collective murmur filled the air as what had just transpired began to register with bystanders. If he walked away now, Ilya could disappear to the north before anyone was the wiser. Instead, the Vympel operative extended his pistol in a two-handed grip, centered the front sight post on the chest of the bobby, and pulled the trigger.

The police officer's shirt jumped.

The bobby staggered.

Spinning, Ilya tracked the pistol to the Asian family. The front sight post passed over the daughter but found a home in the center of her father's chest. Ilya squeezed off two more rounds.

Then the pistol went back into his pocket.

Hunching his shoulders, he sprinted for the alley to his right, chased by a little girl's screams.

CHAPTER 33

BIZERTE, TUNISIA

R APP wasn't sure how he intended to return home from Tunisia, but he knew which modes of travel he couldn't be using.

Boats or planes.

While free of the stomach-churning swells that had made his trip from Barcelona to Mallorca so unpleasant, the flight across the Mediterranean Sea hadn't been much better. The little floatplane seemed to be one step ahead of the storm clouds that had been gathering since Rapp had begun his escape from Spain. Several times during the bouncy trip, he'd turned in his seat to watch as the weather system gathered behind him. Ominous swaths of gray and purple glared back at him as jagged bolts of lightning flickered across the horizon.

He didn't know what a flight in a light plane should feel like, but judging by his pilot, this one had been a doozy. The Hawaiian-shirt-wearing aviator had begun the trip with an almost unbroken streaming commentary that wavered across a half a dozen languages. Once he understood that he wasn't expected to contribute to the pilot's monologue, Rapp had nodded when it seemed appropriate and done his best to keep the contents of his stomach where they belonged. About ten minutes prior to landing, a particularly vicious downdraft had put the float-plane's pontoons a bit too close to the frothing sea for Rapp's taste.

The pilot seemed to share his sentiment. The verbal diatribe changed in cadence and intonation until the words became something Rapp did recognize.

A prayer.

To his credit, the pilot settled the plane onto a stretch of relatively calm ocean and then taxied to a floating dock without incident. Rapp already had his seat belt unbuckled and was out of the cockpit before the propeller stopped turning. Though judging by his actions, perhaps the pilot never intended to kill the engine. No sooner were Rapp's feet on the dock than the pilot spun the aircraft back toward open sea and turned his taxi into a takeoff run. Rapp watched as the little floatplane clawed its way skyward and then banked to the south. While he was glad to have his feet firmly planted on terra firma, Rapp felt the enormity of his situation settle on his shoulders before the aircraft's engine noise faded.

He was here to meet with a Soviet spy.

And not just any spy.

Rapp took a moment to get his bearings as he reviewed Hurley's hurried instructions. He'd delivered them in a staccato burst that somehow managed to convey both seriousness and urgency in just a handful of clipped sentences. There was no doubt in Hurley's mind that Petrov was running an intelligence operation against the United States and they were behind the eight ball. Rapp needed to make contact with Petrov's former deputy, Dmitri Volkov, and begin picking his brain as soon as possible. Despite the unpleasantness of the flight, traveling to the Tunisian city had been the easy part.

Now the real work began.

"Pardon, sir, would you like a ride?"

The question, delivered in French, was voiced by a skinny kid who didn't look older than ten or eleven. He was seated on a contraption of uncertain lineage. Part bicycle and part tram, the conveyance was undoubtedly meant to ferry passengers, but whether the boy's thin legs were capable of transporting Rapp's bulk was another question.

"*Oui*," Rapp said as he clambered into a carriage of sorts that formed the back end of the elaborate tricycle. "Can you take me to the Old Harbor?"

"But of course."

Rapp was seated. While the oversize wheels to his right and left seemed sturdy enough to accommodate his weight, Rapp wasn't as certain that the boy could generate enough torque to get the bike moving.

With a technique that must have been honed from countless passengers, the boy pushed off the ground with his right foot, stood high in the stirrups, and then brought both feet to bear on the left pedal. The uneven application of force caused the bike to list slightly to the left, but the boy expertly steered into the yaw, eking out every last bit of travel. The bike quivered and the boy grunted, but the tires began to turn. The boy placed his feet on each pedal, gave one more monstrous push from the standing position, and then settled onto the well-worn seat.

"First time to Bizerte?"

The question was again rendered in French with the exception of *Bizerte*. The port's name had an Arabic flavor to Rapp's ear, suggesting that the boy was bilingual. His own Arabic was very good but always in need of practice, and as much as he wanted to switch languages, Rapp didn't. Though he'd only been working as a covert operative for a couple of years, he'd already learned that playing into a person's preconceived notions was a great way to remain anonymous. The boy had obviously seen the floatplane's approach and seemed to assume that Rapp was a French tourist; the beautiful port city undoubtedly had many. Better to be thought of as just another wealthy European and forgotten than remembered for his ability to speak Arabic.

"Do you always ask so many questions?" Rapp said.

The boy shrugged narrow shoulders. "Some people just want to go to a place. Other people want to learn about it. I can help with both."

Rapp leaned forward and ruffled the boy's hair. "How much is this ride going to cost me?"

"Depends. Do you want the sightseeing tour or just transport to the Old Harbor?"

"How much for each?"

"The sightseeing tour takes about an hour and it costs one hundred and fifty dinar. Transport directly to the Old Harbor takes about fifteen minutes, so fifty."

The floatplane had dropped him off at the tip of a stone pier that formed part of the man-made protective barrier to the eastern side of the city proper. From the air Rapp had marked the crescent-shaped Old Harbor to the west of the more modern port and guessed that he had around two miles to cover. The math on the sightseeing tour versus the direct ride was a bit suspect, but if the boy really could get him there in fifteen minutes, that would allow Rapp time to conduct a quick reconnaissance of the meeting site before Volkov's arrival.

In true Hurley fashion, the floatplane had been stocked with one of Rob Ridley's Orion team kits. Though he still felt like a stranger in a strange land, the Beretta holstered inside his waistband, extra magazine in his pocket, and four-inch combat knife sheathed at the small of his back had gone a long way toward raising Rapp's spirits. Hurley was a crusty son of a bitch and could be a royal pain in the ass, but he didn't send his operatives into the field unprepared.

"What's the best restaurant in the Old Harbor?" Rapp said, reaching into his pocket for a wad of dinars.

"That is easy. I will take you there."

"Does your dad own it?"

"What? No!"

Rapp had to smother a smile at the boy's indignant tone. Leaning forward, he stuffed the bills into a leather satchel secured to the boy's seat. Judging by the assortment of currency, the kid did a brisk business. "Okay, take me. But I want to hire you for an hour after you drop me off."

"Hire? For what?"

Once again Rapp had to resist the urge to grin at the equal parts excitement and wariness in his chauffeur's response. The boy could sense the opportunity but also understood all too well that no one gave away money for free. Ten years from now, Rapp expected the boy to be running his own taxi fleet.

"I might need you to take me somewhere else. Do you have a mobile?"

"No."

The boy's forlorn tone brought another smile to Rapp's face. "Do you know where to buy one?"

"Yes!"

"Okay. I'll give you the money for the phone and also pay for an hour of your time. Call me once you have the phone so I know the number. If I need you to pick me up, I'll call you and pay you a bonus. How's that sound?"

"Money first?"

"Half ahead of time. You'll get the rest at the end of the hour and you can keep the phone. Deal?"

"Deal!"

The kid's enthusiasm was infectious, but if he was going to have a future as a tycoon, he had a lot to learn, starting with a poker face. "You sure your dad doesn't own this restaurant?"

"Of course! My uncle does."

Or maybe not.

CHAPTER 34

THIRTY minutes later, Rapp sat in a white plastic chair sipping coffee.

Though he'd gone to great trouble to ensure that living his cover job as an international computer salesman in Paris hadn't dulled his edge, Rapp had developed a penchant for Parisian coffee. This was not that. Instead Rapp was drinking the Turkish version that was served boiling hot with the grounds still gathered at the bottom of the cup.

Calling the coffee strong didn't do the brew justice.

He was happy the mixture was served in small cups because an entire mug's worth would probably have caused his heart to explode. Rapp took another sip for appearances' sake while praying that his still-angry stomach could handle the volatile mixture. Fortunately, the waiter had produced some *tabouna*, and the flatbread went a long way toward soaking up the coffee's acidity.

"How do you like my city?"

The man asking the question had approached Rapp's table from inside the restaurant behind him rather than the pedestrian area to the café's front. It was a smart use of blind spots. Then again, if the man was who Rapp thought he was, he'd been on the run from the KGB for almost twenty years.

He probably knew a thing or two about blind spots.

"Not bad," Rapp said. "Kind of a shabby version of Venice."

The Marsa de Bizerte marina curved in from the sea to the east in a crescent that terminated in a wharf lined with fishing boats. Though the murky water smelled of salt and sea life, the entire length was lined with shops, restaurants, and hotels. Rapp was in the area known as the Bizerte Old Harbor and he was sitting on the eastern side of the inlet. The Avenue de Montecarlo it was not, but there was something charming about palm trees paired with cobblestone streets and the hustle and bustle of pedestrians. The storm clouds that Rapp had arrived one step ahead of had dissipated as quickly as they'd come, and cafés were still doing a bustling outdoor business, as evidenced by the multicolored table umbrellas sheltering groups of diners.

The man chuckled as he took the seat across from Rapp. "I hadn't ever thought of it that way, but you're right. That's fine. Shabby is a fair price for anonymity. Besides, I'll take this over a Moscow winter any day."

He was speaking French, but his accent put an unusual spin on the language of love.

His Russian accent.

"Mr. Volkov?"

The man paled. "I haven't used that name in quite some time."

Rapp compared the weathered face looking back at him with Hurley's description—bald with overly large ears, a bulbous nose, and eyes that seemed locked in a perpetual squint. Hurley had called the man chunky, but twenty years later, he'd progressed to fat. Jowls framed his mouth and the shirt buttons nearest his waist looked in danger of popping. His age was hard to determine. Vodka, cigarettes, and stress had all taken a toll on his skin. Rapp would have placed the Russian at anywhere from mid-sixties to late seventies but for his eyes. The cunning glittering from their depths belonged to a younger man.

Or perhaps a man still on the run.

The waiter drifted over to the table and Volkov placed a lengthy and detailed order in Arabic that left Rapp wondering if they were expecting company. He wasn't all that familiar with the local cuisine, but from what he understood, the waiter would be bringing enough food to feed an army.

"Hungry?" Volkov said.

"Nope."

"Too bad. I just ordered a taste of Tunisia. I hope you enjoy it."

"You're not staying?"

The Russian shook his head. "Do you know how many of my countrymen your CIA successfully exfiltrated in the last ten years?"

"No."

"Three. Do you know how many Russian assets were arrested and executed during this same period?"

"I don't."

"Neither do I. I stopped counting at fourteen and that was five years ago. I won't pretend to know how many Soviets were working for you, but I think you'd agree that losing fourteen agents in ten years is certainly beyond the law of averages. Why am I not staying for dinner? For the same reason that I refused your country's help when it came time to choose my permanent home—I do not trust the Central Intelligence Agency. Now, enough about me. Stan Hurley asked for a meeting. I'm here. What do you want?"

That was an excellent question.

Rapp was not an agent runner like Irene or Stan, but it wasn't difficult to put himself in the Russian's shoes. Regardless of what the former KGB officer had communicated to Hurley, Rapp had figured that he wouldn't stick around long. As the old saying went, it's not paranoia if someone really is out to get you. The Soviet intelligence service had a long memory, and Rapp had no doubt that when it came to Volkov, someone still was out to get him.

"Grigoriy Petrov," Rapp said.

Volkov exhaled a deep, rattling sigh. As if his lungs were as weather-beaten as his face. Judging by the yellow stains between his fingers, this was probably true.

"I'd hoped for a different name."

"It's the only one I have."

Another sigh. "I told Hurley everything during my initial debrief. I don't have anything more to add."

"Since Hurley is the one who sent me, I don't think that's true."

Volkov's gray-streaked eyebrows came together, and his eyes narrowed. Before he could respond, the waiter appeared with a bowl of hummus and a heaping platter of warm bread. Volkov looked longingly at the steaming bread, but didn't touch it.

"What is my former comrade doing these days?"

The question irritated Rapp.

Volkov had been one of Hurley's most prized assets. A founding member of the Boys from Berlin. Not only that, but when offered the opportunity to relocate to America, the Russian had declined in favor of setting up his own identity and reinventing himself. These were not the actions of a man who intended to spend his retirement drinking strong coffee and watching the tide roll in. Rapp had a feeling that Volkov knew full well what Petrov was doing these days. Still, this wasn't his area of expertise. He didn't know how to "handle" assets, so maybe this back-and-forth was how the game was played.

"He's a lieutenant general in the FSK. Does that jog your memory?"

"You misunderstand me," Volkov said, his earlier levity gone. "I haven't forgotten about Petrov. The opposite in fact. I didn't choose *shabby Venice* over the Virginia horse country because I loved the smell of rotting fish. Vanishing to a third-world backwater was my best chance to stay alive. Petrov has a long memory and his list of wrongs dates back to the Great Patriotic War. He's an old man now with an old man's view of the world. My guess is that his time is waning, and he's decided to balance the ledger. I want no part of what you and Hurley are working."

Volkov made to leave.

Rapp had other ideas.

"I think you're the one who has misunderstood," Rapp said, snaring Volkov's arm and jerking him back to his seat. "I don't know what arrangement you had with whatever weak-kneed case officer you negotiated with for this deal, and I don't care. I'm not the guy they send to convince some morally bankrupt jerk-off to spy against his own country. The Colombian cartels have a saying—*plato o pluma*. You know it?"

The Russian shook his head.

"It means silver or lead."

"I take it you're not the silver," Volkov said, prying his arm free.

"Smart man."

"I guess that's good because we're both going to need your services."

"What do you mean?"

"That apartment building to your right—the multistory tower. See it?"

Rapp knew exactly which structure the Russian was referencing. The odd construction reminded him of a layered cake made to look like an accordion. Strange design aside, there was another reason Rapp had marked the building on his mental map—it towered over the single- and double-story buildings lining the waterfront. Its whitewashed exterior made for an excellent landmark while navigating the maze of winding side streets and alleys that made up the city proper to his west.

"Yep," Rapp said, never taking his eyes off Volkov.

"There's a red blanket draped across the railing on the top-floor apartment's balcony. It wasn't there a moment ago."

Rapp looked over his shoulder. A crimson blanket flapped in the breeze. "So?"

"For the past day or two, I've suspected that I've been under surveillance. I used this meeting to test my instincts. The person in that apartment is conducting countersurveillance for me. The blanket means he's detected a team. I suggest we bring this meeting to a close."

Once again, the Russian got to his feet.

Once again, Rapp jerked him back to his seat. "Aren't you tired of running?"

"Maybe. But I'm not tired of living."

"Then sit down and stay awhile."

"Do I have a choice?"

Rapp smiled.

CHAPTER 35

F YODOR grinned at the familiar fluttering in his stomach.

The feeling of the hunt.

The Alfa Group operative hadn't experienced the rush that came just before kinetic action in far too long. Or at least the surge of adrenaline that accompanied hunting prey on favorable ground. Fyodor had first deployed operationally to Beirut in 1985, when he'd been part of the task force sent in response to the kidnapping of four Soviet diplomats by radical Islamicists. The brutality of that mission was his baptism in fire, as were the results. The three living diplomats had been released, and not a single Russian diplomat had been taken hostage since. In the ensuing years, Fyodor had stalked his nation's enemies on battlefields ranging from the Middle East to Afghanistan.

But this hunt was special.

Today, he had the opportunity to serve justice to a traitor.

"Five, this is One, target in sight. He is alone. I say again, target is alone, over."

"Five copies all," Fyodor said, whispering into the mic hidden beneath the cuff of his shirtsleeve. "Four, are you in position?"

"This is Four, thirty seconds, over."

Fyodor keyed the transmit button on his low-profile radio twice, indicating that he'd received the assault team leader's transmission. His Arabic was passable, but his accent was horrible. He could have conducted the radio conversation in French, but didn't.

His assault team leader, Sergei, was gifted at a great many things.

Languages wasn't one of them.

Fyodor crouched on the dirty street to tie his shoe. It was one of the oldest tricks in the surveillance book, but like dead drops, chalk marks, and brush passes, the technique was still practiced for one simple reason.

It worked.

As he played with his shoelaces, Fyodor let his gaze wander across the street before settling on the source of his unease—the person who'd been following him for the last block. He'd heard the footsteps but hadn't had a chance to lay eyes on his tail until now. Though the waterfront maintained a veneer of respectability, that shine disappeared within steps of leaving the tourist area. Shops still lined the streets, but rather than windows or doors, most places of commerce had metal accordion-like gratings that could be lowered at the close of business each night. Storefront windows were at a premium, so Fyodor had been unable to catch a glimpse of his pursuer in a reflection.

After securing the final knot, Fyodor allowed his fingers to linger near the cuff of his trousers and the PSS silent pistol strapped to his ankle. His primary weapon, a Makarov handgun, was nestled in the small of his back, but that would be a more difficult draw from a crouched position. With his left hand, Fyodor began massaging a nonexistent cramp in his calf muscle while his right hand unsnapped the concealed ankle holster before sliding around the pistol's grip.

The tail was just behind him and to his left.

His shoulder prickled beneath the person's gaze.

The footfalls grew louder, but their cadence never changed. Then Fyodor saw the tail. He almost laughed. It was a teenager with a soccer ball tucked beneath his arm. The youth gave Fyodor a questioning look but continued shuffling along.

False alarm.

"Five, this is Four, assault team is set. I say again, assault team is set."

"All call signs, this is One. Target is getting up from his table."

Fyodor stood and stretched, trying to contain his nervous energy.

Showtime.

He'd put a great deal of time into planning this operation. Far more time than with the average target, but there was nothing average about the man he was hunting. The traitor had done incalculable damage to the Soviet Union by passing secrets to the Americans. The range of the former intelligence officer's treachery ran the gamut from a list of Soviet assets that had penetrated American intelligence and military targets, to Afghanistan battle plans, to deliberations between the KGB's senior leadership. Even so, Fyodor couldn't allow his thirst for vengeance to cloud his operational judgment. Yes, Dmitri Volkov was an old man and much past his prime, but it would be a mistake to underestimate the spy's wiles. Volkov hadn't just outwitted his compatriots for the years he'd been an active CIA asset. He'd also managed to stay hidden after defecting.

Fyodor assumed the traitor still had a trick or two up his sleeve.

With this in mind, he and his assistant team leader had chosen to take the western edge of the harbor inlet. This side was more congested, but Fyodor intended to use this to his advantage. Throngs of pedestrians meant that the traitor would have a harder time picking up the Russian surveillance team, and the warren of streets and maze of alleys provided multiple opportunities to interdict the traitor away from prying eyes. Volkov might have been a master spy, but he was no match for a team of Alfa Group commandos.

The traitorous KGB officer wouldn't stand a chance.

"Five, this is One, we have a problem."

CHAPTER 36

FYODOR'S stomach clenched.

Every operation experienced problems. This was to be expected. But problems came in a range of severities. The next transmission would determine if this kind of problem was the natural by-product of operational friction or the mission-ending variety. Fyodor hoped for the former. He'd already spent enough time in this African shithole.

A second passed.

Then two.

During a kinetic operation, a handful of seconds could be an eternity, but Sasha should have returned to the airwaves by now.

"Five, this is One," Fyodor said, turning his back to the gaggle of women passing by on the opposite side of the street, "please elaborate."

"Five, this is One, sorry. I'm on the move."

The heavy breathing that accompanied the transmission suggested that this wasn't just a simple reposition.

Sasha was running.

"Five, this is One, the target just hopped into the back of a three-wheeled passenger bike. They're moving southwest toward Rue Bourguiba, over."

Fyodor tried to make sense of what he was hearing. They'd been conducting surveillance on the target for the past two days, and he'd never ridden a bike anywhere. For trips beyond the city's limits, he drove a shabby Yugo.

Otherwise, he walked.

Why the change in routine now?

Pushing this concern aside, Fyodor pulled a city map from his back pocket and unfolded it as he thought through how to best position his team. His plan to interdict the target on the western side of the Old Harbor wasn't without risk. The narrow streets and dim alleys worked to the commandos' advantage, but the entrance to a popular mosque sat just over two hundred yards west as the crow flew from the waterfront. The next call to prayer was still several hours away, but the structure served as a focal point for the community. Congregants came and went all day long, and Fyodor wanted to avoid potential witnesses if possible.

Viewed from this angle, the new development might be helpful. If the target turned left on Rue Bourguiba, he would be moving east, away from the mosque and toward the ocean. Fyodor traced the route on his map with his index finger and found what he was looking for.

"One, this is Five," Fyodor said. "Did he turn right or left onto Bourguiba? East or west? Over."

"Five, this is One, west. He's—"

A burst of static interrupted the transmission. Fyodor waited for his sniper to resume speaking, but the radio remained silent. "One, this is Five, you broke up. Say again, over."

Nothing.

"One, this is Five, do you read me?"

Silence.

Fyodor frowned.

The team's low-profile radios' transmission range was limited to line of sight. As such, the commandos had weathered several communications blackouts while moving through denser areas of the city over the last several days. While he would have preferred to confirm the target's current location with Sasha, he had the information he needed.

"Four, this is Five, have you been monitoring One's transmissions?"

"Five, this is Four, affirmative. I'm moving my team south to Rue Garibaldi, over."

Not for the first time Fyodor found himself thanking his lucky stars for Alexei. The veteran was almost always able to anticipate what Fyodor was thinking and act accordingly. Rue Garibaldi was a one-way street that intersected the southwest-northeast-running Rue Bourguiba from the south. The intersection looked more like a lazy Y canted to its side than a T. This worked to the team's advantage. The diagonal nature of the intersection offered a blind spot to the south.

A blind spot Alexei's assault team could use to their advantage.

"Four, this is Five, I won't make it in time. You have execution authority. I'll provide exfil, over."

Though he'd wanted to help take down the target, Fyodor knew he'd made the correct decision. With Sasha out of radio contact, someone needed to grab the team's van and provide a vehicular getaway for the assault team.

That someone was him.

"Five, this is Four, copy all. We are almost in position. I can see the bike approaching from the northeast. We—*blyat!*"

Fyodor stopped, waiting for Alexei to continue. His earpiece remained silent. "Four this is Five, say again, over."

More silence.

"Four, this is Five, over."

Nothing.

"Any station this net, this is Five, respond if you can hear me, over."

It was not uncommon for a team member to drop off the net when conducting surveillance. Even with the low-profile radios, there were instances when an operative's surroundings prevented them from speaking.

In this scenario, the team member would usually double-click the transmit button on their radio to signify that they could hear but not respond to radio traffic.

Usually.

Even this might be forgone if the operative thought a bystander might notice the movement. Instead, the operative would either wait for the person to move or relocate themselves. But in each contingency, there was one thing a member of the Alfa Group would never do.

Curse on the radio.

"Any station this net, any station this net, this is Five, sound off, over."

Fyodor's stomach clenched.

Something was wrong.

The parking lot with the van was just two hundred yards away, but the distance was deceiving. To reach Alexei's assaulters, Fyodor would have to navigate a maze of one-way streets.

That would take time.

Time that his teammates might not have.

Fyodor raced south, all thought of remaining clandestine abandoned. Alexei was a senior noncommissioned officer. He'd been on the team before Fyodor had even earned his maroon beret.

The commando did not rattle easily.

With the ocean forming a natural barrier to the east, Fyodor had arrayed his team to cover the remaining three cardinal directions that bounded the Old Harbor. Sasha had been in charge of the north, while Alexei and the two other members of the assault team were arrayed to the south. Fyodor had taken up position about two blocks to the west of the inlet. He'd arranged the team this way because the position to the north offered a clear view of the marina, and based on their previous two days running the surveillance, Volkov would probably head south from the café into Alexei's waiting arms. The arrangement also had another benefit. Fyodor could serve as the human goalkeeper between his team and the mosque should the target decide to move west.

While not as experienced as Alexei, Fyodor had been a team leader for several years and had learned to trust his intuition. He sensed that the mosque spelled trouble and wanted to keep the takedown as far from its walled premises as possible. Now his intuition was telling him something else. Rather than follow the most direct route to Alexei's last known position, Fyodor intended to move south on a parallel street and then approach the intersection from the west. This would take longer, but he would be useless to his teammates if choosing the more direct route meant rushing headlong into an ambush.

But that didn't mean he was happy about added transit time.

"Any station this net, any station this net, this is Five, respond, over."

The ensuing silence felt more ominous than before.

Abandoning further attempts at contacting his team, Fyodor concentrated on pumping his legs and arms. Now that he was farther from the more pedestrian-friendly thoroughfares, the streets were far less congested with people, but the space between adjacent buildings had all but vanished. As the city grew denser, the distinction between the sidewalk and street appeared to be up for interpretation. Parked cars sat with tires haphazardly over the curbs, while tables and chairs from cafés and coffee shops battled for supremacy with the vehicular traffic inching along the thoroughfare. Fyodor dodged a motor scooter riding against traffic, hurtled the roots of a massive palm tree sprouting from a sidewalk planter, and slid across the hood of a four-door sedan straddling the walkway.

The driver let loose a stream of angry Arabic, but Fyodor paid the man no mind. He was entirely focused on the intersection of Rue Bourguiba just ahead. With a burst of speed, Fyodor turned right and barreled down the street. He dodged a man seated on a four-legged stool and ignored a throng of shouting children. A cluster of silky oak trees to the right marked the Y-intersection between Rue Bourguiba and Rue Garibaldi. The tiny bit of cover would allow Fyodor to peer around the corner against the flood of one-way traffic to try to determine what had befallen his men.

He halted his headlong rush.

The clump of trees created a perfect hide site. A trio of empty fold-ing chairs sat in the shade offered by the green canopy and the adjacent video-game store was already closed for the evening. He drew the Ma-karov pistol from the concealed holster at the small of his back and held the weapon along his right leg to shield it from onlookers. He thought about screwing on the suppressor concealed in his left pocket but didn't. Threading the metal cylinder onto the pistol's muzzle might attract at-tention. Instead, Fyodor concentrated on calming his breathing as he formulated a plan.

Alexei and his team had been approaching the intersection from the south, or right, in anticipation of intercepting the target traveling west down Rue Bourguiba. Since Fyodor could see no sign of the tar-get or his men, it stood to reason that whatever had befallen them had occurred on Rue Garibaldi to his right. With this in mind, he decided to take a peek down the one-way street while using the trees as cover.

As he drew even with the oak trees, Fyodor's predatory gaze caught his reflection in a pair of rare storefront windows on the far side of the street. The glass panes were enormous and ran the length of the entire store. The clothing inside was surprisingly high-end for this run-down section of town, but Fyodor didn't devote much time to the brightly col-ored Western-style outfits adorning an assortment of mannequins. He was more concerned with the reflection in the glass. The storefront window presented a glimpse of the one-way Rue Garibaldi as well as the opposite side of Rue Bourguiba.

The narrower Rue Garibaldi was packed with vehicular traffic. Cars were parked on both sides of the thoroughfare, while an assortment of sedans and motor scooters turned the space that was undoubtedly meant for a single lane into at least three. Garibaldi terminated into Bourguiba with a stop sign, but this did not deter drivers from merging with the two-way traffic.

Horns blared, brakes squealed, and motorists yelled.

Fyodor could barely think over the pandemonium and the overwhelming chaos brought with it a smidgen of hope. Perhaps there was a benign explanation for Alexei's silence. Maybe the team sergeant quit transmitting because he couldn't hear over the cacophony.

Motion beckoned from his peripheral vision. Glancing left, Fyodor saw a blue gate on the opposite side of the street shivering in the wind. The gate marked the entrance to a walled courtyard ringing a large structure whose purpose Fyodor couldn't discern. White Arabic script flowed across a blue sign mounted above the gate, but Fyodor's eyes were drawn to the entrance's metal bars. A length of twine ran from the bars to an adjacent concrete pillar, preventing the gate from fully opening or closing. Instead it wagged back and forth, continuously testing the twine's strength.

At first, Fyodor didn't get it.

Then he did.

Gripping the Makarov in both hands, he leaned around the largest oak tree's trunk, pointing the muzzle right as he looked south down Rue Garibaldi. The gate was a diversion meant to make him focus left. Therefore, logic dictated that the assault would come from his right.

Fyodor's first glimpse didn't reveal much more than what he'd seen in the reflection from the clothing store's windows. Trees in concrete planter boxes interspersed with gates leading inside walled courtyards dominated the far side of Rue Garibaldi. His side of the street appeared to be more dedicated to commerce. An assortment of cafés and metal racks displaying clothes, handbags, and the like occupied most of the cracked sidewalk. A pair of women hobbling toward him did a double take before braving the traffic to cross to the far side of the street, but most of the pedestrians either didn't notice him among the trees or didn't care.

That was the good news.

The not-so-good news lurked about a block farther south. A small crowd clumped around something. Fyodor couldn't make out what had attracted their attention, but the dark liquid draining from the sidewalk into the street offered a clue.

A body.

Probably more than one, judging by the amount of blood.

Cold sweat popped out along Fyodor's hairline, and he blinked the moisture away, not daring to release his grip on the pistol. He was no longer part of a wolf pack running down prey.

Now he was alone and surrounded by dead men.

Fyodor studied the crowd, trying to get a feel for its energy. It was possible that his team had been caught up in a riot or domestic disturbance. Possible, but not likely. The pedestrians ebbing and flowing around the still-widening pool of blood appeared to be more curious than agitated. Judging a crowd's intent wasn't an exact science, but Fyodor had once seen demonstrators riot outside the Soviet Union's embassy in Kabul, Afghanistan. This gathering looked more like curious bystanders than a mob.

He was in the process of edging around the tree for a better view when a high-pitched chime sounded. Glancing left toward the sound, Fyodor froze. A colorful wagon drawn by two horses was rolling east down Rue Bourguiba toward his intersection. Neither the horses nor the pair of men seated in the wagon gave ground to the stream of trucks, cars, and scooters heading in the opposite direction on the narrow street, though a motorbike passed within touching distance of the lead horse's heaving flank. Traffic behind the wagon had become a snarl of vehicles whose blaring horns did nothing to speed up the plodding animals. One driver rectified the jam by pulling onto the sidewalk while sounding a chime.

The driver of a three-wheeled bike carriage.

Fyodor swallowed, not sure if the tricycle was real or the remnants of a fever dream. Though the number of such conveyances he'd seen today numbered exactly one, he still held his breath as he jostled for a better look into the passenger bench, which was shaded by a flimsy canopy. At first he couldn't see past the boy standing on the bike's pedals. His skinny legs pumped up and down to add a burst of speed as the tricycle pulled even with the wagon. Then the driver sat down, giving a clear view of the passenger bench.

And Volkov.

The bike surged past the wagon and then swung into the road, barely clearing the horses. The maneuver earned a tongue-lashing from the wagon's driver as the mares balked, but the boy paid him no heed. Fyodor watched the tricycle approach for another half second before reaching a decision. His team might be compromised, but he was still in play.

He would complete the mission.

Unfortunately, that was easier said than done. His team's mission brief had envisioned capturing and then renditioning Volkov. Fyodor's commander hadn't explained the rationale behind this decision, but he could guess. Putting a traitor on trial made for great press while sending an unambiguous message—the KGB's memory was long and its operational reach longer still. Spying for the Americans might bring wealth and a chance at relocation in the short term, but all traitors eventually paid for their transgressions.

That said, Fyodor's orders had come with a caveat. Capture was the preferable, but not the only acceptable, course of action. An assassination cost the government political capital and was absent the elegance of a TASS news release, but a dead body still told a story. News of the killing would circle among the KGB elite and trickle down to the rank-and-file officers.

Deterrence would be reestablished.

After looking over his shoulder, Fyodor removed the suppressor from his pocket and screwed the cylindrical tube onto the pistol's muzzle with quick, practiced motions. While the clump of oak trees didn't completely hide him, the brown trunks broke up his silhouette and served as a natural obstruction to the ebb and flow of pedestrian traffic. Most walkers crossed to the opposite side of the street rather than attempt to navigate the leaf-strewn stretch of cracked sidewalk that passed between the trees.

The chime sounded again as Fyodor finished the final turn. The long metal tube changed the pistol's balance, but he'd spent countless hours firing a suppressed firearm. He knew how to adjust his aim-point. He would have to shoot across traffic, but in this regard, the tricycle's strange design helped. Rather than traditional bicycle tires, the bike sported oversize knobby wheels meant to more easily navigate city streets and the rougher terrain closer to the harbor. The tires' larger circumference meant that the passenger compartment sat higher than the surrounding vehicular traffic. He would still be shooting at a moving target, but he wouldn't have to worry about timing the shot around motorists. The distance would be less than ten yards, and he could brace against the tree trunk to steady his aim if necessary.

The shot wasn't simple, but it was doable.

A final check over his shoulder yielded nothing new. The windows in the garment store across the street still showed the same flow of pedestrians and motorists limping toward him down the one-way street. The sidewalk behind him was empty and the blue gate on the opposite side of the street continued to sway impotently in the breeze.

He was clear.

The tricycle edged closer and Fyodor saw Volkov's face. The traitor's features were pinched and his lips drawn into a frown. He looked . . . worried. Fyodor shifted his focus from his target to the pistol's front sight post. He centered the metal sliver on the traitor's chest and then brought the rear sights into alignment. The bicycle's chime sounded repeatedly as they reached the intersection. Fyodor didn't care. He was focused on the pistol's sights and the slow, steady rearward pressure he was applying to the Makarov's trigger.

Any moment now, the shot would break.

Any moment.

Amid the near-constant chiming, Fyodor registered a second sound. The metallic *click* of a door latch engaging.

The video-game store behind him might be closed, but it was not empty.

Whirling, Fyodor brought the pistol to bear while squeezing the trigger.

A blow to his forearm knocked the weapon offline as the pistol spat, sending a round harmlessly into the storefront's stucco wall. Fyodor tried to fight, but a sharp pain radiating from his side stole his breath. Looking down, he noticed the hilt of a knife protruding from his ribs. Then he saw the man who'd stabbed him—thick, uncombed black hair, a beard, and bronzed-olive skin.

And eyes.

Eyes so dark that they were almost black.

The blade turned in his chest and that blackness swallowed him whole.

CHAPTER 37

THOMAS Stansfield was not easily impressed.

He'd seen the very best the European continent had to offer. The magnificent architecture, breathtaking museums, and awe-inspiring cathedrals. There were not many places that still inspired a sense of awe in him.

The Oval Office was an exception.

While the president's workspace was relatively small compared to other heads of state, there was something uniquely American about its simplicity. From the giant Presidential Seal embroidered into the royal-blue carpeting, to the Resolute desk's air of stoicism, to the sculptures and artwork that were selected based on the current president's preferences, there was no question that this office was home to the nation's chief executive. But marble busts, oil paintings, and the other trappings of office were only part of the reason why Stansfield always felt a sense of reverence in this place. The ghosts of his predecessors still inspired awe in a heart that was not yet jaded despite all that he had endured on behalf of that nation he loved.

Thomas Stansfield understood realpolitik not as a diplomat, journalist, or politician, but he had experienced the visceral evil that humankind was capable of unleashing firsthand. More times than he could count, he had been asked to influence the government of a remote country that most Americans couldn't find on a map. And when the political warriors who'd demanded this action lost their nerve, he was left to tally the butcher's bill. The Bay of Pigs was not the only instance in which political cowards had left good men to die on a battlefield of their making.

And yet.

And yet, Stansfield's heart remained optimistic and his spirit unbent. This was not because he believed in the perfection of his nation or its leaders. Far from it. But he did believe in his fellow citizenry and the nobility of America's founding principles even though the men who enshrined those principles had been flawed human beings. As with Lincoln, Stansfield agreed that the better angels of our nature existed, but in this moment, the heavenly cherubs seemed to have taken a back seat to something else.

The devils of politics.

"The president will see you now."

The president's long-serving administrative assistant delivered the news with an even cadence, but Stansfield wasn't fooled. Though he had held a variety of roles during his many years of government service, he was first and foremost a spy. Deciphering a conversation's subtext was part and parcel of the job. The woman was on edge and the source of her anxiety waited on the other side of the still-closed door. Feeling like Daniel about to be cast into the lion's den, Stansfield got to his feet and brushed an imaginary speck of lint from his trousers. "Thank you. If we don't get a chance to speak later, I hope you have a wonderful day."

Stansfield delivered his rejoinder with genuine sincerity. Though she didn't have his nearly five decades of government service, the president's assistant had been guarding the Oval Office for as long as he could remember. She was pleasant to talk with and competent at her job. Stansfield was fond of the woman and truly did wish her a good day.

But that was not why he'd spoken.

The president's secretary was a reliable barometer of his mood, if one knew how to read her. The assistant excelled at keeping tension from her voice and maintaining neutral facial expressions, but there was a single tell to her otherwise ironclad façade. If the current occupant of 1600 Pennsylvania Avenue was in any mood but one, Stansfield's greeting would elicit a *thank you* or at the very least a smile. On the rare occasions when the president was truly angry, the waves of emotion emanating from the Oval Office buffeted even his steadfast secretary. If this was the case, she might nod, but there would be no smile and certainly no spoken reply.

Today she stared at him wearing an expression he'd never seen before. It brought to mind the look a prison guard might give an inmate on death row.

A look reserved for a dead man walking.

"Where is your operative?"

Stansfield paused as he pondered both the question and the tenor in which it was delivered. By his standards, the Oval Office's current occupant was an average president. He was blessed with neither Reagan's oratory gifts nor FDR's vision. He was not the sort to admonish his fellow citizens to ask not what their country could do for them but what they could do for their country and neither was he the kind to forcefully demand the unconditional surrender of America's mortal enemies. Instead, Stansfield judged the nation's commander in chief to be an even-keeled man with a steady hand.

Hopefully, this assessment was still correct.

"I'm not sure I understand, sir," Stansfield said.

Since he wasn't offered a seat, Stansfield remained standing. Nor was he offered a handshake or even a simple hello. Instead, the president glared at him from behind the Resolute desk in the manner of a senior officer calling a junior leader on the carpet for a particularly poor decision. Or perhaps a defender observing the lead echelon of an advancing army from the firing port of his own bunker. The temperature in the Oval Office always felt cool, but today the air was positively frigid.

"Your operative. The one from the Orion program."

Stansfield had never sought the CIA's seventh-floor corner office, but neither had he avoided the job of DCI. He wasn't a natural bureaucrat and had no aspirations to run for elected office, snare a lucrative board position with a prestigious company, or write a tell-all at the conclusion of his government service. His life's work was dedicated to furthering the mission espoused by the CIA, and the OSS before it. He didn't have aspirations for greatness, but he did possess decades of lessons learned the hard way. Lessons that could benefit the organization he loved were he permitted to implement the changes those lessons necessitated. He wanted the director's job.

But not at any cost.

"Mr. President, I cannot speak to my predecessor's position, but I do not utter the names of clandestine officers flippantly. You are the commander in chief and there are no secrets from you, but if perhaps you could add some specifics to your question, I might be able to better answer it."

Stansfield believed every word he'd just uttered.

Almost every word.

He wouldn't be a spy if he didn't recognize the necessity of occasionally bending the rules. As head of the executive branch, the president held absolute declassification authority. There were no secrets from him, but the same couldn't be said of his staff. The Orion program existed as a means to visit extrajudicial justice on terrorists who had American blood on their hands. Terrorists who had proven to be unreachable by conventional means.

Stansfield assumed that every modern president had learned from Nixon not to record conversations in the Oval Office, but assuming wasn't the same as knowing. Unless the president specifically ordered him, he did not intend to discuss the Orion program, let alone the assassins employed by that program.

Especially an assassin named Rapp.

"You haven't seen the news?"

Stansfield shook his head. "No, sir. I was en route back to Langley from the Hill when I received instructions to head here."

Stansfield had spent the first part of the day attending private meetings with numerous senators to try to shore up support for his nomination. He had used the commute back to his side of the Potomac to catch up on cables and the assorted paperwork that came with running the CIA. He neither listened to the radio nor engaged in phone conversations, preferring to make use of what he was already realizing was a precious commodity—time alone with his thoughts.

"I've been on the phone with the British prime minister for the last forty-five minutes," the president said. "Candidly, I don't particularly like him and I'm sure the feeling is mutual, but personal animus aside, this might be the lowest point in our nations' relationship since the redcoats burned the White House."

Though Stansfield still thought his decision to send Irene to Moscow was the correct one, he was already feeling her loss. His adopted daughter occupied no position on the agency's organizational structure, but in the storm of dysfunction engulfing the CIA's executive leadership team, Irene had become his island of calm. She had always been a gifted case officer with a good head for fieldwork. This was why he'd harbored no misgivings about placing the Orion team under the leadership of a relatively junior officer. Lately her role had matured into one of trusted advisor. A de facto chief of staff who could see around corners and find the answers to questions that her boss had yet to ask.

Questions like why the president had requested his immediate presence at the White House, for instance. Stansfield had assumed the president had wanted to hear how critical senators were feeling about his confirmation vote and war-game next steps. A logical but incorrect assumption. Irene would have ferreted out the meeting's agenda instead of relying on suppositions. Stansfield had made a rookie mistake in a job that could ill afford such errors.

"Is this something to do with Latvia?" Stansfield said.

He wouldn't have thought it possible, but the president's face grew darker still. "No. At least not directly anyway, although based on the conversation we just had, I'd place the odds of the British helping us with that predicament at somewhere between slim and none. No, I'm talking about the fact that one of your Orion operatives just murdered two people in downtown London."

Several responses leapt to mind, but Stansfield's thoughts coalesced around a single word—*murdered*. The president understood the Orion's charter better than anyone—he was the one who'd authorized it, after all—so the fact that he was now labeling the killing of a terrorist as *murder* concerned Stansfield. Greatly. This was not the language of a chief executive who had ordered the CIA to do what needed to be done even if it wasn't politically expedient. No, this was the language of a politician.

A politician looking for a scapegoat.

"Sir, I was not the director when Orion was instituted, but I support the program's charter wholeheartedly. I'm not aware of what happened in London, but I do know this: Eliminating terrorists is not murder."

"No shit." The president sputtered. "I'm not talking about the Syrian banker Youssef what's-his-name your assassin gunned down or his bodyguard. I'm talking about the innocent father caught in the crossfire. Not to mention the bobby who took a round to the chest for daring to interfere. What in the hell was your man thinking?"

First the surprise in the congressional hearing. Now this. Stansfield had been in the spy business long enough to understand that sometimes operations went wrong, but this was ridiculous. "With respect, Mr. President, how do you know the London killings had anything to do with the Orion team?"

"Are you saying it wasn't us?"

"I'm saying that I'd like to understand why the British prime minister believes an American CIA officer is gunning down civilians on London's streets."

"I'll give you three reasons. One, witnesses heard the gunman speak English with an American accent." The president held up a slender index finger. "Two, the target was on your kill list. Three, the bodyguard and terrorist were both dispatched with head shots via a suppressed Beretta pistol. Sound familiar?"

It did.

"I can understand how your British counterpart might find such an incident distasteful," Stansfield said, "but I'm still not clear why he called you. Youssef bin Muhammad was a man who lived by the sword and he died the way such men often do—violently. What would prompt the PM to leap to the conclusion that an American covert operative was responsible?"

Stansfield had a feeling that he already knew the answer. A feeling that turned more toward a certainty when the president flushed and looked down at his desk.

"Sir, did you tell the British about Orion?" Stansfield said.

He asked the question softly and without judgment. As if he were a parent attempting to solicit a confession from a misbehaving child rather than the director of the CIA speaking to the leader of the free world. Though the answer was plainly written in the red hue coloring the president's cheeks, Stansfield needed to hear him say the words. If he truly had put untold lives in danger, Stansfield wanted his commander in chief to feel the weight of his actions.

"Not explicitly. Everyone knew that someone had been killing terrorists. That's part of what got us into trouble in Paris. My British counterpart raised concerns about the circumstances surrounding Paul Cooke's death. I assuaged them."

Only a lifetime of handling assets allowed Stansfield to keep his rage from showing. "May I ask about the exact nature of the prime minister's concerns and precisely how you assuaged them?"

Anger battled with embarrassment on the president's face. When it came to conversations with foreign powers, the nation's unitary executive was on his most secure footing from a constitutional perspective. Other than the voting public, there was no one the president answered to in this regard, least of all the interim director of the Central Intelligence Agency.

In theory.

In practice, the president had asked Stansfield to accept the role of director and weather the storm spawned by Paul Cooke's duplicity. Stansfield had pointedly not sought the job, and he was not one of the president's acolytes. Political winds changed direction on a dime, and tomorrow the calculus might be different, but today the situation was clear. The president needed Stansfield, which meant he had to answer Stansfield's questions.

Even if he didn't want to.

"Dead bodies have been piling up all over Europe for the last year. There hasn't been any collateral damage so far, but as the Israelis found out after Munich, nobody's perfect. The prime minister wanted me to know that while he was supportive of the program's goal, he also wanted my assurance that assassinations would not take place on British soil. He was in a precarious spot politically and the opposition party could use the killings to erode his governing coalition. He was prepared to offer certain . . . enticements if I guaranteed that we would keep the nasty business out of his backyard."

Stansfield was tempted to ask about those enticements, but didn't. Heads of state were politicians and trading favors was in their blood. Besides, he had his boss on the ropes and didn't want to squander the opportunity by switching topics. "How did he know it was us?"

The president shrugged. "It wasn't them and it wasn't the Israelis. That doesn't leave too many other options."

"So you gave away Orion?"

Stansfield almost whispered the words, but the president still flinched.

"I did not give away anything. Not that I need to explain myself, but the United Kingdom is our oldest and most reliable ally. The special relationship that exists between our two nations is built on trust, transparency, and shared aspirations. Did I read the British prime minister in on the specifics of a code-word-level classified operation? Of course not. But I did offer him assurances that no assassinations would be conducted on British soil. Assurances in exchange for domestic concessions. Assurances that now appear to have been worthless. So I'm going to ask you a final time—are we behind the shootings in London?"

Stansfield wanted to reply with an adamant no. Orion operatives did not freelance or prosecute targets at their own discretion. Killings were confined to a predetermined list and were supported by agency logistical teams that laid the groundwork for the assassination. Orion team members were not permitted to identify, stalk, and prosecute a target without their handler's approval.

At least that was the official line.

"Sir, when you asked me to take over as DCI, I agreed to do so with one caveat. I would never tell you what you wanted to hear instead of what you needed to hear regardless of the political or personal cost. I can tell you unequivocally that I did not authorize an operation on British soil, but I cannot say with the same amount of certainty that one wasn't conducted. Yet. I'll have an answer for you as soon as possible, but I need to run a few traps first."

"As soon as possible better be before the end of the day. I owe the PM a call."

"Understood. Is there anything else?"

"I hope to God you're right, Thomas. If not, I'd expect the handful of voices currently calling for the CIA to be defunded to become a full-fledged chorus. If both Democrats and Republicans start singing from the same song sheet, the agency will be in real trouble."

Stansfield nodded and then headed for the door.

He wanted to argue that point with the president, but didn't.

His boss was right.

CHAPTER 38

"D o you need help?"

Irene Kennedy did not need help with her bag.

Though she'd just flown across eight time zones and almost five thousand miles, she'd traveled with a single roller bag and her laptop case. This was not so much a reflection of Irene's status as a light packer as it was the urgency with which her boss had dispatched her. After her meeting with Stansfield, she'd rushed home, left a message on her husband's office answering machine, grabbed what she'd found in her closet, and bolted.

Her luggage barely weighed twenty pounds.

She didn't need help with her bag, but she could use a coffee. Flying on an agency business jet was far superior to traveling commercial, but it was now early morning Moscow time and her internal clock was hopelessly off. But she didn't say that to the pleasant young man holding open the door to her black SUV. Instead, she smiled and said, "Yes, thank you very much."

The man took her bags, waited for her to climb inside the SUV, and gently closed the door. This might be the first time she'd traveled to

Moscow on behalf of the DCI, acting or otherwise, but this was not her first time in a crisis. Nothing kept the feeling of helplessness away like being given something to do. Even if that something was as simple as stowing a woman's bags and helping her into the car.

"Great to meet you, Miss Kennedy."

This sentiment came from the husky man who'd just clambered into the front passenger seat. While the driver had met her as she'd descended the Gulfstream's air steps, his companion had taken up a position at the vehicle's hood. Though the wind whipping across the tarmac of Vnukovo International Airport promised that winter was near, he had not buttoned up his suit jacket. Instead, he'd kept his hands at chest level as he scanned his surroundings.

Irene knew what the bodyguard was watching for.

Russian counterintelligence officers.

"Please call me Irene. And what's your name?"

"I'm Fred Burton, and your driver is Brett Maryott. Will you be heading to the hotel?"

"Thank you, but no. The embassy, please."

"Yes, ma'am."

The State's Diplomatic Security Service, or DSS, agents were among the world's best close-protection officers. From the slums of Beirut to the crime-ridden streets of South Africa, the men and women who wore the gold and blue DSS badge proudly kept their diplomat principals safe from threats ranging from criminals, to terrorists, to African warlords. But even America's bodyguards had limits. Guarding against a Hezbollah cell in Beirut was tough but doable.

Thwarting Russian counterintelligence officers on their home turf was in another league altogether.

"When's the last time this car was swept?" Irene said.

"Thirty minutes before we left the embassy for the airport," Fred said, "but I'd still play it safe if I were you."

"Why?" Irene said. Officially, she was here to coordinate the intelligence effort in Latvia, but unofficially, Stansfield had asked her to be his eyes and ears. She had her own theories as to what might be afflicting Moscow Station, but she needed to fact-find, not confirm her biases. As a case officer, she'd been trained to elicit intelligence from assets with access. Nothing said access like the DSS agents who went toe-to-toe with the FSK on a daily basis.

"Because they're eating our lunch, and we still don't know how. Unless you're sitting in the SCIF, I'd treat every conversation as monitored."

Fred gave his assessment in a matter-of-fact manner as if discussing the chance for rain tomorrow rather than the glaring shortfalls of American operational security. If he was worried about disclosing something politically embarrassing, he didn't show it. Instead he kept his head on a swivel, checking side streets, alleys, and passersby with an intensity mirrored by the still-silent Brett.

Irene settled a bit deeper into her seat, happy to be among professionals.

"Understood," Irene said. "Any new developments with Miss Henrik?" Irene had monitored the situation as best as she could during the twelve-hour flight, but updates were hard to come by. Other than the original TASS news release, the Russians weren't saying anything publicly, which was just as well. During tense situations, the most important communication was often conducted informally via long-established back channels.

"Not that I've heard," Fred said. "The ambassador— Left, Brett! Now!"

At first Irene didn't understand the change in Fred's unflappable demeanor. Leaning forward, she saw what had demanded the DSS agent's attention. Two GAZ Volga sedans were parked across the road, nose to nose. The vehicles had no identifying markings, but the luxury cars were synonymous with the KGB and now the SVR and FSK. Even so, Irene wasn't worried. She had a competent security detail and was traveling under diplomatic cover. Under Moscow Rules, she should be untouchable.

Irene slammed against her seat belt as Brett braked and cut the wheel left. She'd attended the CIA's tactical driving course before embarking on her first denied-access assignment, but it had been a while since she'd put a Crown Vic through a J-turn. Even when her skills were still fresh, she would have considered the side street Brett was angling for out of reach.

Not the DSS agent.

Though she wouldn't have thought it possible a heartbeat earlier, the seat belt cut even deeper into her chest as Brett cranked the steering wheel and accelerated. If the young agent ever grew tired of his employment with the State Department, Irene thought he had a bright future as a fighter pilot. With a final squeal of rubber on concrete, Brett did the impossible. The SUV rocketed down the alley, leaving the roadblock behind.

"Shit!"

In contrast to her uncle Stan, Irene usually subscribed to her father's belief that the use of profanity was the by-product of a mind too lazy to think of more suitable adjectives. Not this time. Had the seat belt's nylon webbing not compressed the breath from her lungs, she might have added an expletive of her own to the mix.

Her relief was short-lived.

Another Volga edged from an adjacent side street, blocking their path. A second sedan pulled across from the opposite direction, reinforcing the roadblock. Even with Brett's expert touch on the steering wheel, there was no way the SUV would be able to force its way through the two-car barrier.

The DSS agent seemed to have arrived at the same conclusion.

Popping the transmission into reverse, he spun in his seat to look out the rear window and hammered the accelerator.

They didn't get far.

"Shit!"

This time it was Irene who'd uttered the profanity. The entirety of the SUV's rear window seemed to be occupied by the grille of yet another Volga.

They were trapped.

"Brace," Fred said.

Irene didn't understand at first. Then as the engine began to rev, she got it. Brett had dropped the transmission into neutral and was redlining the RPM. He intended to force his way back out of the alley. For a heartbeat, she was inclined to go along. Had this been Beirut and the men behind her Hezbollah thugs, she would have screamed her encouragement. Prior to the escape-and-evasion phase of training, every class of future case officers was shown clips of the torture and interrogation videos shot by Bill Buckley's terrorist captors. Those horrible excerpts drove home the importance of avoiding capture much better than an instructor ever could. Better to go down swinging than be snatched from the streets of some Middle Eastern back alley.

But she was not in the Middle East.

Irene was on the streets of Moscow in a car bearing the license plates and flags that identified it as a diplomatic vehicle. Even more importantly, she had traveled as an official envoy of the United States of America. An attack on her was an attack against a nuclear-armed sovereign nation.

Even on the streets of Moscow, this designation carried weight.

If she acted the part.

"No," Irene said, putting more confidence into her voice than she felt. "We're not going to run. Put it in park and unlock the doors."

"Ma'am," Fred said, "our instructions were to—"

"I'm issuing new instructions. I am a duly credentialed representative of the government of the United States of America. Americans don't run."

Brett looked to Fred, but Irene suppressed her irritation. DSS agents worked for their State Department principals, but their protectee's safety was their responsibility. In much the same way that a president's Secret Service detail quit listening to their principal once an assassination attempt was underway, her two bodyguards would be well within their rights to tune her out in favor of keeping her safe. To his credit, Fred showed the sobriety for which DSS agents were known.

"Are you sure, ma'am?"

"Positive. If they want to talk, I'm all ears."

Fred looked from her to the car behind them. Then he slowly nodded. "Put it in gear and unlock the doors, Brett. The lady knows what she's about."

Irene sincerely hoped so.

CHAPTER 39

BRETT slammed the transmission into gear and took his foot off the gas, allowing the engine RPMs to spool down to idle. As if on cue, the doors to the trail car opened and three men exited. Two of the suit-clad operatives were what she expected—thick-necked beefeaters.

The third man was something different. He looked to be in his seventies, but his bearing or movements were bereft of the ravages of age. He had a full head of gray hair, and his lined face was kind. He could have played the part of the wise patrician in a film about Rome or perhaps the favorite grandfather on a sitcom.

Irene had a feeling he was neither.

After straightening his suit coat like a politician about to take the stage, the grandfather strode toward her car. He approached her side of the vehicle, stopped, and then rapped a pair of hard knuckles on the tinted glass.

Irene rolled down her window. "Yes?"

"Good morning, Miss Kennedy. Do you have a moment?"

The question that of course wasn't a question was delivered in slightly accented English. Irene's childhood spent abroad had helped her develop a fairly accurate ear for languages. Had she encountered the elderly gentlemen standing at her window anywhere else, she would have pegged him as European. Perhaps German or Swiss. Maybe even Dutch.

Up close, his appearance was even more disarming. Unlike the caricature of the Russian hood in an ill-fitting suit with bad teeth and a veiny nose from too many nights spent in a vodka bottle, the man had a genteel air, freshly trimmed hair, and sparkling eyes. Had she been forced to guess an intelligence service just based on his appearance, Irene might have chosen MI6. He was suave and smooth and looked as if he hailed from a more refined era. One in which Rommel and Montgomery broke off their desert fight each day in time for afternoon tea.

"I'm in a bit of a hurry," Irene said, "but I'd be glad to have my secretary work you in sometime tomorrow. Mr. . . . ?"

"Petrov. Lieutenant General Grigoriy Petrov."

The man paused as if to let his name and title register.

For the first time since Stansfield had handed her this live grenade of an assignment, Irene was grateful that she was not a Russia hand. While she understood the significance of his rank, his name washed over her, making her indifference all that much easier to fake. "Great, Lieutenant General Petrov. My office will be in touch with yours very soon. Now, if you could please move your cars, I'd appreciate it. They seem to have inadvertently blocked my path."

Irene had geared her response toward a reaction, but not the one she received. Instead of anger or indifference, Petrov responded with something unexpected. Laughter. Truth be told, it was a nice sound. No trace of cynicism or snark. Just a genuine chuckle shared between friends.

They weren't friends.

"How is it that I've never heard of you, Miss Kennedy?" Petrov said, wiping tears of amusement from his eyes. "You're good. Very good. No, I'm afraid tomorrow just won't do. Regrettably for your very important schedule, I must insist we have our talk now. Right now. Would you be so kind as to unlock your door so that I might join you?"

"Certainly," Irene said. "It's already unlocked." She rolled up the window before he could reply and made no move to make room for the Russian intelligence officer. It took Petrov a moment to realize what she'd done and sort through the potential options.

Option one meant opening the door and attempting to push Irene to the far side of the car. This was the most direct course of action, but it would mean ending the charade that this was just an amicable conversation between two government officials. Option two required Petrov to walk around the car and enter from the driver's side. This would give lie to the notion that the Russian was in complete control of the situation and potentially cause him to lose face in front of his men.

Neither scenario would likely engender further goodwill.

"Hope you know what you're doing, boss," Fred whispered.

So did Irene. Part of her was tempted to respond to the head of her protective detail, but she didn't. Petrov was still standing just outside her window, and she didn't know how far her voice would carry. Instead she opened the newspaper on the seat next to her and began to read, doing her best to demonstrate that she hadn't a care in the world. The Russian probably wasn't buying her act, but that was fine. She considered it a win that her fingers didn't tremble. She was halfway through the lead article, which happened to be a rather interesting review of Nelson DeMille's latest book, when the light at her window shifted.

Petrov was moving.

A heartbeat later, the driver's-side door opened and the Russian slid into the seat next to her. "You are most interesting, Miss Kennedy. I would love to get to know you better. It's unfortunate that we find ourselves in an adversarial situation."

"I'm sorry, but I don't follow," Irene said. "As I said, I'm a foreign service officer with the Department of State and—"

"Stop."

Petrov's command crackled through the air. The intensity behind the single word was palpable. Fred's shoulders bunched, but he didn't turn toward the Russian.

Good man.

"Neither of us has time for such nonsense," Petrov said. "I need you to communicate something directly to your boss. Word for word."

"I'll be happy to relay a message to the ambassador—"

"Enough! If you persist in this charade, I will have no choice but to communicate through less competent channels. Like Miss Henrik for instance. Do you understand?"

Irene did understand. The person sitting beside her no longer resembled a well-dressed elderly grandfather. Though his visage was no more familiar than it had been before, his eyes were a different story. She'd seen eyes like those earlier.

They were the eyes of a killer.

Fred turned toward the Russian. The burly DSS agent made to reach across the seat, but he was brought up short. By a gun. Irene had been watching Petrov the entire time and she still couldn't say exactly how he'd done it. One moment his hand had been empty. The next, it held a compact, semiautomatic pistol. The muzzle was centered on Fred's forehead.

"You are in my country. Mine. If I wanted you dead, your corpse would already be cooling in the street. I don't want to kill you, but if that is what is required, I won't devote any more thought to pulling this trigger than I would swatting a fly."

Irene believed him. She knew how to spot bluster, and whatever else Petrov was, the Russian wasn't a braggart. If provoked, he would shoot Fred in the face without hesitation.

"Okay," Irene said, slowly reaching for Fred's shoulder. She gave the big man a squeeze and felt hard muscle beneath her fingertips. "You'd like me to deliver a message?"

"To your boss. Thomas Stansfield. Tell my old friend, 'Oranienburg 1945.' Say it back to me."

"Oranienburg 1945," Irene said.

"That's correct. Make sure you relay that message. And if I were you, Miss Kennedy, I would do so quickly."

With the pistol still pointed at Fred, Petrov opened the SUV's passenger door, exited the vehicle, and walked away.

CHAPTER 40

RENE had thought that morale at CIA headquarters had been bad.

It hadn't.

At least not compared to the gloom that permeated the "yellow submarine." The enclosure was nestled within the US embassy and served as the CIA's tiny secure workspace. This was where the men and women who manned the agency's most important station plotted surveillance detection routes, war-gamed recruitment pitches, and identified targets. This was where assets were run, and stolen secrets disseminated in secure cables back to Langley. This unassuming space was the agency's equivalent of the Situation Room.

This was Moscow Station.

Or at least it used to be.

If before the yellow submarine had been the site of triumphant celebrations for missions gone right and a well of positive energy as audacious operations were plotted and war-gamed, now the vibe was decidedly different. Rather than the command post for an advancing army, the sterile confines felt like a different kind of gathering.

A wake.

"Would you like more coffee?"

Irene shifted her contemplation from the folder of documents spread out on the conference table in front of her next to the fire-engine-red secure speakerphone with its flashing green light to one of its would-be warriors. The woman hovering by her shoulder had been assigned the unenviable task of babysitting the Washington visitor until the acting chief returned from his meeting with the ambassador. Relations between the State Department and CIA were almost always tenuous, as their guiding principles were quite different.

At his core, a good diplomat was the kid in high school who fearlessly interposed his body between two of his classmates about to come to blows. State Department employees genuinely believed that every conflict could be resolved through diplomacy if the relevant parties negotiated in good faith. While ambassadors primarily served as the president's spokes-person to a foreign nation's leadership, they also strove to strengthen the relationship between the two countries.

Stealing another nation's secrets tended to have a detrimental effect on this goal.

"No, thank you," Irene said. "Forgive me for asking, but what was your name again?"

"It's Elysia. Elysia Nicolas. And there's no need to apologize. If I'd been through what you'd just experienced, I'm not sure I'd be able to remember my *own* name."

Irene filed that comment away for further consideration later.

The welcome she'd received from Lieutenant General Grigoriy Petrov had been abrupt, but not particularly traumatizing, though this was beside the point. The glimpse into the case officer's mindset was much more troubling. The men and women of Moscow Station were afraid of their own shadows.

No, that wasn't quite right.

It wasn't that the case officers were inflicted with timidity so much as it was an oversize opinion of their adversary. The blown operation had infected this place with doubt, and for an organization that relied on a certain bit of swagger, self-doubt was just as big a killer as Russian counterintelligence officers.

Maybe more so.

"How long have you been in Moscow, Elysia?" Irene said.

The pretty young woman pursed her lips. She was in her early twenties with shoulder-length brown hair and a runner's build. She didn't look young so much as innocent. Irene wondered if she'd ever looked so youthful.

"About four months I guess," Elysia said.

"How much operational work have you done in that time?"

"Very little. I'm still learning the streets. I was scheduled to unload a dead drop last week, but the officer I was assisting called it off."

"Why?"

"I thought the drop site was compromised. Turns out, I was right."

Irene turned to see a newcomer standing just inside the yellow submarine's soundproof door.

"Oh, hi, Duane," Elysia stammered, her face turning red. "I was just getting Irene here up to speed. I thought—"

"I'll take it from here," Duane said. "Why don't you go see if the coffee maker needs refilling?"

Elysia's flush darkened. "Sure." Dropping her head, the woman crossed the room in silence. Duane barely waited for the newbie case officer to exit before slamming the door behind her.

The steel latch engaged with an ominous *click*.

"Who are you and why are you here?"

Irene stared back at the man, considering.

Though she was not an agitator by nature, there was a reason why she'd been selected to serve as a handler for an assassin in the Orion program. Probably the same reason that Stansfield had put her on a plane to Russia to work the Latvia situation instead of choosing any number of more senior executives.

"My name is Irene Kennedy. I'm here because the acting director thought you could use my help."

Irene wasn't sure what Duane had been expecting, but this apparently wasn't it.

"Help? From DC? In case you're not keeping score, our last operation was blown, the Russians are threatening to put the wife of one of my case officers on trial, and my boss and boss's boss have both been kicked out of the country. Oh yeah, I also just left an ass-chewing session with the ambassador, who's pissed that us agency cowboys are making life impossible for his diplomats. Anyway, you'll have to excuse me if I'm not excited to see a babysitter from headquarters. Maybe you could do us both a favor and climb back aboard your shiny jet."

As much as she hated to admit it, sometimes her uncle Stan's way of dealing with a problem was the correct one. Especially when the problem in question was a narcissistic asshole. "Let me apologize for not being clear. I'm here because Thomas Stansfield has lost confidence in Moscow Station. He wants me to provide him with an outsider's perspective of the work being done here and the executives leading it."

Irene thought her directness might cause Duane to back down.

It did not.

"Fuck off. I work for Stansfield, not you. If he wants to talk, he can get off his ass and pick up the phone."

"Irene? I know I'm joining this call late, but perhaps now might be a good time for me to say a few words?"

Stansfield's disembodied voice echoed from the secure phone. Duane looked from Irene to the flashing green light indicating the line was open. Then he swallowed.

"Sir," Duane said, "I didn't realize—"

"Of course you didn't," Stansfield said, "but not because Irene didn't try to warn you. How someone with so little emotional intelligence graduated from the Farm is beyond me. You aren't fit to run a gas station, let alone Moscow Station. Perhaps the archives room at CIA headquarters might be a better fit. If memory serves, there's a flight leaving Moscow for DC this evening. I expect you to be on it."

"Wait a minute, sir. I can help."

"If the way you treated Miss Nicolas is any indication, I don't think your help is warranted anywhere. Your time in Moscow is over. Good day."

Duane's glare shifted from her to the phone and back again as if unsure who should be the recipient of his anger. She thought he might try to press his case again until his face hardened. "I'll see you at Langley, sir."

Without waiting for an answer, the case officer yanked open the door to the yellow submarine and exited the secure space. Irene listened for the door to slam behind him before speaking. Stifling a yawn, she did the time-conversion math in her head. It was after midnight in Washington, DC. If she was tired, her boss had to be exhausted. "That was fun," Irene said after clearing her throat.

"Difficult personalities are part of the job. The CIA asks a lot of our case officers and the type of people who fit our unique psychological profile aren't the sort who make for easy management. Bullheaded spies who are biased toward action will always be welcome as long as I'm in charge. It's stupidity that I can't abide. Speaking of stupidity, please tell me that your favorite assassin didn't take it upon himself to eliminate a target in London?"

"Sir?"

"I had a meeting with the president earlier today. Someone killed Youssef bin Muhammad along with two innocent bystanders. Was it Rapp?"

"I haven't spoken with him in a couple of days, but last time I checked he was in Barcelona. I left a message for him on the answering service to call me, but he hasn't made contact yet. I can't tell you with a hundred percent certainty that Mitch didn't do this, but I think it's highly unlikely."

"Which is what I said to the president. He didn't like that answer. I don't either. Find out for certain, Irene. And fast. The Brits are livid."

"Yes, sir."

Irene had a feeling that the Brits weren't the only ones livid.

If the *Washington Post* and *New York Times* articles she'd read during her flight to Moscow could be believed, Stansfield's confirmation process wasn't going well. The pieces credited the usual anonymous sources, but the reporters were known to be well connected with congressional representatives of both parties. The writers were useful barometers for Washington groupthink, and right now, the Senate didn't seem to be trending in Stansfield's favor. As much as she wanted to ask her mentor how things were going, she didn't. Stansfield had sent her to Moscow for a reason. She needed to concentrate on putting out her fires and leave the old spy to fight his own battles.

Except she was no longer sure which fires counted as hers.

"Sir, you asked me to helm the Latvian intelligence-gathering operation, but that no longer seems to be my number one priority."

"Oh, I disagree. I think you'll find that as chief of station, everything is a priority."

Though she understood English quite well, Irene stared at the phone as if she were trying to decipher a foreign language. After an embarrassingly long pause, Irene responded with the most coherent retort she could muster. "Sir?"

"Come on, Irene. Don't make me spell this out. As we speak, the wife of a CIA officer is languishing in a Russian prison, civil unrest is gripping Latvia, and a cabal of idiots in Congress is trying to muster support to defund the agency and derail my nomination. And did I forget to mention that our British allies think one of our assassins is engaging in gunfights in downtown London? This is an all-hands-on-deck moment. One of the fringe benefits of my new role is that I don't have to care about seniority or any other such nonsense. Until this crisis blows over, I need someone I can trust leading Moscow Station. You, Irene, are that someone. Questions?"

Irene did not have questions so much as objections. Many objections. She'd never been the assistant chief of station or even the chief of base for the types of backwater postings that normally served as training grounds for the more critical stations like this one. Perhaps most important, Irene was not a Russia hand. She didn't speak the language and had never worked the threat. Asking her to assume the role of chief of station was the equivalent of tapping Stan Hurley to lead the Peace Corps.

But she didn't say any of that.

The CIA was not a military organization, but it did embody some paramilitary attributes, chief among those being a fanatical focus on mission. Her boss had just given her a mission. One did not decline a tasking from Thomas Stansfield.

"No questions, sir," Irene said. "I'll check in with the ambassador on Miss Henrik's status just as soon as I get an update from the Latvian intelligence fusion cell I convened."

"Good. Moscow Station has been afraid of its own shadow for far too long and our intelligence-gathering efforts are the worse for it. Something is rotten in the state of Denmark, Irene. I can feel it. Whether the CIA officers under your command need an attaboy or a kick in the pants, I'll leave for you to decide. Either way, I want those men and women hitting the bricks, meeting with assets, and stealing secrets. Understood?"

"Yes, sir."

"Excellent. Then I'll leave you to it."

"Wait, sir, there is something else I need to tell you. Lieutenant General Grigoriy Petrov decided to personally welcome me to Moscow. Do you know him?"

Stansfield sighed. "I do. He's former KGB. Now FSK. We have a rather long history."

"He gave me a message for you. Made me repeat it back to him word for word."

"What did he say?"

It was sometimes difficult to decipher tone on a secure call, as the multitude of encryption devices that rendered the communication secure also made a person's voice sound more sterile. Even so, Irene thought she detected a hint of wariness in Stansfield's reply.

"He said, 'Oranienburg 1945.' Does that ring a bell?"

The answering silence stretched long enough that Irene would have thought that the call had been disconnected were it not for the flashing green light. She cleared her throat and was preparing to speak when her boss's voice returned.

"It does. Are you familiar with Operation Paperclip?"

"The Allied effort to find Nazi rocket scientists and repatriate them to America?"

"Exactly. As you might imagine, there was a Soviet counterpart to our operation. It was called *Alsos* and its objectives were a bit different. Instead of only focusing on rocket technology, Alsos targeted another area of game-changing research."

Kennedy instantly made the connection. "The atomic bomb."

"Right again. The Nazis were frantically trying to develop a nuclear weapon up until the closing days of the war. Allied strategic bombing, along with the heroic efforts of Norwegian saboteurs, prevented Germany from obtaining the heavy water required to control a nuclear reaction, but their scientists had produced something else the Russians desperately needed. Uranium oxide. In the war's closing days, the Nazis hid a large stash of the material in a suburb of Berlin called Oranienburg. The Russians discovered the uranium oxide's location and sent a convoy of vehicles to secure it."

"The Allies didn't stop them?"

Stansfield cleared his throat. "The stash was clearly in the Soviet sector of Berlin. The debate about whether stealing the uranium oxide was worth enraging our Russian partners embroiled leaders on both sides of the Atlantic. While they were trying to reach a consensus, the Russian convoy edged ever closer to Oranienburg. I decided to act."

"You?"

"That's right. By the war's end, I was a young but highly experienced

OSS officer. It was obvious to me, as it should have been to anyone with half a brain, that the Soviets would soon be our adversaries, and that the world would be a much more dangerous place if they succeeded in building a nuclear arsenal. I hoped that if I bought our leaders more time they would come to the correct decision, so I blew up a bridge as the Russian convoy was crossing it. It sounds barbaric, I know, but it was war. In order for my subterfuge to succeed, I had to ensure that there were no Soviet survivors."

As Stansfield spoke, Irene pictured the scene in her mind's eye. That's when the remaining pieces tumbled into place. "But there was a survivor. Grigoriy Petrov."

"His scout car had broken down several miles west of where I'd set up the ambush. He arrived in time to see me shoot the lone survivor as the man tried to swim for shore, but he was too far away to do anything. I later learned that the man I'd killed was a brilliant Russian physicist. His name was Nikolai. Nikolai Petrov."

For the first time since the conversation had begun, Irene was grateful that it wasn't occurring in person. She managed to stifle her gasp, but there was no hiding the look of horror she knew was etched across her face. "You killed Grigoriy's brother?"

"Yes. As you know from personal experience, the statement 'War is hell' isn't just a colorful expression. After the operation, I led my partisan band back into Allied territory without incident, but the team's good fortune didn't last. My aide-de-camp was a sixteen-year-old French boy named Andre. He spoke German like a native and continued to poke around in the Soviet sector on behalf of Allied intelligence even though I admonished him not to do so. Petrov eventually caught and killed him, but not before torturing Andre long enough to learn about my role in Nikolai's death."

"War is hell," Irene said.

"Indeed. Even the so-called cold ones. Perhaps now you better understand Petrov's animosity."

As always, Stansfield had a gift for understatement. Irene knew the hatred she felt for the Islamic terrorists who'd murdered her father along with sixty-two-odd people in April 1983 when a suicide bomber detonated a van full of explosives outside the U.S. embassy in Beirut, Lebanon, and she hadn't watched him die. "I can see why Petrov might hate you, but I still don't understand his timing. If he is settling a vendetta, why now?"

"That is an excellent question for which I don't have an answer," Stansfield said. "Fortunately, there's a new chief of Moscow Station, and I've heard she's extremely capable. Now, unless you have anything else, I'm going to catch a few hours of sleep. Tomorrow has the makings of another long day."

"Nothing else, sir. I'm on it."

"I know you are, Irene."

Stansfield ended the call.

Irene leaned back in her chair, alone with her thoughts at last.

What had seemed manageable moments before her call with Stansfield now felt different. Moscow Station was in crisis, Europe might be on the brink of war, a lieutenant general in the Russian counterintelligence service was hell-bent on settling a forty-year-old vendetta, and once again blood was flowing down a European ally's streets. Blood that implicated her assassin. Irene eyed the yellow submarine's unassuming, foam-covered walls imagining some of the conversations that must have occurred in this sacred space.

Here was where agency officers had tried to determine whether Nikita Khrushchev was bluffing about Cuba or ready to lead the world into nuclear war. Here was where her predecessors had simultaneously missed the Soviet invasion of Afghanistan and brainstormed how to aid a brave Polish cardinal who'd been elevated to pontiff. This room had been the scene of gratifying victories and stinging defeats, but that was the way of the intelligence business. Irene wasn't so much cowed by the enormity of her task as distressed by what little she could bring to the battlefield. She didn't have her usual allies like Dr. Thomas Lewis, Stan Hurley, or even Mitch Rapp. No doubt word of her predecessor's unceremonious recall back to Langley had already spread through the station's personnel. Some might welcome his departure, but on the balance, human beings prized stability, and of that Moscow Station had seen precious little. Were she a betting woman, Irene would place odds on her welcome as the new acting chief being a bit muted, to say the least.

She was alone.

"Miss Kennedy?"

Irene turned to see the woman Duane had so rudely dismissed standing hesitantly in the door. What was her name? Something unusual and perhaps a bit whimsical. Elise? Eloise? Elysia—that was it.

"It's just Irene, Elysia. Please, come in."

The young woman's answering smile warmed the room.

Perhaps Irene wasn't without allies after all. Maybe she would be able to take a beat to figure things out before embarking on a one-woman crusade to right the listing ship that was Moscow Station.

"Sorry to interrupt, Irene, but I thought you should see this."

Elysia extended a folded piece of stationery that Irene reflexively took. Unfolding the paper, she found a message typed in English.

```
I am a ranking staff officer in the Russian
intelligence service. I have vital information for
Moscow's chief of station that could help avert a
war in Latvia. I will only provide this information
face-to-face. Acknowledge receipt and intention to
proceed by leaving the light in the chief of
station's office on your embassy's fifth floor
illuminated all night. If you signal your intention
to proceed, I will leave further instructions and
proof of my bona fides on the following day in the
same manner I provided the note.
```

Beneath the paragraph were two handwritten words.

Please hurry.

So much for taking a beat.

CHAPTER 41

IRENE read through the message twice more to ensure there wasn't some nuance to the phrasing she'd missed. Then she turned her attention to the handwritten words.

Please hurry.

"How was this delivered?" Irene said.

"Do you know the gas station a block away?"

Irene shook her head.

"I guess if you've never been to Moscow there's no reason why you should. It's reserved for foreign diplomats. The DSS folks refuel our vehicle fleet at that station exclusively. Anyway, two days ago, someone slipped this message into the open window of one of our diplomatically tagged SUVs."

"Two days ago?"

Elysia wilted. "I know. I'm sorry. Our working relationship with State has been . . . strained as of late. To be fair, the note was thrown into the back seat while the DSS agent was inside paying. A foreign service officer discovered it this morning."

Irene added another item to the mental list of subjects she

intended to discuss with the ambassador. While it was not uncommon for CIA and Department of State employees to find themselves at cross purposes, the relationship between the two organizations in Moscow seemed to be unusually antagonistic. No doubt part of this could be laid at the feet of the CIA's string of blown operations. Even the most patient diplomat grew tired of being repeatedly raked across the coals by his foreign counterparts for the operational inadequacies of his CIA contemporaries.

Irene nodded as she read through the message yet again. If there was some hidden intention beneath the banal language, she was missing it. Not that there needed to be. A member of the Russian intelligence service wanted to meet with their American counterpart. At the very least, this could be an attempt to establish the type of back-channel conduit often fostered between rival intelligence services. At best . . . at best, a high-ranking Russian intelligence officer was offering to provide information to a crippled Moscow Station, just when the CIA needed the information most.

Hope battled with cynicism as Irene carefully placed the message on the conference table. Whoever coined the adage that when something seems too good to be true it often is could have been describing the profession of espionage.

Most of the time.

But every now and again, lightning really did strike and it was the job of the men and women who manned the ranks of the clandestine service to be ready when it did.

"Okay," Irene said, turning the letter over in her hands, "can you please let the station's case officers know that I'd like to meet with them en masse later today?"

Elysia paused with her fingers on the door handle. "All of them?"

Irene nodded. "I need to know the heat status of every handler left in Moscow Station. We're going to start working the op plan to meet whoever this is."

Elysia frowned.

"Something the matter?" Irene said.

"Yes. I mean no, but . . ."

Irene sighed. "I don't pretend to understand what's been happening over here, but it's apparent that this station's leadership has been less than stellar. That aside, I need you to unlearn whatever you've been told and remember that you are a Farm-trained clandestine officer working against one of our nation's most skilled and determined adversaries. If there's something you think I need to know, I expect you to tell me. Understood?"

Elysia nodded. "It's just that whoever sent that message said that they are a ranking staff officer." The case officer stared at Irene expectantly.

"Sorry," Irene said after it became apparent the woman wasn't going to continue, "I'm still not seeing your point."

"Oh, I thought you knew. Moscow Station's standing policy is to never attempt to recruit staff officers."

Irene was dumbfounded. "Why on earth not?"

Elysia shrugged narrow shoulders. "I'm not sure who originated the order, but it's been in place for a long time. The thinking was that by the time a KGB officer reaches such a high rank, they have too much at stake to betray their country."

"Meaning that the potential recruit must be a dangle?"

"Yes."

Once again, Irene had to school her features in order to hide her true feelings. While she understood the logic behind such a policy, the diktat was sharply at odds with the purpose of the clandestine service. Was there risk in attempting to recruit a senior member of the Soviet intelligence service? Of course. But was the risk worth the reward? Absolutely. Wild Bill Donovan, the agency's operational father, once said that the ideal OSS candidate was a PhD who could win a bar fight. That the most important station in the agency that was his legacy was now operating by a philosophy that prioritized risk over reward was unthinkable. How many of the men and women who'd labored under

Moscow Station's foolish restrictions had matriculated to other duty assignments and infected new personnel with their foolishly risk-averse attitudes?

But that was only the tip of the iceberg.

The real tragedy was in opportunities lost. Russian assets in possession of potentially game-changing intelligence had been shunted aside because of an inane rule whose origin had been lost to the sands of time. The damage was almost impossible to calculate. But that was a problem for later. In the here and now, Irene needed to focus on the tactical problem—how to structure a clandestine meeting with the volunteer.

"Give your fellow case officers a heads-up that I'm about to announce a policy change," Irene said. "Starting now, it's open season on all Russian governmental officials regardless of their rank or position. Moscow Station is in the business of recruiting spies."

Elysia nodded. Hope warred with trepidation.

Hope won.

"Right away, Chief," Elysia said. "I'm on it."

"I know you are, Elysia," Irene said with a smile.

As the young woman exited the room, Irene thought she might have just recruited her first ally. She hoped this boded well for her meeting with the ambassador. Either way, Moscow Station was back.

CHAPTER 42

STAN Hurley swallowed a mouthful of black, bitter coffee. Though the java was plenty hot and freshly made, it somehow still tasted stale. Or maybe that was just him. Though he wanted to pour the mug down the drain and brew a fresh pot, he didn't. He was expecting company any minute and they were on the clock. As the shabby safe house's bare-bones accoutrements attested, this was not about five-star accommodations or gourmet beverages. This was the spy's equivalent of roughing it, and while the coffee was not good, it served its purpose. After half a mug, Stan could already feel his mental fog lifting, though if he were being honest, the coffee served another purpose beyond just as a source of caffeine.

Penance.

A hard knock rattled the flimsy door against its frame. The sound followed a specific rhythm—a sharp staccato of three quick raps followed by two slow ones. After a pause, the pattern repeated with a slight variation. Instead of two slow ones, the knocking ended with three. Stan set his cup on the grimy table and scooped up the second tool that was integral to this morning's activities.

A pistol.

Taking a centering breath, Stan got up from the table and covered the short distance to the door with his rolling stride. The pistol was in his right hand and angled at the floor. A Glock wasn't his preferred carry, but it was the best he was going to do while engaged in a spontaneous operation conducted without the logistical benefits provided by Rob Ridley and his CIA advance team.

Besides, it beat the alternative.

Sliding up to the door, Stan kicked the rubber stopper free from where it was wedged beneath the doorjamb. Positioning his torso behind the wall, he reached up to unhook the chain lock before disengaging the dead bolt. Then he turned the doorknob and yanked, allowing the door to open away from him. The knock pattern confirmed that his visitors were not random guests who'd wandered to the wrong apartment, but the sequence did nothing to validate that the knock was not done under duress, or worse still, been extracted from its intended recipient.

He could have used the filmy peephole to validate who was standing on the stoop, but that would have required positioning his entire body behind the door. Stan had learned many hard-won lessons, but the most basic remained the most important—never do what your adversary expects. Stan brought his pistol up to the high ready position, but kept his left hand free. In an engagement this close, it was better to have a hand ready to deal with a potential physical altercation.

Yet another lesson learned the hard way.

The door swung past the halfway point and Stan waited for the unexpected. Best case, he'd get to assess how his mentee entered an unfamiliar safe house.

Worst case, things were about to get interesting.

The Russian came through the doorway first, not quite a tactical entry, but not a simple stroll either. Dmitri Volkov passed beneath the doorjamb and stepped deep into the apartment, squinting in the darkness. Stan tracked the former KGB officer with his pistol for no more than an instant.

It was an instant too long.

An expertly delivered blow to Stan's bicep knocked his gun arm offline at the same moment the point of something sharp jabbed against his shirt just under the lowest rib.

"Not bad, kid," Stan said, feeling a twinge of pride at Rapp's performance. "Now put the knife away before someone gets hurt."

A pair of eyes so dark as to be black stared back at him. "You're the only one in danger of getting hurt."

"I don't think so," Stan said. With a not-so-gentle prod, he pressed the point of the tiny push dagger he'd drawn from his belt into Rapp's liver. "You're good, but not ready for a shot at the title just yet. Now, join your Russian friend and pull up a chair at the table. We've got a lot of ground to cover and not much time."

Rapp's gaze drifted down to the dagger before refocusing on Stan's face.

That he had gotten the drop on Rapp was true, but the outcome of their fight was far from certain. At best, he and his apprentice might have given each other dueling terminal wounds. At worst, Rapp could have slid his longer blade into Stan's vitals before he would have been able to reciprocate with the push dagger. Even if the attack didn't kill him outright, the shock of a blade entering his heart or lung cavity might have prevented him from pressing home his attack. The most charitable analysis would be to label the engagement a draw with the advantage going to Rapp. A more accurate assessment was that Rapp had gotten the drop on him.

But that wasn't what Stan saw in the kid's face.

Instead, the assassin seemed to be replaying everything that had just happened and internalized the lessons learned as if he were watching film from one of his college lacrosse games. Then, with a nod, Rapp squirreled away the knife and stepped past Stan into the apartment. Hurley had no idea what was going through the young man's mind, but he was fairly certain of one thing—Rapp would never fall for that trick again.

• • •

"You did what?" Hurley said, trying to keep his voice even.

The debrief was being held in front of the Russian which was un-avoidable but not ideal. Still, it would not do to give the former KGB officer the impression that he thought Rapp had lost his mind.

Even if that was true.

"I took out the Russian direct-action team."

Rapp delivered his response in the deadpan tone one might use to tell a supervisor that you'd correctly filled out your time card. Stan couldn't detect even the slightest hint of bravado. Just a clinical state-ment of the facts.

Perhaps he'd misunderstood Rapp's update.

"By 'take out,'" Stan said, "you mean—"

"They're dead."

Nope. No misunderstanding.

Hurley stared at his assassin, coming to several realizations in rapid succession. One, Rapp really was his assassin. Stan had trained Rapp, pushed him to his limits, tried his damnedest to drum him out of the Orion program, and then provided tacit approval and assistance for Rapp's decision to kill Cooke, a French DGSE operative, and several others in a Paris hotel room.

For better or worse, Rapp was his.

Two, Rapp was more than just good. He was the best the program had ever produced. Probably the best assassin any program like this had ever produced. The kid had nearly bested Hurley in hand-to-hand com-bat on his first day of training at the Lake Anna facility. But that hadn't been Rapp's peak performance.

Far from it.

Much like a newly drafted Michael Jordan, Rapp's skills had contin-ued to improve the longer he'd plied his craft. Exponentially so. Killing terrorists wasn't easy. Killing terrorists protected by bodyguards was straight-up hard. Single-handedly killing multiple Russian paramilitary operatives on unfamiliar terrain bordered on the mythical.

Three, Hurley had imagined that he was creating the human equivalent of a fire-and-forget missile. Someone who could hunt down and kill terrorists with no oversight and little to no logistical help. In that respect, Hurley had succeeded, but it turned out that he'd been using the wrong analogy.

Fire-and-forget missiles did not select their own targets.

Rapp did.

Hurley had a thousand questions.

He didn't ask them.

The disconnect he felt with Rapp was profound. No, that wasn't quite true. The disconnect he felt between himself and the life he'd lived for the past thirty years was a chasm so wide as to be uncrossable. Hurley had been wrong. Wrong about Rapp's fitness to be an assassin, wrong about his protégée-turned-traitor Victor, wrong about Irene's ability to lead the Orion program, and most critically, wrong about himself. He'd instructed Rapp to lie low after the Cooke killing on the pretext that the young assassin needed to give him time to smooth things over with Stansfield and Irene, but the rationale he'd provided wasn't the whole picture.

While it was true that the violent murder of a CIA director in waiting wouldn't just blow over in a news cycle or two, Hurley needed time as well. Time to take an honest look at his mistakes in order to plot a new path forward. He was stubborn, but he wasn't stupid. He had some crow to eat if he hoped to earn his way back into Stansfield's good graces and he owed Irene an apology.

A massive apology.

That shit sandwich wasn't going to taste better with time, so Stan figured he might as well take the first bite.

"You were the guy on the ground," Hurley said, forcing the words past his thick tongue. "The Russians were your call."

"Who are you and what have you done with the man I knew as Stan Hurley?"

Hurley had been bracing himself for a question like this from Rapp, but it was Volkov who'd landed the verbal jab. The exact moment he'd decided that a little humble pie was in order, he found himself saddled with not one but two sons of bitches more than happy to make him grovel. He wanted to cry out to the Almighty at the injustice of it all, but didn't. There was a reason why he was joined at the hip with these shitbirds.

Penance.

"I've grown older and wiser since we last met," Hurley said, eyeing the Russian. "You're just fatter."

Hurley might be on the "making amends" step of a twelve-step program, but that didn't mean he couldn't sprinkle in a little truth with his newfound humility. Besides, watching the smile slide off the little fucker's face almost made up for missing an opportunity to chew Rapp's ass.

Almost.

"No need to be rude," Volkov huffed. "I'm here voluntarily and at considerable risk."

"Wrong," Hurley growled. "You're here because that was our deal. Smuggling you out of East Berlin was one of my greatest tactical accomplishments. Persuading the agency's seventh floor to turn you loose with a bank account full of money and no minders was my biggest political achievement. If you recall, there was a condition to our deal—if I ever came to you for assistance, you would help with no questions asked. Sound familiar?"

"*Da.*"

"Good. Then let's stop with the bullshit. You're here because I bought and paid for you twenty years ago."

Volkov smiled, revealing a familiar gap between his front two teeth. While there was no telling where the Russian had spent the millions Stan had funneled to his offshore accounts, it had certainly not been on dental work.

"This is the Stan Hurley I remember," Volkov said. "I will of course aid your efforts in any way I can. There is just the slight issue of compensation. I had a thriving business that took years to build in Bizerte. After the messiness of our exit, I'm afraid I won't be welcome back anytime soon."

"Messiness?" Stan said.

"Your friend didn't just kill a Russian team. He slaughtered them in broad daylight and left their bodies for the locals to find on one of the port's busiest streets. And he used me as his distraction. I'm afraid my time in Tunisia is at an end."

Hurley wasn't sure what annoyed him more—the mournful way in which Volkov voiced the last sentence or that when he looked to Rapp for confirmation, the assassin merely shrugged. If this conversation dragged on for too much longer, he was going to have to trade his coffee for something stronger.

Like heroin.

"Three million," Hurley said, "and two more as a success fee."

"Very generous, but there's the matter of my legend. I'm afraid that my emergency clean passport is no longer so clean. If I could trouble you for a half a dozen more aliases, I—"

"Three," Hurley said. "Two of your country of choice, but the third has to be German."

"*Ja.* That will work nicely."

"Fan-freaking-tastic," Hurley said, his words dripping with sarcasm. "Now, if there are no more contractual issues to discuss, how about we get down to—"

An electronic warble interrupted him. Rapp reached into his pocket and withdrew a cell phone. Hurley gave the kid his best scowl, but Rapp ignored him as he answered the call and held the phone to his ear.

"*Allo?*"

Rapp stared at the table for a beat as he listened. Then his black orbs found Stan.

"It's Greta."

CHAPTER 43

HURLEY digested the news his protégée had just relayed in silence.

Up until this moment, Rapp had only experienced the physical hardship that came with his newly chosen profession. Sore muscles from long hours of physical conditioning, bruises that were the by-products of combative sessions on the mats, and the like. He'd even weathered the type of damage that could be life-ending in the form of a gunshot wound to his shoulder, but he'd yet to navigate the type of pain that time never really healed.

The pain of relationships ending.

Hurley couldn't hear Greta's end of the conversation, but he could see thunderclouds forming on Rapp's features. Hurley had given up on marriage after multiple attempts, and he didn't even try to count the non-matrimonial relationships that had gone up in flames. This job was an unforgiving mistress—a truth Rapp might be about to learn firsthand.

"Hang on," Rapp said as he stood. Holding the phone against his chest, he turned to Hurley. "Bedroom?"

"Down the hall," Hurley said, pointing to the right. "She okay?"

Rapp gave a curt nod as he brought the cell back to his ear. "Run me through that once more." The assassin continued to voice encouraging sounds as he headed for one of the flat's two bedrooms.

"My, my, my," Volkov said, "intelligence work has changed since I've been out of the game. I didn't realize the new generation took calls from home while working in the field."

Hurley shot the Russian a surly glance, but didn't bother to correct his assumption. The less the former KGB officer knew about Rapp's personal life, the better.

Besides, Volkov wasn't wrong.

Each of the women who'd held the title of Mrs. Hurley had known he'd worked for the CIA—attempting to hide your employer from your spouse was a fool's errand—but none of his ex-wives knew what he actually did for the agency. With each, he'd used some version of the story that he worked in an administrative role. One of the legions of paper pushers for whom employment at Langley wasn't all that different from laboring at any other federal bureaucracy. Even then, he'd never taken a call from home while on the job. Instead, he'd directed his wives to use an answering service set up for this very purpose. The idea of fielding a call from a significant other while sitting in a safe house in a foreign nation was preposterous.

But here they were.

"I appreciate the relationship tips," Hurley said, reaching for the pack of cigarettes in his shirt pocket, "but maybe you should sit this one out." He shook out one for himself, lit it, and then slid the pack and Zippo across the table to the Russian.

"That was uncalled-for," Volkov said. "I appreciate what you did for me in Berlin, but there's no cause to rub my face in it." His accent thickened as it always did when he was angry, but he still accepted Hurley's peace offering. Snaring a cigarette, he placed it in his mouth and lit the end in one practiced motion. Snapping the silver lighter shut, he inhaled and then blew a sweet-smelling cloud toward the ceiling. "I'd quit this disgusting habit, you know."

Stan did know.

That was the point.

Volkov loved the Indonesian *kretek*-style clove cigarettes for reasons that probably had more to do with their scarcity than their flavor. For a nation that had ostensibly been consumed with seeking a communal egalitarian existence for its citizens, the old Soviet guard had certainly enjoyed flaunting their inequality. The cigarettes were nearly impossible to get except through black-market channels, and the KGB officer had smoked them incessantly.

As would any good intelligence officer, Hurley had used this eccentricity to his advantage by presenting the Russian with hard-to-find brands of the foul cigarettes each time they met. Besides engendering a bit of goodwill, Hurley had also been conditioning his asset to associate the flavored death sticks with providing information to his CIA handler. By lighting up, Volkov had just signaled that he was once more on the clock.

Time to get to work.

"I'm not rubbing your face in it," Hurley said. "You said you'd handle Stefanie, and you did. I'm just reminding you that getting caught in an East Germany honeytrap almost cost you your life. I helped you then. You'll help me now."

Volkov's pinched forehead and narrowed eyes suggested that the Russian had more to say on the matter, but instead of speaking, he took another draw from the cigarette. To this day, Stan didn't know whether the affair between the East German woman and her KGB lover had started innocently or had been a Stasi machination from the start. Either way, Petrov had discovered the liaison and was preparing to have Volkov arrested for his lapse in professional judgment when Stan had come to the rescue.

Volkov had responded to Stan's warning by murdering his young lover and then reporting the attempted Stasi orchestrated honeytrap to Petrov and their joint boss, Mikhail Ivanov. Thoroughly impressed by Volkov's ruthless practicality, Ivanov had promoted Volkov on the spot, effectively ending Petrov's attempt to sideline his deputy. When Stefanie's body was found floating in the Spree the next day, the Stasi learned a very important lesson—running intelligence operations against their KGB patrons wouldn't end well.

Stan thought there was a second lesson to be learned as well: Love and espionage do not mix. He fervently hoped that this wasn't a truism his assassin would find out the hard way.

"What do you need?" Volkov said.

Hurley took a final pull from his cigarette and then dropped the butt into his coffee cup. He was all about building rapport, but the cloying film that now coated his tongue made him want to vomit. How the Russian could smoke *kreteks* by the pack was beyond him. "I paid a visit to one of our mutual acquaintances. Muller—remember him?"

Volkov ashed his cigarette into Hurley's cup. "Of course I remember Hans. How is my former Stasi friend?"

"Dead."

Hans Muller, along with Felix Bauer, Carl Ohlmeyer, and Volkov himself, had been a member of Hurley's East German spy ring—the Boys from Berlin. Muller and Volkov had both been intelligence officers, while Ohlmeyer and Bauer were bankers. Now Muller and Bauer were dead and Volkov and Ohlmeyer were on the run.

It didn't take a genius to connect the dots.

Someone was settling old scores.

The Russian paused with the cigarette halfway to his mouth. Foul-smelling smoke spiraled toward the ceiling in gray wisps. "How?"

"Officially, he fell down his apartment's stairs two days ago."

"Unofficially?"

"His German apartment building has no stairs."

The cigarette hissed as Volkov added his butt to Stan's cup. The Russian's face was blank. The face of a master spy. The face of a man who knew nothing about recruiting a Stasi officer named Hans Muller before turning him over to be run by hotshot CIA handler Stan Hurley.

His trembling index finger said otherwise.

"Who?"

Hurley shrugged. "Not sure. My visit wasn't in an official capacity, so I couldn't formally ask my contacts in the BND or BKA about Muller's death."

Volkov shook his head. "Our Deutsch friends don't have much of an appetite for Cold War intrigue. I'm not sure Germany's foreign intelligence service and national police force agree on much, but in this instance, I'd be willing to bet that they'd both concur your Stasi asset died of natural causes."

"Might be a tough sell, since his head was bashed in with a blunt object, but you're mostly right. I still have a friend or two in the newspaper business, but even they couldn't get anything out of the police."

"They're likely not any more interested in getting to the bottom of what really happened than their uniformed countrymen. Germany was reunified less than a handful of years ago. Digging up stories about East German misdeeds is a bit like lifting up a rock only to discover a coiled viper. Some things are best left in the past." Volkov brushed an imaginary piece of lint from his shirt. Then he looked back to Hurley. "Who killed my friend, Stan?"

Hurley's fingers itched for another cigarette, but he didn't reach for the pack. While he'd welcome another nicotine hit, enduring the sickly-sweet smoke wasn't worth it. "Ohlmeyer gets a package with Felix Bauer's head inside, our best former Stasi asset takes a long fall down a nonexistent staircase, and a Russian kill team pays a visit to your retirement home. Who do you suppose might be the common denominator between these otherwise completely unrelated events?"

"Grigoriy Petrov."

"That wasn't so hard now, was it?"

Petrov had been responsible for recruiting and running CIA officer Alexander Hughes while Hughes had been assigned to the Berlin Operations Base. When the opportunity to recruit Volkov, Petrov's deputy, had fallen into his lap, Hurley had jumped at the chance to return the favor. Volkov had recruited Stasi officer Muller, who in turn had flipped

Bauer, an East German banker who helped the Stasi finance operations against West Germany.

And just like that, the Boys from Berlin had been up and running.

While Hurley's East German espionage cell hadn't been able to bring back the dead assets that Hughes's treachery had exposed, their invaluable reporting went a long way toward evening the score. Best of all, Hurley successfully exfiltrated all three of his assets from behind the Iron Curtain before the Stasi or KGB discovered the spy ring. In a rarity for the clandestine world, the Boys from Berlin had escaped their dangerous exploits unscathed.

Until now.

"Why is Petrov doing this after twenty years?" Volkov said.

"My guess is that he's been planning his retribution for a long time," Stan said. "Maybe he watched the coup against Gorbachev fail and learned a few lessons. Maybe he thinks the new Russian president is a drunk who won't notice if he starts knocking off a couple of former Cold War adversaries. I don't have a fucking clue, but you're going to help me find out."

The Russian looked at Stan as if he'd lost his mind. "You can't be serious."

"Of course I'm serious. You're about to pay a visit to a couple of your former KGB friends here in Vienna. Then you're going to politely ask them what the fuck Petrov is thinking."

"They will kill me."

"Nah," Stan said. "This is Vienna. Nobody kills anyone in Vienna."

"The KGB killed a defector here in 1975."

"Shit, that was almost twenty years ago. Besides, you won't be meeting them alone. Rapp and I will protect you. And in case you hadn't noticed, Rapp's pretty damn good in a fight."

"I'm leaving."

Stan turned to see Rapp standing in the hallway with his backpack slung over his shoulder and the cell phone pressed against his chest.

CHAPTER 44

Y ou're what?" Stan said.

"Leaving. Greta needs me."

"What the fuck?"

Rapp flushing with embarrassment was something Hurley never imagined he'd see, but the expression was gone a heartbeat later, replaced by the clenched jaw and drawn eyebrows he knew too well. "Something's off with her bodyguards. I'm going to get her."

"Is she in danger?"

"She thinks so."

"Do you?"

"Here's what I think," Rapp said. "Somehow, the Russian team in Barcelona knew I would be at the airport. They were also able to track my phone. I think the penetration is on Ohlmeyer's end. I know he hired outside help to protect Greta. He's a good banker, but that doesn't mean he knows shit about mercenaries."

"That still sounds kind of thin."

"I'm going to get her."

Rapp spoke with a finality that brooked no argument, but Stan still got up from the table and interposed himself between his assassin and the door. Rapp didn't try to push past, but violence radiated from the kid like heat from a potbelly stove.

"The job is here," Stan said.

"There is no job. Nothing about this is sanctioned by Irene or Stansfield. Greta's life was threatened, so I asked for your help. You sent me to retrieve Volkov. I did. Now the situation has changed. Whatever Cold War bullshit you guys are reliving is not my problem. When everything went sideways in Paris, I was laid up in a fleabag hotel with a bullet wound in my shoulder. Greta showed up, no questions asked. Now I'm doing the same for her. Once I know she's safe, I'll check in with you."

Left unsaid was the reason why Rapp reached out to Greta after Paris instead of his CIA mentor, Stan, or handler, Irene. Rapp had nearly been killed because the Paris operation had been compromised, and Stan was responsible for the mishap. He knew he'd fucked things up with Rapp. Badly. Were he in the assassin's place, he wouldn't trust anyone from the agency any farther than he could throw them.

But he wasn't in Rapp's place.

As much as the kid didn't believe or was pretending not to see it, this wasn't just Cold War intrigue. Petrov was still a high-ranking member of the Russian intelligence service. While Stan hadn't sussed out the threads of Petrov's spiderweb yet, he recognized the hallmarks of an intelligence operation when he saw one. The Russian certainly wasn't above personal vendettas, but a former KGB officer of Petrov's stature thought bigger than petty score-settling. The Russian's actions had been blatant. Petrov wanted his American counterparts to know that he was moving pieces around the chessboard. Stan could only guess at the Russian's motivation, but he was certain about one thing.

Something big was coming down the pike.

The key to discovering that something lay in Moscow. True, eliminating Petrov and potentially Hughes wasn't a sanctioned Orion mission, but that was just semantics. When the full scope of Petrov's meddling was discovered, Irene and Stansfield would be clamoring for someone to put a bullet in the former KGB officer's head.

Surely he could make Rapp see this.

"Listen," Stan said, placing his palm flat against Rapp's chest, "I know how you feel, I—"

"You don't have a fucking clue how I feel."

Stan felt Rapp's pectoral muscles tense beneath his fingers. "No? You think I've never been betrayed? Or had to choose between my personal and professional lives? I have multiple ex-wives, and too many former lovers to count. Good women who would have made great life partners had I been in another business. I'm not in another business and neither are you. This is the job."

Rapp slapped his hand away. "There's more to me than just this job. I'm not you."

And with that, the future of the Orion program walked out the door.

CHAPTER 45

I can talk now," Rapp said, putting his cell back to his ear after he'd shut the safe house's door.

"That didn't sound good," Greta said.

"Just work stuff, darling. Tell me again why you're worried."

"You know that feeling you said I'd get? The one where my subconscious is trying to tell me I'm in trouble? I'm getting it."

Greta sounded calm.

Dispassionate.

Like she was complaining about freeway traffic on her drive home from the office rather than the true purpose of her call.

Men who might be trying to kill her.

"Where are you?" Rapp said.

The moment he asked this question, Rapp knew everything would have to change. The protection afforded Greta by his ignorance would be gone. There could be no continuing his Russian adventures with Stan until the situation with Greta was sorted.

He didn't care.

He'd been powerless to stop the men who'd killed Mary.

He wasn't powerless now.

"Zurich. In the mountains just outside the city limits."

He'd guessed as much. Carl Ohlmeyer might be a fantastic banker, but he wasn't a spy. The impulse to keep Greta close would have been almost impossible to ignore.

"Are you currently in danger?"

Rapp hustled down the steps leading to the street. The safe house was in a rougher part of town. This was great for maintaining the operational privacy that came with staying off the beaten path, but a bit more problematic when it came to hailing a cab.

"No. Or at least not yet. I spend most of my time indoors and our food gets delivered, but something feels . . . off. A tension among my bodyguards that wasn't there before. The team quiets down whenever I'm around, but I've heard them arguing more and more frequently. Something's not right."

Rapp angled west, away from the dingy apartment building and toward a park he'd seen while completing a surveillance detection route, or SDR, on the way to the safe house. While Reumannplatz was still a far cry from Martyrs' Square in Beirut, there was no denying the grittier feel to the neighborhood. Graffiti tags covered the concrete barriers denoting the entrance to the U-Bahn and pedestrians gave wide berth to the clusters of angry-looking men clumped at street intersections. Three such men detached themselves from where they'd been leaning against a bus shelter's glass walls and headed toward him.

"What changed to make you call?"

Greta sighed. "It's too quiet. Before, I could always hear the off-duty men joking or teasing each other. You know?"

Rapp did know. He'd spent a disproportionate amount of his teenage years and early twenties in locker rooms or riding on team buses. Men, especially the types of men drawn to physically demanding sports and vocations, liked to bust each other's balls.

"When did the quiet begin?" Rapp said.

"About an hour ago. We're at a little estate in the country. My grandfather's had the property for years. There's a guest wing with its own kitchen and bedrooms and that's where the security detail members go when they're off duty. I didn't sleep much last night, so I was in the kitchen preparing coffee during their shift change brief. While I couldn't make out their words, I did hear the conversation's tenor. Something had them on edge and they couldn't agree on how to handle it."

Rapp stopped walking. The three rough-looking men increased their pace, positioning themselves between him and the park.

"How long ago was this meeting?" Rapp said.

"Thirty minutes or so. They always check in with me after shift change, so I didn't get a chance to call until now."

"Can you get outside unnoticed?"

"I think so. My room's on the second floor, but it's a short drop to the ground. I used to sneak out as a child. There's a village with a pub just a short hike down the mountain."

"Do it. Pick up a new phone at the village and call me. Is there somewhere you can go? Somewhere public that no one would think to look?"

The men fanned out with coordinated movements, cutting off potential escape routes unless Rapp decided to retreat.

He wasn't much on retreating.

"Umm . . . yes. I can call a taxi once I get my new phone. There's a hostel in Rheinfall, about twenty miles to the north. My friends and I used to go there when we were in high school. It has a café that's usually full of backpackers and students."

Were the situation not so dire, Rapp might have pursued this revelation in more depth. Sneaking out of her grandfather's estate for clandestine visits to the village pub and slumming with university students at a hostel. Neither of these was an activity he would have associated with his girlfriend.

But the situation was dire.

The biggest of the trio stared at Rapp with hard eyes as his shoulders bunched.

"Go now," Rapp said. "Call me once you're safely out of the woods."

"Okay. Are you all right?"

"Fine, darling. I'm heading to the airport now. I'll pick you up in Rheinfall in four or five hours. I love you."

"I love you too."

Greta ended the call.

The biggest of the three men flicked open a knife.

CHAPTER 46

GIVE me your money."

Or at least that's what Rapp assumed the hood said. Words aside, the tough's body language spoke volumes. As did his folding blade.

"Not today," Rapp replied.

He responded in Arabic.

This was not lost on the would-be robber.

Though the knife was just as tightly clenched in his right hand, the hood's scornful expression lost some of its certainty. To blend in with his European counterparts, Rapp was wearing slacks and a button-down shirt. But upon closer examination, his dark complexion didn't match the Germanic stock common to this Austrian city. Sure, this was a rougher part of town, but a mugging attempt in broad daylight at a busy intersection suggested that what was happening was more shake-down than violent crime. Rapp's gut told him that the thugs were opportunistic scavengers looking to prey upon well-heeled Viennese who take a wrong turn.

Hyenas rather than lions.

Unslinging his backpack, Rapp tossed the satchel at the knifeman. The bundle smacked into the man's chest. He reflexively grabbed at the nylon strap with his left hand while cupping the bottom with his right.

Rapp followed the backpack's flight path.

Without breaking stride, he launched a vicious uppercut with his right elbow while pinning the knife arm against the hood's chest with his left hand. Elbow connected with jaw in a satisfying crunch.

The mugger crumpled.

Rapp stripped away the blade in one fluid movement. Then he stomped on the prone man's wrist. The bones crunched. Spinning, he dropped into a knife fighter's crouch and faced the remaining toughs. "Are we done?"

Again, the question was asked in Arabic.

Again, Rapp's choice in languages seemed to register.

Or maybe it was the sight of their comrade splayed across the concrete moaning through the blood streaming from his broken jaw while cradling his wrist. Both men raised their hands palms facing upward and backed away. Slowly. Rapp gave each a hard glare. Then he picked up his backpack, slipped it over his shoulders, and continued on his way.

The men did not follow.

A hundred yards and a world apart from the earlier violence, Rapp emerged from the alley and found himself at the park. Forgoing the first two cabs idling at the curb, he opened the back door to the third and climbed inside.

"Aéroport, s'il vous plaît."

If the cabdriver was at all irritated that his new passenger had broken protocol by ignoring the line of cabs, the wad of schillings Rapp pushed across the divider seemed to do the trick. The Volvo accelerated in a smooth purr as the cabbie studiously ignored the angry gestures and shouts from the drivers lounging outside the first two cars. Rapp had found that a liberal enough application of currency could smooth over most misunderstandings.

"You're bleeding, monsieur."

"*Merci*," Rapp, said noticing the splotch of crimson on his elbow. "I took a fall back there."

The cabbie nodded, but his grim expression suggested that Rapp wasn't the first passenger who had emerged from the Reumannplatz after experiencing a fall. All the better. He preferred to remain unnoticed. The cabbie passed back a stack of napkins, and Rapp padded his elbow dry.

The blood wasn't his.

This time.

CHAPTER 47

W HO are you and where is Duane?"
Irene was no stranger to hostile receptions. CIA officers were thieves charged with stealing another nation's most closely guarded secrets. On the rare occasions when she traveled without a legend, no one was happy to see her. From the extra attention she received from customs workers, to side glances from police officers, to aggressive surveillance teams manned by counterintelligence operatives, Irene was accustomed to frosty introductions.

She just wasn't used to receiving them from fellow Americans.

"Good afternoon, Mr. Ambassador," Irene said. "My name is Dr. Irene Kennedy and I'm with the Central Intelligence Agency."

"I know who employs you. What I don't know is what you've done with Duane Patterson. Where is he?"

Irene sighed.

Unlike many of her fellow spies, Irene understood the need for diplomats, and she respected their place in the world. Because her father operated under State Department cover, she'd grown up as part of the extended diplomatic family. She knew firsthand the dedication of her nation's foreign service officers and their tireless efforts, but that did not mean she saw eye to eye with her counterparts. At their core, diplomats wanted to smooth out differences between the US and their foreign hosts, while the activities of CIA officers often incited tensions, especially when espionage operations went south and the American ambassador was left holding the bag.

In Moscow, a good many operations had gone south.

"Mr. Patterson was unexpectedly recalled to Langley."

"You mean fired. I don't pretend to understand how you people make decisions, but this is an asinine move if I ever saw one. One of your officer's wives is still in a Russian jail, the chief of station and his deputy were both PNG'd, and now you show up and fire the third in command? Seems to me this shitstorm calls for a little continuity while we ride out the squall rather than throwing more leaders off the boat."

And that in the nutshell was the underlying difference between her organization and the ambassador's. He wanted peace and stability and was willing to compromise operationally in order to get it. She wanted to conduct an intelligence action against her nation's adversary and intended to make use of the chaos to camouflage her activity. If the ambassador thought the road was bumpy now, wait till he heard what she was here to propose.

"Sir, I appreciate your concern for Miss Henrik. Acting Director Stansfield has asked me to personally relay his thanks for your work lobbying the Russians to release her." Irene wanted to add that those efforts, while well-intentioned, had proven to be wholly ineffective. Too often diplomats fell into the trap of confusing diplomacy for results. Talk was well and good, but if those feverish meetings didn't translate into tangible outcomes, the dialogue was just hot air. But out of respect for the ambassador, she didn't say that. Despite his less-than-welcoming introduction, she was hoping they could still work together. "As for Mr. Patterson, I won't speak for the acting director, but I'd be happy to set up a call with Thomas Stansfield if you'd like to voice your concerns personally."

The ambassador smashed his fist down onto his desk, startling Irene and sending a wave of coffee cresting over the lip of his mug. "You don't get it, do you? I'm trying to prevent the situation with your officer's wife from becoming an international incident at the same time I'm navigating rising tensions between Russia and one of its former Soviet republics. I've got a meeting with the Russian foreign minister in two hours to try to unfuck the damage your blown operation has done, and my phone is ringing off the hook. Apparently, Miss Henrik's father is a bigwig in Minnesota politics and now every Gopher State elected official from the governor on down has called to offer their thoughts. I'm waiting for the local PTA to get in on the act."

The ambassador reached for a napkin and began to mop up the spill. "All of that I can handle. It's part of the job. What I can't handle is dealing with more fallout from busted CIA operations. I know you have a mission. I'm just asking that you refrain from doing it until we get the issue with Miss Henrik resolved. Does that sound reasonable?"

It did sound reasonable.

It was also completely untenable.

"I understand, sir," Irene said.

"Good," the ambassador said as the red hue faded from his cheeks. "Welcome to Moscow. I hope you get to see some of the city."

"Me too," Irene said as she shook the ambassador's hand before getting to her feet, "but I'll probably be too busy."

That was a lie.

Irene intended to see a great deal of the city.

CHAPTER 48

SIR, Irene is on the phone for you."

Thomas Stansfield closed the folder on his desk before acknowledging his assistant.

The cover sheet glared back at him, adorned with a combination of abbreviations in capital letters meant to announce its classification level. In theory, there were fewer places on the planet more secure than the office of the acting director of the Central Intelligence Agency.

In theory.

In practice, classified operations had begun to unravel with startling alacrity. That the majority of these operations involved Russian assets seemed to suggest that the security breach was localized to the CIA's Near East, or NE, Division, but that was scant comfort to the agents who'd embarked on one-way trips to Lubyanka Square or the agency handlers who'd lost them. Only after ensuring that the paperwork was properly shrouded did Stansfield look up.

"Thank you, Meg. Please put her through."

"Yes, sir."

Stansfield was a spy and so he approached the penetration from a spy's perspective. It did not escape his notice that many of his agency's most prized recruitments had been low-level functionaries with access to vital information. People who worked adjacent to the real decision-makers.

People like Meg.

Stansfield had known his assistant for almost two decades. While not on the level of his relationship with Irene, he felt a familial affection for the mother of two. Meg was not his adopted daughter, but she could have been a much younger sister or perhaps a favorite niece. He no more suspected Meg of passing secrets to the Russians than he did his own wife.

Which was exactly why she would be perfect for the job.

With a sigh, Stansfield made a mental note to ask the agency's counterintelligence division to refresh Meg's background investigation. This was what it truly meant to live as a spy—questioning a twenty-year friendship because the leak had to be coming from somewhere.

One of the two phones resting on Stansfield's spotless desk trilled. The red phone. He reached for the handset a bit too eagerly, just as much because he was anxious for an update from Irene as he was relieved to have an excuse to abandon the dark path his thoughts had been traveling. It would rend his soul if counterintelligence found cause to believe Meg was a Russian asset, but part of him would feel relieved. Until the source of the burnt operations was discovered, the hemorrhaging would continue.

Hemorrhaging and dead agents.

"Irene?"

"Good day, sir."

Whether this was actually the case remained to be seen.

His counterpart at MI6, Rollie Smith, had forwarded him the CCTV footage of the shooting in London. While Irene still hadn't heard from Rapp, Stansfield was now reasonably certain the assassin was not the newest member of the Orion team. On the not-so-positive side of things, someone had leaked Youssef bin Muhammad's name from the

Orion's supposedly secret kill list, the Senate Select Committee on Intelligence had formerly requested that he return to testify a second time, and the wife of one of his CIA officers was still in a Russian jail. This was not a banner day to be the acting director of the Central Intelligence Agency. Even so, he refused to allow his pessimism to infect his interaction with Irene. Things weren't good at the moment, but as a veteran of World War II, Stansfield had a unique perspective on what was truly bad.

"How is Moscow Station?"

"I apologize for jumping straight to the chase, but I've sent a rather urgent cable. I'd appreciate it if you could read it and respond as soon as you are able, sir."

Stansfield frowned as he read between the lines.

That she was speaking to him on the red phone meant that she was calling him from the secure bubble deep within the CIA's annex inside the embassy. Her words would be scrambled at her handset and then further encrypted before they were transmitted. The same was true for his side of the conversation. Even if the Russians somehow intercepted the coded signal by hacking into a landline, it would take the equivalent of the entirety of Fort Meade's supercomputers working around the clock for a solid year to break the encryption protocols. Short of her standing in the room with him, this was the most secure voice communication available on the planet.

Knowing all this, Irene still refused to divulge specifics. Stansfield was equal parts intrigued and terrified. Either she'd stumbled onto intelligence of monumental importance, or she had reason to believe that the most secure voice communication in existence was no longer secure.

"Understood," Stansfield said. "You'll have my response within the hour. Anything else?"

"Actually, yes. As you suspected, morale here is . . . poor. I'm instituting changes as we speak, but there is one item that is severely affecting my team's performance. I could use your help with it."

"If you're referring to Miss Henrik's detention, I share your frustration, but the secretary of state has convinced the president to give him the opportunity to resolve this diplomatically. I have argued for a harder tack against the Russians, but I'm afraid my counsel doesn't hold much weight at the moment."

This was putting the situation mildly.

A more accurate assessment would be to say that with the current uprising in Congress and anger from the Brits, the president was reassessing Stansfield's value to his administration. Reassessing it on what felt like an hourly basis. Even though Stansfield had nothing to do with Cooke and the French debacle, politics was politics. If throwing his candidate for DCI overboard was what it took to calm the partisan storm, Stansfield had no doubt that he would soon find himself treading water. He didn't voice this to Irene, because he knew he didn't have to. His mentee was also very skilled at reading between the lines.

"Yes, sir. I understand, but my request goes beyond just Kris Henrik's well-being. As you know, fully half of my case officers have spouses and family members residing in Moscow with them."

"And they're afraid that theirs might be next," Stansfield said, shaking his head. "I should have seen this coming. How bad is it?"

"Bad. The station is effectively paralyzed."

Stansfield's gaze lingered on the single personal item displayed on his otherwise sanitary desk.

A family photograph.

Stansfield was a husband, a parent, and now, to his wife's great delight, a doting grandparent. Without question, his lifetime of service had taken a toll on his family. Between holidays missed, birthdays absent, and too many sporting or school events unattended to count, his children and wife knew what it was like to share him with the unforgiving mistress that was the Central Intelligence Agency. Even when he was home, his thoughts were often far away, and while his family never suffered physical or emotional abuse at his hands, there was no question that the decades of conflict had changed him. In any honest reckoning of his adult life, his wife and children had paid an outsize price for his service.

But what would he have done if they'd ever been threatened directly?

"I understand your concern."

"Thank you, sir. You'll understand it even better after you read my cable."

Stansfield felt his heart accelerate.

Irene was on to something.

Something that required her entire team of case officers to execute, not just the ones in Moscow without family members. Though the intelligence service and the military were completely different animals, the organizations did share much in common. While part of the OSS, Stansfield had worked with Resistance cells manned with partisans as young as twelve and as old as eighty. Sometimes entire families were involved in the fight. On more than one occasion, he'd seen the handiwork of the German SS in the form of men, women, and even children lined up against a wall and shot. It was within his writ to order the intelligence officers of Moscow Station into the field regardless of the threat to their families.

He would not.

"I will take care of this, Irene. You have my word."

"Thank you, sir. Please send a reply to my cable as soon as you're able. I'll be preparing things on this end."

"Will do. Godspeed, Irene."

"Thank you, sir."

As the secure call ended, Stansfield realized he'd been wrong earlier. Most of his family was ensconced in America safely out of reach of the Russian menace.

Most, but not all.

After saying a quick prayer for his surrogate daughter, he considered how to proceed. The president was a good man, but also a politician. A politician fighting for his job. While Stansfield couldn't rule out going to him for help before this disaster was resolved, it was too soon to do so now. This was a problem best handled internally, but the solution he had in mind required a certain delicacy.

Federal law enforcement was the most obvious answer, but Stansfield thought this might prove to be counterproductive. He needed an entity with the requisite authorities for what he was thinking, but without the nation's top cops' penchant for flashy press conferences, presided over by serious-looking Special Agents in Charge eyeing their next promotion to assistant director. No, Stansfield required an entity comfortable with playing for keeps while staying away from flashbulbs and television cameras.

Unlocking and then opening a desk drawer, Stansfield withdrew a leather-bound address book. Spies might be famous for their memories, but his wasn't quite in the same shape it had been fifty years earlier when he'd memorized entire radio cyphers before parachuting into Nazi-occupied France. The address book had been a gift from his wife when he'd officially joined the CIA shortly after its inception. She'd joked that it was the last time she expected to see it because Stansfield would fill its pages with secret names and numbers. This wasn't far from the truth. While the multiple pencil-annotated entries weren't classified per se, the information was sensitive. The book had never left his office, and Stansfield didn't expect it ever would.

The first page contained an abbreviated organizational chart of the governmental agencies and bureaus Stansfield most often had cause to communicate with. The names annotated in his distinctive hand beneath each agency had changed many times over the years, as had the numbers, but for the most part the departments had stayed the same. People came and went, but governmental bureaucracy was forever. Stansfield slid his neatly trimmed fingernail past the Secret Service, continuing down the page in search of greener pastures. He still wasn't sure exactly what he was looking for, but he felt confident that he'd know it when he saw it.

Three entries from the bottom of the page he did just that.

Reaching for his secure phone, Stansfield punched in a series of digits and then waited for the call to go through. On the third ring, someone answered.

"Commissioner Fay speaking."

"Bill, this is Thomas Stansfield over at CIA. How are you today?"

"Director Stansfield? This is a surprise. How can I help you?"

"First off, just 'Thomas' is fine. I'm not officially director yet and may never be, but I'm quite certain the Thomas thing is going to stick. No one wants to cross swords with my mother."

The answering chuckle sounded convincing if hesitant. Bill Fay had a critical, albeit unglorious, role in the federal government. The average American had probably never heard of the commissioner and likely never would, unless Bill failed to do his very important job. Then everyone would know his name. But important job or not, Commissioner Fay did not regularly receive calls from the director of the CIA.

Even if that person was only the acting director.

"No disrespect to your mother, but I sincerely hope your nomination sails through, Thomas. Regardless of what those fools in Congress are saying, your agency is vital to our national security, and the men and women who work thanklessly from the shadows deserve the kind of leadership I know you would provide."

Thomas Stansfield was not a man overly given to sentiment.

If offered the opportunity to choose differently, he would still have volunteered to serve the nation he loved as an OSS operative, but that service had not come without cost. As with many men of his generation, he'd entered combat barely a man and he'd returned from Europe old beyond his years. While he hadn't landed on the beaches of Normandy or nearly frozen to death during the Battle of the Bulge, Stansfield's version of the war had been no less horrible. Though his targets were soldiers, his fellow partisans were not. Early on he'd had to learn to steel his emotions or else risk coming undone. Fifty years later, he was not a man easily moved to tears, but Fay's comment stirred something deep within him. Perhaps it was because in a town so consumed with superficiality in the name of career advancement, the commissioner's praise was genuine. Fay had nothing to gain by voicing his support and everything to lose if his comments were made public. This, more than anything else, confirmed that Stansfield had called the right man.

"I very much appreciate that, Bill. You've been at this a long time, and I'm grateful for your trust."

"Absolutely. Now, what can I do for you?"

"I need your help with a delicate situation that must be handled with the utmost of discretion."

"Hmm. That's one hell of a lead-in, Thomas. Is this the kind of situation that has the potential to get me jailed or fired?"

"Jailed? No. Fired? If it goes right, potentially. If it goes wrong, certainly."

A raspy chuckle echoed from the phone. "For a spy, you're pretty honest. I take back what I said earlier—you might not have a future at the agency after all."

Static filled the line for several seconds, leading Stansfield to wonder if the connection had somehow severed. Then Fay's voice returned.

"Sorry about that. I had to close my office door. Sometimes the walls have ears. Too damn many of the next generation think they're in government service to star in Bob Woodward's next book. Pisses me off. Now, tell me what you need."

Prior to making this call, Stansfield had been wrestling with how much to tell Fay. While the commissioner had an excellent reputation, Stansfield knew him only slightly. He had decided to hold back some of the pertinent information both in the name of operational security and to provide Fay with protection in the form of deniability if this blew up in their faces.

Now he felt differently.

Fay would be putting his career and reputation on the line based on the say-so of a man he barely knew.

He deserved to know why.

"Here's the situation," Stansfield said before relaying everything that had happened in Moscow with a handful of terse sentences. He left nothing out. Fay needed to make his decision with a clear-eyed view of both the risks and the potential reward. The commissioner listened without interrupting, then Stansfield asked if he had any questions.

He voiced one.

"So lemme guess, you want me to send a message?"

"Just so. A message that will be impossible to misunderstand."

"I can see why you think this might get me fired."

"If this is too big of an ask, I understand. I just—"

"Holy hell, Thomas. I didn't say I wouldn't do it, I just said it would probably get me fired. Of course I'll help. I just need to get some things in order so that whoever replaces me can hit the ground running. When do you need this done?"

Stansfield smiled. Men like Fay were the reason his cohort had been labeled the Greatest Generation. "Immediately would be great."

"Then you'd better buckle up. This flight's about to get bumpy."

CHAPTER 49

SORRY I'm late," Irene said, shutting the yellow submarine's door. "The ambassador was running behind."

A series of guarded looks were exchanged between the six men and four women gathered around the yellow submarine's simple conference table. Irene was no mind reader, but she'd spent enough time running agents to be able to make a pretty educated guess at what her fellow case officers were feeling.

Relief.

"How did it go with the ambassador?"

The question came from a man seated to her right. Irene matched his angular face with the picture in the personnel files she'd hurriedly reviewed on the flight over. "It's Jason, right?"

"Yes, sorry. Jason Bailey. I've been at Moscow Station the longest, so I have the most experience weathering the ambassador's storms."

Irene frowned at his choice of words. She found it interesting that Jason touted his experience with regard to the ambassador rather than his familiarity with the Russians that the CIA officers were here to target.

"Yes, well, while I appreciate that, I'm not concerned about the ambassador."

Another flurry of looks. Irene watched dispassionately, genuinely curious who would step into the breach next. She caught Elysia's eye, and the pretty brunette gave her a half smile. Something that more resembled an apology than encouragement.

How had this station drifted so far off course?

"Um, just to be clear, I'm assuming we're no longer pursuing the volunteer from the note, correct? The Russian staff officer?"

Jason again. Irene wasn't sure if he was the group's spokesman because of his seniority or because he was the chief pot stirrer. Either way, she intended to keep him close.

"Why would you think that?" Irene said.

She'd debated asking how Jason knew what had been said during a private conversation between her and the ambassador, but didn't. Embassies were notoriously gossipy, and the ambassador had made a performance of her dressing-down. No doubt the story of him pounding his desk in the face of the acting CIA station chief had spread like wildfire before she'd even left his office.

Besides, good spies should want to snoop.

Now she just had to hope that the men and women in the conference room with her were committed to gathering more than just gossip.

"Because the ambassador—"

"The ambassador does not run this station. I do. A Russian intelligence officer expressed his intention to provide vital information to stop a potential war in Latvia. Unless the president himself tells me otherwise, we are going to collect that information. Any other questions?"

Irene looked at each of her officers rather than focusing on Jason. This was partly because she wanted to allow him to save face and partly because if her assessment had been incorrect and he was just the spokesman and not the resident troublemaker, she didn't want to alienate a potential ally. But more than that, she needed the case officers gathered around the table to internalize the reality that the days of playing it safe were over.

"Just one—Kris Henrik is still in a Russian prison, correct?"

Jason again.

Her first impression was definitely correct.

"The ambassador and his team are working tirelessly on this issue," Irene said, "but yes, Miss Henrik is still detained."

"That's what I thought," Jason said with a somber expression. "Look, everyone in this room knew the risks when we signed up for this job. We accepted them. Our families did not. Maybe we should hunker down until Kris has been released. Or bring our spouses and kids onto the embassy grounds until this blows over."

Irene nodded.

What Jason was proposing was infinitely reasonable.

It was also completely wrong.

The Russian counterintelligence officers were some of the best in the world and this was their backyard. Even absent those advantages, only the most incompetent of spycatchers would miss the significance of the embassy staff's families suddenly relocating. As soon as vehicles full of women and children started rolling through the mission's gates, the FSK would know what was up. Every asset was precious, but the man who'd surreptitiously dropped a note in an American's car wasn't just another asset. The opportunity to recruit someone at his level came along once in a career. Even without the trouble brewing in Latvia, she would have put much on the line to meet with him.

Given their current circumstances, Irene was willing to go all in.

"Moving dependents onto embassy grounds would tip our hand to the Russians," Irene said. "We can't run that risk, but I'm also not discounting the danger to your family. We're going to run an operation to link up with this Russian, but we won't use anyone's spouse for the meet the way Kris was used. Good?"

"What if the Russians don't see the distinction. What if they decide to detain another spouse, or God forbid, a child? What then?"

"Then the Russians will have made a critical mistake. There are rules to the way this game is played."

Jason snorted. "Not from where I'm sitting. Kris Henrik is in a cell, and her husband is back in DC. If there are rules, the Russians haven't suffered any consequences for breaking them."

Irene looked from Jason to the row of clocks mounted along the wall above their heads. Her gaze lingered on the one labeled WASHING-TON, DC before shifting back to Jason. "That was true earlier today. It will not be true by the time we execute our operation to link up with the volunteer. The Russians are about to receive a very unambiguous message. There will be no more American spouses taken into custody."

"How—"

"How isn't important, Jason," Irene said, interrupting the case officer. "You expressed your concerns, and I addressed them. That part of the conversation is over. Understood?"

Judging by the set of his jaw, Jason did not think the conversation was over, but he gave a curt nod. Not an apology accompanied by a promise to be a team player, but she would take what she could get. Moscow Station was undermanned as it was. She really couldn't afford to bench any more of her players, no matter how much they might deserve it.

"Good," Irene said. "Then let's get to it. I need to know each of your heat states. Please tell the group whether or not you are currently under surveillance. If you are, for how long. If you're not, then give us the last time you did have watchers. Elysia, let's start with you."

CHAPTER 50

D AMIEN Lipovsky loved his job.

Or to be more precise, Damien loved his job while stationed in the United States. The Ministry of Foreign Affairs, or MID, like its American Department of State counterpart could be a thankless mistress. For every posting to London there were ten missions located in backwater third-world countries of dubious strategic importance to the Russian Federation or its predecessor, the Soviet Union. As a young, single man, Damien had found the assignments to the African subcontinent or Southeast Asia full of adventure and possibilities.

Now, as a middle-aged, married father of three, he thought them considerably less so. In his fourth decade of life, his taste in adventures ran more toward exquisite restaurants, fine symphonies, engaging theater, and good schools for his children. He was also partial to cities in which the electricity ran uninterrupted twenty-four hours a day and which one could navigate streets free of protesters or criminal gangs. In this regard, his posting as the deputy chief of mission to Washington, DC, did not disappoint.

Mostly.

Crime in the District had recently catapulted the city to the top of a rather undesirable list—murder capital of the United States. While none of the mission's personnel had experienced this scourge firsthand, Damien had seen the writing on the wall and instituted several administrative changes. Most of these changes had been made with an eye toward making his staff feel more secure.

Most, but not all.

As the second-highest-ranking Russian diplomat in America, and the person who oversaw the majority of the mission's day-to-day functions, Damien's position warranted a driver. Normally, this function was filled by a low-level MID employee.

Normally.

But after the crack cocaine–fueled murder epidemic surfaced in the form of a triple homicide just blocks from the embassy's Wisconsin Avenue address, Damien had instituted a switch. His new driver, Bogdan, was a former paratrooper on loan from the SVR. Bogdan's almost two-meter height and nearly one-hundred-kilogram mass made for a ready deterrent whenever Damien found himself in a less desirable section of the District.

Fortunately, today was not one of those days.

"When do you think we'll be done, darling? I have an engagement later today."

Damien stifled a sigh.

If he'd grown to appreciate the finer things in life, his wife, Irina, had begun to feel entitled to them. His promotion to deputy chief of mission had come with a slew of social obligations. As per the norm, the ambassador handled the glitziest of engagements, but Washington, DC, was a nexus for foreign governments, as the almost two hundred missions located within its confines could attest. A diplomatic event of some sort or another occurred almost every day of the week and Irina had become something of a regular fixture on the tony streets of Embassy Row. His wife spoke English, Russian, French, and German fluently, had a vivacious personality that was the life of any party, and looked stunning in an evening dress. She was a much-sought-after invitee for boozy brunches, cozy coffees, afternoon teas, and the ever-important formal dinner.

Today was no exception.

"The museum is magnificent," Damien said. "Truly one of the greatest of its kind in the world. Our visit will last several hours. Minimum."

Irina sniffed.

Loudly.

Damien didn't care.

The Smithsonian's National Air and Space Museum was the ultimate experience for an aviation buff like Damien. Until his vision had taken a turn for the worse as a university student, he'd planned on serving as a pilot in the Soviet air force. Though his dreams of streaking through the sky at the controls of a MiG-29 had long since faded, he still loved aviation in all its forms and had been planning a visit for weeks.

Irina would deal with it.

"Look on the bright side. We won't have to wait in line."

Irina tossed her golden curls in response, but Damien knew the reaction was just for show. She loved the pomp and circumstance that came with her role as wife to the second-most-important man in her nation's most important diplomatic mission. While they were entering the museum via the Independence Avenue doors used by the general public, nothing else about their grand arrival was usual.

Bogdan had dropped them curbside just feet from the museum's glass façade before sliding the black Lincoln Town Car into a makeshift and highly illegal parking spot on the opposite side of the street. Damien's staff had of course called ahead with his visit request, and so the chief curator, the head of the visitor services team, and the museum director were all waiting in a tight cluster next to the facility's open doors.

As a rule, the people who called Washington home weren't overly impressed with the plethora of black limousines, security details, or VIPs who frequented it. The same couldn't be said of the visitors who flocked to the nation's capital hoping to catch a glimpse of powerful politicians or heads of state in the same manner in which a tourist in Los Angeles looked for a movie star behind every pair of glittering sunglasses.

Knowing Irina as he did, Damien had timed their arrival to coincide with one of the museum's busiest periods, and he wasn't disappointed. The line of patrons waiting for visitor passes snaked down the sidewalk. Murmurs accompanied their appearance. Irina flashed the tourists a high-wattage smile and added a touch of sway to her walk as she played to her impromptu audience. She was dressed in a formfitting cocktail dress and heels in anticipation of whatever *engagement* she'd slotted into her busy social calendar for later. Hardly typical museum-going attire, but Irina wasn't a typical museumgoer, and she wanted everyone to know it.

As they drew even with the crowd, a middle-aged woman stepped from the visitor line. Irina's smile widened, no doubt anticipating the interaction. Photographs from her many social appearances often found their way into the lifestyle sections of the local papers. She was approached by admirers on a regular basis and had been asked for her autograph numerous times. Even people who didn't know who she was could sense that there was something special about the exotic woman dressed in the latest fashions. As he'd told his wife more than once, Irina would have made an excellent diplomat.

"Excuse me," the woman said, "but aren't you the Russian ambassador's wife?"

Irina laughed and the sound echoed down the street like tingling bells. "No, my husband is the deputy chief of mission, but I'm delighted to meet you."

Damien knew she wasn't exaggerating. Irina really was delighted to be recognized even if the woman had confused her title. The ambassador's wife was a troll of a woman with a perpetually sour expression.

No one ever remembered her name.

Irina had offered her hand for the customary American shake. It didn't happen. Instead, the woman's features hardened.

"You Russians should be ashamed of yourselves. You're holding an American diplomat's wife hostage. Maybe you should go home."

The murmurs Damien had assumed were the typical fawning that normally greeted Irina took on a more ominous tone as individual words became recognizable. *Russians*, *thugs*, and *kidnappers* all made an appearance. Irina's smile faded, replaced by a look of puzzlement. She genuinely couldn't understand why the Americans weren't happy to see her.

Damien did.

"Come, darling," Damien said, grabbing her by the hand. "Let's go inside."

"No," the woman said, planting herself in Damien's path. "I think you should go home."

"Go home, Russkie!" someone shouted.

"Get the fuck out of here."

"Russkie, go home."

"Free Kris."

"Free Kris!"

"FREE KRIS!"

Where the earlier exclamations had come from the visitor line with the randomness of exploding popcorn kernels, the *free Kris* began to gather momentum as the crowd coalesced around the single phrase. Damien interposed himself between his wife and the visitor line as he felt the energy shift. He knew Americans were angry about the decision to detain the CIA officer's wife, but he'd thought it had been the abstract kind of anger expressed by talking heads and journalists. Something manufactured by DC's political class, but not anything the average citizen paid much attention to.

He'd been wrong.

The sharp *crack* of a slamming car door cut through the crowd's chants. Turning, Damien saw Bogdan sprinting toward them. The former paratrooper bowled over a demonstrator standing in his way without breaking stride. Catching Irina by the waist, Damien steered her toward the charging paratrooper, thankful he'd insisted on a change to his driver. The crowd was restless, but they weren't stupid. No one would dare stand against the refrigerator-sized bodyguard whose mallet-shaped hands were already clenched into fists.

No one but the three police officers who suddenly appeared on the sidewalk.

"Excuse, are you Mr. Damien Lipovsky?"

"Yes, and this is my wife," Damien said. "If you could help us to our car, I would appreciate it."

The presence of the uniformed officers seemed to mollify the crowd. The *Free Kris* chants continued, but the sense of menace dissipated. The hard looks and angry expressions remained, but the patrons moved back into a rough approximation of their original queue.

Crisis averted.

"Otyebis ot menya!"

Or perhaps not.

Damien turned to see a second set of police officers between him and an enraged Bogdan. They probably didn't understand the Russian curse, but they certainly seemed to comprehend the paratrooper's state of mind. The biggest of the three officers had his arm outstretched, palm up in the universal gesture for *stop*, while his partner was fingering the Taser holstered at his belt.

"Bogdan—calm," Damien said in Russian. "These men are here to help."

The former paratrooper could be forgiven for not understanding. In Russia, the sight of government officials, uniformed or otherwise, was rarely cause for relief.

"Thank you for verifying your identification," the officer closest to Damien said. "Now if you'd please come with me."

In rapid succession, Damien realized several unsettling facts. One, the policeman speaking with him wore a different uniform than the trio corralling Bogdan. Rather than identifying him as a District of Columbia police officer, the man's uniform featured three letters.

Three unsettling letters.

I-N-S, which Damien knew stood for Immigration and Naturalization Service.

Two, rather than shepherd him and his wife left toward their waiting Lincoln Town Car, the men were angling right. Right toward where an unmarked sedan sat idling.

"I am a member of the Russian Federation's consulate, and I don't intend to go anywhere with you," Damien said, standing his ground. "I have diplomatic immunity."

"Of course you do," the officer said with a smile, "but I wasn't talking to you. The questions I have are for your wife."

"What questions?" Damien said.

"Routine ones, I'm sure. We noticed several irregularities on her visa paperwork. I'm certain she'll be able to clear them up in an hour or so."

Damien put his arm around Irina's shoulders. "She's not going anywhere."

The officer continued to smile, but as he leaned closer, Damien realized that the gesture was at odds with his cold, hard eyes. "Listen up, you Russkie son of a bitch. Your wife is coming with us. She can walk over to that car or be carried. Doesn't make a bit of difference to me. If you, or your ape, try to interfere, you'll both be facedown on the concrete quicker than you can blink. Got it?"

Damien did get it.

All too well.

"Darling," he said to Irina in Russian, "go with them. I'll be with you shortly."

Irina's face was a mask of rage, but to her credit, she merely nodded. Like all Russians, she was no stranger to the secret police.

"Great choice," the officer said, pitching his voice so it would carry. "I'm sure this is all just a big misunderstanding. Just like the situation with Kris Henrik."

CHAPTER 51

ONCE again, Irene Kennedy found herself sitting alone in the yellow submarine massaging her temples. While the room's meager three hundred square feet had felt homey when she first began to work in the space, she would now use a different word to describe her feelings.

Claustrophobic.

To be fair, this adjective might better describe her state of mind than her surroundings. The meeting with her clandestine team had not gone well. Between legitimate concerns about their individual heat states, worry about family members still in Russia, the drain on morale driven by Kris Henrik's continued imprisonment, and the operational churn that had resulted from the almost one hundred percent leadership turnover in the last couple of days, Moscow Station's contingent of case officers was not in a great headspace. Irene had serious doubts about her team's ability to pass the Farm's final training exercise at the moment, to say nothing of working a complex approach to a high-level Russian intelligence officer in a denied-access environment.

But her team's shortcomings were only part of the problem.

Despite Stansfield's confidence in her, Irene was less than ten years out of the Farm herself. She had never held a senior leadership role at any of the CIA's overseas bases or stations, and she was not a Russia hand. She was woefully unprepared for the position in which she found herself and perhaps one bad decision away from igniting a full-fledged mutiny among her staff. As each of her case officers had explained why their heat state with respect to the Russian counterintelligence officers charged with surveilling them would not allow them to conduct a linkup with the Russian volunteer, Irene felt her spirits free-fall. Stansfield had sent her here to provide direction and guidance to the single station that might just be able to unravel whatever Russia was planning in Latvia before the European continent plunged into war. Instead, she felt like she was standing on the bridge of the *Titanic* as the ship slid beneath the Atlantic's icy waters.

"Irene? You have a call."

Irene looked up to see Elysia standing in the doorway.

The woman had become her de facto aide and though her help was invaluable, Irene was now worried that such proximity to a failing leader might tarnish the young case by association. Pushing the dispiriting thought aside, Irene forced her lips into a smile.

She could almost hear Stansfield's fatherly tone.

One problem at a time, Irene.

One problem at a time.

"Thank you, Elysia. Who's on the line?"

"Not sure. It's a secure call from the embassy in Vienna, so the initial handoff was just from their communications team to ours. I can route the call here if you'd like."

"That would be great."

Elysia nodded and left, shutting the door behind her.

After Moscow, Vienna Station was probably the second-most-important posting in Europe. Vienna had long been a crossroads for espionage, as reflected by its nickname "City of Spies." In her admittedly limited experience, secure calls from one CIA station to another rarely heralded good news. After clearing her throat and mind, Irene activated the secure speakerphone.

"This is Irene."

"Irene, it's Stan."

She had never been happier to hear the familiar, gravelly basso. Hurley's voice felt like home.

"Stan—it's good to hear from you."

"Likewise. Sorry that it's taken so long to return your call to the message service. In answer to your question, I am one hundred percent certain Rapp had nothing to do with the London shooting."

The euphoria that had accompanied hearing a friend's voice faded as the reality of the situation began to register. Stan Hurley was calling her from the CIA station in Vienna. Chances were, he wasn't phoning to discuss the schnitzel. "How do you know?"

"Because he was with me."

"In Vienna?"

"It's a long story."

It was.

For the next ten minutes, Irene listened with minimal interruptions as an operative who was at least nominally supposed to be under her supervision regaled her with tales of the unsanctioned operations he and another member of her Orion team had undertaken. She almost stopped Stan to clarify that she'd heard correctly when he mentioned in passing that Rapp had eliminated an entire Russian direct-action team in Bizerte.

Almost.

As Hurley himself had taught her long ago, don't ask the question if you don't want to know the answer. Be that as it may, there were still some questions she had to ask whether she wanted to know the answers or not.

"I think I understand where you've been, but I'm still not clear as to why you're in Vienna with a former KGB officer turned defector."

"Shit, sorry. That's the best part. Volkov's come out of retirement to help us crawl into Petrov's head."

Irene frowned. "I get that Volkov was once Petrov's deputy and that the men continued to work closely until Volkov defected, but that was, what, twenty years ago? I'm not certain how much insight your former asset can provide into Petrov's thinking today."

"Volkov said the same thing. That's why we're in Vienna. Outside of Washington, DC, this city has the largest contingent of Russian intelligence officers abroad. It's by far the most important espionage-related city in Europe. I told Volkov to drop in on some of his former coworkers."

Irene stared at the speakerphone as if the inanimate device could provide context to Stan's answer. He wanted to use a defector to strike up a conversation with current Russian intelligence officers? Surely she'd misheard. "I think using Volkov to spot and assess potential SVR officers for us to target is fantastic out-of-the-box thinking, but we don't have weeks or months to go through the recruiting process. We need answers now."

"Agreed," Hurley said. "That's why I told Volkov to think unconventionally."

Irene felt her headache return with a vengeance. The words *Stan Hurley* and *conventional* did not belong in the same sentence. If the man whose default setting was to play fast and loose wanted someone to think unconventionally, she could only imagine what chaos might ensue. "What exactly does that mean, Stan?"

"It's like this. I'm betting Petrov has gotten out over his skis and he's making his contemporaries nervous."

Irene stopped massaging her temples. "Why do you say that?"

"Gut feeling backed up by a couple of facts."

"Start with the facts."

Hurley laughed. "You never did think much of my gut. Okay, stick with me. The effort to oust Gorbachev was, what, two years ago? The coup had the backing of the KGB's leadership and the army along with a whole bunch of Communist Party bigwigs, but it still failed. When push came to shove, the KGB's and Soviet military's rank-and-file members refused to follow their orders to storm the Russian parliament building. After the dust settled, the coup's leaders were imprisoned or executed, the KGB broken apart, and the Soviet Union dissolved."

"I'm with you so far."

"Great, because that takes us to today. Russia is no longer a communist totalitarian state, but it's not a bastion of democracy either. Corruption has run rampant, many former KGB officers have become instant oligarchs, and Russia's first democratically elected president begins his day with a vodka and orange juice and switches to straight vodka by lunch. Things are not going well for the Motherland."

"And you think what—Petrov is mounting another coup?"

Hurley sighed. "I think that some of the same people who stopped the coup against Gorbachev a couple of years back might have buyer's remorse. Look, Petrov has always been a mover and shaker. Had the coup not happened, he'd probably be running the KGB today. But it did, and the KGB was split in half. Petrov is one of the leaders of the FSK and now works the counterintelligence mission. Foreign intelligence collection is handled by the SVR, meaning that the Russians in Vienna don't work for Petrov and may not be on board with whatever the hell he's doing."

"You think Volkov might be able to open a back channel to the SVR?"

"We're flying blind, Irene. We missed the coup against Gorbachev and dodged a bullet when it wasn't successful. We got lucky once. We shouldn't count on getting lucky twice."

Irene agreed. She glanced at the clock that displayed Moscow time in uncompromising red LED digits. Only a few hours until nightfall and her opportunity to signal the Russian volunteer. Now was the time to throw everything at the wall and hope that something stuck. "This plan of yours, it's not without significant risk to Volkov."

"I know. So does he. We've already come to a financial agreement. I'm going to provide security for him during his meets, but like you said, the sense of urgency doesn't allow for finesse. Things might get rough."

Irene refrained from pointing out that Stan Hurley had never been known for his finesse. Instead, she focused on what was actually transpiring in this conversation. Only weeks ago, Hurley had all but questioned her fitness to be Rapp's handler. Now he was coming to her for approval when he could have just run the operation without her knowledge. Stan Hurley might really be turning over a new leaf.

Or maybe the world was about to end.

"Thank you for letting me know, Stan. I think your reasoning is solid and your plan, while risky, is worth the potential reward. I'm working something here too. Hopefully between the two of us, we'll get answers for Stansfield."

"Count on it, Irene. Good hunting."

"Good hunting, Stan."

Only Stan could give her a kick in the ass by being nice. Her team of case officers were certain that they were compromised by FSK watchers. That might be true, or it might be that the men and women under her charge had been badly rattled and were now jumping at shadows. One way or another, they were about to find out.

Moscow Station was done sitting on the sidelines.

CHAPTER 52

"WHAT was your guy thinking?"

Zeke Williams let the question hang in the air as he poured himself another helping. He wasn't normally big on traditional martinis, but the Texas version was quite the rage at the Lone Star State–themed Davy's Tavern.

"My guy?"

Zeke pointed at his dinner companion with his newly filled martini glass as he answered. "Stansfield is your guy, right? You told me the rank-and-file officers loved him, and that my boss should help him over the finish line. We made the rounds with the right senators and teed up the committee hearing expecting him to hit a home run. Instead he struck out on national television. Is he the right guy or not?"

The man seated across the table from Zeke leaned forward, his margarita still untouched.

This was a good sign.

Though the restaurant was one of the District's hottest eateries,

Zeke paid a sizable monthly tab to ensure that his table was always available. Tucked away in a dark corner far from the bar, restrooms, and exit, this space served as an office, entertainment venue, and, when necessary, confessional.

If his dinner guest felt he had to whisper, the man was about to deliver a doozy.

"Stansfield is the right guy, but this thing in Moscow caught everyone flat-footed. Nobody in the division has ever seen the Russians arrest an American spouse."

Division was short for the Near East Division, a CIA directorate responsible for several geographical regions across Europe and South Asia. Max Powers was the division chief and the man joining Zeke for cocktails, Jeremy Olson, was Max's deputy.

Zeke paused with the martini halfway to his mouth before setting the drink back on the white linen tablecloth. "We're friends, so I'm going to be blunt—what kind of shit-show operation are you guys running? You're the Central Intelligence Agency. Nothing is supposed to catch you flat-footed. Here's the deal: Stansfield has to go back in front of that Senate Select Committee before his nomination gets a full vote. If you want my boss's help getting some of the Senate fence-sitters to find their courage, you're gonna have to give me something. Something that shows your guy isn't just rolling over for the Russians."

"Come on, Zeke. You know I can't—"

"Jeremy, stop. My boss and I both have clearances. You know that. Hell, I just finished my five-year poly. I would never ask you to divulge anything secret, especially here of all places. Just give me something to whisper into the ears of your two most problematic senators. Remember—this is all pro bono. You aren't my client and I'm not your lobbyist. I'm just a patriot who wants to ensure that the right man gets to sit in the seventh floor's corner office."

Jeremy eyed him for a long moment, his fingers drumming out a staccato beat on the table. Zeke waited without speaking, allowing his argument and impassioned expression to do the work for him.

Everything he'd just communicated was true.

After a fashion.

"Here's what I can say," Jeremy said, his voice barely a whisper. "We have not rolled over for the Russians. Stansfield has hand-selected an interim chief of station, and she's about to do something big. Hopefully Stansfield will be able to report the results of her operation to the committee in the SCIF prior to his open hearing, but if not, you can take this as gospel—the Russkies are about to get their asses handed to them by Moscow Station."

Jeremy looked across the table expectantly.

Zeke sighed.

Loudly.

"I hear you, but this is you and me talking. In my business, your word is your currency. I can't go back with whispers of something big only to have whatever it is you're working on self-destruct on the launchpad again. Are you sure about this?"

"Positive," Jeremy said. "It's going to happen in the next twenty-four hours. You won't hear about it on the news, but the classified cables from Moscow Station will bear me out. I'll do what I can to get the Senate Select Committee on Intelligence a redacted version of the operational summary before Stansfield testifies. Barring that, I'll see if there's a morsel or two I can throw your way. This is big, Zeke. Maybe the biggest thing to come out of Russia in years."

Zeke held Jeremy's earnest gaze for a beat.

Then he slowly nodded.

"Okay," Zeke said, holding up his hand, "Okay. I don't need details. My boss has been working this town for fifteen years. He has a back pocket full of IOUs, and we're prepared to cash them all in for Stansfield. Sorry to cut our cocktail hour short, but I need to start working the phones."

"No apology necessary," Jeremy said with a smile. "We're grateful for your help."

Zeke waved to the waiter to let him know they were done and then got to his feet.

He did need to start working the phones.

Just not the ones Jeremy expected.

CHAPTER 53

ZEKE Williams put his car in park and dashed into the convenience store.

The overcast skies had finally delivered on their threat, and rain was coming down in fat droplets. Nodding to the man behind the register, Zeke walked to the back of the establishment, where he pulled a six-pack of beer from the refrigerated display. After bundling the beer under his arm, he turned to the true purpose of his visit.

A wall-mounted pay phone.

Zeke tucked the handset between his shoulder and cheek, slipped a quarter into the coin slot, and dialed a local number.

The phone rang four times.

On the fifth, someone answered.

"Eddie's Dry Cleaning."

The speaker sounded American.

He was not.

"Yes," Zeke said, "I was calling to see if my suit and tie were ready?"

"Name?"

"Brad Smith."

"Just a minute, Mr. Smith. Lemme check."

Zeke turned toward the front of the store. The man behind the register had gone back to his paper. In a city that ran on leaks, there was nothing particularly unusual about a well-dressed man ducking into a gas station to use a pay phone.

At least that's what Zeke hoped.

"Okay, sir, I've got your slip right here. You can pick up any time after five tonight."

"Great, thank you."

Zeke hung up the phone, paid for the beer, and ran back to his car.

The rain was coming down harder now, which made his job more difficult. Difficult, but not impossible. Ideally, he would wait a day or two before making the drop, but the urgent nature of his conversation with Jeremy left him no choice. Moscow was eight hours ahead of DC.

The clock was ticking.

After pulling out of the gas station, Zeke shot west across the Potomac River into Virginia. He didn't have time to run a full SDR, but with DC traffic, it wasn't hard to fake missing an exit in order to justify looping back onto the highway to check if he was being followed. Eventually his travels brought him to Quincy Street in Arlington and the Central Library. Ducking inside, he asked for and was quickly granted permission to use one of the public internet terminals.

After taking his seat in a worn plastic chair, Zeke opened up an internet browser. Then he launched the computer's word-processing software. In simple, concise language, he transcribed his conversation with Jeremy. Then he reviewed the document for accuracy and printed the single page. Closing out both the browser and the word processor, Zeke stopped by the circulation desk to pay the dime for his printout. With a final smile for the pretty librarian, Zeke accepted the paper, ensuring he only touched the document by its bottommost edge. After exiting the library, he got behind the wheel of his BMW.

This was the point at which he felt most vulnerable.

Zeke did not consider himself a traitor.

A traitor steals secrets from his own country, and this definition did not apply to him. Though his passport said otherwise, in his heart he was a citizen of his mother's birth nation—the Soviet Union, or now Russia. As he'd affirmed to the examiner numerous times during his polygraph, Zeke had never passed information to foreign intelligence officers.

He had, however, passed information to Russian intelligence officers.

Reams of it.

Zeke wasn't a traitor, but he was a spy.

The BMW again took Zeke west, this time toward a little park in Wolf Trap, Virginia, about fourteen miles from Arlington. Though his periodic lie detector tests had never given him a problem, Zeke was not so glib about the counterintelligence capabilities of the many three-letter agencies that actively hunted people like him. He thought of himself as Russian, and planned to relocate to his homeland someday, but he was not about to trust his safety to the KGB.

Accordingly, he'd never met face-to-face with his handler, nor did he plan to do so until he was ready to leave America for good. Instead he'd volunteered to spy via letter and had insisted on dictating his contact procedures rather than allowing the KGB, now SVR, to take the initiative.

One of those procedures had been the partially drawn blinds in the row house across the street from his favorite pub. Another had been the call he'd just placed to the fictional dry cleaner. In the first instance, his Russian handler had been signaling a need for immediate information to follow up Zeke's last dump. In the second, he'd told the Russians to expect something at the dead drop tonight.

In a bit of luck, the rain had mostly stopped by the time Zeke arrived at Foxstone Park. After parking the BMW next to a paved footpath, he pulled on a pair of gloves taken from his jacket's pockets, folded the paper, and then carefully ripped away the portion containing his fingerprints. Next he folded the remaining document several more times before placing it in a Ziploc bag he'd removed from the glove box. After sealing the plastic bag, he exited the car and followed the asphalt into the trees. The footpath roughly mirrored a twisting creek, and he strolled along contentedly until he came to a small bridge that spanned the stream.

This was the moment of truth.

After confirming he was alone, Zeke left the trail and clambered beneath the bridge. Withdrawing the Ziploc bag containing the document from his jacket pocket, he checked his surroundings for watching eyes a final time and then deposited the bag under the bridge.

Fifteen minutes later, he was back in his BMW driving east.

He'd done his part.

Now it was up to his countrymen to do theirs.

CHAPTER 54

FOUR hours later, Rapp pulled to a stop on Zentralstrasse.

All in all, he hadn't made bad time. There were several flights between Vienna and Zurich each day and the transit took only a little over ninety minutes. After arriving in Zurich, Rapp had secured a rental car and hit the road. He would have made it to Rheinfall sooner but for the need to visit one of his safe-deposit boxes. In addition to the cash, passport, and documents that Ohlmeyer had provided when the banker had originally set up the box, Rapp had added something more germane to his line of work.

A loaded Glock and two spare magazines.

The comforting feel of a pistol in his waistband and magazines in his pockets did much to improve his state of mind. As did the town of Rheinfall. The charming Swiss city looked as if it had been lifted from the pages of a travel guide. The town was full of quiet parks, cafés, and shops. The streets were clean and multiple scenic overlooks provided opportunities for hikers to catch their breath while watching the Rhine River flow lazily by. It was the sort of place that attracted bohemian backpackers and sophisticated holiday-seekers in equal number.

Rapp was neither.

He was debating whether to try his luck with the Autobahnpolizei by parking illegally or circle the block in search of a *Parkplatz* when the decision was made for him. No sooner had he pulled even with the row of chairs marking the hostel's café than the front door opened and Greta bounded out. Rapp shifted the transmission into park and exited the vehicle.

The Swiss beauty jumped into his arms.

"I missed you," Greta said.

"Me too," Rapp said, pulling her tight.

She felt . . . wonderful.

The press of her tight body against his chest was certainly pleasant enough, but his sense of satisfaction was more than just sexual. Her hair smelled of lavender and her skin like vanilla. The warmth of her breath tickled his skin and the touch of her nose against his neck sent a jolt of electricity arcing through his nervous system, but the whole of her was greater than the sum of her parts. The weight of her presence filled the void left by her absence.

He felt . . . complete.

A two-note wolf whistle split the air, suggesting that their hug had not gone unnoticed. Looking over Greta's shoulder, Rapp spotted a group of men gathered around one of the café's outdoor tables with backpacks resting by their feet. Seeing that he had Rapp's attention, a backpacker lifted a stein in salute.

Rapp smiled.

Even dressed in an oversize sweatshirt and jeans, sans makeup, with her hair pulled back in a ponytail, Greta attracted the male eye.

"Made some friends I see?" Rapp said.

Greta snorted as she released her hug. "Boys will be boys."

Before he could reply, she threaded her fingers through his hair and then stood on her toes to kiss him full on the lips. If the touch of her nose against his throat had sent a shock through his nervous system, the feel of her mouth on his almost short-circuited it. He slid his hands down to her hips and was in the process of pulling her closer when she pressed her palm flat against his chest.

"Enough," Greta said with a chuckle from deep in her throat. "Get me out of here."

"Of course," Rapp said, the words coming out a bit more breathless than he'd have liked. "Where are we headed?"

"Home."

Thirty minutes later, Rapp was driving south on the Autobahn and was almost to Zurich.

Zurich and Greta's waiting grandfather.

After climbing into the car beside him, Greta had fastened her seat belt and promptly fallen asleep. He hadn't blamed her. Between the lack of sleep the previous night and the anxiousness and stress of today, she must have been exhausted.

But now, his sleeping beauty was stirring.

"It's so good to be with you," Greta said, stifling a yawn.

Rapp smiled. "Let's see if you still think that once we face your grandfather. How'd he take it when you ditched his security detail?"

Greta gave a faint smile. "About how you'd expect. He was upset that I didn't just call him with my concerns and angry with himself that he might have inadvertently put me in danger. He said that he would terminate their contract and hire a new security firm. I told him not to bother because you were coming for me. Problem solved."

At that, she reached over, slid her fingers through his, and squeezed.

Rapp squeezed back, but he didn't agree.

If Greta's guards had been about to do her harm, this problem was far from solved. Rapp added the topic to the long and growing list of things he intended to address with the Ohlmeyer family's patriarch once they were face-to-face.

"How are things with you and Stan?" Greta said.

"I don't think he's very happy."

Greta chuckled. "Even I know Uncle Stan better than that. If he's unhappy, you'd know."

"True, but he's in good company. No one in our lives is happy right now."

"I am." Greta kissed the back of his hand. "Are you?"

He was.

Ridiculously happy.

He'd been given a second chance. Though he'd only been twenty-one when he'd lost Mary, they'd been together since their teens. He wouldn't have been able to articulate it at that time, but when Mary died, he'd believed that the part of him that could be happy had died too. Sure, there'd been other girls after her, but no one had come close to filling the void left by her absence.

No one until Greta.

"Happier than I've ever been," Rapp said.

He'd spoken without thinking and now the heaviness of his words settled on his shoulders. He'd been truthful, but his response felt unfaithful to Mary. As if her memory were slowly drifting away as surely as the smell of her had faded from the sweatshirt she'd left in his car.

Was he really ready to finally let go of his first love?

"Hey," Greta said, her words soft, "it's okay if—"

"No," Rapp said, turning to face her, "it's not. I love you. You are the most important thing in my life. You. Not Mary's ghost and sure as hell not my job. You are what matters."

He felt the conviction in his words. Did he love his job? Yes. Did he feel like he'd been created to do it? Absolutely. And would he miss dealing out vengeance to the shitbags who had killed and maimed innocents in the name of radical Islam? Again, yes. But would he give that up if that's what it took to keep Greta?

Yes.

Most people were lucky to find true love once. Though he was only in his twenties, Rapp had discovered it twice. He hadn't had a choice with Mary. A coward had taken her from him. He wouldn't allow anything to take Greta from him.

Not even his career.

Greta's blue eyes filled with tears. She leaned over to kiss him, but a shrill sound brought her up short.

Her phone.

"*Scheisse*," Greta said, fumbling with the handset. "I gave this number to my grandfather. He's probably calling to make sure you arrived. Should I answer?"

Rapp nodded.

Greta smiled at him as she lifted the handset to her ear. "*Grüsse, Opa.*"

Rapp stared at the woman he loved.

He couldn't help it.

Greta always looked stunning, but in that moment her face was radiant.

And then it fell.

"*Was? Opa? Opa!*"

Rapp reflexively hammered the accelerator as he tightened his grip on the steering wheel. Greta took the phone from her ear and dialed.

"Put it on speaker," Rapp said.

She looked at him, nodded, and then pressed the appropriate button.

The phone call went unanswered.

Greta made to dial again, but Rapp reached over and covered his hand with hers. "What did you hear?"

The face that had been so full of life just moments ago was now drawn and pale. "He said my name and then something else."

"What?"

"Run."

CHAPTER 55

IRENE Kennedy counted up five floors on the US embassy building as she drove past. As per the Russian volunteer's instructions, a single light remained lit in the chief of station's office. The sun had set about an hour ago, and with darkness shrouding the city, the light could have been cast by a distant star rather than a simple desk lamp. Irene liked that analogy. A single star in an otherwise dark sky was cause for making a wish. As her SUV carried her west on Bolshoy Deviatinsky, Irene fervently wished for luck in tonight's operation.

Her team was going to need it.

"Ma'am, are you sure we can't talk you out of this?"

Irene smiled at the honorific.

She'd made such progress in prodding her protective detail to call her by her first name, but that headway had been lost the moment she'd proposed something crazy to her agents.

"We've been over this, Fred," Irene said. "I understand your concern, but my entire team is putting it on the line this evening. I've got to do my part."

"You're the boss, Chief," Fred Burton said from the front passenger seat.

Her driver, once again Brett Maryott, didn't say anything at all, but he did activate his right-turn signal in order to merge with the traffic on Konyushkovskaya Street.

She considered his silence a win.

Like her team of case officers, her protective detail was not big on her decision to participate in tonight's festivities. Brett completed his turn and goosed the SUV's accelerator, pressing Irene back into her seat. "We've got company."

"Confirmed," Fred said as he looked in the side-view mirror. "Our Russian friends are out tonight in force."

"Not to worry," Irene said. "I have it on good authority that the FSK will be on their best behavior."

The DSS agents' lack of response spoke volumes.

Stansfield had phoned just prior to her leaving the embassy to confirm that the Russian deputy chief of mission and his spouse were being expelled based on an issue with the spouse's visa. Since the pair hadn't been formally declared persona non grata, the interaction hadn't risen to the level of an international incident, but a message had been delivered all the same. The pair were going to be flown back to Moscow on a State Department jet, and the jet would not return to America until Kris Henrik was aboard. The CIA's Moscow Station should be free to operate this evening without fear of the employees' families bearing the repercussions for their actions.

At least that was the hope.

"Okay, ma'am," Fred said. "Four more turns and it will be your show. Ready with the jack-in-the-box?"

Irene eyed the contraption on the seat to her left. "I push the button and get out of the way, right?"

"Exactly. Just make sure you slide it into your seat before you exit the vehicle. The idea is to keep your silhouette exactly the same."

While technology had revolutionized the profession of espionage, sometimes the old ways were still best. The jack-in-the-box was a perfect example. When the activation button was depressed, a person-shaped balloon rapidly inflated, giving the impression that the seat's previous occupant was still in the car. The jack-in-the-box couldn't withstand close scrutiny, but for a mobile surveillance team trying to follow the SUV, it should do the trick.

"Two minutes," Brett said. "Your drop-off's coming up on the right, ma'am."

Irene peered into the night searching for the industrial building. Tonight was just a rehearsal, but Irene intended to go through each step as if it were the real deal short of exiting the SUV.

A moment later, the boxy structure's outline materialized.

"In sight," Irene said.

"Okay," Fred said. "Remember, if we were doing this for real, I'd want you to duck behind the bushes in front of the building and stay frozen for at least five minutes. The Russians are probably using more than one tail vehicle. After your five minutes are up, walk at a normal pace to your car. Brett and I should be able to keep them from getting close enough to determine that the jack-in-the-box is a fake for at least thirty minutes."

Irene did remember.

All of it.

This was partially because she had a photographic memory, but mostly because the plan had been hers. She still nodded anyway, as though she were committing the details Fred had just recounted to memory. Tonight's goal was twofold: One, to see if her case officer's heat state was real or the product of an overactive imagination. Two, to stretch and test the Russian surveillance team.

Though she had no way of knowing if her volunteer was still checking the embassy windows after two days of silence, Irene was acting on the assumption that she would meet with the Russian tomorrow. This meant that tonight might be her only chance to practice before she'd have to lose the FSK surveillance team for real.

The plan to do so was simple.

Her case officers had left work this evening as they normally did in ones and twos, but rather than go home to their families, the men and women began to execute SDRs that would take them across Moscow's four cardinal directions, dragging their surveillance teams with them. Though the Russians certainly had the home-field advantage, their resources were finite. Irene hoped that by forcing Russian counterintelligence operatives to pick and choose whom to follow, she would dilute the surveillance net currently ensnaring her CIA officers.

Especially the Russians assigned to watch her.

"Thirty seconds, ma'am."

Irene released her seat belt and grasped the door handle with one hand while resting the other on the jack-in-the-box. After Brett made the next turn, a multistory industrial building on the right would briefly obscure the SUV from the pursuing surveillance team. This blind spot would allow her to activate the decoy, exit her vehicle, and hide behind the hedges. Once the Russian surveillance team drove by, she would walk to the parking lot, where a car had been pre-positioned for her.

Simple.

"Okay, Irene," Brett said. "Five, four, three, two—"

Light shattered the darkness, nearly blinding her.

Irene turned toward the headlights, registering the presence of a massive truck.

Then her head connected with the passenger window accompanied by the sounds of buckling metal, squealing tires, and breaking glass.

CHAPTER 56

ZURICH, SWITZERLAND

S HOULD I call the police?" Greta said.

Rapp powered into a turn before riding the brakes as he tore through the outskirts of the village that sat just south of Ohlmeyer's estate. Like most Swiss towns, this one consisted of orderly groups of houses bordered by greenery. Even this close to Zurich, the town had an agrarian feel, with pastoral wheat fields providing a backdrop to the settlement. Rapp didn't slow in concession to the speed limit as much as he did to the reality that houses meant children and children didn't always look twice before crossing the street.

After nosing the BMW around a hairpin ninety-degree turn, he exited the village proper for the smaller back road leading to Ohlmeyer's estate. With open road to his front and rolling fields to his left and right, Rapp floored the accelerator. Though he couldn't see it yet, he knew the turnoff to the mansion was waiting just beyond the next bend.

"No," Rapp said. "We're almost there."

Greta nodded, her fingers still clutching the phone.

Though he wanted to comfort her, Rapp kept both hands on the steering wheel. Last time he'd consulted the speedometer, the needle had been north of 130 kilometers per hour and climbing. Getting to the estate as quickly as possible was important, but he would be no help to anyone if his driving put them into a farmer's field.

Or worse.

As if summoned by his thoughts, a sedan shot from the opposite side of the blind turn. Rapp jerked the wheel right. Greta screamed as the hillside filled the BMW's windshield. Rapp ran the front tire up on the edge of the embankment and gritted his teeth. He made eye contact with the sedan's driver as the vehicle flashed by and had the image of a clean-shaven man with brown hair parted to the side and piercing blue eyes.

Piercing blue *asymmetrical* eyes.

The man's right eye was opened wider than his left. Almost as if that half of his face had registered surprise while the other portion had continued with business as usual.

Then, the road was clear.

"*Mein Gott,*" Greta said. "He nearly killed us."

Rapp risked a glance in the rearview mirror, but the vehicle showed no signs of slowing. Its brake lights flashed briefly as the car approached another turn and then disappeared from sight. Then the turnoff to Ohlmeyer's estate appeared. When he'd come here with Stan, the private drive had been blocked by a reinforced gate.

Not today.

The gate was open, and the gatehouse empty.

"Oh no," Greta said, clutching the dashboard as she leaned forward to peer out the windshield. "No, no, no."

"Lock the doors behind me and stay in the car," Rapp said, unbuckling with one hand and steering with the other. "Do you hear me? Stay in the car."

If she heard him, Greta gave no indication. Instead she continued her steady monotone of *no, no, no.* Rapp powered up the long drive before slamming to a stop at the roundabout even with the mansion's imposing entrance. Though he currently resided in Switzerland, Ohlmeyer would always be German at heart. His choice of pets reflected this sentiment. During earlier visits to the estate, Rapp had become acquainted with the banker's two giant German shepherds.

One of them was sprawled in a puddle of fur across the front entrance.

"Greta," Rapp said, shaking her shoulder. "Did you hear me?"

For the first time since she'd seen the open gatehouse, his words seemed to register. Turning, Greta regarded him with tear-filled eyes.

"Stay in the car," Rapp said. "If I'm not back in five minutes, call the police and wait for them at the gatehouse. Do you understand?"

Greta slowly nodded.

"I need to hear you say it, darling. What are you going to do?"

"Stay in the car. Wait for you. Call the police."

Not perfect, but it would do.

Rapp pressed his lips against her forehead. Then he exited the BMW, closed the door, and drew the Glock from his waistband. The sound of the BMW's locks engaging gave him hope that his instructions had penetrated Greta's shock-clouded mind, but that was the extent of the good news.

Of bad news there was plenty.

Like the gatehouse, the mansion's massive oak door stood wide open.

Rapp flowed up the sidewalk, his eyes and the pistol's sights moving in tandem. The German shepherd lay motionless, sprawled on the blood-soaked ground. Its open, unblinking eyes told the story, but Rapp still crouched and touched its fur.

Warm.

Judging by the gaping exit wounds on its back, the dog had been felled by multiple gunshots. Its lips were pulled back in a snarl, revealing a set of massive teeth. The animal had gone down fighting.

Rapp angled left as he approached the door and then cleared the foyer by sliding right in increments. The maneuver was known as slicing the pie, and the slow and deliberate methodology, while effective,

was the opposite of what Rapp wanted to do. His bloodlust was screaming for him to make entry in a wave of sound and fury, but doing so
alone without the aid of flash-bangs or frag grenades was akin to suicide. Instead he finished his sweep of the foyer, peering as deeply into
the foyer's recesses as possible while trying to ignore the crimson-
stained marble tile.

Then he made entry.

Rapp buttonhooked left, both because it was his dominant side and
because most shooters were right-handed and would have chosen the
opposite direction. The pistol's Tritium night sights glowed green in the
semidarkness as Rapp swept the three orbs across the room, resting for
a moment on the two chairs and the figures tied to them before clearing
the rest. The second German shepherd was sprawled across the foyer,
its breath coming in labored, wet-sounding pants. As much as he felt for
the dog, Rapp ignored the animal in favor of the chairs.

He had immediately recognized what the open gate and empty
gatehouse signified and had spent the seconds it had taken to hurtle up
the driveway fortifying himself for what he would find in the house
proper. He thought he'd done a reasonable job.

He hadn't.

Carl Ohlmeyer and his beloved wife were each tied to a chair.
Chairs that were facing each other. The unspeakable things done to Elsa
Ohlmeyer were matched only by the look of horror on Carl's dead face.
The implication was obvious—the banker had been forced to watch as
his wife was tortured to death. The rage that had been building since
the gatehouse now threatened to burst free of the bulwarks Rapp had
erected to contain it. He wanted to scream. To rend things end to end.
To vent his anger on anything and everything within reach.

He did not.

Instead, Rapp kept his pistol oriented down the long hallway leading to the still-uncleared house while he forced himself to check Carl's
neck for a pulse. There was no need to do the same for his wife.

There wasn't much left of her neck.

Greta's grandfather was mercifully dead, but he hadn't gone easy. As with his wife, Herr Ohlmeyer had been tortured. But unlike her wounds, which served only to cause pain, his had been meant to send a message. The banker's shirt was unbuttoned and a word was carved into his bare chest. Rapp was studying the letters, trying to make sense of their unfamiliar meaning, when a footfall sounded.

From behind him.

Turning, Rapp centered the pistol on the figure framed in the doorway.

"No!"

Greta's wail was more animal than human.

She ran toward the chairs.

Rapp caught her by the torso as she tried to push past and spun her into the air. "You don't want to see this," he said, pressing her face against him. "Trust me—you don't want to see this."

He carried her outside as she sobbed against his chest, only setting her down once they reached the BMW. "Why didn't you stay in the car?"

"You had a phone call. They said it was life-or-death."

For the first time, he realized that she had his cell clutched in her hands. Prying the mobile from her fingers, he put the phone to his ear.

"Hello?"

"It's me."

The cigarette-saturated voice was instantly recognizable.

Stan Hurley.

"What?" Rapp said, his tone reflecting his anger.

"Tough day?"

"I'm at Ohlmeyer's place."

"Shit. Is it bad?"

"Just a sec." Rapp opened the passenger door and helped Greta inside. "It's Stan," he said, pointing at the phone. "I need to take this."

Her vacant stare provided no recognition that she'd heard, let alone understood, him. Rapp buckled her seat belt, kissed her forehead, and then gently closed the door. After putting some distance between himself and Greta, he held the phone back to his ear.

"Really bad," Rapp said. "Ohlmeyer and his wife are both dead. I think they tortured her and made him watch. The things they did to her make the Hezbollah thugs from Beirut look like card-carrying members of the Geneva Convention. Greta saw it before I could stop her."

"Motherfuckers. Any idea who?"

Rapp eyed the door, considering his answer. "They killed his dogs too. One of them is still dying. The other's body was warm to the touch. I think we just missed the hitters."

The image of the car that had nearly run him off the road flashed through his mind. Rapp pictured the driver. The man with the asymmetrical eyes.

"Why?"

"Why what?" Rapp said.

"Why torture them to death? That goes beyond just settling a score. Someone's trying to send a message."

"Not trying. Did. What does *Verräter* mean?"

"It's German for 'traitor.'"

"They carved it into Carl's chest."

A wind tumbled down the hillside, plastering Rapp's shirt against his torso. The doorway eased open a bit farther as if the house were inviting him back to experience the horrors a second time. Rapp had killed in anger before, but the rage coursing through his blood at that moment felt different. The atrocities visited on an aging man and his dementia-stricken wife weren't business as usual.

This was personal.

"Those motherfuckers. Volkov was right."

"Right, how?"

"Not over the phone. You and I are about to go to war."

"I already have a war," Rapp said, watching the door swing back and forth in the breeze. "I don't need another."

"It's the same fight. The shit they carved into Ohlmeyer's chest proves it. Drop Greta off at the US consulate in Zurich. I'll make sure a detail of DSS security folks and Marines from the embassy in Bern drive down to collect her and then bring her back. She'll be safe on embassy grounds until this is over."

"I'm not leaving her again."

"Kid, I know I haven't always been straight with you. I was a shitty mentor and an ungrateful son of a bitch. I realize this is a hell of a thing to ask, but I need you to stop with the questions and trust me."

Rapp felt like he was at the edge of a precipice.

Did Stan Hurley deserve his trust? There was a pretty compelling case to be made that the answer was no. Hurley had deliberately tried to wash him out of the Orion program and then assumed the worst about him when the Paris job went off the rails.

But.

But Hurley had also admitted he was wrong and green-lighted Rapp's request to kill Cooke and the double-dealing French intelligence officer. Not only that, but he'd been the getaway driver after Rapp completed the job. When Rapp had needed off-the-books help in Barcelona, Hurley had come, no questions asked. Ohlmeyer and his wife were dead, but the original threat to Greta remained. There was no reason to think that whoever had begun this killing spree was going to stop. He could protect Greta in the short term, sure, but at what cost? Was she prepared to spend the rest of her life looking over her shoulder?

The question he'd asked Volkov in Tunisia now taunted him.

Aren't you tired of running?

If Hurley was correct, there was only one way to protect the woman he loved.

But what if Stan was wrong?

"What does Irene think?" Rapp said.

A long, tired sigh echoed from the phone. "Irene isn't able to weigh in on this."

Rapp's blood ran cold. "Is she—"

"Alive? Yes. Still in the fight? No. It's just you and me, kid. Now, are you in or not?"

Rapp stared at the BMW.

He knew it was Greta sitting in the front seat, but that's not who he saw. He'd been just sixteen when Mary had upended his entire world with that first, shy smile. Some people went their entire lives without finding a soulmate. Rapp had discovered his at sixteen and then lost her at twenty-one. What was he willing to do to ensure that Greta didn't end up like Mary?

Anything.

Everything.

"What do you need?" Rapp said.

"Get to the airport and buy a ticket with a clean legend."

"Where?"

"Doha."

CHAPTER 57

As safe houses went, this one wasn't the worst Rapp had inhabited.

Neither was it the best.

The apartment complex was a blocky design with a focus on functionality rather than aesthetics. Each unit had a balcony, two bedrooms, a single bathroom, and a living area adjoining the kitchen. The furniture was plain but serviceable, the floors were clean, and the air-conditioning kept the apartment at a reasonable temperature. Club Med it was not, but indoor plumbing and a toilet that flushed put the place light-years ahead of Beirut. Funny how this was the comparison to which he always returned.

Funny, but understandable.

Beirut had been his baptism in fire.

Rapp looked from where he was lying on the apartment's sofa to the clock hanging on the wall and then to the cell phone resting on the coffee table in front of him. His sense of time and circadian rhythms were both hopelessly off. Doha was only two hours ahead of Zurich, but the sheer amount of traveling he'd done over the last several days was wearing on him. Starting with Barcelona, Doha was the sixth city he'd visited in less than a week, and if he knew Hurley, not the last.

Thinking of his mentor prompted him to check the cell for missed calls. Only two people had the new device's number, and neither was supposed to use it except for emergencies. Then again, the past couple of days had been one emergency after the other. To add insult to injury, neither Hurley nor Greta was known for following instructions. The Nokia's LCD display remained reassuringly blank, and Rapp was considering a catnap when a knock sounded at the apartment's door.

Rolling off the couch, Rapp stood as his fatigue vanished.

A length of wood that had until recently served as the handle to a rubber toilet plunger leaned against the sofa. He snagged the improvised baton and crossed the tiled floor to the apartment's door. As per Hurley's request, he'd traveled to Doha on the first available flight from Zurich using a new legend. While this had allowed him to arrive at the city most expeditiously, the rapidity of his travel meant there had been no time to arrange for Rob Ridley's advance team to preposition an operational cache with documents, money, and, most important to him at the moment, weapons. Rapp had made do with what was available, but if the person on the other side of that door wasn't Stan Hurley, the ensuing melee would be pretty one-sided.

Sidling up to the entrance, Rapp switched off the apartment's lights and positioned himself to the right of the door frame so that the door could swing open unimpeded. After waiting for the agreed-upon knock pattern to sound a second time, he unlocked the dead bolt. "It's unlocked."

The door swung open, and Stan Hurley stepped inside.

"Hey, kid," Hurley said, his eyes unerringly tracking to Rapp despite the room's dim interior. "Nice stick. Gimme a hand."

Hurley tossed a messenger bag to Rapp before closing the door behind him and locking it. He pulled a doorstop from the plastic bag in his hands, dropped it to the floor, and wedged it in place. "That's better."

"What else did you bring?" Rapp said.

"Something more suited for the job than a broom handle. Open the bag."

Rapp undid the satchel's metal buckles and dumped the contents on the coffee table. Most of what tumbled out appeared to be the makings of a new legend—passports, credit cards, pocket litter, and currency.

Most, but not all.

The two plain belts that fell onto the table seemed out of place, but Rapp wasn't fooled. Grabbing one of the lengths of leather, he twisted the buckle and pulled, revealing a matte-black three-inch blade.

"Composite material," Hurley said. "It'll pass through an X-ray machine."

Rapp turned the blade over in his hands before resheathing it. "Not bad. Are there pistols in your other bag?"

"Nope. Can't take those where we're going."

"Where's that?"

"Moscow."

Rapp felt his face flush.

The chaos of the last several hours combined with a gut-wrenching parting with Greta had thrown him for a loop. He'd completely forgotten to ask about the person who was arguably becoming the second-most-important woman in his life.

"Cut yourself some slack," Hurley said. "You've been through the wringer. Irene was in a car crash. She's banged up and has a concussion, but no bleeding on the brain. The Russian docs are keeping her in the hospital for observation, but the ambassador has already been to see her. She's in good spirits and should be discharged in a day or two, but she's sitting this one out."

"What kind of car crash?"

"The kind that happens when the FSK is trying to send you a message."

"How'd you hear?"

"I got on the horn with Stansfield to pass along Volkov's update before I left Vienna. He gave me the news."

Hurley opened the second bag, removed two liter-sized bottled waters, and gave one to Rapp. "Drink up. Air travel is dehydrating."

Rapp accepted the bottle, unscrewed the cap, and took a long pull. "Why are we going to Moscow exactly?"

"To stop a war in Europe."

CHAPTER 58

R APP had to hand it to his mentor.

Hurley never thought small.

"A war in Europe. Is that all?"

Hurley shot him a surly look. "I know this thing with Greta is hitting you hard, but you're not the only one who's pissed. Ohlmeyer was my close friend for more than twenty years. In this business, that's saying something."

Rapp wanted to respond with an equally sharp comment about the maelstrom he'd been forced to weather with Greta. In what was a surprise to no one who knew the Swiss girl, the woman he loved had been less than enthused with his decision to leave her with strangers while in the depths of grief. It hadn't helped that he was at a loss to explain why he was leaving or how it would eliminate the ongoing threat to her life. Instead, he'd asked her to trust him, given her his cell number, kissed her forehead, and left for the airport. He wanted to hold the crushed look on Greta's face against Hurley, but he knew that wasn't fair.

He'd chosen this life, just as he'd chosen to involve her in it.

Decisions had consequences.

"You said something about an update. What did Volkov learn?"

Hurley's pinched features slowly relaxed as he seemed to recognize Rapp's olive branch. "I've got to give that Russian son of a bitch credit. Once we came to an agreement on the financials, he was absolutely fearless. In the space of a couple of hours, he bumped three different SVR officers, including the Vienna resident."

"How'd that go?"

Hurley shrugged. "Some of the meetings were better than others, but he got intel from everyone. Taken in sum, his reporting helped us understand at least directionally what Petrov is thinking."

"Why would his former colleagues talk to Volkov? He's a traitor and a defector."

"That's precisely why. They knew Volkov was a direct conduit to us. Don't get me wrong, their organization might have a new name, but the SVR officers in Austria are the same KGB operatives I went head-to-head with during the Cold War. But they're also different. Or at least have chosen to be different. During the attempted coup against Gorbachev, they could have sided with the hard-liners in favor of the status quo. They didn't. Instead, they chose their country over the Communist Party."

Rapp thought this assessment might be giving the former KGB officers a bit more credit than was due, but he pushed his cynicism aside in favor of asking the most important question. "What gives with Petrov?"

Hurley fished a pack of cigarettes from his pocket and offered one to Rapp. He took it. Nothing says bury the hatchet like burning a Marlboro Red with the person who'd once wanted to kill you with his bare hands.

"He's an old man with scores to settle and dwindling time to settle them. Petrov and Stansfield have a beef that extends back to World War Two. Stansfield killed Petrov's brother."

"Holy shit."

"That about sums it up," Hurley said, exhaling a stream of smoke toward the ceiling. "But setting their personal vendetta aside, the way the Cold War ended had to have been a slap in the face to Petrov. He spent almost fifty years fighting to advance communism. Then the Soviet Union collapses, and the KGB is disbanded in the space of three months."

"I get why he hates us," Rapp said as he lit his own cigarette, "but he's felt that way for half a century. Why's he settling old scores now?"

Hurley shrugged. "No one seems to know for sure. My guess is that he saw the negative publicity around the clusterfuck that was Cooke's death as an opportunity. An opening to drive a wedge between the United States and Europe while mortally wounding the CIA in the process. And if his actions brought down his old nemesis, Stansfield, in the process, so much the better."

Rapp considered this as he took a massive drag from his cigarette. He'd dabbled with smokes just to be cool in high school, but as an athlete, he'd never been tempted to pursue the habit in earnest. This particular cigarette, however, had him second-guessing that decision. The nicotine buzz banished his fatigue and ordered his scattered thoughts.

"I hear what you're saying," Rapp said, "but Petrov is one guy. How's he doing this alone?"

"He's not. Petrov spent the majority of his KGB career assigned to Department S working as an illegal. This made him a great fit for his final KGB assignment—overseeing Directorate Five."

"The Vympel units," Rapp said.

"Exactly, though they were called Vega when the units were still part of the KGB. Anyway, they might have a new name, but their specialty hasn't changed—wet work. That's who we think you encountered in Barcelona and Tunisia. They're probably also the ones setting bombs in Latvian bars. And that shit's working, by the way. Stansfield said the first Russian military transports have already landed at the air base near Daugavpils. Anyway, one of the top Vympel assassins is a guy named Ilya Lebedev. Most Vympel units work in hunter-killer teams, but Lebedev is more of a lone wolf. Based on a tip from Volkov, we relooked at the CCTV video from Youssef bin Muhammad's assassination in London. The shooter was wearing a disguise, but we think it was Lebedev. Take a gander."

Hurley opened a false bottom in the messenger bag, withdrew a photograph, and set it on the coffee table. "This is from his personnel file. It's at least fifteen years old, but it's all we've got."

Rapp picked up the photo and swore. The rest of Lebedev's features had changed with time, but there was no mistaking his asymmetrical eyes. The assassin's right eye opened wider than his left.

"I take it you two have already met?" Hurley said.

"A car nearly ran us off the road just short of the turnoff to Ohlmeyer's estate. Lebedev was behind the wheel."

"That tracks. He's Petrov's operative of choice."

"I still don't get how Petrov's operation is unsanctioned. If the SVR officers Volkov bumped know about it, then surely the director of the FSK does too. What's his name again?"

"Barannikov." Hurley ground his cigarette butt into the coffee table before dropping it into his empty water bottle. Apparently, he wasn't worried about collecting the apartment's security deposit. "I'm not saying he didn't know about Petrov's op. I'm saying he didn't approve it. Look, there's no love lost between the FSK and SVR, so some of the reporting Volkov gathered is probably slanted, but I wouldn't be surprised if Barannikov is just watching to see what happens. If Petrov is successful, he can claim credit. If the old guy fails, he gets moved out, and Barannikov has plausible deniability."

"I don't understand. Counting Lebedev, there are at least three operational Vympel teams working for Petrov, maybe four. That's way too big of an effort for Barannikov to be able to claim plausible deniability. Either he knew about Petrov's operation and authorized it, or Petrov did this without Barannikov's knowledge, which means that the FSK director is incompetent. Where's the plausible deniability?"

"Simple. The operational Vympel teams aren't working for Mother Russia. They're freelancing."

CHAPTER 59

Rapp stared at Hurley, convinced he'd misunderstood. "Mercenaries?"

"Exactly."

"Who's paying them?"

"That's the genius part. Remember how the SVR got into trouble because of the slush fund Ivanov was running with Hezbollah shitbags?"

Of course he remembered.

The *trouble* Hurley was referencing was the impetus for Rapp's trip to Beirut and all that followed. Mikhail Ivanov had been the deputy director of Directorate S back in his KGB days, but unlike Petrov, he'd moved to the SVR when his old intelligence service had been disbanded. While in that role, he'd convinced his superiors to fund a Hezbollah terrorist cell operating in Beirut. As dirtbags were prone to do, Ivanov starting skimming money, which in turn got him into trouble, which in turn eventually got him dead.

"Let me guess," Rapp said, "not to be outdone by their sister service, the FSK also has a slush fund and Petrov runs it?"

"Yes, but it gets better. The SVR used outsiders to manage their dirty money. Sketchy banks in Switzerland, Germany, and the Caribbean. The kind of financial institutions known for accepting deposits and not asking questions. Petrov works differently. He runs his operation in-house."

Rapp looked at Hurley in disbelief. "He has his own banker?"

"Not just any banker. Florian Schmidt. He's former Stasi, but his specialty was rather unique. When most of his fellow East German intelligence officers were attempting to steal Western military and state secrets, Schmidt was focused on industrial espionage until he moved on to an even more lucrative target—West German banks."

"That was a thing?"

"It's still a thing. Think of him as Ohlmeyer's equivalent. He and Petrov worked together when Petrov was stationed in East Berlin. After the wall came down, Schmidt accepted Petrov's offer to join him in Moscow. Schmidt still works for the FSK today. Right now, his portfolio includes paying Vympel teams to run off-the-books operations against Petrov's enemies."

"This really is some *Tinker Tailor Soldier Spy* bullshit," Rapp said. "You had the Boys from Berlin in Volkov, Muller, Bauer, and Ohlmeyer. On the other side of the Iron Curtain, Petrov was working against you with Schmidt, Lebedev, and that CIA-turncoat piece of shit, Alexander Hughes. Two competing espionage cells, each manned by spies, traitors, and cutthroats."

Hurley gave a slow nod. "That was the Cold War in a nutshell, kid."

"But what about Hughes? Where does he fit?"

"I think Alexander Hughes was a distraction from the start. Does he still work for Petrov? Maybe. But a lot has changed in the CIA since he defected back in the seventies. His information has long since been exhausted. I think he was a stalking horse to distract Ohlmeyer, and by extension, Stansfield."

Rapp took a final puff from his cigarette before following Hurley's example.

The security deposit was definitely not getting returned. "Then it all points back to Petrov?"

"That's how I read things," Hurley said. "He's a pretty smart fucker, but the Latvian false-flag operation is his weakness. I'm willing to bet the Russian president doesn't have a clue that his domestic intelligence service is blowing up bars full of ethnic Russians as a pretext for an invasion. Before the FSK took her out of commission, Irene was trying to link up with a Russian volunteer. He claimed to be a high-ranking intelligence officer with information that could avert a war in Latvia. He's the key to all of this."

"And we're going to bring in the volunteer?"

"Exactly," Hurley said. "Stansfield gave me his assessment of Moscow Station. It's a shit show. The case officers are under constant surveillance and jumping at shadows. With Irene out of commission, there's no one left to take charge. We're gonna enter Russia dark, meet this volunteer, and then pass his information to Stansfield."

"That's why we're in Doha?"

"Yep. Despite the jackassery that's occurred since the KGB split into the SVR and FSK, the Russians are still the best intelligence officers in the business. We'll come in separately and link up in Moscow. My cover will be as a German businessman fresh off a meeting with his Qatari investors. Business is good and I'm thinking of expanding into Moscow."

Rapp could guess where this was headed, but he asked the question anyway. "What about me?"

Hurley upended the plastic bag, and the contents spilled across the coffee table. At first Rapp thought Hurley had brought a mophead into the apartment. Then he saw the wig tape, adhesives, and prosthetic nose. "I'm going to the party as a jihadi?"

"Not just any jihadi. You're a Hezbollah moneyman looking for new investment opportunities."

Beirut.

It always came back to Beirut.

"Sounds like a good plan, Stan. There's just one problem."

"What?"

"I'm not doing it."

CHAPTER 60

HURLEY sat frozen with the plastic bag still clenched in his hands.

Then his eyes narrowed and his jawline hardened. Turns out the old Stan Hurley was still in there somewhere.

"The fuck you say?"

"Listen," Rapp said, trying to defuse the brewing thunderstorm, "everything about your approach checks out except for one thing."

"Please," Hurley snarled. "Enlighten me."

"Your focus on the Russian volunteer. He could have the goods, or he could be a ghost. And even if he's real, and we manage to link up with him, there's no guarantee that what he considers proof of the false-flag operation will convince anyone else. Russian transports are already landing at the air force base in Lociki. Once Russian soldiers start rolling into the street, the game's up. We can't risk betting everything on the volunteer."

"I'm still waiting for the part where you tell me your plan."

"Petrov. You said it yourself—Petrov is the key to everything."

Hurley frowned. "I know that, dipshit. What are you saying—that we should have a talk with the old man?"

Rapp shook his head. "We're well past talking. We'll both go to Moscow. You meet with the volunteer. I'll kill Petrov."

Hurley opened his mouth. Shut it. Opened it again. "Look, kid, I appreciate your initiative, but I think that's a little easier said than done. Setting aside the repercussions of assassinating a high-ranking FSK officer on his home turf, this isn't an operation we can just wing. We'd need to establish a pattern of life, figure out where he lives, all the shit we don't have the time or resources to do."

"Ordinarily I'd agree, but in this case, we don't have to do any of those things. We know exactly where to find Petrov—his office."

If Stan had looked surprised before, he now seemed positively shell-shocked. "Are you fucking kidding me? You want to walk into FSK headquarters and cut Petrov's throat?"

"Not me," Rapp said, pointing at the disguise components still scattered across the coffee table, "a Hezbollah shithead looking for a new investment opportunity. I bet Petrov would love to meet with another potential contributor to his slush fund."

Hurley's jaw was still clenched, but his face no longer shouted disbelief. Instead his expression looked thoughtful. "That's not half bad, but Petrov isn't going to meet with just any jihadi. You'd need an introduction."

"Surely you've got some jihadis on the payroll," Rapp said. "Get one of them to set it up."

Hurley rubbed his chin as he stared off in the distance. "That's a good idea. I'll ask Stansfield to lean on Max Powers, the Near East Division chief. Lebanon falls within his area of responsibility. I'm sure one of his case officers has an asset that could be persuaded to reach out to Petrov on your behalf. This could actually work."

Hurley looked back at Rapp.

"It'll be hairy. Even if you pull this off, we still need to figure out the exfil and a bunch of other logistical details. Meeting with a Russian volunteer under the FSK's nose is dangerous. Waltzing into FSK headquarters to assassinate one of their senior leaders is borderline suicidal. You sure you want to try this?"

Rapp locked eyes with Hurley. "You sure Petrov had Carl and Elsa Ohlmeyer killed?"

Hurley dipped his head. "As sure as I can be."

"Then so am I."

CHAPTER 61

E LYSIA Nicolas pulled her Ford Explorer up to the service station, expertly navigating the confined space between the gas pumps and curb. Moscow, as was the case much of Europe, hadn't been constructed with American gas-guzzlers in mind. If nothing else, her parallel-parking game had taken an exponential leap forward over the last three months.

If only she could say the same thing about her espionage skills.

Stifling a yawn, Elysia put the SUV in park, unfastened her seat belt, and grabbed her purse. The Explorer's massive fuel tank was still half full, but she wasn't here just to top off. In spite of everything else that had gone wrong, the desk lamp in the chief of station's office had remained illuminated.

Now it was time to see if the price Irene had paid was worth it.

Elysia's shiver as she exited the SUV was only partially due to the morning's brisk temperatures. She hadn't learned about the chief's accident until returning to her apartment at close to midnight. Her SDR had lasted for five hours and encompassed much of the northern section of Moscow. A trip through a museum, dinner, some light shopping, and a nightcap might not have been such an unpleasant way to spend an evening had she not been continuously on the lookout for surveillance.

She'd glimpsed watchers at least once, but hadn't made any effort to shake them. The exercise's purpose had been to determine if she was being followed, and if so, stretch the FSK team assigned to keep track of her. All in all, she'd been satisfied with the way she'd worked her shadows and had come back to her flat tired, but content.

That feeling vanished the moment she'd seen her answering machine's flashing red light. The news about Irene's accident and subsequent hospitalization had been delivered in the no-nonsense, slightly bored tone of an embassy administrative worker. Someone who didn't know the fledgling chief of station and certainly didn't comprehend the significance of her hit-and-run car accident.

Elysia understood both.

After imagining the woman she'd come to admire lying alone in a hospital bed surrounded by strangers, she had rushed to the medical center to show her support. This had been a mistake. For one thing, Irene's room had been bristling with DSS agents. For another, the sight of the unconscious woman's bandages, tubes, and bloodstained clothing drove home a rather uncomfortable truth—the Russians were still playing for keeps.

Even after being assured by Irene's protective detail that the chief's injuries looked worse than they were, Elysia camped in the hospital's waiting room until 2:00 a.m., when exhaustion won out. After dragging herself home, she'd tumbled into bed and tossed and turned until her alarm sounded, unable to escape the image on her boss's broken body. But exhausted or not, nothing was going to keep her from filling up at the exclusive gas station reserved for foreign diplomats just blocks from the US embassy.

The same gas station the Russian volunteer had used to pass his initial message.

After pumping the gas, Elysia replaced the nozzle and went into the station to pay. She tried to catch a glimpse of her car in the glass door's reflection, but the early light wasn't cooperating. She wasn't much for fishing, but imagined that this is how it must feel to throw a lure into the water and hope for the best.

After handing the cashier her government credit card, Elysia poured herself a cup of coffee from the aged pot and added cream and sugar. She thought the acid might be too much for her already sour stomach, but she took a cautious sip anyway.

"Good, yes?"

The man behind the register asked his question with a wide grin, and his English, while heavily accented, was understandable. Elysia graced him with a smile she didn't feel, added a bit more cream, and took another swallow. The java wasn't any more tolerable, but that hadn't been the point.

It was hard to catch a fish if your bait didn't spend any time in the water.

"*Spasibo*," Elysia said.

The man nodded, ran her card, and then handed the plastic back across the counter. Elysia replaced it in her purse and stepped outside. The biting wind rose goose bumps on her arms. Her Explorer sat at the pump looking exactly as she'd left it. As bobbers went, the SUV was probably a bit unsuited for the job.

She crossed her arms beneath her breasts, warding off another shiver. Though traffic still meandered along Rochdelskaya Street, the gas station's parking lot was devoid of vehicles. This entire exercise had been nothing but a waste of time. Hunching her shoulders against the breeze, Elysia threw open the Explorer's door and climbed inside.

A scrap of paper lifted from the seat on invisible vortices.

With a display of hand-and-eye coordination completely out of character to her distance-runner self, Elysia snagged the paper as it tried to escape. Slamming the door closed, she started the car, fastened her seat belt, and popped the transmission into drive. She did her best not to rush these actions in case anyone was watching, but she also only had the benefit of one hand.

In no universe was she unclenching the other.

In a feat approaching magic, Elysia managed the five-minute drive to the embassy without hitting a single traffic light. The Marine guarding the vehicular entrance waved her through after a cursory check of her face. Then the security gate was closing behind her. With a breach of protocol that risked incurring lasting damage to her career, she pulled into the first available parking spot, which happened to be reserved for the ambassador. She slammed the gearshift into park before the Explorer was fully stopped, eliciting a groan in protest from the transmission. As the SUV rocked back and forth, Elysia unclenched her fist and then unfolded the paper.

It was from the volunteer.

Moscow Station was back in business.

CHAPTER 62

STAN Hurley sipped with caution.

Rochelt made some of the finest fruit brandies on the planet, and this apricot blend was no exception. The Austrian-brewed beverage also packed quite the punch, and Hurley was at the distinct disadvantage of not knowing how long he would be waiting in the hotel bar until his party arrived. He could have chosen to nurse a beer instead, but as a successful German businessman staying in one of Moscow's most prestigious hotels, that just wouldn't do. Besides, he kind of enjoyed the idea of a Langley bean counter stroking out in their cubicle after receiving the receipt for Hurley's bar tab. It wasn't often that he partook of cocktails that priced out at close to one hundred dollars per snifter.

"Would you like something to eat, *mein Herr*?"

"No, thank you," Hurley said.

The question had been delivered in Russian-accented English. Hurley answered in the same language, but his consonants reflected a harsher, Germanic influence. Even here, in the heart of the old Soviet Union, the staff at the Hotel Peking spoke English. It wasn't hard to see who had won the Cold War, but whether or not the victors could keep the peace was a different matter.

The waiter nodded and returned to the far side of the bar, leaving Hurley with his morose thoughts and his increasingly depleted brandy. The Peking was the hotel of choice for many foreign businessmen. It also had been a hotbed of KGB activity during the Cold War. Much of the staff had been paid informants and the hotel rooms were wired for sound. Now that the FSK had assumed responsibility for Russia's counterintelligence mission, this was presumably still the case. Viewed from this perspective, the Russian volunteer's request to meet at the Peking was a stroke of genius—the epitome of hiding in plain sight.

Or at least it would be if the son of a bitch ever showed up.

Hurley took another cautious sip as he wondered how much longer he could afford to let this play out. In addition to dinner and more alcohol, he'd already been offered drugs, his choice of female or male companionship, and a tour of Moscow's hottest nightclubs. The hotel bar was elegant in a distinctly Russian fashion—overstuffed red chairs trimmed in gilded gold flourishes, polished wood tables, and a sparkling marble floor.

Even so, businessmen did not stay at the Peking for the décor.

This was the place to be if you wanted to experience *all* that Moscow had to offer, and while Hurley wasn't above taking a walk on the wild side for the sake of his legend, the clock was ticking. By now Rapp was in the air bound for Moscow, and the latest update from Daugavpils suggested that the Russian forces were prepared to venture outside the wire on their first peacekeeping patrol.

The mysterious volunteer needed to get this show on the road.

Hurley let his gaze play across the mostly empty room before coming to rest on the newspaper situated next to his brandy. Before boarding his flight in Doha, he'd dialed one of the Orion program's message services for a final check-in. To his delight, instructions to meet the Russian volunteer had been waiting. In coded language, he was told the time and place to meet along with the recognition signal—a newspaper divided into two stacks with the half to his right displaying the front page. Stansfield had done as instructed, but the meet time had come and gone thirty minutes ago. Either the volunteer was a no-show, or the entire exercise had been a dangle.

Neither option boded well.

A cold breeze ruffled Hurley's pant legs.

He turned to see the bellhop holding open the hotel's door for someone. Several someones, by the sound of multiple voices speaking Russian. A moment later, a phalanx of well-dressed men barreled into view. The point of the wedge, a gentleman in his forties wearing a suit he hadn't bought in Moscow, paused to survey the bar.

His visual sweep stopped on Stan.

Then he smiled.

CHAPTER 63

THE man's smile wasn't what anyone would term pleasant.

Though the gesture was wide enough to show teeth and seemed to convey a genuine sense of merriment, Hurley wasn't fooled. On more than one occasion, his life had depended on his ability to read body language. This wasn't the smile of someone who had unexpectedly run into a friend. Instead it brought to mind a hunter who'd just discovered a rabbit in his snare.

Hurley reached for the newspaper.

He needn't have bothered.

No sooner had his fingers touched the newsprint than the hunter was standing in front of his table.

"What are you drinking?"

The question was delivered in Russian-accented English.

"Rochelt," Hurley said.

"Fine selection."

Turning over his shoulder, the man snapped his fingers and delivered an authoritative-sounding stream of Russian to the bartender. The man didn't salute, but he might as well have. His earlier languid mannerisms were a thing of the past, replaced with a precise economy of motion that would have been at home on a military parade field. He poured the brandy but was intercepted before he could bring over the drink. Instead, one of the Russian's entourage, a thin man with a long face and a sharp nose, took the glass and carried it to the table. After depositing the snifter on the shiny wood, he and his companions withdrew out of earshot. One of them stood in front of the hotel's entrance, while the others took up positions at the elevator bank, front desk, and hallway leading to the ground-floor rooms.

Apparently, the Peking was no longer open for business.

Hurley's tablemate pretended not to notice. Instead he downed the brandy in a single swallow before slamming the glass onto the table. "Austrians. Not much for fighting, but they make damn fine liquor."

"Can I help you?" Hurley said.

The Russian smiled. The gesture didn't look any friendlier. "My name is Colonel Zhikin from the Federal Counterintelligence Service. You and I have five minutes to avert a war and stop my country's descent into chaos."

Many responses leapt to mind, but Hurley discarded most of them.

Ordinarily, he would live his legend until an interrogator beat the truth from him. Not tonight. As he'd told Rapp in Doha, there were instances in which Russian KGB officers had used their status as spies to their advantage. Under the guise of meeting with American diplomats or the CIA officers they professed to be targeting for recruitment, Russian turncoats had instead passed along vital intelligence. Hurley wasn't sure what was going on here, but he did know two things: A supposed Russian volunteer had called this meeting, and Zhikin's minions wouldn't be able to hear their discussion.

"I'm listening," Hurley said.

"I am Petrov's deputy. He's instigated the situation in Latvia using Vympel operatives without the knowledge of the FSK director or the Russian president."

Hurley reached for his snifter and took a swallow, deliberately at odds with the Russian's sense of urgency. "That makes for a compelling, not to mention convenient, story, but I'm not hearing anything that would remotely qualify as proof."

"Then shut up and remember these words—Allied Solutions. Did you get that? Allied Solutions."

"I got it."

"That is the name of the front company through which Petrov is funneling the Vympel operatives' payments. Have your forensic accountants follow the money and you'll see that it points back to Petrov. Then have your president call mine. It's the only way to stop a war in Europe and the return of the hard-liners here. Now, we're done."

"Not quite," Hurley said, snaring the Russian's sleeve as Zhikin tried to stand. "A friend from the Middle East is coming to see your boss tomorrow. Nine a.m. sharp. I need you to help him get to the correct office."

"You are not in a place to make demands."

"The hell I'm not. You think the situation in Latvia is bad now? Wait until NATO gets involved. You ensure my friend gets to where he needs to go, and I'll make sure your information does the same. Deal?"

In a surprising show of strength, Zhikin ripped his forearm free from Hurley's grasp. "Deal. Now I need you to do something regrettable."

"Why?"

"Because I'm going to arrest you. You'll be transported under guard to the airport and put on a flight to Berlin that departs in forty minutes. You'll see a bank of public phones next to the departure gate. I suggest you use the third one from the left to make a call before you board the plane. Now, get on with it."

"Gladly," Hurley said. Grabbing his snifter, he tossed the brandy into Zhikin's face.

The FSK officer sputtered and rubbed his burning eyes, which made Hurley think of Irene lying in a hospital bed. Standing, he leaned across the table and snapped a right hook into the Russian's jaw. Hurley had almost two complete seconds to enjoy the stunned look on Zhikin's face. Then he was tackled by several members of the colonel's entourage. As a Russian fist slammed into his cheekbone, Hurley savored a single thought.

It was worth it.

CHAPTER 64

R APP had done some dumb things in his life.
Voluntarily walking into FSK headquarters might just rank among the dumbest.

He examined the Lubyanka building from where he was standing just west of the structure on the corner of Pushechnaya Ulista. Though he wasn't much for architecture, he had to admit that the building's exterior exuded a certain charm. The structure's first two levels were constructed of stone that was colored a bland shade of gray, but the remaining stories were built from yellow bricks. The trimming and windowpanes were done in a rust-colored paint vaguely reminiscent of a Moscow sunset. Taken in whole, the Lubyanka was an island of color in a sea of drab slate and uninspiring construction.

Not bad for one of Moscow's most notorious prisons.

"Prostite menya."

Rapp shifted to allow someone to move past him on the sidewalk. For reasons known only to the Russian psyche, Lubyanka Square was somewhat of a tourist attraction and a steady stream of passersby meandered along the broad, tree-lined pedestrian walkway that bordered the building. While no one was stopping to take pictures, more than a few families strolled hand in hand past the coral-colored double doors leading to the building's interior.

Rapp couldn't easily come up with a Western equivalent to the Lubyanka's dark history. The number of political prisoners who'd been dragged through the entrance only to be dispatched via a bullet to the back of the head in the infamous ground-floor prison were too numerous to count. He didn't know if Muscovites viewed meandering by the Lubyanka as an act of bravery similar to whistling past the graveyard or if perhaps the general populace simply refused to believe that the stories of what transpired inside the cheerful building were true. Either way, Russians didn't seem to feel the dread that radiated from Lubyanka's cold stones.

But he did.

Rapp glanced at the clock mounted on the Lubyanka's top story and confirmed what he already knew. It was time. According to Russian dark humor, the Lubyanka was once referred to as the nation's tallest building because Siberia was visible from its basement detention cells. Rapp thought this bit of lore was too optimistic. Most Russians unfortunate enough to be guests in the Lubyanka didn't live long enough to see Siberia.

Rapp planned to be the exception.

When he and Hurley had constructed this plan, it had seemed possible. Not easy by any stretch of the imagination, but doable. Once again, Volkov's help had been enlisted, this time to provide an overview of the Lubyanka building and what he remembered of its layout and security. Much was still up in the air, but the operation's broad strokes had been addressed to Rapp's satisfaction.

A Hezbollah asset would broker Rapp's introduction to Petrov. As befitting a groveling terrorist financier, Rapp would arrange his own transportation from the airport to the Lubyanka building, where he would supplicate himself on bended knee before his soon-to-be Russian patron.

And then he would kill him.

Which left the issue of how to escape the building.

Here again, Volkov earned his CIA stipend.

The former KGB officer suggested that they take a page from the mysterious bombings in eastern Latvia with one of their own. Or at least the threat of a bombing. Someone claiming to be a member of a Latvian nationalist group would phone the building's switchboard and deliver the warning. Volkov assured Rapp that in its long and ignoble history, the KGB's headquarters had been subject to many bomb threats, and while the actions had never materialized, standard operating procedure for this contingency was ironclad—evacuate the building so that Explosive Ordnance Disposal (EOD) techs could conduct a floor-by-floor sweep.

Before entering FSK headquarters, Rapp would phone the Orion answering service from his cell. This would trigger a countdown. Exactly ten minutes later, the bomb threat would be delivered. Hurley, who would arrive in-country well before Rapp, would be responsible for any operational logistics and for coordinating their joint exfil from Russia. During the operation itself, he would loiter close to the building and retrieve Rapp in the ensuing chaos as the workers evacuated.

Simple.

Or at least as simple as a job this audacious could be.

Except that now there was one very large problem—Stan Hurley had gotten himself declared persona non grata. Rapp had learned the bad news by checking in with the Orion answering service shortly after landing in Moscow. The coded update had been vague on the reasons why Hurley had been tossed out of Russia but specific on the fact that Rapp would be met by an FSK colonel named Zhikin, who would just happen to be waiting in the Lubyanka's lobby.

Zhikin would then convey him to Petrov's office.

The recorded message was also specific on one more item—operational execution was now at his discretion. As per Hurley's earliest guidance, Orion team members were not suicide bombers. If an assassination could not be conducted without a reasonable expectation that the operative would escape, then it should not be conducted at all. Without Stan to assist Rapp, Petrov's killing had now reached that threshold. Execution authority was now vested in the man on the ground.

Rapp.

Pressing forward had been a pretty easy decision when he'd still been in the phone booth's sterile confines.

It was considerably harder now.

The enormity of the task seemed to mirror the Lubyanka building's stalwart construction. A structure that had weathered the rise and fall of empires while serving as the backdrop for death on an industrial scale. If he went into that building, there was a good chance he would not come out. Pushing away the thought, Rapp squared his shoulders and made for the crosswalk separating him from his destiny. Put in the correct context, his decision was simple.

If he went after Petrov, he might die.

But if he didn't, Greta most certainly would.

A horn blared from the far side of the street as an eggshell-blue bus tried to hustle him along. Rapp locked gazes with the driver as he reached the crosswalk's midpoint, refusing to alter his pace. The puffy-faced man touched his thumb and index finger together as he glared through the windshield.

The gesture didn't mean "okay" here like it did in the West, but Rapp didn't take the bait. The bus hadn't encroached any farther into the crosswalk and he was almost to the opposite street. Besides, he wanted to see whether the changes to his appearance were having the desired effect. His olive skin, dark complexion, and almost black eyes provided a great start, but the wig, fake beard, and a prosthetic nose from Hurley's disguise kit completed his transformation. He was an Arab of Lebanese descent. In a city as homogeneous as Moscow, he would stick out like a sore thumb. Rapp let his eyes reflect a freedom fighter's rage, while his posture and stride exuded menace. The bus driver was a sample size of one, but judging by the man's restraint, Rapp was achieving the desired effect.

He curled his lips into a sneer and spat at the bus's grille.

The driver's face reddened, but the bus didn't move. Maybe his restraint was a function of Rapp's intimidating appearance or maybe it was because the man thought that anyone heading for the Lubyanka's entrance of his own accord was best left alone.

Either answer was fine.

Crossing the remaining feet in three quick strides, Rapp paused in front of the door's polished handle and withdrew his cell phone. He was preparing to dial when the device did something unexpected.

Ring.

CHAPTER 65

RAPP stared at the handset.

Only two people had this number. Hurley wouldn't be calling, which meant the person on the other end of the line had to be Greta. He took a deep breath and thumbed the answer button.

"Alo?"

"Can you talk?"

It was Greta.

Her voice was calm, and she was speaking in French. Both of these were good signs. French was spoken widely in Lebanon, meaning that Rapp could answer and still remain in character. Additionally, Greta's calm tone meant that she probably wasn't in immediate danger. On the not-so-positive side, she wasn't calling to chat about the weather.

"Non," Rapp said, "I'm in the middle of something."

"Then I'll make this quick. I've been doing some work and—"

Strains of music drifted through the air. For a moment, Rapp thought he was imagining the melody. Then he realized the song's origin—the Kremlin Clock was chiming in nearby Red Square.

He was late.

"*Ma chérie*, I must go—"

"What they did to my grandfather and grandmother—" Greta's voice broke and her stifled sob tore his heart in two. "It was for money. They needed the accounts' information. It was a robbery. Do you understand?"

He did understand.

Carl and his Alzheimer-stricken wife had been tied to chairs and made to face each other. At the time, Rapp had attributed the actions to wrath. A white-hot rage that had manifested as a sadistic enjoyment taken from forcing a man to watch as the love of his life was tortured to death. He'd been on the right track, but he'd picked the wrong entry on the list of Seven Deadly Sins. It wasn't wrath that had motivated Petrov.

It was greed.

Herr Carl Ohlmeyer was more than just a banker. He and his family owned or had controlling interest in multiple banks. Ohlmeyer also managed a number of large accounts used to finance the Central Intelligence Agency's clandestine activities along with smaller "retirement" accounts for the operatives themselves. In this regard, Hurley and Rapp were both beneficiaries of Ohlmeyer's largesse.

"How badly was the family business damaged?" Rapp said.

"Not as bad as it could have been. We've lost ten or so million, but my grandfather held back the most important accounts. Even in the face of—"

Another muffled sob.

Rapp didn't know the total worth of Ohlmeyer's portfolio, but $10 million was a drop in the bucket. If Ohlmeyer had given up all the account numbers, Petrov could have looted ten times that much, but the old German had hung on despite the horror visited upon his wife.

There could only be one reason for that level of grit.

"He knew," Rapp said, as gently as he was able. "He knew they would kill Elsa no matter what. Your grandfather loved your grandmother with all his being. If he'd believed that money could have bought her life, he would have given away everything without a second thought. But he knew."

Greta was weeping openly now, but still forced words past the sobs. "Make them pay. Do you hear me? Make the men who did this pay!"

"I hear you, *chérie,* and I will. I swear it."

Greta ended the call.

Rapp studied the phone for a minute, half expecting it to ring a second time. When it didn't, he thumbed the number for the message service, waited for the automated answering machine to pick up, and spoke three words.

"Start the clock."

Then he grabbed the polished door handle and shoved.

Time to honor his vow.

CHAPTER 66

R APP pushed aside the swirl of emotions and questions that Greta's call had generated. There would be time to dissect the robbery's implications later. He had a job to do and a legend to maintain. Anything that diverted his mental energy from these two tasks might cause him to lose his focus, and by extension, his life.

The door to the Lubyanka building swung inward easily, as if on oiled hinges.

It had seemed odd to Rapp that the exterior to the building that housed Russia's domestic intelligence organization would be unguarded. Then again, he wasn't Russian. Presumably someone born in the Motherland would understand in their very marrow why the Lubyanka's entrance needed no sentry. Posting a guard outside the building would have been the equivalent of stationing demons at the gates of Hades.

No one tried to sneak into hell.

But if the FSK was content to leave the outside unguarded, this sentiment didn't apply to the building's interior. Once inside Lubyanka's granite walls, Rapp found himself in a lobby that could have been taken from central casting for any government bureaucracy worldwide. To his front, a pair of guards flanked a tandem conveyor-belt X-ray machine and a walkthrough scanner. Several more guards waited on the far side of the lobby near a single door. A bank of elevators dominated the far wall and a desk sporting a phone and a bored-looking woman sat adjacent to the elevators.

At Rapp's appearance, the woman looked decidedly less bored.

He saw no one who resembled an FSK colonel.

Perhaps Zhikin was running late, or more likely, the Russian had grown tired of waiting for his tardy Arab guest. Either way, Rapp was on his own. Ignoring the line of four men and two women snaking from the walkthrough scanner to the building's entrance, Rapp made for the nearest guard. The man barked something at him in Russian and pointed to the end of the line. Rapp shook his head. "I'm here to see Lieutenant General Petrov."

Rapp delivered the statement in perfect Arabic, but his performance appeared to be lost on the guard. In the way of bullies everywhere, the pudgy man grabbed Rapp by the shoulder and pushed him toward the end of the line.

Or at least he tried to.

With a snarl, Rapp wrenched his shoulder free before delivering his statement a second time in louder, slower Arabic. Then he tried again in heavily accented English. "Lieutenant General Petrov."

This roused the woman at the desk from her stupor. Her voice cut through the air with what Rapp assumed was a rebuke based on the guard's reaction. One moment, the beefy fellow had been reaching for the pistol holstered at his belt. The next, he pointed a stubby finger toward the scanner and motioned for Rapp to go to the head of the line. This could not have pleased the men and women he was cutting in front of, but other than a few hard glances, no one reacted.

Perhaps Muscovites could pretend to accept the banality of this building while standing outside its premises, but inside was a different matter. The air felt colder, and the walls looked harder. Rapp wasn't an overly religious man, but as with Auschwitz, there was a sense of menace to this place. An evil that permeated the walls and wafted up from the floor.

Rapp's stomach tightened as he passed through the scanner's archway. The composite knife that was worked into his belt buckle hadn't triggered the airport's metal detectors, and there was no reason to think this sensor was any different. Even so, he didn't think he'd ever be able to pass beneath an X-ray machine without his gut clenching.

Instruments like this were designed for men like him.

Something above him chimed and Rapp's heart skipped a beat.

The guard pointed at Rapp and then the conveyor belt. Shrugging out of his coat, Rapp placed it on the belt and then stepped into the walkthrough scanner a second time. The device beeped again, but somehow sounded less urgent. The beefy guard gestured at the single flashing amber light, and the woman nodded. Apparently, electronic devices manufactured by companies in the former Soviet Union did not always operate flawlessly.

"You are here for Lieutenant General Petrov?" the woman said.

Rapp nodded as he picked up his coat from the far side of the scanning machine. "Yes. A Colonel Zhikin was supposed to meet me here."

A chime sounded from the bank of elevators to his left, and the doors hissed open.

"You just missed him," the woman said. "If you'll take a seat in one of those chairs, I'll ring Colonel Zhikin and let him know you've arrived."

"No need for that. I'll take him up."

Rapp turned toward the elevators, expecting to see the FSK colonel.

Instead, he was confronted by a pair of familiar eyes.

Asymmetrical eyes.

CHAPTER 67

AFTER you."

If walking through the metal detector had made him anxious, preceding Ilya Lebedev into the elevator was enough to make Rapp want to claw his eyes out. He complied with the instructions anyway. His Hezbollah financier persona would not have known who the Russian assassin was and would have had no reason to feel uneasy. Also, Lebedev had spoken in Arabic so there could be no misunderstanding.

Perfect Arabic.

Stan Hurley was a cocky son of a bitch who disparaged a whole lot more than he praised, but even Hurley held a grudging respect for the Russians. Stansfield took things a step further. He'd once told Rapp that Americans too often characterized Russian intelligence officers as thugs and this arrogance could be deadly. The Russians were better at the espionage game from a fieldcraft perspective and possessed linguistic capabilities often lacking in their counterparts.

Apparently, these capabilities also applied to their Vympel assassins.

"Have you ever been to the Lubyanka before?"

Rapp eyed Lebedev as he decided how to respond.

If he'd had any doubts about the man's identity earlier, they were now gone. Up close, he could better see the resemblance between the man standing before him and the photo from Lebedev's personnel file. His cropped hair was now graying at the temples and his features were more weathered. Rapp had put the man in the picture as in his early twenties, but this version of Lebedev was closer to forty. Still, the clefted chin and crooked nose remained the same. As did his eyes. His right one appeared to be open wide in surprise, while the left looked sleepy in comparison.

This was the man who'd murdered Greta's grandparents.

"Of course not," Rapp said.

"That's strange. You look familiar."

"We Arabs all look the same."

He'd hoped the scorn he'd heaped onto his reply might discourage further attempts at conversation.

It did not.

"This building has a long and bloody history. Countless political prisoners were brought here. Many never left. The prisons once housed in the basement have been closed, but some of the features used to disorient detainees remain. Would you like to see one of them?"

"No. I would like to conduct my meeting with Lieutenant General Petrov and then leave your cold, Allah-forsaken country."

Rapp had delivered his remarks with the intention of prompting a reaction from the Russian. In this he succeeded, but it wasn't the one he'd imagined. The Russian's bellowing laugh filled the elevator's tight confines.

"You are an interesting man. It takes courage to insult my country to my face. Courage or perhaps madness. Are you sure we've never met?"

Tendrils of uneasiness snaked from Rapp's stomach. Lebedev certainly could have marked him in the same instant he'd made the Russian, but the human mind tended to see what it expected. There was no reason for Lebedev to associate the Hezbollah financier standing next to him with a man he'd glimpsed for a fraction of a second back in Switzerland. At least for an ordinary person there would be no reason.

Assassins were not ordinary people.

When Rapp remained silent, the Russian shrugged. "No matter. I'll show you anyway." Without breaking eye contact, the Russian tapped a button adjacent to the lit one indicating which floor the elevator was traveling to. Rapp couldn't read the Cyrillic adjacent to the button, but he assumed it served an administrative function like closing or holding open the elevator's door.

The elevator shuddered to a halt.

Then the opposite wall slid open.

"Isolating the detainees was of paramount importance," Lebedev said. "Special alcoves were built into the prison's hallways so that guards could push detainees into them at a moment's notice to shield them from other people. Flashing lights mounted to the walls illuminated every time a prisoner was transported from their cells. Even the elevators were carefully designed to prevent occupants from gaining a sense of where in the building they were being held. Half floors like this allowed guards to seclude prisoners from the building's population and ensure they never saw a random human face. Once a prisoner entered this building, time and space ceased to exist."

Stale, cool air flowed into the elevator.

Meeting Lebedev had not been part of the plan. Rapp was sharing a cramped elevator with the man who murdered the grandparents of the woman he loved. A man who was taking perverse pleasure in detailing the dark building's gruesome history. The assassin seemed determined to provoke a response.

Rapp obliged.

"Is this supposed to impress me?" Rapp said. "A dirty building that was once a prison? Have you ever been to Lebanon? This place and all its sordid history could not hold a candle to the killing houses back home. Once-beautiful structures now filled with shit, blood, and corpses stacked from floor to ceiling. If you've never visited Martyrs'

Square in Beirut, you have no real concept of suffering or death. Now be a good dog and take me to Petrov. He and I have business."

Lebedev's smirk slowly slid from the Russian's face as Rapp spoke. The man's features had hardened into an expression that looked much more at home.

Rage.

The Russian reached for his waistband.

Rapp kicked him in the chest.

CHAPTER 68

RAPP'S kick was meant to create space between himself and the Russian.

Perhaps bounce the assassin off the elevator's wall, scramble his thoughts, and maybe even cause Lebedev to drop whatever it was he was trying to draw from his waistband.

It didn't.

With a fluidity impressive for a man of his size, the assassin eeled around Rapp's leg.

Pain flared in Rapp's calf as silver flashed from the Russian's other hand. The one that hadn't been reaching for his waistband. Rapp cursed his stupidity. He'd fallen for the oldest trick in the book. Lebedev had baited him into focusing on his moving hand instead of the one holding a knife. If he didn't want to die in this dingy elevator, he needed to get his shit together.

Now.

Ignoring the burning sensation in his leg, Rapp planted his foot and launched forward in an awkward right-handed Superman punch. Electricity shot the length of his wounded leg, suggesting that he didn't have many flashy moves left. For the second time, his intended strike caught only air. Lebedev slipped right, flowing beneath Rapp's outstretched fist.

Which lined him up perfectly for Rapp's left hand.

His dominant left hand.

Rapp fired a fist into the man's chest aiming for just below his left nipple. He had to take the knife out of play. A strike to the Russian's bicep was the textbook way to cause Lebedev's fingers to involuntarily open, but the bicep was a small and moving target. If he missed, the Russian's blade would find his ribs or throat. A blow to the torso could have the same effect, if delivered with enough force.

Or as Hurley liked to say, if you can't strike accurate, as least strike hard.

Rapp swung with everything he had, and the jarring impact ran the length of his arm. The Russian grunted, but he didn't drop the knife. Instead Lebedev thrust the glittering point at Rapp's unprotected right side. Rapp twisted, groping for the assassin's knife arm. A line of fire opened across his flank at the same moment his fingers closed on the Russian's wrist. Ignoring his new wound, he ripped the Russian's arm toward him and pummeled Lebedev's torso with three quick hooks, hunting for the liver.

The Russian's sleeve tore away and Rapp's knuckles found ribs, not flesh.

Broken ribs were painful, but not fight-ending. Desperate to stop the next knife thrust, Rapp crashed the Russian's shoulder with both hands and drove him toward the elevator wall. If he could smash the assassin against the wall hard enough, Lebedev might drop the knife. Rather than fight Rapp's two hands with his one, the assassin cupped the base of Rapp's neck and brought his skull down in a vicious head-butt. Rapp tried to turn his head into the blow, but the assassin's iron grip held him in place.

A constellation of stars exploded across his field of vision.

He tried to hold on to the knife arm.

Tried.

His hands fell away like limp noodles. Rapp bit down on his tongue as the world faded, and the bright flare of pain brought things back into a hazy focus.

Laughter greeted his return to semiconsciousness.

Deep, rolling laughter.

"Not bad. Not bad at all. But nowhere near good enough."

Thick fingers gripped his hair and yanked his head back, exposing his neck. The knife descended toward his throat in a mesmerizing blur. Rapp tracked the blade's glittering serrated edge, wondering how much this would hurt. Then he snapped his head downward.

The ties binding the wig to his hair tore free.

Lebedev was left holding a bundle of stringy black curls.

Rapp's fingers were wrapped around something else.

The Russian's testicles.

With a ripping twist, Rapp tried to separate flesh from bone. The assassin's face contorted as something between a screech and a wail emanated from his lips. Rapp yanked downward on the man's distended ball sack like he was pulling a lawn mower's starter cord. Then he fired a vicious hook into Lebedev's throat. The assassin's head whiplashed to the right and his mouth opened into a silent O. Rapp slipped a hand up the man's body, grabbed a handful of hair, and jerked down while scything his elbow up.

The first blow ruptured the assassin's nose.

The second cratered his temple.

Lebedev went limp.

Releasing the body, Rapp took a deep, shuddering breath.

Then another.

By the third, the world had regained its focus. Grabbing the assassin by the shoulders, Rapp dragged him to the still-open elevator doors and draped him across the threshold. The compartment beyond looked as advertised—small, dark, and dingy. Perhaps half again as big as the elevator itself. Rapp patted down the assassin and removed the Makarov pistol holstered at Lebedev's waist as well as a cylindrical suppressor that he screwed onto the muzzle. He looked at the body, considering. He'd never fired the weapon and didn't know how much the suppressor would attenuate the pistol's report, but he was probably safe.

Probably wasn't good enough.

Rapp placed the pistol on the ground, picked up Lebedev's knife, and slit the Russian's throat. Then he rolled the assassin into the compartment. After wiping his fingerprints and blood from the knife on the Russian's pant leg, he tossed the blade after the man. Then he used his knuckle to push the button that had opened the compartment what seemed like a lifetime ago.

The doors slid shut with a tired sigh.

After a prolonged shudder, the elevator began tracking upward.

Rapp removed his coat, draped it over the pistol, and retrieved the bundle from the floor. One of the men who'd killed Greta's grandparents was dead.

The other awaited.

CHAPTER 69

"Aʀᴇ you okay?"

The questioner's expertly tailored suit, predatory smile, and perfectly coiffed salt-and-pepper hair all suggested that he was a high-ranking member of the Russian counterintelligence service. But there was one detail that didn't fit—the purple bruise spreading across the man's cheek. Had he not known better, Rapp would have thought the speaker had taken a haymaker to the jaw. Still, the time for subtlety was well past. The clock was ticking and he needed answers.

"Are you Colonel Zhikin?" Rapp said.

The man nodded.

Rapp breathed a sigh of relief. He'd arrived at the correct floor. After his elevator ride with Lebedev, perhaps he was due a bit of luck.

"You were supposed to meet me downstairs," Rapp said.

"I sent someone else. Did he find you?"

"Did you see anyone else get out of the elevator?"

Zhikin's dazzling smile dimmed. FSK colonels were not accustomed to enduring the rough side of someone's tongue. "What happened to your face?"

"I tripped. Where is Lieutenant General Petrov?"

Zhikin pointed to the corner office at the end of the hall.

"You sure you're okay?"

"Positive."

Rapp was not okay, but neither was he dying. The remainder of his elevator ride, while short, had been long enough to perform a quick triage of his injuries. The cuts to his leg and ribs hurt and would need stitches, but they were shallow and non-life-threatening. Lebedev's headbutt had thankfully missed his nose, but his forehead was hot and swollen to the touch. An injury that, while painful, was not cause for immediate concern.

The same couldn't be said of his wig.

Where before it had looked like a convincing mop of hair belonging to a Lebanese Arab, it now more resembled . . . well . . . just a mop. Somehow his nose prothesis was still attached, but his overall aspect was now more drug-addled homeless person than fearsome Hezbollah financier.

Rapp pushed past the FSK officer, forcing Zhikin to tag along behind him.

The floor was arranged like it was home to a corporation's C-suite rather than a nation's counterintelligence service. The hallway opened into a pod of sorts in which several offices branched off from a common area containing a wet bar, conference table, several richly upholstered leather chairs, and two sofas. A single desk was positioned in the center of the common area and behind the desk sat a very large Russian woman.

Rapp assumed she was a receptionist of some sort. Someone whose importance was derived by her proximity to power and the access she controlled to the people who resided in the trio of corner offices. The woman took one look at him and then directed a stream of angry-sounding Russian toward Zhikin. Rapp's ability to speak the language hadn't magically improved since his arrival in Moscow, but based on her tone and tenor, the woman was probably asking why the FSK officer had allowed a street bum onto such hallowed ground. Ignoring her, Rapp was striding toward Petrov's office when he heard a curse from the office to his left.

A curse rendered in German.

Leaving Zhikin to sort out the woman, Rapp turned left and followed the *Scheisse* to its source. The office's owner had done well for himself. Floor-to-ceiling windows gave an unobstructed view of Lubyanka Square, while an oil painting hung on the far wall side by side with a framed flag from the now-defunct German Democratic Republic, aka East Germany. Custom-made shelves held hardback books by German authors along with pictures and mementos from a country that no longer existed. Plush leather chairs abounded, and soft lighting muted whatever remained of the stodgy, government atmosphere. The office's centerpiece was an ornate hardwood desk that probably cost twice Rapp's monthly salary.

Behind the desk sat the man who'd uttered the curse word.

The *German* curse word.

"Herr Schmidt?" Rapp said.

The man behind the desk looked from his computer monitor to Rapp. "*Ja?*"

Greta's words came back to him in a rush.

It was a robbery. Do you understand?

He hadn't understood then.

Not completely.

He did now.

Digitally stealing money from a bank wasn't the same as sticking a gun in the teller's face and demanding that they open the vault. Ohlmeyer's holdings would have had account numbers, passwords, and security protocols. Someone would have had to verify the information Lebedev was extracting. Someone who had been on the phone with the assassin as he'd tortured to death an elderly woman with dementia while her husband had been forced to watch.

Ideally, that someone would have been a banker.

Or an operative who had once targeted West German banks on the Stasi's behalf.

"Good to meet you," Rapp said.

His job had always been purposeful, but never personal. He nibbled around the edges of the organizations who had funded or trained the men who had blown up the plane carrying Mary, but he'd never been face-to-face with her assassins. This was partially because the actual triggerman had perished in the crash and partially because Irene, Hurley, and Stansfield had constructed his target list with the idea of going after the low-hanging fruit first. While everyone he'd killed so far had deserved to die, he hadn't felt a personal connection to them.

Until now.

Schmidt removed his gold-plated wire-rim glasses and set them on his desk. "Do I know you?"

"No, but we have a mutual friend."

"Is that so? Who?"

"Herr Carl Ohlmeyer."

Schmidt's eyes widened.

He was reaching for something sequestered beneath his desk when a pair of suppressed 9mm rounds thudded into his chest. He jerked and then tumbled from his chair. Rapp stepped around the desk, lined up the stubby suppressor on Schmidt's forehead, and pulled the trigger.

Kill shot.

"What have you done?"

Turning, Rapp saw Zhikin standing just inside the office's doorway.

"Settled a business dispute," Rapp said, pointing the pistol at the Russian's midsection. "A dispute between my organization and Herr Schmidt. It will not concern you unless you decide otherwise." Leaving the pistol leveled at the Russian's midsection, Rapp draped his coat back over his pistol arm, shrouding the weapons. "Do we have a problem, Colonel Zhikin?"

Zhikin slowly bared his teeth in a predatory smile. "You'll never get out of this building alive."

The gonging of a fire alarm rang through the air.

Zhikin narrowed his eyes.

"They're playing our song," Rapp said.

CHAPTER 70

Rapp crossed the distance to the Russian in four easy strides. "We exit this building with everyone. Then I go one way, and you go another. Or I shoot you now and take my chances. Which is it going to be?"

For a long moment Rapp thought Zhikin might just call his bluff. Then the SVR officer slowly backed out of the office, allowing Rapp space to follow him. Once in the common room, the Russian's lips twisted into a feral smile. "Which way?"

Rapp didn't understand what Zhikin was asking at first. Then he got it. To the right lay the bank of elevators and safety. To the left, a final office.

Petrov's office.

The Klaxon continued to sound, and the desk once manned by the receptionist was now empty. He had the time and the opportunity. A quick stroll followed by three equally quick trigger pulls and it would be done. The man who had torn out Greta's heart would be dead and the fifty-year battle he'd waged against America over. Rapp's gun hand trembled beneath his jacket with the need to see Petrov's brains splattered across the office's floor-to-ceiling windows.

He'd never in his life wanted to kill someone so badly.

"Elevators," Rapp said. "Let's go."

The Russian's smile faded, replaced by a look of confusion. He lingered for a moment as if he were the devil offering a wavering soul a final temptation. Rapp prodded Zhikin in the ribs with the pistol's suppressor. "Move."

With a shake of his head, the Russian started toward the elevators. Rapp's skin crawled at the notion of leaving Petrov alive, but he still followed Zhikin into the elevator's open doors. He'd been on the verge of entering Petrov's office when his intuition had stopped him. As if he'd been standing on a lacrosse field watching a play develop, he'd seen what would transpire if he gave into his bloodlust.

His job was to finish wars.

Not start new ones.

The elevator doors hissed shut.

"Where to?" Zhikin said.

"Lobby. We walk out of this building together. Then we part company."

"You know that's not going to happen, right?"

Rapp sighed and gestured toward a patch of discolored carpeting on the elevator's floor. "See that?"

The Russian looked where he was pointing and frowned. "Yes?"

"That was from the last man who underestimated me."

Zhikin swallowed.

The remainder of the elevator ride passed in silence.

Thirty seconds later, the doors hissed open to a much busier lobby. The Klaxon had stopped ringing, but the Lubyanka's occupants were still evacuating the building in twos and threes. Rapp nodded for the Russian to lead the way toward the door. Once again, the FSK officer paused as if assessing his odds. Rapp nonchalantly scratched an itch behind his ear with his gunless hand, revealing the bloody section of shirt stretched across his ribs.

Zhikin started for the door.

Six strides later, Rapp was out of the building. The biting Moscow wind had never felt so good. He tilted his head left and Zhikin obliged, leading them away from the crowd. Zhikin turned a corner, stopped, and then muttered something in Russian. He'd ushered them to a loading dock tucked away from the main pedestrian areas.

A deserted loading dock.

"You killed a Russian intelligence officer inside the FSK's headquarters. You just started a war."

"Wrong," Rapp said. "I just prevented one. I killed a German thief. No one else. The actions the FSK chooses to take to address a rogue lieutenant general who actively facilitated this thief's work by paying Vympel operatives to mount a false-flag operation in Lativa do not concern me." Rapp paused, allowing what he'd said to sink in. "In fact, without his banker, I'm willing to bet the lieutenant general in question will have a hard time accessing the funds he stole. Which means his Vympel units won't be paid for their work."

"Which means they'll be willing to talk," Zhikin said slowly.

Rapp nodded. "I'm sure the FSK's crack forensic accountants will get to the bottom of the lieutenant general's undoubtedly unsanctioned operation once they've completed a proper audit of the financial records stored on the German's computer."

Zhikin stared at him for a beat. "You may be right, but that doesn't help me. Letting a jihadi murderer walk away won't be good for my career. Not to mention my life."

"I've got you covered," Rapp said, taking a step closer and dropping his coat. Raising the pistol, he aimed it at the Russian's shoulder. Zhikin turned his head to track the stubby suppressor, and Rapp fired a right cross at the FSK officer's jaw. His knuckles crunched into Zhikin's chin exactly where the purple bruising began.

The Russian collapsed.

Picking up his coat, Rapp jogged away from the fallen intelligence officer, turned another corner, and followed a narrow alley that dumped into the street. Since the majority of the building's occupants were still clustered around the entrance, Rapp turned right, away from the crowd.

The enormity of his situation set in.

Hurley was supposed to have retrieved him after the job and arranged their exfil. Despite what he'd said to Zhikin, he knew the FSK wasn't going to just sweep an assassination that had occurred in their headquarters building under the rug. As soon as Zhikin recovered, he'd put the full weight and power of the Russian counterintelligence service into finding the rogue Hezbollah shooter. And since Zhikin's cover story depended on Rapp's silence, the FSK operatives would undoubtedly be issued instructions to shoot him on sight.

He was in trouble.

Rapp came to a crosswalk and was preparing to dart across when a well-used Lada sedan slid up to the curb next to him. The driver, a woman wearing a hijab, leaned across the seats and shouted through the open window, "Get in!"

While the offer seemed tempting and the woman was speaking American-accented English, Rapp worried this fell into the "too good to be true" category. He could see a hint of brown hair and the woman's pretty face, but nothing else.

"Shit," the woman said, "I forgot the first part. Stan Hurley said to ask if you needed a ride."

Which was word for word what Hurley had said to him on the streets of Paris after the Cooke debacle.

Rapp opened the door and piled inside.

The woman accelerated away from the curb accompanied by blaring horns from angry motorists. She hung a quick right followed by an immediate left, fleeing the scene of the crime at an impressive pace. "My name is Elysia and I'm with Moscow Station. There's a bag of clothes in the back seat. You need to change. Now."

Rapp grabbed the bag and began shucking his shirt and disassembling what was left of his disguise. "What's the rush?"

"You have a plane to catch."

CHAPTER 71

KRIS Henrik wasn't sentimental.

Much to her husband's delight, she didn't swoon over romantic movies or pack away keepsakes in stacks of cardboard boxes. She was a practical Midwestern girl who wasn't overly given to displays of emotion, but as her vehicle pulled onto the airport's tarmac, her eyes filled with tears.

It was really there.

A beautiful business jet painted in a familiar blue and white livery with the words UNITED STATES OF AMERICA centered above a row of porthole-style windows. And just to make sure there was no misunderstanding, a stenciled version of Old Glory was affixed to the plane's tail.

She was going home.

The car stopped and the two men she was sharing the back seat with exited. In a final bit of humiliation, she'd been forced to ride between the Russians as if she were a little girl who'd lost the battle for a window seat to her older brothers.

She didn't care.

Kris would ride on the car's hood if that's what it took to get out of this country.

A biting Moscow wind swept into the car, ruffling her hair. She wasn't normally one for cold weather, but she wouldn't have traded the breeze's icy fingers for anything. There were low points during her captivity. Moments when she began to wonder whether she would ever leave her detention cell.

The breeze felt like freedom.

"Do you need assistance, Miss Henrik?"

She probably could use some assistance getting out of the low-slung sedan, but she wouldn't accept it. Kris would fall flat on her face before she allowed another Russian brute to touch her. Instead of answering, she ignored the Russian's outstretched hand in favor of grabbing the seat in front of her. Then she pulled herself from the vehicle.

"This will be over in just a moment, Miss Henrik. Then—"

Kris stepped past the Russian attempting to talk to her and started walking toward the plane. She knew she was supposed to wait for some kind of ceremonial exchange, but she didn't care. Kris was done listening to Russians. The business jet with its extended stairway was just twenty yards away.

She was getting on it.

A pair of men in suits flanked the bottom of the airstairs. She assumed they were State Department Diplomatic Security Service agents. One of them appeared familiar. She thought his name was Frank. Or maybe Fred?

The second man looked . . . different.

"Miss Henrik—you will stay with us until told otherwise."

A meaty hand grabbed her shoulder, spinning her around. Tears filled her eyes again, but for a different reason.

They weren't going to let her go.

"Take your hands off her. Now."

Kris shivered, and this time not from the cold. The command had been given in a calm, even tone, but it somehow dripped dangerous intent. Turning, she saw that one of the DSS agents had somehow covered the sixty feet that had been separating them and now stood at her shoulder.

The *different* DSS agent.

"This is Moscow," the Russian said. "You are not in a position to—"

The agent's hand blurred. The motion had been too fast for her eyes to follow. All she knew was that one moment the Russian had been gripping her shoulder with thick fingers, and the next he was cradling his hand with a look that promised murder.

"You don't want this. Believe me."

Again, the DSS agent spoke almost deadpan. Again, the frigid air seemed laced with menace. The American couldn't have been much older than she was. Mid- to late twenties. Certainly not yet thirty. In contrast, the Russian who'd grabbed her shoulder was at least ten years more senior and fifteen pounds heavier. He should have laughed off the DSS agent's threat.

He didn't.

Up close, Kris could see what was different about the American. His thick, uncombed head of black hair and beard were at odds with the buttoned-down image DSS agents typically conveyed, as was his deeply tanned, olive skin. His face looked a bit swollen, almost as if he'd been in a fight, but his penetrating eyes were what had drawn her attention.

Eyes so dark as to be black.

The Russian half-heartedly edged forward, but halted when his companion commanded him to stand down. The FSK officer looked almost relieved to be put in check.

"Come on, Miss Henrik," her DSS savior said. "It's time to go home."

Resting his arm gently on her shoulder, he shepherded her to the staircase.

This time, no one tried to stop her.

CHAPTER 72

ZEKE Williams pulled into the side street leading to his favorite pub at a crawl.

This was his second time frequenting the establishment in the same week. If this pace continued, he might have to ask the owner about getting his own parking spot. As things stood, he'd already done four loops around the block while waiting for something to open. Normally, the wasted time would have sent his blood pressure spiking.

Not today.

The third time he'd passed the pub's crowded lot, Zeke had forgotten to even check for an empty space. Instead his attention had been devoted to his radio and the NPR host's monotone voice. The reporter had been summarizing what was happening in Latvia as if she were reading a grocery list.

Or perhaps it was more accurate to say what was *not* happening in Latvia.

The Russians had apparently loaded up their troop transports and flown home.

Interesting.

A woman exited the pub and made for a black Volvo. Zeke slowed even more and activated his turn signal, much to the irritation of the motorist behind him. An angry horn sounded, but Zeke kept his eye on the prize. The parking lot's entrance and exit was only wide enough for one vehicle to pass through at a time. The Mercedes behind him was going to have to suck it up for another couple of minutes.

Welcome to the District.

The woman slid into her car, started the engine, and pulled out. Zeke gave her a friendly wave and then took her space. The Mercedes's driver rolled down his window and extended his middle finger as he rolled past, just in case his earlier horn blast hadn't been clear. Usually Zeke would have taken the gesture as an invitation to respond in kind.

Today, he didn't.

He was once again distracted, but not by the radio this time. Instead his attention was focused on the newly painted row house across the street. Or more precisely, the drawn blinds on the row house's second-floor window.

Zeke turned off the car, his hands functioning on autopilot as he frantically tried to sort through the ramifications of what he'd heard on NPR combined with the request from his Russian handler for more information. Though he'd spied for the Soviets, and now Russians, for years, he'd always done so on his own timeline and with his own safeguards. There had been periods during his espionage career when he'd produced intelligence prodigiously and intervals when he'd gone dormant, but his peaks and valleys had never been driven by his handler.

Zeke considered himself a patriot and he passed information to help his mother country, but he was also a realist. No one was ever going to care as much about his safety as he did. Real or imagined, he'd always let his intuition guide him, and while there was no way to validate the effectiveness of his sixth sense, he felt vindicated in the most important way.

He was still alive and not rotting in a supermax prison.

Zeke took a final look at the row house before arriving at his decision. He'd helped his countrymen as much as he could, but things didn't feel right at the moment. He was going to lie low for a while and see how things shook out. His handler would be angry, but when he was ready to spy again, he knew the Russians would welcome him back with open arms.

They always did.

CHAPTER 73

COLONEL Zhikin was not accustomed to feeling afraid.

At least not in Vienna.

Next to Moscow, this was where he'd always felt the most at home operationally. For decades the city of music had served as a crossroads for espionage professionals. Austria, both culturally and geographically, was the boundary between East and West and so was the Cold War's de facto ground zero. But as the drizzle that had been turning the city's dirty streets into treacherous spans of slick asphalt finally became a full-fledged rain, he couldn't ignore the prickling at the back of his neck or his clenched stomach. The prideful part of him, the Russian part, wanted to chalk the feeling up to unease.

It was not.

Zhikin was terrified.

"Would you like another?"

Shifting his attention from the bay window that offered an unob-structed view of the busy avenue, Zhikin considered his empty glass. As was befitting a spy, he had arrived at the bar early. He'd consumed the first vodka to ward off the afternoon's chill and the second to take the edge off his tension. While he could no doubt fabricate a similar medicinal reason for a third shot, this would not be a good idea. Prime ministers and presidents made much of their fancy summits and photo ops, but everyone knew that the real work between nations took place in quiet alcoves, back alleys, and the occasional dimly lit bars.

Like this one for instance.

"*Nyet*," Zhikin said, covering his empty glass with his palm, "but perhaps when my companion arrives."

The waiter gave a deferential nod before retreating to the far side of the empty room. Empty because Zhikin had switched the sign dangling in the window from OPEN to CLOSED the moment he'd entered the establishment. A quiet word with the proprietor paired with his charge card had done the rest. This might be Vienna, but the bar, like its owner, was Russian. Zhikin's lips formed a wan smile. Just a handful of years ago, his KGB credentials would have been enough to send the bar owner scurrying to do his bidding. Now that was accomplished with a piece of plastic emblazoned with one of his nation's many newly formed energy conglomerates.

To paraphrase his favorite American singer, *times they were a-changin'.*

The bar's door swung open to the tinkling of the cluster of bells hanging atop the hinge. A blast of cold air swept into the room, bringing with it the man for whom Zhikin was waiting. Though he'd selected the table nearest the window and had been checking the street almost continuously for the last thirty minutes, he still hadn't seen the man approach.

This shouldn't have been surprising.

Stan Hurley had made a career out of sneaking into places he didn't belong.

Hurley hesitated just inside the bar's entrance to shake the water from his overcoat. Or at least that was the pretense for his pause. While fat drops of Viennese rain did spill onto the floor, Zhikin wasn't fooled. The American was surveying his surroundings. Noting the exits and occupants and gaining a sense of the flow and atmosphere.

Watching the man work really was like attending a master class on espionage. Hurley was not some sort of superspy, but he'd been operational for more than three decades. If the admittedly spotty file on the CIA operative was even partially correct, Hurley had spent much of the last half decade or so targeting the rising menace of Islamic terrorism, but he'd cut his teeth in East Berlin.

A good spy never forgot his roots.

After a final shake, Hurley shucked his overcoat and draped it over his forearm. His left forearm. Hurley was right-handed, and while Zhikin was reasonably sure the American wouldn't risk the current détente by bringing a pistol to this meeting, that did not mean he wasn't armed with something less ostentatious but every bit as deadly. Though to be fair, even a fountain pen was dangerous in Stan Hurley's hands.

Zhikin did not rise to meet his guest, but he did signal the waiter with a wave. Had this been a traditional rendezvous with an American operative of Hurley's reputation, Zhikin would have seeded the bar's staff with fellow FSK or Alfa Group operatives. In this case, Zhikin was the only representative from his nation's intelligence service, and the bartender was just a bartender. Still, the bespectacled man approached his table with the rapidity and reverence his position deserved.

Or at least, he tried to approach Zhikin's table.

Hurley intercepted him before he could complete his journey of fealty. "I'll take that," Hurley said, snatching the vodka bottle from the man's hands. "Now beat it."

Zhikin didn't know what annoyed him more: the fact that Hurley gave the order in perfect German, or that the bartender instantly obeyed. On second thought he supposed the young man's obeisance made sense. Zhikin was the Russian equivalent of a made man. Anyone who could show up to a meeting late with an FSK operative and then commandeer his bottle of vodka was not a person to be trifled with.

After ensuring the screw cap was securely sealed, Hurley flipped the bottle around so that he was holding it by the neck. Then he covered the distance to the table in a smooth rolling gait. "Give me one reason why I shouldn't smash this into your skull and call it a day."

Not the greeting he'd imagined, but not such an unforeseen way to begin a conversation with Hurley either. "For starters, that bottle contains a particularly fine vintage, and it would be a shame to see it spilled all over my clothing. Perhaps you could sit so we could share a glass?"

In a motion almost too quick to follow, Hurley slammed the bottle down in a vicious arc and shattered Zhikin's shot glass.

"You think this is funny, motherfucker?" Hurley said. "Ohlmeyer was my friend."

"I don't think anything that occurred is funny. Because of Petrov's arrogance, we have both lost comrades. Their deaths were needless, but there is nothing either of us can do to bring them back. We do, however, have it within our collective power to decide something else—whether the senseless killings will continue."

Zhikin's voice never wavered. He ignored his racing heart, the vodka running down his cheek, and the almost irresistible urge to reach for the pistol he'd Velcroed beneath the table. Instead he locked gazes with the human wrecking ball poised to murder him with a vodka bottle and waited. He supposed that if he did meet his end in the next several seconds, being bludgeoned to death with a Beluga Gold Line was a very Russian way to go. In fact, it might be preferable to what his superior, FSK Director Barannikov, might arrange.

"What then?" Hurley spat, still standing. "You want to make nice?"

Ignoring the American, Zhikin stretched across the table for the second shot glass. The one he'd intended for Hurley. After running his napkin around the interior to make sure it was free of glass fragments, he turned his attention back to his adversary. "If you're not going to punch me in the jaw again, I'd appreciate it if you filled my glass. It really is a fine blend."

Hurley glared at him for a moment longer and then slowly shook his head. "That's a hell of a bruise. I didn't even hit you that hard."

Zhikin refrained from explaining that he'd actually been punched in the chin twice. Instead, he smiled tightly and bit his tongue while Hurley unscrewed the bottle and began to pour.

"Thank you," Zhikin said. "I'd offer you some, but I seem to be a glass short."

"No problem. I'll drink from the bottle. *Vashe zdoroviye.*"

Hurley clicked the bottle against Zhikin's upraised glass and then took an impressive swallow. Many impressive swallows. Russian blood must flow in the American's veins.

"How is Miss Kennedy?" Zhikin said after placing his glass on the table.

Hurley eyed him over the bottle's lip. "With the exception of some bumps and bruises, fine. What about Petrov?"

"Neither the SVR nor the FSK were happy when the full scope of Lieutenant General Petrov's deeds became known. An inquiry was ordered. Regrettably, Petrov died before he could provide his testimony."

Hurley snorted. "Natural causes I assume?"

"I am told he took a long fall down a short flight of steps."

Hurley took another swallow of vodka. "How about Alexander Hughes?"

"Heart attack. Too much red meat I'm afraid."

Hurley slammed the bottle onto the table. "So what? You think we're even?"

"Here is what we propose," Zhikin said as he refilled his glass. "Our nations may never be friends, but we needn't be active combatants. Let us return to the old way of doing things."

"Moscow Rules?" Hurley said.

Zhikin nodded. "Our intelligence services will look for ways to work together when we can. When we cannot, we will behave as adversaries, not enemies. Intelligence officers will do what intelligence officers must, but families and civilians will remain off-limits. Agreed?"

Hurley stood. "You're right—this was a good vintage. Enjoy."

"Do we have an understanding?"

The question came out harsher than Zhikin had intended.

Not desperate perhaps, but certainly urgent. Barannikov had agreed to let Zhikin handle negotiations with Hurley on the premise that the two men would be able to engage in the type of candid conversation that often eluded the directors of rival intelligence services. But he'd also made clear that more than just Zhikin's future depended on the outcome of this unofficial summit. Zhikin might have convinced Barannikov that he hadn't been privy to Petrov's plans, but as the lieutenant general's deputy, he hadn't completely escaped the stain of his predecessor's actions either.

"No," Hurley said, "we don't have an understanding. Thomas Stansfield had the same bullshit heart-to-heart talk with the SVR director awhile back. As you can see, it got us nowhere. Besides, this Moscow Rules horseshit has always been too one-sided for my liking. You heard of the Chicago Way?"

Zhikin shook his head.

"Don't you people have movies in Russia? Fine, I'll summarize the terms of our new rules of engagement this way: You don't fuck with my guys, and I won't fuck with yours. But if your guys start with the rough shit again, my response will be exponential not incremental. Capisce?"

Zhikin did not capisce, but he still nodded.

"Good," Hurley said, shrugging into his overcoat. "Oh, and one more thing, this arrangement doesn't apply to those Vympel fucks who worked off-the-books for Petrov. I won't actively hunt them, but if I catch one of those sons of bitches in a dark alley, I will stick a knife in their brainpan and stir. Make sure you pass that along. Have a great evening."

Hurley strode out of the bar without waiting for a reply.

For that Zhikin was grateful, because he didn't have one.

CHAPTER 74

CONGRATULATIONS on the new office, sir."

Thomas Stansfield gave his visitor a wan smile. Irene Kennedy knew him better than anyone outside his immediate family, but it wasn't just her familiarity that encouraged Stansfield to drop his professional demeanor even if only for an instant. Kennedy truly understood his motivation for assuming the position of DCI.

She understood because she shared it.

"Thank you, Irene. It does have a nice view from this side of the desk."

Stansfield had been an employee of the Central Intelligence Agency since its inception, and he'd held the role of deputy director of operations for years. As a member of the intelligence organization's executive leadership team, he'd been in this office more times than he could count, but he'd never sat behind the director's desk. Even when he'd been serving as acting DCI, he'd let the office sit empty rather than move in before his confirmation. While not a military organization, the CIA was rife with traditions and customs. Stansfield respected the agency's heritage and his predecessors' accomplishments too much to occupy the director's office as a squatter.

"I'm very glad the confirmation vote went your way, sir. For what it's worth, I think my father would have enjoyed seeing you in that chair."

This time, Stansfield didn't smile.

It wasn't because his protégée's words hadn't touched him. They had. Though they'd both been intelligence professionals, Stansfield considered Irene's father more brother than coworker. The day Stansfield had received news of his tragic death was the second hardest of his life.

The first had been telling Irene's mother.

Now, a decade later, his dearest friend's daughter had taken up the family business and the risks that came with it. Though she'd no doubt tried to dampen its effect with makeup, the bruising around Irene's right eye still stood in stark contrast to her fair skin. In a break from the norm, she had resisted her near-constant urge to tuck her auburn hair behind her ears in favor of allowing it to hang freely around her face. Stansfield suspected this was not an attempt to hide her youth so much as it was to obscure the finger-sized, livid blue splotches along her cheek and temple. Most days, he caught glimpses of her father's face when he looked at Irene.

Today, he saw his friend's broken body in his daughter's bruises.

"Stop staring. I'm fine."

Stansfield raised an eyebrow at his visitor's sudden change in tone. "Most officers treat their boss with a bit more respect."

"I'm not most officers."

This was true in more ways than one.

Irene had never been just another agency officer. Her photographic memory, keen analytical mind, and aptitude for fieldcraft had put her on the fast track from seemingly the moment she'd graduated from the Farm. Though he was not her patron in the sense that he'd intervened on her behalf to protect her from career-ending mistakes, Stansfield had worked to ensure that Irene was presented with opportunities to demonstrate her considerable skills.

When the time had come to implement the Orion program, selecting her to lead it had been a no-brainer. No doubt she viewed Hurley's presence as operational training wheels to keep her on track, but in Stansfield's mind the opposite had been true. Stan had been too much of a cowboy for too long. Though he had the cunning, ruthlessness, and intelligence to be one of the agency's greatest case officers, the man was brash and impulsive. Like a good handler, Stansfield had paired the two in order to leverage their personal relationship. Hurley might not like the thought of Irene peering over his shoulder, but he'd tolerate her.

Until he hadn't.

"You are definitely not like most officers," Stansfield said. "You are my goddaughter, the mother of a young child, and an exceptional spy. My interest in your career will always be intertwined with my affection for you and your father. I know you are aware of these things, but I want you to know that I am also aware of them. Understand?"

Irene nodded.

"Good. Then we can move on to the second part of this conversation. The portion where we answer the most pertinent question—*what next.*"

"What do you mean?" Irene said with a frown.

Stansfield chuckled. "Relax. This isn't an attempt to convince you to choose a less dangerous path. Quite the opposite in fact. Your performance in Moscow was masterful. You arrived to find a dysfunctional station in crisis and a brewing conflict in Latvia. By the time you'd departed, war in Europe had been averted and a threat to this nation's safety neutered. The vote for my confirmation as director went well because I was able to go back to the Senate Select Intelligence Committee with a story to tell. At the closed-door hearing, I presented the classified version of how this agency preserved peace on the European continent by unraveling a Russian intelligence operation. Even Senator Jefferson Rutledge is no longer questioning the CIA's necessity. The committee also agreed to close their ill-advised public investigation into the circumstances surrounding Cooke's murder. You did this, Irene. You."

Stansfield paused on the pretext of giving Irene a chance to reply. In reality, he was interested in her response to his praise. The CIA did not recruit church mice. The idea that one could waltz into an adversarial nation and convince its citizens to put their lives at risk by stealing their homeland's secrets required a certain amount of confidence.

Confidence that too often became arrogance.

Irene had just notched what should be considered a career-defining accomplishment by any objective measure. Would she bask in the warmth of Stansfield's praise, brush it away under the pretense of false modesty, or do something else entirely? Polygraphs were great, but in his experience nothing provided the measure of a person more accurately than their response to a well-earned compliment.

"Thank you," Irene said after the silence built for several seconds. "I did what needed to be done."

Just so.

"Yes, you did," Stansfield said. "As the newly minted director of this organization, it does not escape my attention that there are a great many things that *need to be done*. Which of them would you like to tackle next?"

Irene's features contorted into a look that was so unfamiliar it took Stansfield a moment to name it.

Confusion.

"Sir?"

"You're really going to make me spell this out? Fine. You stand at a crossroads. Down one path lies promotion to the senior executive service, assignments as the chief of base and station to our most important postings, an office on the seventh floor of this building, and perhaps one day, this very chair. This is the path to fulfilling your gift for leadership."

Had he given this speech to just about anyone else in the building, they would have been euphoric. Sure, they might have tried to mask their joy with a quiet smile followed by a serious question or two, but there would have been no hiding the jubilation in their eyes.

Not Irene.

Instead, his protégée gave a quick nod as if he'd just relayed the cheapest place in DC to buy gas. But while her external appearance remained one of cool detachment, Stansfield didn't believe her internal monologue was quite so serene. Irene was nothing if not a planner. He imagined her thoughts were even now proceeding down the path and all its potential branches and sequels like a runaway freight train, exploring their collective potential. In the time it took him to reach for the ceramic mug emblazoned with the CIA's seal seated on the corner of his desk, they returned.

"What about the other path, sir?"

Stansfield had anticipated this question, but he still took a swallow of tea before replying. "The other path leads to more bruises and blood. Separations from your family, hard-fought battles lost, lonely vigils waiting for nameless assets to surface, and searing sessions of self-reflection when they don't. Your other choice is to remain operational, Irene. Normally, a good field hand makes a terrible administrator, and vice versa. For most people, these sets of skills are exclusionary. Not you. You have the ability to do both. So which is it going to be?"

Stansfield honestly had no idea which option she'd choose. Selfishly, he wanted her in leadership. While Moscow Station had proved to be in a class all its own, far too many bases and stations were led by timid and ineffective executives more concerned with their next promotion than preventing a cataclysmic intelligence failure. Yes, the Iron Curtain had fallen, and the Cold War was won, but Stansfield couldn't help but think that they were on borrowed time.

Hurley, for all his faults, had a head for seeing which way the winds of conflict were blowing, and he'd been harping on the dangers of radical Islam for years. The Orion program was a good start, but Stansfield needed more PhDs who could win a bar fight and fewer Ivy League–educated thought leaders. Irene could help revive the agency's warrior culture and recruit the next generation of bruisers who were unafraid to get their hands dirty on their nation's behalf.

Those were his wishes, but perhaps not hers.

"By operational, you mean what exactly, sir?"

"I mean you get back in the field and start recruiting assets. Maybe do a tour down at the Farm to pass on your knowledge to the next batch of case officers. Either way, I'd want you on the front lines developing agents where none exist right now."

"What about Orion?"

Stansfield leaned back in his chair, confused by the question. "What about it?"

"Who is going to run the program?"

"You mean who is going to run Rapp?"

Irene nodded.

Stansfield sighed. "I'm not sure. Stan will need a strong hand, and Rapp will require someone he trusts. In an agency that preaches a truism that the mark of a good handler is the ability to pass an asset off to another handler, I've managed to create the opposite of that in the Orion team. Don't worry—I'll use Dr. Lewis as an unbiased arbitrator. He might just have some ideas about who we should look at to replace you."

"That won't be necessary."

Stansfield raised both eyebrows. "You already have someone in mind?"

"No. It won't be necessary because I'm not going anywhere. You said that I was at a fork in the road. Maybe so. But I'm not ready to take either of those paths. Not yet. I lobbied you to implement the Orion program and put me in charge. I lobbied even harder to be allowed to run Rapp the way I saw fit. Now that Stan is finally on board with me and Rapp, and the program is bearing fruit, you want me to move to something else? I'm sorry, sir, but I can't do that."

"Can't or won't?"

Irene didn't answer. At least not right away. To the casual observer, she was completely unfazed. No flushed face or aggressive posture and no anger sparking from her eyes. Just an intelligence professional dispassionately stating her case.

Stansfield was not a casual observer.

As someone who'd known Irene her entire life, the set of her jaw said volumes.

"I'm not saying no, sir. I'm just saying not now. Please."

Stansfield turned from his protégée to the expansive window. He spent a long moment surveying the grounds of the agency to which he'd devoted his adult life. An agency full of people who accomplished the impossible while navigating the unthinkable on a daily basis. People like the case officer sitting across from him.

His decision made, Stansfield turned back to his surrogate daughter.

"This office really does have quite the view. I think you'd like it."

"Maybe so," Irene said, getting to her feet, "but I'll stick with the view from mine for now. Good day, Director."

Her words hung in the air long after she'd left, and Stansfield couldn't shake the notion that they had a familiar ring.

Perhaps because he'd once said the very same thing.

EPILOGUE

D R. Thomas Lewis stared at his patient, waiting for the man to speak.

As a psychologist, Lewis's job was to help people see the parts of themselves they would rather keep hidden. While pop culture had propagated the stereotype of an all-knowing therapist who deftly guided patients on journeys of self-discovery, this did not match his experience. It was true that he began each session with the broad strokes of what he thought a patient needed to confront in order to make progress, but these notions served more like a compass rather than a road map.

A directional azimuth for his opening questions, not a detailed script.

Lewis knew that most of his patients ranked coming to see him only slightly higher than a visit to the dentist. As such, he'd found it instructional to allow the patient to make small talk in the beginning of the session, since these seemingly throwaway comments sometimes hinted at deeper issues.

Not this patient.

The man seated on the other side of his office possessed almost a preternatural ability for stillness. He was barely out of college and his shaggy hair and scruffy beard should have brought to mind a beatnik poet or maybe a fraternity brother just back from a spring-break jaunt to Mexico. His lax grooming standards should have dulled the man's edges or added some warmth to his unnerving black eyes the way a pink dog collar might soften a German shepherd's appearance.

They did not.

Instead, the intensity radiating from the man elicited a different response.

Fight or flight.

"Do you know why you're here?" Lewis said after it became obvious that Mitch Rapp was content to pass the morning in silence.

"Greta."

Lewis scratched something indecipherable onto the yellow legal pad he was balancing on his lap. This was not so that he could remember what Rapp had said. Instead, he was writing to mask his own reaction.

Surprise.

"What makes you say that?" Lewis said.

"Give me a little credit, Doc. You brought me back to the place where it all began to remind me what I'd sacrificed to get this job. Now you want to know whether I intend to keep it."

Lewis's reply was interrupted by a bloodcurdling scream. The voice wasn't recognizable, but the gravelly basso that followed it certainly was. In a nondescript-looking barn on the other side of the property, Stan Hurley was imparting some rough wisdom to the next crop of candidates slated to join the Orion program.

"How long is he going to be back in the schoolhouse?" Rapp said.

Lewis shrugged. "Believe it or not, he's here of his own accord. After returning from Moscow, he asked for a meeting with me, Irene, and Stansfield. He said he had fences to mend and requested to oversee the training of the next batch of recruits."

"Hurley volunteered to come in from the field? If that's not a sign of the Apocalypse I don't know what is."

Rapp made the comment with a ghost of a smile, but Lewis kept his features carefully neutral.

He was good, this kid.

Good and getting better.

Where before Rapp had been primarily concerned with the martial aspects of the job, Irene's prize assassin now seemed to be picking up a few HUMINT tricks of the trade. As a former Green Beret and now employee of the Central Intelligence Agency, Lewis was used to playing for the varsity team. A colleague considered average in Lewis's world would be a top achiever in any other organization. But even on this extended talent scale, Rapp stood head and shoulders above the rest. The question Lewis was trying to answer this morning wasn't whether the assassin could still do the job for which he was trained.

It was whether he still wanted to.

"Then let's cut to the chase," Lewis said, crossing his legs. "How do things stand with you and Greta?"

The smile vanished and the icy silence returned.

This time, Lewis was determined not to be the one who broke it. Losing Rapp would be a horrific blow to the Orion program and the nation's security writ large, but what they were trying to build was bigger than any one man. As George Washington had so elegantly displayed by resigning from the presidency, no one was irreplaceable.

Not even Rapp.

"We broke up."

The three words landed with the force of three granite boulders.

Rapp was one of his most guarded patients, which was saying something, since Lewis's clientele was made up almost exclusively of spies. Trying to peer behind Rapp's walls was nearly impossible, but he knew that the assassin's relationship with Greta wasn't a youthful fling. Rapp did not love quickly or easily. In fact, Lewis was willing to bet that he hadn't used this word in the context of a romantic relationship since Mary.

"Why?" Lewis said.

Rapp's expression changed to something Lewis couldn't quite read. No longer the stoic assassin, but neither was there any hint of the earlier mirth. Had he been pressed to name the emotion paired with the assassin's features, Lewis would have used one he'd never before associated with Rapp.

Resignation.

"Her grandparents' death rocked her to the core."

"And she blamed you?"

Rapp shook his head as he gave Lewis an annoyed look.

Lewis realized that he'd just violated a therapist's cardinal rule—never interrupt your patient. It wasn't so much that he'd broken in because of rudeness as surprise. Rapp seldom revealed what he was truly thinking, and on the rare occasions when he did, his feelings came in staccato bursts. It had never occurred to him that Rapp might continue speaking.

"I'm sorry," Lewis said. "Please continue."

"She didn't blame me. The opposite in fact. Her grandparents' murder drove home the true nature of the world in very personal terms. Her grandfather had worked with Hurley and Stansfield. She understood that he was a combatant after a fashion. Carl might have been killed unjustly, but he'd died because he was a pseudo-soldier."

"Those who live by the sword risk dying by it."

Rapp nodded. "Her grandmother was a different story. Elsa was a civilian suffering from Alzheimer's disease. Her periods of lucidity were growing shorter and shorter. She was a noncombatant in every sense of the word. Her death wasn't collateral damage. It was murder. Like Mary."

Lewis scratched more nonsense onto his yellow pad. This time, instead of a single jumble of words, he went on for several sentences. Rapp almost never brought up his girlfriend by name.

About the time Lewis was beginning to believe he might have to fill an entire page with mumbo jumbo, Rapp continued.

"Greta didn't blame me, but she didn't want me part of that life anymore. She said that everyone retires at some point, and even though I'd only been in the game for a couple of years, I'd already done more than most. She wanted me to quit."

Lewis gave a slow nod. "She makes a pretty compelling argument."

"Even more compelling in person."

Though Lewis had never met the Swiss beauty, he'd seen pictures. The woman could have been a model. Listening to Greta read the phone book was probably compelling.

"Not just because she's beautiful," Rapp said, as if reading his thoughts. "As we were standing in the lobby of her grandfather's house, I could see it."

"What?"

"Everything. In the span of a couple of seconds, I visualized our future lives. Our wedding, our house in Switzerland, our kids, even our grandkids. It sounds crazy I know, but it's true."

It did not sound crazy.

Not to Lewis.

While much had been made about Rapp's raw athleticism and linguistic prowess, in Lewis's opinion it was the assassin's ability to wargame multiple courses of action in a fraction of a second that made him so formidable. For someone capable of analyzing a target and his bodyguards the way Joe Montana could read the opposing team's defense, imagining his future would be no great feat.

"Was it a good life?"

Rapp looked at the floor in silence. Then he slowly nodded. "A great one. But it wasn't mine."

"What does that mean?"

In a blur of motion Rapp snatched the legal pad from Lewis's lap. He examined the top page for a moment before settling the pad on his knees. "I'm not even mad that everything you've written down is utter gibberish. Know why?"

Lewis shook his head.

"Because you're a great shrink. You are uniquely suited to be a therapist for the CIA's clandestine service. Partially because your military background gives you a special vantage point into the lives of the men and women who do what we do, but that's only part of the reason. You were born to be a shrink. It's in your genetic makeup. This isn't a job for you. It's your purpose."

Every time he thought he had Rapp figured out, the assassin proved otherwise. Like a multifaceted rock, there was always some new depth or dimension to his personality that had previously been hidden from view. "And you're born to be an assassin?"

Lewis had chosen the word *assassin* intentionally. Irene liked to refer to the Orion program members as counterterrorism operatives, while Stan called them door-kickers. Neither euphemism was correct.

Rapp, and the men like him, were killers.

"Our society is based on the principle that justice is equally distributed to all, but for far too long, that hasn't been true. Blame it on a lack of political fortitude, or realpolitik, or just that the shitbags who needed killing the most tended to live in places where it was really hard to get to them. Whatever. The result is the same. People like Mary went unavenged. Men, women, children, innocents. They died, but their killers were allowed to go on living. Not anymore. Would my life with Greta have been spectacular? Yes. But it wasn't mine. My life, my purpose, is to be an avenging angel for people like Mary."

Rapp had laid out his raison d'être in calm, unemotional tones. He could have been explaining to a friend why he'd given up a lucrative career as an investment banker to take a job teaching underprivileged kids how to read. But Rapp wasn't a teacher or an investment banker.

He was an assassin.

"That's it, then? You're going to spend the rest of your life skulking about in the shadows and shooting unarmed men in the face?"

Lewis had asked the question with the intent of provoking a reaction.

He succeeded.

With a flick of his wrist, Rapp tossed the legal pad at Lewis in a flutter of yellow pages. The notepad hit him in the chest. Lewis looked down to grab it before the pad slid off his legs. By the time he looked back up, Rapp was standing over him.

"I'm going do the job for which I'm uniquely qualified until it no longer needs to be done. Any other questions, Doc?"

Lewis had never felt personally threatened by Rapp, and he didn't feel threatened now. What he did feel was healthy respect for the man in front of him, almost as if he were standing on the North Rim of the Grand Canyon. One wrong step and he could find himself hurtling toward the rocky floor's jagged embrace.

"Nope," Lewis said.

"Then maybe write my last answer down. It was a good one."

Without asking for permission to leave, Rapp ghosted out the door.

Lewis expected nothing less.

There was still work to be done.

ACKNOWLEDGMENTS

THIS is a novel, meaning that as much as I tried to ground the book in the world in which we live, it is still a work of fiction. With that in mind, I confess to occasionally taking liberties with events, timelines, locations, and the like. For instance, though the Barcelona Museum of Contemporary Art exists much as it was described in the book, it was not constructed until several years after *Denied Access* takes place. By the same token, though both the Lubyanka building and its dark history are real, details have been altered for the purposes of this story. **Please don't tell Mitch Rapp**.

Writing a novel is a team effort, and the Mitch Rapp team is staffed by all-stars. Special thanks to Emily Bestler, Lysa Flynn, and Sloan Harris, who continue to be faithful stewards of Vince's legacy. Publicist David Brown keeps finding innovative ways to get Mitch Rapp into the hands of new readers, while Ervin Serrano and Jimmy Iacobelli designed a truly spectacular cover. **Thank you, Team Mitch Rapp**.

When I realized that *Denied Access* was shaping up to be an espionage novel, I called the best spy novelist I knew for advice—David McCloskey, author of *Damascus Station*. David provided insightful counsel for a particularly vexing plot problem, suggested that I read the nonfiction book *The Main Enemy*, and put me in contact with one of its authors, Milton Bearden. Milt is a former CIA officer and old Russia hand who could have been plucked from the pages of *Tinker Tailor Soldier Spy*. Milt graciously allowed me to ply him with questions, and his real-world experience added veracity and depth to *Denied Access*. **Thank you, Milt and David.**

My opportunity to tell stories in the Mitch Rapp universe is due in no small part to the efforts of my incredible agent, Scott Miller. Tragically, Scott recently passed away after a long battle with cancer. His beautiful family remains in my prayers. May his memory be a blessing. **Thank you, Scott.**

As always, my wife and children were constant sources of encouragement and inspiration while writing this book. **Thank you, Angela, Will, Faith, and Kelia**.

Finally, I'd like to thank the legion of Vince Flynn readers who sent *Capture or Kill* to the number two spot on the *New York Times* bestsellers list. Mitch Rapp fans are the best fans. **Thank you, faithful readers, for welcoming the new guy!**

DENIED
ACCESS